PLAN OF THE THIRTEEN

Chronicles of the Imperial Rangers

BARBARA J. ROBERTSON

PLAN OF THE THIRTEEN - Chronicles of the Imperial Rangers

DEDICATION

The "Chronicles of the Imperial Rangers" series is dedicated to the men and women of the United States Marines, Navy, Army, Air Force, and Coast Guard, whose hard work and sacrifice continues to provide us with the freedoms we enjoy and hold so dear.

Thank you for your service!

ACKNOWLEDGMENTS

Many thanks are owed to my close friends, sisters, and advisors:
To Denise Robertson, RN, and Debbie Hilst, RN, my sisters, for patiently providing medical advice during the creation of this series, and for reading the finished works. Love you!
To RMCM Marie Vellis, for her support for this project. Her leadership and dedication to duty and country during an exemplary 30-year career in the US Navy helped open the doors for women to achieve ranks and careers previously not available to them. Thank you for your friendship.
To Bonnie Copeland, for reading my works, and providing commentary and gentle criticism during the creation process. Thank you, thank you!
To Mara Kalcheim, for her encouragement and holding my feet to the fire. Thank you!
To Roe Andersen, my proofreader, for her excellent skill and constructive criticism.
To Bettina Moss, for helping drill down to the essence of our heroes. Time in conversation with you was priceless.
To John Lenzi, for his encouragement, wit, and humor. Thank you, my friend.
To Rosalie Bruce, for her invaluable advice and assistance during the publishing process.
To the many veterans who shared their memories of military service, confrontations, and battles with me. You are a priceless treasure. As you requested, your names have not been disclosed. But your stories of victories and defeats in battle will stay alive..

PROLOGUE

Located in the far corner of the T'Cetyl galaxy is the solar system known as "R'Genra." Four inhabited planets orbit their sun: Ban'Ti, the jungle planet, third from the sun; M'Wati, called the Planet of Islands; Home World, the center of the Empire, with eight billion calling the beautiful planet home; and massive K'Halon Prime, the source of human life in the R'Genra System. For nearly 2,500 years, the Empire has ruled K'Halon Prime and Home World, and later M'Wati. Ban'Ti was populated last, being on the inside of the asteroid-filled White Belt.

K'Halon Prime is the largest inhabited planet in the R'Genra solar system. A Great Catastrophe was responsible for the current state of the large planet. One side of the planet is densely forested, with three billion people, and even more large mammals, birds, and many other animals. The other side of K'Halon Prime is barren desert, with sparse fresh water sources, and thus, absent diversity of plant and animal life. Only vermin, reptiles, vultures, and poisonous insects call the desert side home.

Prior to the Catastrophe, humans lived only on K'Halon Prime. The chilly forest planet was divided among many kings, who warred against each other for land, riches, and power. After the Catastrophe, the Star People came, and surviving kings formed the Empire. Peace and order were established. A great awakening of knowledge occurred during the next centuries. Fantastic technological advances in flight in the second millennium of the Empire enabled the people to reach beyond K'Halon Prime to its beautiful neighbor, which they named Home World.

The climate of Home World is mildly temperate and its soil very fertile, with many lakes and rivers providing fresh water. Its oceans are dotted with large and small islands, making trade easy and abundant. Its diverse array of plants, land mammals, fish, and birds provided food for the settlers. The human population grew rapidly. The orbit of Home World took one year, whereas K'Halon Prime spent 2.65 years orbiting around the sun. The people relocated to Home World in transport after transport, seeking more favorable living conditions, and much milder winters.

Rapid advancements were made in science and technology, and ships sent out for exploration discovered M'Wati, and eventually, the little jungle planet of Ban'Ti. The Empire expanded to include the four inhabited planets and beyond, to the outer reaches of the R'Genra System. A thriving arrangement of trade and commerce developed rapidly. Six space bases were established within the system to provide protection for the four worlds and their interdependent commerce.

Beautiful M'Wati was called the "Planet of Islands." With only two major large continents and thousands of islands, the world is barely half the size of Home World. The planet produces many types of ocean fish, fine wines, and grains for export. The primary profits for the Empire on M'Wati are the gold and diamond mines, all of which belong to the Great Empress Kayla. The lovely planet is a paradise for vacationers, weddings, and retirees, and those who love all types of water sports. Its moderate climate provides year-round enjoyment for permanent residents and the many visitors to the watery world.

The last twenty years of the reign of the former Great Benevolent Emperor P'Lau witnessed the rise and fall of the Rebellion, led by his half-brother, Duma Wat. The Rebellion was officially over now. The recent appointment of Empress Kayla by the powerful Vee Lok Lords established the new dynasty. Not everyone agreed with the Galactic Lords' selection, however. The mysterious "Plan of the Thirteen" to overthrow the Empress was still at work. The Empire was being corrupted from within, unbeknownst to its people.

From the first days of the Empire, the Imperial Class System has been the social structure for all peoples of the R'Genra System. The Warrior Class holds the uppermost tier of the Imperial Class System. Since the beginning of the Empire, all emperors and empresses have come directly from the Warrior Class. The Mother of the new dynastic bloodline is Empress Kayla. The highest-ranking warriors are the Rangers, sworn by blood oath to the Empress for their service, will, and their lives. The males are the Borgund Rangers, and the females are the Kaylan Rangers. The Rangers are sworn to obey and enforce the will of the Empress.

Herein begins the third of the Chronicles of the Imperial Rangers: Plan of the Thirteen.

I

Home World

Gentle evening breezes playfully tossed the snowflakes beginning to fall, making the delicate, frozen shapes spin and twirl in the Courtyard lights. The bright evening lights came on at precisely 5:00 p.m., and the tower bells sounded their chimes. Closing the tall, narrow window, Empress Kayla took one more look at the brightly lit Courtyard and smiled at her Guards. This was the last Main Court event of the year, and everyone was anxious for the Honors Banquet to begin. The Palace doors opened wide and the Warrior Class relatives of the Rangers and Imperial Guards quietly streamed inside.

Heavy boot steps of one hundred sixty-four marching Borgund Rangers resounded throughout the Main Court of Home World Palace. The men halted next to the fifty-five women Kaylan Rangers, all Rangers wearing their finest formal uniforms, standing in perfect presentation formation. Two hundred Imperial Guards followed, lining the walls and balcony of the Main Court, and the space surrounding the throne. The only guests here tonight were the proud parents, relatives, and Life Partners of the Rangers and Guardsmen. No wealthy aristocrats, courtiers, or military brass were allowed at the private Honors Banquet. Unlike the military, neither the Rangers nor the Imperial Guards wore any medals, merely rank insignia at their collars. Their awards were kept in their service files.

The Great Warrior Empress Kayla entered, flanked by her personal Ranger guards and six Imperial Guards. She faced her Rangers and Guardsmen, as the voice of Commander Superior (C.S.) G'Rosk announced: "The Great Empress Kayla, Ruler over all Known Worlds and Conqueror over the Unknown Domain. All Hail our Great Empress Kayla!" The audience hailed their Empress three times, then everyone knelt before her.

"Draw swords!" C.S. Javette commanded. Each Ranger drew their plasma sword, and the fiery white-hot swords gleamed and crackled pure energy, as they held them high above their heads with both hands. "Salute!" She cried. They sharply pulled their swords down to their left breastplate with both hands, in the Royal Salute.

"Sheathe swords!" C.S. G'Rosk ordered, and they returned their swords to their backplates, extinguishing the energy weapons. The Rangers stood, awaiting their Empress' voice. She was the youngest Empress in the history of the Empire, an intense, beautiful, raven-haired woman with rare green eyes. Still a Master Commander Ranger, the Empress Kayla loved and respected her Rangers and Imperial Guards. During the first year of her reign, the woman Rangers petitioned to change their longstanding name from "Shi'Lon" to "Kaylan" Rangers, to honor their Warrior Empress, the Mother of the new dynastic bloodline.

Empress Kayla said, "Our bravest and finest warriors, tonight is your night. Honors, awards, commendations, and bonuses will be presented to several Imperial Guards, and our Borgund and Kaylan Rangers. Our thanks and praise to each Ranger and Guardsman is made from our heart, for your dedication, your unwavering loyalty, and your service to our Creator and our Empire. Let the Honors Begin!"

High Ranger Lord Vu'Duc presented the many promotions, awards, and bonuses to the Imperial Guard recipients, the protectors of the Empress. The men and women in their Royal Purple uniforms and long cloaks carried deadly pulser spears, their primary weapon. When the last Imperial Guard accepted his award and returned to the ranks, they were all applauded loudly by everyone in the Court.

Presenting the Borgund and Kaylan Ranger awards, the High Ranger Lady Bette was efficient and spoke with authority, as Lord Vu'Duc had done. Yet when she announced the last award winner, her voice showed her pride, "Ranger Tish, you are awarded a commendation for Excellent Performance in saving young Prince Lukus' life, with the gratitude of our Empress Kayla. You are also promoted to Commander Tish!" Her fellow Kaylan Rangers cheered the Ranger, as her Grandmother, the Lady Bette, smiled with Lord Vu'Duc. Then, everyone applauded the Ranger award recipients loudly, and cheered for those promoted.

Dressed in his formal Borgund Ranger uniform and black cloak, Royal Consort Master Commander Dan'L and four Novice Rangers handed out Holiday gifts from Empress Kayla to all Rangers and Imperial Guards. The Empress held out her left hand to little Prince Lukus, who climbed the throne stairs gingerly. Lukus stood by his Mother's side, raised his arms, and proclaimed, "Let the feast begin!" The smiling three-year-old Prince was showered with applause and laughter from all the Rangers, Imperial Guards, and the happy audience.

Servants brought in sumptuous roasted meats and large platters of all kinds of delicious foods. Wine and hard cider were served, and live musicians played. Empress Kayla spared no expense to celebrate her bravest protectors tonight. "We're almost through, Consort Dan'L. Please take our Son and his Grandmother with you and go ahead of me. Lukus will probably sleep the entire trip to the Imperial Command Battle Cruiser," Empress Kayla quietly said. Her Consort Dan'L, Grandmother C.S. Javette, and C.S. G'Rosk, Javette's Life Partner, left with Prince Lukus for their New Year's Holiday trip to K'Halon Prime, their home planet.

After another hour, Empress Kayla walked back to her Royal Suite in the North Wing with her two Kaylan Ranger personal guards, Master Commanders Shanna and L'Van. She changed out of her formal red Ranger dress and high-heeled boots, the same uniform all her Kaylan Rangers wore tonight. Her attending ladies handed her the black trousers and blouse of the daily Ranger uniform, and stood back a prudent distance while Kayla put on her breastplate and backplate armor, and arm bands. "I'm not flying for three and a half days in those high heels," she quipped, and her Rangers laughed with her, watching her put on her fancy black boots—definitely not regulation footwear.

"Now, my last order of the year is for both of you to enjoy the Year-End Holidays with your loved ones. Four years as my personal guards must have taken their toll on you. In January, you get to rejoin our Kaylan sisters with regular assignments befitting your ranks. I'm certain you'll be relieved to be free of me!" Kayla said with a smile, "My heartfelt thanks to both of you, Shanna and L'Van." She touched her heart and bowed her head to her personal Rangers, and they bowed deeply to her. She handed them each a special Holiday gift and dismissed them.

The Empress left the Palace with six Imperial Guards and boarded her large Imperial shuttle to the Capital City Space Base. They lifted up and flew off. In a few minutes, Empress Kayla, a warbird space pilot for many years, looked out of the view window, and realized they were flying the wrong way to the Base. "First Commander T'Let, please check the pilot's course with him. I do not see the harbor," she asked the Guard seated across from her. She saw his head drop in sleep, and said, "First Commander T'Let?" Her Guards' heads dropped one by one.

"What's going on here? Guards!" She yelled, and tried to unbuckle her harness, but it would not unbuckle. Then, her eyes rolled back in her head, and the Great Empress Kayla went unconscious.

The shuttle pilot said to his concealed guest in the cockpit, "It's been twenty minutes. They're gassed and unconscious, Baron. You can step out and buckle into your seat now. They'll be out at least one hour." Both men wore gas masks.

"Then, fly to your coordinates now," the Baron ordered, with a devious smile on his face. Both men began to laugh as the Imperial shuttle flew into the night with their captives. A few minutes later, a hidden door opened along a hillside, and the shuttle slowly flew inside. The shuttle lowered ten meters and landed, and the concealed door closed. The beautiful Empress Kayla was hoisted over the pilot's shoulder and carried to a cold, dark cell, and dumped on the floor like a sack of potatoes.

II

Dim amber lights greeted her eyes, as Empress Kayla blinked several times, attempting to focus clearly. Metal walls, white ceiling, and a concrete floor. Vibrating energy bars glowed brightly to her right. She was locked in a cell, somewhere. The cell was four meters long and three meters wide, with a height of three meters. The musty smell indicated the cell was underground. Beyond the energy bars was a large storeroom but she could not see how long or wide it was in the very dim light. Her wrist comm link had been removed. She reached into her cloak, but her scanner was gone. The nano-titanium breastplate and backplate were still on her body; no one could touch them other than her, without a severe shock. Her body armor was coded to her DNA.

Fighting her initial panic, Empress Kayla breathed deeply and exhaled slowly to calm herself. *Whose captive am I?* Then she answered her own question aloud, "Figure Thirteen, are you there?" She stood and faced the energy bars, the only opening.

The sound of a chair being pushed back preceded footsteps approaching. He looked at his Royal Captive and said, "Good evening, former Empress Kayla. I hope you're uncomfortable." He wore a mask over his eyes. She discreetly touched the vid recorder on her breastplate.

She recognized her captor. "No need for the ridiculous mask, Baron Tri'T. Please tell me why you have done this to me," she said, and stared into his eyes. He took off his mask.

"You know why. You called me 'Figure Thirteen,' so you know who I am. Therefore, you know why you are here. In thirty days, I will be Emperor, in accordance with Imperial Law. Our 'Plan of the Thirteen' will be executed as originally designed many years ago. The rule of the Warrior Class is at an end. Your reign was brief and is over. No one will find you here, former Empress. If you are cooperative, I will consider releasing you, once my coronation is passed, of course. If you cause me any problems whatsoever, I will gas you again, and end your life. Are we clear, former

Empress Kayla?" He asked.

"Clear as water, which I need now, Baron Tri'T. And some food as well, if you please," Kayla requested politely. *Get the basics first, then see what else he wants.* He walked away, then returned with a bottle of water and two snack bars. He touched keys on the control panel, and a small opening formed in the energy bars.

"Make them last. I have many things to do before I return," the Baron said, and passed the water and snack bars to her through the opening. "By the way, your cell is magnetically sealed, and lined with mirrored titanium. Any weapon fired inside will see you killed from the ricocheting fire. Your hidden pulser and laser pistols, and your famous plasma sword hidden inside your armor are useless. We thought of everything," he said with a sarcastic smile.

She looked him directly in his eyes and said, "I made a very special and expensive effort to locate and rescue you from the devastation on M'Wati, Baron Tri'T," Kayla said, taking the bars and water from him. "I spared no expense. Many lives were lost searching for you. And we gave you a Royal Homecoming to celebrate your recovery, Baron," she added.

"And for that, you are still alive, former Empress. My colleagues wished to kill you immediately, but I convinced them otherwise," he answered. He programmed her cell's energy bars and began to walk away.

"What about my Son? Where's Prince Lukus? And my Royal Consort Dan'L?" She asked, first with a demanding voice, then repeated, pleading with the Baron. But no answer came, only the sound of a heavy door closing. She was alone in the near darkness.

En Route to the Imperial Command Battle Cruiser

"This is my third call, Captain. I demand to know where the Imperial shuttle containing Empress Kayla is, right now. I am Royal Consort Dan'L, and you'd better tell me where she is this instant," he demanded, with anger in his voice.

The Space High Command Captain answered, "As we already reported, Royal Consort: Our Empress Kayla has not arrived, and her Imperial shuttle is missing. All efforts are being made to locate her and the shuttle. I'm sorry, sir, but that's the only information we have. We simply do not know where the Empress is now," the Captain answered, frantically handling call after call. "Her shuttle dropped off the scanners right after launch."

"Dan'L, he doesn't know anything. Go sit next to Lukus and let me handle this. You're too distraught right now," C.S. G'Rosk said. "Go on, Son. Let me do my job." G'Rosk was the Life Partner of Dan'L's Mother,

Javette. He had also been Dan'L's mentor during his and Kayla's Phase 2 and 3 Ranger Training, over ten years ago. G'Rosk knew Dan'L well.

Javette sat in the pilot's seat after Dan'L left the cockpit and buckled in. She looked in the overhead mirror at her Son and Grandson, worried about them. "G'Rosk, if this is another coup against our Empress Kayla…"

"Of course, it is, Javette. And I'm afraid whoever is behind this has our Kayla either in captivity, or she is…"

"Don't say it, G'Rosk. Don't you dare say it," Javette said firmly to her Partner. "I refuse to believe our Creator would let her die like this. She is alive, I know it. And if there is any way under the sun she can escape, Kayla will find the way. She is a Ranger!" Javette said and tilted her head back to fight tears. "She will survive!"

Home World Ranger High Command, Military Advisors, and Imperial Guard High Command were furiously working, every man and woman contacting every possible landing site, each emergency channel. There was no sign of Empress Kayla, her six Imperial Guards, or the Imperial shuttle. They had lost contact with her six hours ago.

Lord Vu'Duc, Lady Bette, and Field Marshall General Blatan looked at their former Emperor P'Lau, now the Chief Advisor to the Empress. "There is no other choice. We must declare a solar system-wide state of emergency. Full Red Alert. It is Imperial Law. The protocols are clearly defined," P'Lau stated, sounding like the Emperor he used to be.

Gen. Blatan said, "I'll order up the Imperial Army, Navy, Air Corps, and Space Cadre to Red Alert. The Empire is under attack—from where or whom is unknown. You are correct, Chief Advisor. Six hours have passed. We must do what is necessary."

"Then, we will lock down here and at K'Halon Prime," Vu'Duc said. He signaled Red Alert within both Palaces and ordered every Ranger and Guardsman to their respective Main Courts. It was 3:45 a.m. on December 25th. Lord Vu'Duc implemented the solar system-wide state of emergency. All personal and holiday leaves were cancelled.

Chief Advisor P'Lau ran to the command control system in the North Wing of the Palace, logged in under his authorization codes, and keyed in the state of emergency command. Every door in both the Home World and K'Halon Prime Palaces closed and locked automatically. Every Imperial Government Building on all four planets locked. All water purification plants, desalination plants, power plants, communications stations; every hospital; and each military base were under Emergency Control. Only three people had the authorization codes at this state of emergency level: Empress Kayla, Chief Advisor P'Lau, and High Ranger Lady Bette.

"A solar system-wide state of emergency has been declared, Commanders Superior G'Rosk and Javette. You are to return to Home World Capital City Base at once and bring Prince Lukus to the Royal Palace

Ranger High Command for sequestering. You and Royal Consort Master Commander Dan'L are to report to me for your assignments. Lady Bette out." Javette looked at G'Rosk and took his hand.

"We have failed our Empress Kayla, Javette. If this turns out badly, I will never forgive myself," G'Rosk whispered. "Never!"

From behind the pilot's seat, Dan'L listened to his Mother and G'Rosk talk in whispers. He heard Bette's orders and their conversation. He was a Borgund Ranger—a master of stealth. G'Rosk felt his presence and turned around to see him standing there, listening. Dan'L put his hand on his Mother's shoulder, and said, "My Empress was correct. She said only last week: The Plan of the Thirteen was still being implemented, even after four years of her rule. 'Figure Thirteen' is behind this. I know he is, Mother. I'm sure of it."

"If you are right, my Son, then we have to do everything in our power to protect the only one blocking Figure Thirteen's path to the throne. We must protect the heir, Prince Lukus. If Empress Kayla is absent from her throne for thirty days, Imperial Law demands a new Emperor be crowned. Her heir is Prince Lukus, and you are his Father, Dan'L. Both of you are vulnerable, my Son," Javette said quietly, and looked at him. She left the pilot seat and Dan'L sat down.

After buckling in, Dan'L punched in the comm link number on the secure line for High Ranger Lady Bette. After she answered, he said, "This is Royal Consort Master Commander Dan'L, Father of Prince Lukus. With all due respect, High Ranger Lady Bette; the state of emergency protocols are too widely known. The heir to Empress Kayla's throne will be sequestered in a place known only to me and our Creator. Please notify Admiral Mur of the Imperial Command Battle Cruiser the Commanders Superior G'Rosk and Javette will be dropped off on his main hangar bay, and will require a fighter for return flight to Home World Capital City Space Cadre Base."

A few seconds passed, then High Ranger Lord Vu'Duc came on the line and said, "I cannot approve of your plans to violate emergency protocols. We will protect Prince Lukus here, Royal Consort Dan'L."

"Like everyone protected Empress Kayla? I will not have my Son suffer the same fate as his Mother! I swear on my honor to keep him safe. Lukus is my Son, as well as the Royal Heir. He will be safer if our whereabouts are unknown!" Dan'L said emphatically. "Please, Lord Vu'Duc and Lady Bette. Please trust your Ranger, Lord and Lady," he pleaded.

"He's going to do it anyway, Vu'Duc. May as well give him permission, so he is not breaking Imperial Law and considered a fugitive," Bette said wisely. The two highest Ranger authorities in the Empire acquiesced.

Vu'Duc leaned into the vid screen and said, "Master Commander Dan'L, we expect you to fulfill your Ranger duty and protect your heir to the throne. You will signal Commander Superior Javette every three days to let us know Prince Lukus is safe. You will succeed at any cost! Return the Prince to this Palace in twenty-eight days. Vu'Duc out!"

Dan'L flew straightaway to the Imperial Command Battle Cruiser, orbiting above Home World. He landed, and G'Rosk and Javette ran down the hatch. The techs fueled up his ES-317 warbird, loaded it with missiles, and Dan'L launched at full throttle. In ten minutes, they accelerated to hyperspace eight.

Little Prince Lukus walked up to his Father, rubbing his sleepy eyes. "Hello, Father. Where's Grandmother and G'Rosk?"

Dan'L patted the copilot seat, and Lukus climbed in and fastened his harness. "I will not lie to you, Son. Your Mother has not arrived at her ES warbird. We are afraid a bad man has captured her, Lukus. Grandmother Javette and G'Rosk are joining all the other Rangers to find your Mother, our Empress."

The boy's eyes opened wide. He sat up very straight, and said, "The Rangers will find my Mother. They must find her! Grandmother will make them find her, won't she, Father?"

Dan'L smiled at his Son and replied, "The Empress' Rangers will do everything in their power to find her. And I will do everything in my power to keep our Prince Lukus safe!"

They talked for a long time about the situation. For a three-year-old, Prince Lukus was quite advanced and intelligent. Neither of his parents had ever "talked down" to him or treated him as a simple child. The Prince asked, "Where will we hide, Father?"

"In the White Belt, Lukus. The most dangerous place I can think of, Son. Are you ready for an adventure?" Dan'L asked with a twinkle in his eye.

Prince Lukus excitedly said, "An adventure—how wonderful! Full speed ahead, Master Commander Dan'L!"

III

The Cell

Scratching another tic mark into the cement floor, Empress Kayla counted off her fourth day of captivity. The breastplate and backplate body armor kept her torso at 98.6 degrees, but her legs and feet were cold. She looked at her body armor and snickered. The armor was full of hidden weapons and knives, plasma pulser pistols, and the plasma sword; yet it was useless in here, with the magnetically sealed walls. The water bottle was nearly empty, and her last snack bar had only one bite left. A 20th-degree Master of T'Ly, the highest of the martial arts, Kayla used deep meditation to keep her focus sharp, and her will to survive strong. But the human body required clean water and food to live, whether Empress or vagabond. Vagabond…

Kayla recalled meeting a vagabond many years ago, Kend'R. He was a disgraced Borgund Ranger, banished to a jungle moon by the Empire. She was sent by then-Emperor P'Lau to pick up Kend'R and return him to Home World. She listened to Kend'R tell his story during their long flight. Over several days, he revealed his underserved fate, and she knew he told the truth. Upon his return, Kend'R was absolved of any crimes, and reinstated as First Commander.

When she ascended the throne, Kayla promoted Kend'R to Master Commander, and one of her personal guards. They were good friends. During his banishment, Kend'R made a meager living charting horoscopes. He even plotted hers, but Kayla didn't believe in horoscopes. She believed in the Creator of All Things, and the human spirit.

Stretching out her long legs, Kayla remembered Kend'R's last prediction for her two weeks ago: "A slippery slope is ahead of you, my Empress. It cannot be avoided, but it can be traversed with much care and wisdom." She poo-pooed the horoscope, as always, preferring to take each day as a blessing from the Creator. But wonder of all wonders—Kend'R was once again correct. She was on a slippery slope, indeed. Would Baron Tri'T come back and release her, or bring her more water and food, soon? Or would he let her starve, continue the Plan of the Thirteen, and take her throne?

Bowing her head, Kayla said another prayer for her six Imperial Guards and their souls. Any man corrupt enough to plot the capture of his Empress would not hesitate to kill her unconscious Guardsmen. She began to slowly pace in her cell, to keep her blood flowing. How could she get word to Dan'L or Javette she was alive? Reminding herself of the Imperial protocols, Kayla knew a state of emergency had been declared. If she could only let them know where she was; but it was futile. She had no idea where Tri'T kept her.

For four years, Empress Kayla had ruled the Empire. On the night of her official coronation, original "Plan of the Thirteen" signer, former Baron Z'Lun, orchestrated a coup d'état with Space Cadre Fleet Admiral U'Ret, and the Baron's son, D'Reg. Empress Kayla and her Rangers soundly defeated the coup. Z'Lun, U'Ret, and D'Reg were imprisoned and interrogated repeatedly about co-conspirators working with them against the Empire. During these interrogations, the Plan of the Thirteen was mentioned, and several original signers' names were divulged. But not all.

One of the original signers died before the Vee Lok Lords returned to select the next Emperor/Empress. The ailing Baron chose his replacement without disclosing the man's name to the other Plan members prior to dying. The name of the new "Alternate" replacement was unknown to Baron Z'Lun, or the others captured after the attempted coup. All the captured traitors knew of the replacement was that he was given the notebooks and keys to the safe deposit boxes of their deceased co-conspirator, and the information and vast wealth contained therein. The replacement was known only as "Figure Thirteen."

The mysterious Figure Thirteen was finally revealed to Empress Kayla as Baron Tri'T of M'Wati, the only known participant in the Plan from that planet. Tri'T was now her captor, jailer, and, if her Rangers and Imperial Military failed to rescue and release her in time, the new Emperor.

Determined to survive, Empress Kayla began her T'Ly martial arts workout. She would stay alert and strong as she could be and find a way to survive. She would succeed at any cost.

Home World

The Great Council of Barons met in an emergency session at the mansion of Baron S'Tan. "We must discuss the absence of Empress Kayla today. The Military Advisors and the Lord and Lady High Rangers assure me everything possible is being done to locate the Empress. We all know she has been abducted, and may already be deceased," Baron S'Tan opened. "None of us can afford to ignore the situation, much as we'd like to."

"We cannot sit on our thumbs and do nothing. Imperial Law states a new Emperor must be chosen by this Council if the Sovereign is absent for thirty days," the Elder Baron T'Sur said, stating the law they all knew. "I am well past the age of seventy. Therefore, I withdraw my name from consideration. Two of my Brother Barons should also withdraw: Baron S'Tan, and Baron T'Lec. Then, we are left with four candidates from which to choose. It is prudent we discuss this grave matter tonight and wait until our next meeting to vote. On the twenty-eighth day, if our beloved Empress has not resurfaced, we will meet to choose the next Emperor."

"But, what of Prince Lukus? He is her heir, and next in line. We cannot displace the first-born Son of Empress Kayla!" Baron Tri'T said, pounding the table.

"I will not swear a blood oath of loyalty to a three-year-old boy! It is unconscionable! His Father will make all the rulings, another Borgund Ranger," S'Tan said bitterly. "We will choose the next Emperor, not the Rangers!"

The discussion continued into the late night, over many bottles of Brandywine. The Great Council of Barons agreed on two points: the three of them over the age of seventy withdrew from consideration; and whichever of the four remaining Barons was chosen would formally request Prince Lukus to abdicate. The "eternal loyalty" each Baron swore by blood oath to Empress Kayla was forgotten. It was December 31st.

The Emergency High Command meeting continued at the Palace of Home World. Four Commanders Superior sat at the long conference table checking off their lists of actions taken in the last two weeks with the Military Advisors. None of them was one millimeter closer to finding Empress Kayla. "She could be anywhere in the solar system!" A frustrated General L'Mar exclaimed. "How do we know she is still on Home World? No communications with her or the Imperial shuttle. No DNA-tracking signatures. Nothing! The proverbial needle in a haystack," he said in a defeated tone of voice. "We tried LIDAR, GPR, and satellite scans. My Air Corps fighters have scanned every sector of Home World, K'Halon Prime, and M'Wati."

Their discussion continued for two hours. Then, C.S. G'Rosk received a text from M.C. Kend'R, requesting five minutes of their time. G'Rosk agreed, and Kend'R was admitted.

Standing at attention, M.C. Kend'R said, "Honorable Sirs and Madams: our Empress Kayla utilized many methods two years ago when she ordered the search for Baron Tri'T after the M'Wati Disaster. In addition to all the methods we have used in the last two weeks, she also ordered GPR—

ground penetrating radar—sonar pinging, and scanning with underground scan-tubes, searching for heat signatures."

"Yes, we are aware of the methods used, Master Commander," C.S. T'Anh said abruptly, interrupting him.

"We also used amplified telepathy, and Ground-Penetrating Radar with ultra-sonar waves," Kend'R revealed. "I believe we should try this at once, Commanders Superior."

The leaders looked at Kend'R as if he was crazy. Then C.S. Javette asked, "Did you participate in this 'amplified telepathy,' Kend'R? I know you are a telepath. But no human other than those living on M'Wati helped in Baron Tri'T's discovery and rescue," she stated.

"I beg to differ, Commander Superior Javette, with all due respect. Empress Kayla had me fly over the Baron's property and adjacent lands below our scanner range. I used the amplified techniques to detect a survivor in the wine cellar next door to the Baron's vineyards. The robotic borers were sent into tunnel, and the wine cellar was discovered, with Baron Tri'T still alive. The technique worked then; why not now?" Kend'R bravely asked.

"Did you know of this search, Commander Superior B'Von?" T'Anh asked accusingly.

B'Von answered quietly, "Yes, of course. Master Commander Kend'R is my twin brother. I was ordered to keep his mission secret. Only Empress Kayla, Kend'R and I knew. The methods utilized were too unconventional for others to know. But Kend'R found the Baron in only three days," he shared. "We discussed this last night. When Kend'R requested permission to use the technology from the Military Advisors, he was denied. We decided to ask your permission to try it to find Empress Kayla."

Javette slapped the table and said, "Then why haven't we done this already? We've tried everything else. I want this 'amplified telepathy' put to work tonight!"

"But where do we start? We've looked everywhere. All sectors of Home World; K'Halon Prime; even on Ban'Ti!" General Blatan said.

"Would you show me where the searches took place? Maybe I could help, sirs, madams. Empress Kayla is my Sovereign, and my friend. I am her astrologer," Kend'R announced. "I will help as much as I can, if permitted."

Projections came up above the table, and the areas covered by GPR, DNA-tracking, and scans were shown. Concentrating on Home World by sheer instinct, Kend'R asked, "Please zoom in another fifty percent here," and examined open spaces not scanned. "Why were these areas not scanned, if I may ask?"

Gen. Blatan answered, "They are farmlands, mostly owned by Baron S'Tan. The harvest is at hand. The Baron asked that we not put our GPR machines in his fields until after the harvest." The Military Advisors and

Ranger High Command leaders looked at each other, not saying what each one feared.

High Ranger Lady Bette ordered, "Then begin your 'amplified telepathy' over the areas you wish to cover at once, Master Commander Kend'R. You will report your results to C.S. B'Von or G'Rosk daily. We will provide a fighter and a pilot for you, so you can concentrate. And may the Creator help you find our Warrior Empress Kayla!" She dismissed Kend'R, and he left to begin his search. Bette turned to the Military Advisors and asked sternly, "Now, which one of you intentionally kept Kend'R's information from this High Command group?"

The Cell – 20th Day

Weak from hunger and thirst, Kayla leaned against the wall. Her survival training taught her how to survive in the desert, snow and ice, and in the jungle. But all tactics had to be considered now, in her underground prison. Her new tall boots were used to collect her own urine, the only liquid she had to drink for ten days. After throwing up the first time, she could swallow and keep it down. Hunger pangs gnawed inside her belly, causing intense muscle spasms. She curled into a fetal position to alleviate the contractions of her intestines. Starvation was a very effective, slow torture. Two weeks and six days in here, and she was still alive.

Laughing softly, she thought of how many times she wished for a little more time to herself since becoming Empress. "Be careful what you wish for," she reminded herself aloud. She prayed to her Creator once again for her Son Lukus' safety, and for Dan'L to keep him safe. Lukus and Dan'L were the only ones blocking Baron Tri'T's path to the throne.

Would Javette, G'Rosk, Bette, and Vu'Duc swear allegiance to Tri'T, if he took her throne? If not, they would be banished; or more likely, be killed instantly. Would her fourteen billion people of the Empire be treated fairly by Baron Tri'T? No way. Anyone who would be part of the Plan of the Thirteen would not consider the well-being of the people of the Empire. He would take the throne, kill anyone who did not swear loyalty to him, and do whatever he pleased. The Empire would become his personal playground, and its wealth his to enjoy.

Suddenly, scratching sounds came from the floor, and her weary eyes opened. A little field mouse squeezed under the wall and began sniffing around the floor of her cell. The cute little brown mouse checked out the toilet hole in the corner, and then slowly approached the limp body of the Empress in the far corner. Silently Kayla drew a thin knife from her breastplate, waited until the field mouse was close enough, and stabbed it. "Hello, lunch," she said. She crawled to her cells' energy bars and turned the mouse in the rays, cooking her lunch. Another day of life was hers.

The next day, Baron Tri'T came through the storeroom door and walked up to the energy bars of Kayla's cell. "Still alive, former Empress Kayla?" He asked.

She sat up as best she could and replied hoarsely, "By the grace of our Creator, yes, I am. Are you here to release me, Baron?" Her face was ashen, and her cheeks sunken and drawn. She gathered her cloak and touched the vid recorder on her breastplate.

"No, not yet. When your Son, Prince Lukus, abdicates the throne to me, I will release you. You and he will spend your lives on K'Halon Prime, working the Fringe Lands for me. I will enjoy watching both of you scratching the desert ground, trying to convert it to farmland," he sadistically said. He opened a wine bottle, and took a long drink, knowing her throat was contracting, just by watching him swallow the liquid. "By the look in your eyes, I assume you have managed to survive on your own water and waste. Wine tastes so much better than piss," he commented, and drank from the bottle in his hand. "Much better, in fact."

Kayla stared at him, then asked, "So, tell me, Baron Tri'T: how did you survive for nearly three years in the wine cellar on M'Wati? We found empty cans everywhere and hundreds of empty wine bottles. Most think you survived on fine wine. But, after being in here for three weeks, I know you must have eaten something. So, please tell your dying Empress, how did you survive?" She asked, watching him drink more wine.

The Baron looked at the ashen woman on the floor and snickered. He said, "Very well, former Empress. Since you did have me rescued and treated as a hero, I will tell you." He took another drink of fine wine and told his story: "When the nuclear bomb exploded in N'Well, I was at my barrister's home. He called his servants to gather all the food, water, and candles, and take them to his wine cellar. My barrister, six of his women servants, and his butler and I holed up in the wine cellar. We pulled a mattress against the door for insulation against the radiation."

The Baron pulled over a chair and continued, "For two weeks, we shared the food equally, lighting the candle for our only light. The butler tried to pick up broadcasts on his comm link, but there was nothing. We toileted in the trash can, and took turns going out to empty the can every day. We were very civilized, at first. Then, the barrister forced one of his servants in sex. She screamed like hell. The butler took another woman and forced himself upon her. We all were so drunk on the wine, you understand. It's all we had after the first month."

He took a long drink and said, "When my barrister beat another servant and raped her, the butler jumped him and killed him with a wine bottle. Blood ran everywhere. The butler then cut his body up and roasted his flesh over a fire of broken-up wine boxes. We all ate the meat. The next day, I ran to the back of the cellar to hide from the butler, and found a cell, just like you're in now, containing highly expensive vintage wines. The blood-thirsty butler tried to attack me, and I trapped him inside, and locked the door."

"Two of the younger women who'd been raped ran outside to die. Four women were left," he said. "They agreed to take turns giving me sex, and I agreed to not force them, or beat them. After another week, we killed the butler," he disclosed, and drank more wine.

Kayla saw his face change. She quietly asked, "And which wine did you drink with his flesh, Baron?"

He laughed and answered, "We ate his legs and arms, and drank syrah. When we roasted his heart, belly, and liver, we washed the meat down with port. When we ate his brain, the pink sparkling wine tasted better." Another tilt of his wine bottle, and then he finished his story:

"After another three months, the women were so weak, I put them in the vintage wine cell. It's amazing how long a human body can stay alive when appendages are cut off, arm after arm; then one leg; and the second leg. I survived on the flesh of my barrister, his butler, and his women servants! There, I've said it, former Empress Kayla. And I'd do it again. I'll do whatever it takes to survive. Your Son, Prince Lukus, will give his throne to me. One way, or another!" The Baron stood and threw aside the empty wine bottle. He reached into his bag and pulled out another bottle of wine and a loaf of bread and passed them to Kayla.

"I assume you will stay alive a few more days, now. Long enough to watch my Royal Coronation. Fare thee well, former Empress Kayla!" The Baron stumbled out of the room, and she heard the door slam shut. Then Kayla touched her vid cam to shut it off.

The wine bottle was sealed. She saw her reflection in the bottle glass. She looked like a beggar, a trashy vagabond. A vagabond… A telepathic vagabond…

"Kend'R," she called aloud, "Hear me, Kend'R. Find me. Release me. Save your Empress, my friend Kend'R," she cried. All evening, she called his name, as a mantra. She broke off some bread and ate little pieces slowly. The crumbs were placed around the cracked brick to attract another little mouse-morsel. She used her big knife to cut off the bottle top and drank some wine. *It is better than piss*, she thought. "Kend'R, come find me. Kend'R, find me," she chanted all night and the next day. "Kend'R," she cried. "Come find me, Kend'R."

IV

Home World

The Main Court at the Palace on Home World was packed; over five hundred aristocrats, courtiers, military brass, and every available Ranger was present. It was the thirtieth day of Empress Kayla's absence. The Great Council of Barons walked in, all eight titled, wealthy men dressed in their finery. They stood next to the women Kaylan Rangers.

"Presenting Prince Lukus and Royal Consort Master Commander Dan'L," the High Priestess announced. Dan'L brought his Son forward. The audience whispered so loud, it sounded like a storm to Dan'L. *Where was Kayla? Was she dead?* He was trying to be strong for his Son. The boy was next in line for her throne, but he was only three years of age. Prince Lukus tried to stand with his head high, but the child was full of fear.

Baron S'Tan stood and said, "It has been thirty days since our Beloved Empress Kayla has held the throne. Imperial Law demands the throne be given to another this very day," he stated. The cheers from the Main Court audience were few, but loud.

The Chief High Tribunal Justice stood and said, "We are obliged to agree with the esteemed Baron S'Tan. A new Emperor must take the throne today."

Prince Lukus was escorted to the steps before the throne. The High Priest held Dan'L back, as Baron Tri'T approached the boy. He quietly threatened, "Your mother is alive and waiting for her Son. If you give your throne to me, she will live, and hold you in her arms again. If you do not give your throne to me, Prince Lukus, your Mother will die a slow and painful death, as will your Father, your Grandmother, and all those you know. Now—abdicate," he whispered. "I am not kidding, boy. We have your Mother, and she will die today if you do not give your throne to me."

Dan'L tried to reach his Son but was restrained by the High Priest and Palace Guards. They held Dan'L while the audience in the Main Court watched the struggle for power between a grown man and a little boy. They could not hear the Baron. "My Mother will be released, and come home to me?" The little Prince asked.

Baron Tri'T answered only, "Yes. Now do you abdicate your throne to me, or will your Mother die screaming in horrible pain?" The Prince broke free and ran crying to his Father. The audience was silent. No one heard the Baron's threats to Prince Lukus, but they saw the boy being intimated by Tri'T.

"The Prince has abdicated. The new Emperor is to be chosen by the Great Council of Barons. Whom do you choose as Emperor, my Barons?" The High Tribunal Justice asked.

Baron S'Tan stood and answered, "We choose the survivor of the M'Wati Disaster. We choose Baron Tri'T!"

The Main Court audience did not applaud or cheer. They were stunned the events in front of them were taking place. "What did he say to make Prince Lukus run away?" They asked.

"Where is our Empress Kayla? We want our Empress Kayla," the voices began, and turned into loud, raucous chants. "Empress Kayla! Empress Kayla!"

But the Baron walked up to the throne and stood in front of the High Priest and High Tribunal Justice. They tried in vain to quiet the audience. The High Priestess refused to participate, walked down the throne stairs to the Rangers, and joined the people, "Empress Kayla! Empress Kayla!" The Borgund and Kaylan Rangers then loudly joined the cheer, "Empress Kayla! Empress Kayla!" Everyone felt the treachery at play.

"I demand you give me the crown! Crown me now!" An angry Baron Tri'T yelled at the top of his voice. The Main Court yelled and chanted "Empress Kayla!" even louder.

The High Priest motioned for the High Priestess to join him, but she raised her arms and chanted loudly, "Empress Kayla!"

The Baron screamed, "Crown me! I am the Emperor now!" The High Priest looked at the Main Court audience, everyone shouting at him. He tried to calm them by raising his arms, but his efforts did not work. Their shouting grew louder. Baron Tri'T yelled in his face, "Crown me, I said! I am the legal emperor! Crown me now!" The High Priest then blessed Baron Tri'T and told him to kneel. He raised the crown above his head and began the prayers. The audience kept chanting for their missing Empress, while the High Priest continued.

The thirteen-meter-high metal doors blew apart with a deafening crash, as an attack chopper flew into the Main Court. The two riders on the chopper flew between the ranks of the Borgund and Kaylan Rangers. Empress Kayla jumped off the back of the chopper, drew her plasma sword, and twisted its handle in a flash, extending the sword into a spear.

She threw the plasma spear between the High Priest and Baron Tri'T and yelled, "That crown is MINE!" Kayla leaped up the steps, and the startled High Priest placed the crown on her head. The Main Court audience roared with cheers and applause. Imperial Guards grabbed Baron Tri'T and held him away from her.

"Baron Tri'T, you are under arrest," Empress Kayla ordered. Imperial Guards took the Baron off the steps, kicking, screaming, and demanding for her to step down.

The Empress looked a fright. But she sat on her throne and ordered the side vid screens to be lowered. She touched her breastplate vid recorder and downloaded it for everyone in the Main Court to view. The audience watched as every word spoken by Baron Tri'T to Empress Kayla was played for them. When he confessed to consuming the flesh of his barrister and the women servants piece by piece, shouts came from the audience to have his head on the Palace gates. The Main Court audience was shocked, appalled, and disgusted with the Baron. Only two years ago, he was lauded as a hero survivor of the M'Wati Disaster.

"Thank you for your support, my people. Our absence the last twenty-nine days was not by our choice, as everyone has seen," Empress Kayla said weakly. She was handed a cup of water and downed it at once. Then, she continued, "We will not delve into the darkest parts of our captivity. Suffice the record to reflect our return on this day, by the hard work of our Rangers and Military, Master Commander Kend'R, and by the mercy of our Creator."

Once again, the Main Court cheered and applauded their distressed Empress. From the attack chopper, Kend'R slowly walked to the table where the shocked Council of Barons sat. He stared at Baron S'Tan as he slowly walked toward him, reading his mind. Kend'R raised his arm and pointed his finger, saying loudly, "You! You knew where she was. It was your secret place. You knew where our Empress was the entire time! Traitor! TRAITOR!"

Baron S'Tan jumped up from his seat and tried to run, but Master Commander Shanna caught him, and put a choke hold on the traitor Baron. Imperial Guards took him from her, put S'Tan in restraints, and led him away.

Empress Kayla said, "Baron Tri'T, you have deceived our Council of Barons, our High Priest, and our people. You abducted our person and killed six of our bravest Imperial Guards. The crimes you committed on M'Wati have shocked and sickened us. Put this traitor in prison. Take this cannibal away!" She yelled. Baron Tri'T was taken to a prison cell below the Palace.

The High Tribunal Justice stood and apologized to Empress Kayla, and then said, "This Imperial High Court Tribunal petitions our Great Empress

Kayla to expedite the legal proceedings against former Barons Tri'T and S'Tan. Since everyone in Main Court and the Empire watched their treachery, reaching a verdict will be a swift process." The Empress bowed her head and agreed to the expedited legal proceedings.

Empress Kayla received blessings and anointing from both the High Priest and High Priestess, then was helped to her Royal Suite. Kayla refused to let any of her ladies touch her, or her filthy clothing. For the first time in thirty days, she removed her breastplate and backplate. She stayed under the cleansing water of her shower for over an hour, with tears streaming down her face. The Royal Physician examined her and prescribed treatment for her starved body. Immediately, a med droid was brought to her suite, and fluids, fresh blood, and supplements were given to her intravenously.

After the Royal Physician left, Prince Lukus was allowed in to see his withered Mother. The boy rushed to his Mother and held her with all his might. When Royal Consort Dan'L came to Kayla and saw how emaciated she was, he could not hold back his tears. She managed to say, "Our family is together again, at last. The Creator be praised." Dan'L held her gently, and all three of them cried together. The ladies-in-waiting huddled in the corner, each of them in tears for their beloved, starved Empress. They called for food to be sent up right away.

"I'm sorry I stepped down, Mother. But the Baron said he was going to make you hurt and kill you, and Father, and Grandmother, and everyone I knew," little Prince Lukus revealed, the tears rolling down his cheeks. "He was so mean, Mother." She comforted her Son until he stopped crying. Grandmother Javette entered and held Lukus, rocking to soothe him.

The servants pushed in three carts of various foods for them. But Kayla could only eat little "mouse-sized" bites, and drank cup after cup of clean, cool water. It would be many days before she could eat a simple meal. She sipped liquid protein, ate fresh yogurt and some buttered white bread. Her entire digestive system groaned loudly, and Lukus laughed hearing her belly. He tried to mimic the sound and Kayla had to laugh with him. It brought them all some relief and served to quell the elevated level of emotions in the Royal Suite.

The last order from the Empress before going to sleep was to incinerate her filthy clothing and boots worn for thirty days. Dan'L made an appointment with her bootmaker for new boots the next day, and a new dark red breastplate and backplate fitting was scheduled.

One week later

The ladies-in-waiting carefully dressed Empress Kayla for her third Main Court appearance since she retook the throne. Javette was visiting her before the Court session and the conversation was amiable. Rich pastries were on the serving tray with fresh fruit and yogurt, and the ladies enjoyed the time before having to depart for Court. Everyone was light-hearted and happy to see their Empress putting on some much-needed weight. Her cheeks were beginning to have some color in them, and Kayla looked much less gruesome. As her dress was being fastened, Kayla felt an overwhelming pain in her abdomen sharply attack her. She held her belly, and then fainted. Javette immediately called for the Royal Physician T'Sel.

"Give her some air, please. Stand aside now," the Royal Physician cried, making his way to the stricken Empress, lying in a pool of blood. Quickly scanning his Sovereign, he called for a gurney and ordered her shuttled to the Imperial Naval Base Hospital.

Royal Physician T'Sel and Imperial Navy Physician Captain Mae stood next to the Empress, discussing her condition after the emergency surgery. Royal Consort Dan'L paced in the hall like an angry lion, watching the scene in the secure Emergency Room.

Slowly, Empress Kayla began to blink her eyes, and tried to focus. "Easy, your Majesty, now go slowly," the white-haired Royal Physician said softly. "We have you in the ER at the Imperial Naval Base, at the harbor. You're recovering from a sedative. Consort Dan'L is outside, anxiously waiting on you to awaken," he said, patting her hand.

The room began to spin when she sat up, and Kayla nearly fell forward off the bed. Captain Mae caught the Empress just in time and helped her to lie down again. She said, "Please move slowly, my Empress. You've been through a lot. Just lie back," Captain Mae said. The attending nurses propped up her body a little so Empress Kayla could relax, yet slowly awaken.

Consort Dan'L was allowed into the room. He took Kayla's hand and kissed her cheek. The Royal Physician stepped back and sat in a chair, completely exhausted, and signaled for Captain Mae to take over for him. She asked, "My Empress, do you understand me?" Kayla nodded, while a nurse sponged off her sweaty brow.

Captain Mae looked at Dan'L, then said to her Empress, "I am very sad to tell you this, but we were not able to save the child. We tried everything, your Majesty. We saved you, but not your baby," the Captain said with genuine remorse. "You miscarried violently. I'm certain it was from your weeks of starvation, my Empress."

From the look in Empress Kayla's eyes, the Navy physician knew Kayla was unaware of her pregnancy. "You did not know, your Majesty?" She asked softly, to confirm. Kayla shook her head "No," and the tears streamed down her face. The medical personnel left, giving Kayla and Dan'L time alone.

Dan'L held Kayla while she cried for her lost child. "You were starved,

Kayla. Too weak to carry our child, they said. The Baron killed our baby," he said vehemently. A respectful time was given to the Royal Couple, then a soft knock preceded her room door opening.

"My Empress, there have been many advances in medicine since the Vee Lok Lords blessed us with advanced knowledge. We now have the ReGen-Pod, and Captain Mae's specialty is Regenerative Medicine. With your permission, Captain Mae will take over your medical treatment, my Lady," the Royal Physician T'Sel said. "We were going to let you recover slowly and naturally from your starvation, but the violent miscarriage you suffered has changed things. I strongly recommend this new treatment for your Majesty. Otherwise, you could be bedridden for months, Empress Kayla," he said softly.

Captain Mae said, "It will not be easy, but the ReGen-Pod treatments will accelerate your healing. I recommend we start right now, Empress Kayla." She nodded in acceptance, and her head fell back on the pillow. Consort Dan'L kissed her again and left the room.

The Empress was prepared for ReGen-Pod treatment. The med techs moved Kayla to the dark room where the large machine resided. "It looks like a giant cryo tube," Kayla muttered, and Captain Mae agreed. They carefully lifted Kayla off the gurney into the ReGen-Pod and removed all her IV tubing. "Your extreme dehydration and malnutrition shrunk several of your organs, most notably your kidneys, and your uterus, my Empress. Your liver and pancreas aren't too happy either," she said, and Kayla smiled at the corner of her mouth. "Now please lie back. We will give you a mild sedative gas now, Empress." A strange smell of oranges filled Kayla's nose and lungs, and then her eyelids closed. They shut the machine's heavy cover and began.

For three hours, Consort Dan'L waited, paced, and worried while his Kayla lie in the ReGen-Pod. The newest technological wonder targeted her damaged kidneys, uterus, liver, and pancreatic cells, and rebuilt them at the sub-molecular level. Captain Mae supervised and monitored the procedure, assisted by a team of surgeons ready to correct any error, or take over with traditional surgery. Upon completion of her treatment, another full-body scan was taken and analyzed. The procedure worked.

The Great Empress Kayla awoke, and discovered she was surrounded by Dan'L, her brother Olm, and her family. She was exhausted but managed a smile. "Did my loyal Barons elect someone else to replace me yet?" Kayla asked Javette.

A soft round of laughter filled her room. Then Javette answered, "No, my Empress. The Great Council of Barons was fresh out of cannibals."

Kayla laughed until her monitor beeped and her stomach ached. A worried Captain Mae ran into her room and found the Empress smiling, surrounded by her concerned, loving family. "You must rest now, your

Majesty. We have several more, smaller treatments over the next few days. Your family can claim you in three days, Empress Kayla," the Navy Physician said. Everyone said their good-nights and left.

"I've never seen such an incredibly positive reaction to the ReGen-Pod treatment. She was so emaciated. I feared we would have to resort to old-school organ replacement. Our Empress is truly remarkable," Captain Mae told Dan'L. He agreed with her, and went home to his Son, Prince Lukus.

V

Within three days, Empress Kayla was shuttled back to the Royal Palace. The third bedroom inside her Royal suite was set up as recovery room, complete with a state-of-the-art med android. After a few hours' rest, the Royal Physician and Captain Mae scanned and examined their VIP patient.

The Empress sat up and said, "I have to hold Court. I haven't been there for my people in many days. They need to know their Sovereign is still capable and ready to serve them."

Her doctors approved three half-day Main Court sessions a week, supervised by one of them, of course. Cpt. Mae said, "Your Majesty, the best trajectory to complete recovery is patience. Your body needs rest, mild isometric exercise, and a calorie-rich diet, heavy with proteins. I urge you to consider the long-term effects of a successful recovery. Pushing your body at this time will not only slow down your recovery; you may permanently scar your new organ tissues. Please, Empress Kayla, I beseech you: Please take it easy, my Empress," she pleaded.

Kayla waved away her attendants and everyone but her doctors. "Are my organs too damaged to conceive and bear another child?" Her green eyes focused intently on Cpt. Mae.

"I will be frank with your Majesty. At this point in time, we do not know for certain. But with rest, proper diet and very mild exercise, we should be able to put you into the ReGen-Pod in three more weeks. Another treatment should restore your reproductive organs completely," she answered.

The Royal Physician added, "You must refrain from sexual intercourse of any kind for at least two months, I'm afraid. Your organs are in the rebuilding and healing process. No physical exertion, no bending, and no lifting. And no marital activities, Madam Empress. It's for your own good, Empress."

"So, Baron Tri'T is still controlling our life," she said, and rolled her head to the side. She tapped her wrist comm link, and her Kaylan guards entered, followed by four Imperial Guards. "Please summon Chief Advisor P'Lau," she asked, and sighed heavily.

Several minutes later, a concerned P'Lau stood next to her bed. "Please announce we will attend Main Court the day after tomorrow for one-half day, then twice a week for two weeks. All petitions are to be submitted in writing prior to presenting them in Court. All banquets and dinners are postponed for two months, but mid-morning refreshments will be served. The thought of dealing with the aristocrats before their tea unnerves me," she said. "When does the High Court Tribunal expect to announce their verdict for former Barons S'Tan and Tri'T?"

"Next week, Empress Kayla. But you are not required…"

"I will be there, P'Lau, even if I have to stay in this bed! My abductor will face me when the verdict is announced!" She declared, and the vital sign monitors began to beep. The med droid adjusted her IV controller and sent a mild tranquilizer into the Empress' vein.

P'Lau added, "The Imperial Prosecutor added the charge of murder of your unborn baby. Former Baron Tri'T will meet the Creator very soon, my Empress," P'Lau added bitterly. "Too bad he can only be executed once!"

"And Baron S'Tan?" She asked weakly, beginning to feel the effects from the tranquilizer.

He answered, "He is complicit, without a doubt. But his attorney claims S'Tan knew nothing of Baron Tri'T's plan to abduct and starve your Majesty."

"The bloody liar," she responded, and fell fast asleep. Chief Advisor P'Lau left her room.

Master Commander Kend'R told the Inquiry Board every detail of his search for missing Empress Kayla. His recordings from each search and written reports were discussed, along with testimonies of the Air Corps pilots who methodically flew over the farmlands with Kend'R in the copilot seat, telepathically "Listening."

"This Board has heard your testimony, Master Commander Kend'R. But, quite frankly, your 'Amplified Telepathy' seems far-fetched," the leader, Space Cadre Admiral C'Dur, said. "Almost unbelievable, in fact."

C.S. B'Von stood and said, "Master Commander Kend'R's telepathic ability has been well-documented since the Royal Academy, Admiral. His 'Amplified Telepathy' technique was used secretly on M'Wati to locate several pockets of survivors, including Temple priests, priestesses, monks and nuns. Soldiers surviving underground at the Imperial Army Base were also found and rescued," B'Von stated.

"Are you certain you knew nothing of this underground building previously, Master Commander Kend'R?" Another Inquiry Board officer asked, in an accusing tone.

Kend'R remained at attention and suppressed his emotions. He calmly replied, "I was imprisoned on Ban'Ti three years, then banished to A'Wan another eight years. Upon my return to the Emperor's service, I was sent to the Temple of the Creator on Xau for over eight months. Although my Brother and past friends have welcomed me back, those Borgund Rangers who are more recently in service avoid me. I have not been present in the Main Court for duty since my reinstatement. How could I possibly have known about a secret, underground building on lands owned by a Baron unknown to me?"

Most of the Inquiry Board accepted Kend'R's response. But the still-disbelieving Adm. C'Dur said, "Your claim of telepathic communication with our Empress is still hard to believe. It's ludicrous!"

Turning to look at the Admiral directly, Kend'R replied, "I will prove my gift from our Creator, with this Board's approval." Every man nodded in agreement, and Kend'R began:

"You awoke at 4:17 a.m., got out of bed, and took a piss. Then, you returned to bed, mounted your still-sleeping lover, and forced the boy in anal sex. For breakfast you had green tea and boiled eggs. Then, you hired a shuttle cab to take you to the Base and arrived by 6:57 a.m. Shall I continue, and tell of your episode in the Palace storeroom with the delivery boy prior to attending this meeting, Admiral C'Dur?"

Everyone stared at the now-revealed Admiral C'Dur. The newest believer in Kend'R's telepathic ability turned red-faced and stormed out of the meeting.

The Official Inquiry Board struck Kend'R's revelation about Adm. C'Dur from the record and accepted his testimony. The meeting was adjourned.

Kend'R's discovery and rescue of Great Empress Kayla resulted in a broadly inclusive search warrant being issued for all properties of the Baron S'Tan. When Kend'R pinpointed the location of Empress Kayla last week, it was in the middle of a vineyard. Big GPR machines were used to identify and mark the location and size of the underground building. But no entrance was found.

Imperial Army commandos were dropped in the vineyard with robotic boring machines, and they penetrated through ten meters of soil and concrete into the building. They rescued the emaciated Empress, and she was evacuated to the Royal Palace in the Air Corps fighter with Kend'R. Their blasting into the Main Court on an attack chopper and the Empress retaking her throne was watched by her people live on all the broadcast and Imperial networks.

As a result of the Official Inquiry Board ruling and far-reaching warrant, the hidden, underground building was searched by investigators with a fine-toothed comb. Baron S'Tan's mansions and all his properties were searched. Every record, computer file, document, and data crystal were taken into evidence. All the "dirty laundry" of Baron S'Tan was made public. His innocent family moved into seclusion and changed their names.

The secret underground building housed contraband; field-grade weapons and ammunition; jar after jar of pleasure drugs; various chemical grenades outlawed for decades; and old-fashioned torture machines and tools. Hundreds of new Rebel uniforms were boxed and stored, along with boots, helmets, and thirty-year-old space suits.

The building was so far underground, no scanning device registered the shuttle. Access to the building was by either a secret tunnel connecting the underground building to the wine storage warehouse, or a false hillside hangar entrance, where the Imperial shuttle was flown inside, and remained parked. The underground building was immense. The six Imperial Guards' bodies were in body bags in a walk-in freezer, along with eight other unidentified bodies. They were removed for identification of remains by coroners.

When the Army Commando Major was making his final search through the now-empty underground building, he methodically shined his xenon light along each wall and floor joint, while his men scanned every millimeter. "Bring the scanner over here," he ordered. His flashlight revealed a wider-than-usual gap where the wall met its ninety-degree joint.

Scanning revealed a room behind the wall. When a special brick was touched, the wall opened to a forty by fifty-meter room, decorated throughout with occult symbols, dried bones, various crystals, and black candles. A long satin cape was hanging on a hook, with a black mask, like the mask Baron Tri'T first wore when he captured the Empress. Behind a painting of men copulating with women, boys, and beasts, was a large safe.

It took a master safe cracker over two hours to open the high-tech lock on the safe. The Major recorded the safe being opened, witnessed by High Ranger Lord Vu'Duc and Baron T'Sur. Inside the large wall safe was a treasure trove of 10,000-credit bars, many property title documents from the last several hundred years, and a long gilded box.

"Remove the box and scan for prints. Then open it very carefully," Lord Vu'Duc ordered. He focused his vid camera as the box was opened. Lying inside was a parchment scroll.

"Lord Vu'Duc, close the box and bring it to my private study at once. You have all done well," Empress Kayla said, watching from her study in the Palace. The parchment scroll was carefully unrolled while being recorded from every angle. At the top of the document were the words: "Plan of the Thirteen."

The scroll was taken to the secret Imperial lab for full analysis, supervised by lead scientist, Dr. D'Vre. Dozens of recordings were made of the infamous scroll. Written in the ancient language from K'Halon Prime spoken now only by the priests, a copy of the document was made to be translated for the Empress by her trusted friend, Priest K'Ramm.

Home World Royal Palace

Baron T'Sur escorted Empress Kayla into the Main Court for the session with the High Court Justice Tribunal. Surrounded by her personal Borgund Ranger guards and Imperial Guardsmen, the Empress slowly sat on her throne. The High Priest handed the Royal Scepter to her, then blessed the Main Court audience. The High Priestess blessed Empress Kayla.

The High Court Justices stood and the senior Justice announced: "Former Baron Tri'T of M'Wati, you have been found guilty of high treason; abducting and abusing our most high Empress Kayla; unlawful imprisonment and intentional starvation of our Sovereign; indirect murder of her unborn baby and heir to the throne; murder of six Imperial Guards; murder, and consuming the flesh of your barrister, his butler, and four household servants; rape of four women; deceiving the Great Council of Barons, and the High Court Tribunal Justices. Your other charges number over one hundred sixty-four, and you have been found guilty of each charge."

The Senior Justice put down his com tablet and said, "Never in our history has one man been convicted of so many heinous crimes against our Creator; against Nature; and against women. To sentence you to death by injection is an affront to this court, our Great Empire, our Empress Kayla, and your victims. Therefore, it is the decision of this High Court Tribunal to sentence the former Baron Tri'T to death by the 'Walk of the Unrepentant,' in the jungles of Ban'Ti!" The Baron raised his head high and smiled arrogantly at them.

The audience within the Main Court was stunned. Then, the voices began to rise in the Court. The people began questioning each other what the sentence meant.

"What is the 'Walk of the Unrepentant?' I've never heard of it," Master Commander Kend'R asked C.S. G'Rosk in a whisper.

"Tri'T will be dropped into the deepest, darkest heart of the Ban'Ti jungle, naked, without food or water. His body will be drenched in fresh blood, and his tongue cut out, so he cannot cry out for help. He will be consumed by the jungle," G'Rosk whispered. "It is not enough. The Creator alone will see that the balance is restored," he said. "Fiend!"

As the audience in the Main Court slowly discovered what the sentence entailed, the mumbled voices began crying out: "He tried to deceive all of us and rule our Empire!"

"Abductor of our Empress! Ban'Ti is too far away!"

"Cannibal! Most unclean!"

"Murderer!"

"Killer of innocent babies and women!"

"Rapist! Misogynist! Cannibal!"

"Kill the cannibal! Kill him now!"

Empress Kayla sat stoically on her throne, her eyes focused on the former Baron Tri'T, who refused to look at her. When the High Court Tribunal Justices left their bench, the Main Court audience stormed the floor, and surrounded the arrogant, guilty man. Palace Guards tried to keep the people away, but could not, and were pushed away. The high-priced defense attorney for Tri'T ran out of the Court, fearing for his life. The aristocrats, landed gentry, and courtiers attacked Tri'T, taking turns punching and kicking the Deceiver Cannibal. Only then did Tri'T's face show fear.

The Main Court audience became a mob. Surrounded by her Imperial Guards and personal Rangers, Empress Kayla slowly stood. Imperial Guard M.C. An'Ton picked up her frail body, swiftly walked out of the Court with the Empress, and carried Kayla to her Royal Suite, followed closely by Chief Advisor P'Lau. The mob in the Main Court beat and tore Tri'T limb from limb, ripped off his genitalia, and drug his mangled corpse out of the Court to the Palace Main Gates. They impaled his body pieces on pikes of the high fence. Cheers and applause thundered for nearly fifteen minutes. Justice was served by the people.

The Main Court doors were closed and locked.

Baron T'Sur and the other members of the Council of Barons visited former Baron S'Tan in prison immediately after the Main Court's fury was released. S'Tan was found by his prison guards later, with a sharpened wooden stake through his heart—the deed committed by falling on the stake by himself, the security vid showed. His body was also impaled on the high fence by the Main Gates that evening, by persons unknown.

Empress Kayla looked out her windows and saw the bodies of former Barons Tri'T and S'Tan impaled on the high fence of the Palace Gates. She recalled her firsthand experience five years ago, witnessing the Rebels of Duma Wat turning against him, and offering their former leader to her for surrender. The scene turned her stomach.

"I've never been so shocked and disgusted," Captain Mae said, turning away from the window. "How could such highly educated, civilized people do this, Empress Kayla? Could you have stopped it?" She asked, her face showing total disgust.

Kayla sat carefully in her big chair and let the med droid start yet another IV in her arm. "Captain Mae, fortunately, you weren't in Court today to witness the mob. There was nothing my Imperial Guards or Rangers could have done to stop the six hundred incensed members of the Main Court. Yes, I could have ordered my Imperial Guards to fire on them; but then, hundreds of innocent people would have been killed. And I would have been the Evil Empress for ordering their slaughter."

She leaned her head back and said, "I have twice witnessed civilized people turn into a mob. Mob mentality is shocking, brutal, and appallingly deadly. It is a swift tidal wave of violence. The mob executed Baron Tri'T. In three days when Main Court reopens, the wealthy aristocrats, courtiers, and VIPS will be dressed in their finery, with smiles on their faces again. Today's event will be justified rationally as deserved punishment of a monster," the Empress observed. "Justice is avenged."

After scanning her Royal Patient, Captain Mae asked, "How can anyone rule, knowing what their members of the Court are capable of doing? How can you calmly walk into the Court after today, and look at them without fear? It is beyond my comprehension, Empress Kayla," she commented, and made notes on her com tablet.

"We were appointed to serve the people. We are their Monarch, true. But we also belong to the people, Mae. Any Sovereign who does not remember who he or she serves is destined to either rule an Empire of slaves as a despot or suffer a fate worse than death. I choose to serve our Creator and my people, and put them first in everything I do," Empress Kayla stated firmly.

After the blood transfusion and liquid protein infusion completed, the Empress said, "We have conferred at length with our Royal Physician, who has faithfully served three Sovereigns in his career. He has been promoted to Chief Medical Advisor. You are hereby appointed as our Royal Physician, Admiral Mae, if you can tolerate us going forward," Kayla said with a smile.

Newly promoted Admiral Mae bowed and replied, "It would be my greatest honor to serve you, my Great Empress Kayla."

VI

K'Halon Prime, T'Anju Temple

The early morning rays of the rising sun shined through the magnificent stained-glass windows on the east side of the Temple. From his private study, Priest K'Ramm meditated on his prayer rug, and let the rays of colored light fill his face and his mind. This was a wonderful, blessed day from the Creator, and the priest was filled with energy and purpose. It was truly a glorious morning.

Winter had come with all its force early this year on K'Halon Prime, bringing fierce winds and storms both north and south of the equator. But at T'Anju, it remained mild, with sporadic, light snowfall, and more sunny days before winter claimed the seaport and harbor. K'Ramm relished every sunny day, knowing many months of grey stormy days lie ahead.

The Temple of the Creator would be completed soon. A big Grand Opening was being planned, to coincide with the opening of the fancy ski resort and casino in the mountains to the west of the Temple: "Mount Regency." The three hotels near the Temple were almost ready to welcome pilgrims. Even the High Priest was attending the Grand Opening, bringing several new priests, priestesses, and nuns for assignment to the new Temple. Brother D'Avid had more than fifty monks assigned here already. Twenty-one acolytes were serving the Holy Men and Women, helping prepare the new Temple for the people.

Rising from his meditation, K'Ramm stood, stretched his muscular body, and walked to his office. He buzzed for an acolyte and requested breakfast. So far, it was a peaceful sunny morning. The red light on his private comm link suddenly began flashing, demanding his attention. The incoming message was urgent and top-secret. It had to be his Empress Kayla. His heart beat a little faster.

Trying to be cool and "priestly," and not show his excitement, he answered, "This is Priest K'Ramm. How may I serve our Great Empress

Kayla today?"

The video opened and he projected her face onto his large screen. She was still thin, but so beautiful, even after her trials of abduction and near starvation. She smiled graciously at him and said, "Good morning, Priest K'Ramm. May the blessings of our Creator fall upon you, and all those at His Temple. In respect of your time, I will cut to the chase. A special document has been discovered, written in the ancient language now used only by your Holy Caste Order of priests and priestesses. Your Empress requests you to personally translate this document, sharing the transcription only with us. No other eyes must see it. No one else must know of its existence. Will you assist us in this matter?" Empress Kayla asked.

"I am always at your service, my Empress, and am honored to be chosen for this task," K'Ramm answered. He saw the serious face of the woman he once held in his arms for several days of bliss. *This must be very important to her*, he realized.

She managed a warm smile for her priest, and said, "Thank you, K'Ramm. You are within the highest circle of those I trust. I await your return call."

The top-secret, "Eyes Only" encrypted file downloaded on his comm link, and K'Ramm looked at the projected scroll: "Plan of the Thirteen." Even in the Temple on T'Anju, rumors of "the Thirteen" were heard. These were the men who tried to take over the Empire during the first week of his Empress' reign, the night of her coronation. Were they connected to the evil Baron Tri'T, from K'Ramm's home planet of M'Wati?

The acolyte knocked and brought in his breakfast. K'Ramm instantly shut down the file and waited until the young acolyte left before reopening it. The long scroll was nearly one meter in length. He went to his supply cabinet and brought out a new com tablet, and immediately began transcribing the document. After checking it three times, K'Ramm encoded his transcription, and keyed in the secret comm link number to his Empress.

K'Ramm said, "Before I send my translation to your Majesty, a few observations must be made. The grammar of this document is high-level, like the Holy Books. The writing is that of a Temple scribe; perfectly written, with measured spacing between each word and sentence, and a large flourish on the first capital letter of each paragraph. This document had to be written by a Temple scribe, a seminary teacher, or a priest, my Empress," K'Ramm said, with a worried look on his face.

Kayla recognized the look of deep concern on her friend's face and made notes of his observations. Then she said, "Please continue, Priest K'Ramm."

"This document is exactly one thousand, three hundred words; thirteen hundred, my Lady. The first half of the Plan described the history of

K'Halon Prime as the original seat of the Empire. The original ten Barons of K'Halon Prime and the gifts of land, title, and riches given to them from their Royal Benefactors are mentioned."

He rubbed his forehead and continued, "The Plan goes on to reveal the resentment of the current Barons of the seat of the Empire's power being moved to Home World. While Home World flourished and became the focal point for each successive Emperor, K'Halon Prime languished, and fell behind in importance. As more than half of its people relocated, the 'Parent' of the R'Genra System fell into third place, after Home World and M'Wati."

Then he read directly from his transcription: "We pledge our lives, our lands, and our wealth to restore the might of K'Halon Prime, by taking the throne for one of our pure-blooded brothers of K'Halon Prime, restoring the seat of Empire to its rightful planet." He summarized the next section, where the Plan threatened death to any signer who revealed the Plan to an outsider.

Then the priest leaned forward and quoted, "Upon the return of the Vee Lok Lords, this Plan will be enacted. If one of us is chosen, all will support him. Any other chosen by the aliens to rule will be eliminated by any means possible, until one of us, or our sworn, loyal Alternate Lords, takes the throne. Our 'Technicians' have sworn loyalty to the death and will continue the Plan if we are discovered and fail to complete our objective. The Fount is made to overflow for them. The Old Engine will be rebuilt and restored to its magnificence. The Plan will succeed at any cost. Signed this day in blood, we dedicate our lives to the Plan of the Thirteen." K'Ramm laid down his com tablet and looked into the vid cam.

Empress Kayla and K'Ramm shared a look of high concern, both realizing this evil Plan was still at work. K'Ramm said quietly, "My recommendation is to re-interrogate any prisoners connected to this Plan for information relating to 'Technicians,' 'The Fount,' and especially the 'Old Engine,' my Empress. The Holy Caste Order must uncover its conspirators, as well. This is most disconcerting, Empress Kayla," K'Ramm said.

"Thank you for your observations and transcription, K'Ramm. Send over the file securely at once. There is much work to be done. The fifth anniversary of our coronation is in six months; a perfect time for action," she said softly. "Please pray for the people of our Empire, Priest K'Ramm, and many thanks to you," she said, bowed her head, and signed off. The transcription downloaded in seconds. She read the translated document in its entirety several times. All she worked for during the last four years as Empress was at risk. Peace; Reconciliation; better schooling; advancements in science, medicine, and technology. Her life, and the lives of her Son Lukus and his Father Dan'L were still in someone's crosshairs.

It was time to design a Plan of her own. She would not sit idly by and let the Technicians, Alternates, and other members of the Plan of the Thirteen usurp her reign. The highly advanced, powerful, Galactic Vee Lok Lords must have known her sovereignty would be challenged, even four years after her ascension to the throne. Vee Lok Lord Ceen gave her advanced knowledge when they appointed her Empress, and she continued to study and grow the best she could. Kayla wrote for hours on a new com tablet, designing new, non-protocol defensive strategies to protect her Empire.

What was the "Old Engine?" The "Fount;" what and where was it, and what purpose did it serve? They had better find out soon. The Plan would require saboteurs working within the Imperial Military to be successful. She conferenced together her Ranger High Command and Chief Advisor P'Lau, and commanded, "Ready our Imperial Command Battle Cruiser and appropriate personnel for travel to K'Halon Prime. Departure in two weeks. Trip duration: one month." After further consideration, she added M.C. Kend'R to the "Essential Personnel" roster.

The first rule of interrogation is to ask the right questions of the subject. After the failed coup d'état the night of Empress Kayla's coronation, the guilty traitors Baron Z'Lun, his son D'Reg, and former Fleet Admiral U'Ret were arrested and questioned day and night. The former Baron revealed the "Plan of the Thirteen" under truth serum, and eventually divulged the names of those who had signed the document in blood. The only name not revealed was that of the mysterious "Figure Thirteen," the unnamed replacement for the Baron who died prior to the Vee Lok Lords' return. Figure Thirteen turned out to be Baron Tri'T.

All named co-conspirators were tried and sentenced by the High Tribunal Justice Court, but no one was executed. Empress Kayla sent Z'Lun, D'Reg, and U'Ret to M'Wati, sparing their lives, but punishing them harshly, nevertheless. The former Baron Z'Lun was one of the Thirteen; his was the first signature, in fact. His son D'Reg helped his Father, deluded by dreams of power fed to the seventeen-year-old boy by his Father; but D'Reg was not one of the Thirteen. U'Ret was a paid traitor, loyal to the Baron for years. He was not one of the Thirteen, either.

The remaining names were titled landowners, Royal Beneficiaries of land and title grants hundreds of years ago. The Lords and Ladies working in alliance with the Thirteen were the majority of titled beneficiaries on K'Halon Prime. Millions of square kilometers of land, mansions, many houses, hotels, resorts, factories, and vineyards were taken back by their current benefactor: Great Empress Kayla.

The Great Council of Barons numbered twelve when Emperor P'Lau ruled. Within the second week of Empress Kayla ascending the throne, there were seven. There were more than forty titled Lords and Ladies during the reign of Emperor P'Lau, on all four planets. After the unsuccessful coup, only twenty-seven remained, four of them on K'Halon Prime. The price of their failure was very high.

The one Baron the Empress trusted was the Great Council leader, Baron T'Sur of Home World. He was invited to a special meeting with Empress Kayla in two days. The only new titles she had bestowed were to High Ranger Lord Vu'Duc and High Ranger Lady Bette, and they were Life Partners for over thirty years. Kayla granted them a beautiful mansion and estate on a land parcel on Home World, a few hundred kilometers from Capital City.

Much of the Royal Hierarchical System required realignment, and the Empress wanted the valuable input of Baron T'Sur. The elderly Baron lived and breathed the Royal Hierarchy. T'Sur knew every Royal Beneficiary and their history for hundreds of years. But the unfortunate man never married. He had no heir to succeed him, not even one niece or nephew.

Those imprisoned former Barons, Lords, and Ladies were to be re-interrogated by senior Kaylan Rangers. A new set of questions was prepared for them to pose to the prisoners, specifically names of "Technicians," "The Fount," and the "Old Engine." They were also questioned for the name of the scribe or priest who hand-wrote their Plan on the long parchment scroll. These questions had not been asked in their nearly five years of captivity.

The Commanders Superior met with Empress Kayla in their underground conference room, with C.S. T'Anh and C.S B'Von conferenced from K'Halon Prime. The Empress also brought in her Chief Medical Advisor, her Weapons Master, and the Royal Scientist, Dr. D'Vre. "My trusted Rangers and honored guests, Dr. D'Vre would like to share his newly-discovered information with you," the Empress said. "Please recall we gave the original 'Plan' parchment to Dr. D'Vre to study."

Dr. D'Vre projected a holographic picture of the gilded box and its parchment inside. "For several days, we studied the scroll; scanned it; translated it; took small samples of the parchment to date it; and so on. On the back side of the scroll were faint markings, initially assumed to be ink transferred from rolling the scroll. But reverse-negative analysis revealed something else," he said excitedly, and the holograph of the scroll turned over.

"The reverse of the scroll revealed more writing in the ancient language when reverse-negative analysis was applied. You will notice the handwriting here is the same style, identical script flourishes, and spacing. Priest K'Ramm from the Temple at T'Anju translated the reverse for us, and his translation was astonishing, to say the least," Empress Kayla revealed.

Much more specific information was contained on the reverse side of the scroll, written in special ink visible only under black light. Names of the Lords sworn to the Thirteen were listed, the type of contribution each made, and their code name. All the code names were common animals, such as Boar, Steer, Buck, Rattler, etc. "There are three Lords on the list who escaped detection and are still at large. Two of them attended Main Court last week," the Empress said. "Please see to their arrest and interrogation immediately, Commander Superior G'Rosk. They are presumed innocent, of course, pending investigation."

Dr. D'Vre continued, "We also scanned the gilded box and found nothing; until Empress Kayla ordered us to remove the gold and re-scan it again. As she suspected, more information was written inside the box itself, along with this." He held up a long, flat key. "It's rigid plastic, which is why we missed it during the first scans. Our analysis reveals the type of lock it fits is ancient. It is obviously for one-time use only, since any lock that old would break off this key if used," he said. "We presume there is a steel master key in use."

The Royal Scientist was thanked and excused from their meeting. "The fastest and best way to continue our investigation is to obtain more information from those incarcerated. Our Chief Medical Advisor recommended a trained physician accompany our Kaylan interrogators to K'Halon Prime and Ban'Ti Imperial Prisons to hypnotize the prisoners. It is imperative we draw the information from these men soon. Each of them has received visitors in the last five years, and all are now under investigation. One man in particular met with each prisoner in the last six weeks. But he is no ordinary man. He lost every agent we sent to follow him. Even our Borgund Rangers," the Empress revealed. She signaled for her Weapons Master.

"As you know, we are attempting to incorporate minimally-invasive methods of spying and interrogation. These have recently been developed, on recommendations from our Empress Kayla," he said, and opened a small box of seemingly-dead flies. "Insects are everywhere and operate unnoticed by most humans, unless we happen to be eating something fragrant or greasy. Then flies try for morsels on plates, and cockroaches invade the food preparation places at night. Bugs are the perfect spies!" He removed a fly, pinched its wings, and it flew around like a real fly, trying to land on their cups. When C.S. Javette shooed the fly away, it flew off, and landed in the air duct.

The Weapons Master showed everyone the fly's transmission. Each face at their table was recorded, and fingerprints on their cups were scanned in detail. The fly spy was now recording the meeting, transmitting their actions live. He quipped, "We now have the veritable 'fly on the wall' to broadcast to us live any place we plant it, inside any room," he said proudly.

Empress Kayla thanked her Weapons Master, and he left. "My friends, our investigation has now changed. Perhaps the prisoners assumed we would never acquire the information we now hold and have continued their original plans. It is prudent to assume one or all of them know we now have the late Baron S'Tan's 'Plan of the Thirteen,' and have translated it, both front and back. We must ask the right questions to get the right answers," she said, quoting her Phase 2 teachings. Senior Rangers around the table nodded to their Empress.

"You will assign Master Commander Kaylan Rangers to perform the initial interrogations. Send them to K'Halon Prime and Ban'Ti Imperial Prisons today. They are to report to our Weapons Master prior to departure for flies and cockroaches," she said. "Also assign Borgund Rangers as undercover prison guards for the prisoners. They will escort the prisoners to meet with their visitors. Each visitor will have this affixed unknowingly to his or her person after the visit." She held up a sheet of transparent plastic, with tiny, clear dots attached. "Each dot is coded for DNA tracking. No electronics or detectable homing device," she said.

The Commanders Superior, and High Rangers Lord Vu'Duc and Lady Bette had their tasks laid out for them. The Empress stood to leave, and then asked, "Have you prepared the personnel lists for our trip to K'Halon Prime? Please make certain Master Commander Kend'R accompanies us. We have appointed him our Royal Astrologer," she said, and left in a hurry.

"Royal Astrologer?" Lady Bette asked.

From the vid screen on K'Halon Prime, C.S. B'Von answered, "Kend'R is blessed with a rare gift from our Creator. Our Empress Kayla is wise to enlist his help in this situation."

C.S. Javette said. "This malevolent Plan is still being implemented as we speak. We need all the help we can get."

VII

Seven courses of gourmet food and wine were consumed over a two-hour time span by Baron T'Sur, Chief Advisor P'Lau, and Chief Medical Advisor T'Sel. Empress Kayla skipped the wines and could barely eat more than one bite of the rich food. Her appetite was satiated after a few bites of bread and potatoes, knowing she could digest them easily. Her Chief Medical Advisor nodded silently at her food choices, slim though they were.

Empress Kayla began, "I remember my Father telling me stories of the old Empire, the mighty Earl of Wil'Ont, the Barons of K'Halon Prime, and the Lords of the Realm. He made the ancient Empire seem almost magical," she said with a smile.

Baron T'Sur sat back, and began his tale: "When I was but a lad, my Father and I rode out on horseback all day across the land. From the mountains of the East, across the hardwood forests, and to the Great Winding River we rode with our men. Being young and naive, I asked, 'Will this someday be my land, Father? It is vast and wonderful!'"

He leaned forward and said, "My Father took the reins of my horse and made me dismount at once, and we walked the horses for over an hour. 'We are stewards of the gifts given to us by the Emperors and Empresses. This great, vast land belongs to the people of Home World, and their generations to come. It is not mine to give to you, my Son. It is my title and responsibility I bequeath to you, entrusting you to shepherd our people. This is my legacy to you.'" Baron T'Sur took a sip of his Brandywine.

"As a student in the Royal Academy, we learned the Royal Hierarchical System; who controlled which lands on their planet; and the legacy of their title. The Hierarchy must be restored to strengthen the aristocracy, and the Imperial Class System itself," P'Lau offered.

Chief Medical Advisor T'Sel added, "Without a strong aristocracy, many within the middle and lower classes would not be provided the opportunities to achieve and excel as they now do. I myself attended Medical School on a scholarship from the Great Council of Barons," he revealed.

Baron T'Sur framed the main question: "Our shame and aspirations to disrupt the Royal bloodline and break our ancient agreement with the Vee Lok Lords have brought us to this moment. My utmost respect and admiration of your strength of will and tolerance go to our Empress Kayla. Many Emperors past would have ordered all the aristocracy put to death after the initial coup d'état failed the night of your coronation. It has happened before. I confess; I fully expected Borgund Ranger steel to slice my throat upon hearing of the failed coup. After your abduction and near starvation by former Baron Tri'T, I stand in complete amazement of my being allowed to live, along with my fellow Royal Beneficiaries. But, thanks to your grace and mercy, here we are today, Great Empress Kayla. What will you do with our aristocracy now, my Warrior Empress?"

Kayla carefully worded her response to the most powerful remaining Baron in the Empire. "As you all know, I was born a daughter of K'Halon Prime, and in the Warrior Class. My late Father, Master Commander Tom'S, once said our class was chosen to rule the Empire because we had the fewest members and were the strongest. He said we were born, bred, and trained to protect the Emperor, and serve the Creator. Our Emperor served the people of the Empire and our Creator. I am here before you by the grace of our Creator, protected every second by our loyal Rangers and Imperial Guards. It is my appointed life task to serve the fourteen billion people of this Empire. I would welcome the assistance of dedicated stewards of the Empire, gentlemen. But, unfortunately, my personal experience with the members of the aristocracy has been…less than desirable. You, Great Baron T'Sur, have been the one blessed exception, which is why I seek your wise counsel today," she answered honestly.

He responded, "An Empire is as strong as its supporters and its military. The aristocracy should be your direct beneficiaries and staunchest supporters, my Empress. An Empire without an aristocracy is a dictatorship. Power must be held at the top and merited to those our Empress trusts to carry out her wishes. We need more stewards for your people, my Empress. Otherwise, you must increase your military, Rangers, and Imperial Guardsmen by ten-fold, or more. We all stand on the shoulders of those beneath us, either by sharing power, or by force. You alone must choose, my Great Empress," he closed.

Standing with some effort, Empress Kayla said, "The Vee Lok Lords chose a Warrior Empress to lead this great Empire. We dedicate our life and rule to serve the people in a New Dawn of Peace and Reconciliation. We choose to restore the Royal Hierarchy, one beneficiary at a time, guided by your wise counsel. To demonstrate our commitment, we bestow upon our esteemed Chief Medical Advisor T'Sel the title of 'Lord T'Sel,' and the lands and property listed in this deed," she said, handing him a scroll from her inside cloak pocket. He took her scroll and bowed his head.

"For our next appointment, we turn to our most trusted Chief Advisor P'Lau, to whom we swore a blood oath to serve and obey as a Novice Shi'Lon Ranger. To honor your twenty-six years of wise rule of this great Empire, we bestow upon P'Lau the title of Baron, and grant you the K'Halon Prime lands from the ice shelf, to the great Eastern Mountains, to the Great River, and to the fifteen-degree parallel above the equator," she said with a big smile, and handed her newest Baron his scroll. "We give you one-half of the lands formerly controlled by Baron Z'Lun." P'Lau was in shock; he bowed and took the scroll from her.

The tired Empress stepped behind her chair and held onto it tightly. "And finally, my last appointment is for you, Baron T'Sur. Your lands and properties on Home World are already vast. To add to your property holdings would only burden you at this time. Therefore, your Empress chooses to place you above the other members of the aristocracy and appoints you our Viscount T'Sur!" She signaled an Imperial Guard, who brought out a fancy red box holding a long, gold necklace from the Royal Heirloom collection to her. She placed the necklace around him.

"Our formal ceremony will be held in the Main Court on K'Halon Prime in two weeks, Baron P'Lau, Lord T'Sel, and Viscount T'Sur. Plan to accompany us on our Imperial Command Battle Cruiser in eleven days, gentlemen. We await your suggestions for further beneficiaries of our Empire," she said. Many thanks and heartfelt gratitude were offered to their Empress. She smiled and graciously accepted the men's gratitude, then retired to her Suite, exhausted.

Viscount T'Sur looked at his necklace medallion and commented, "No man has worn this necklace for over seven hundred years, if memory serves me correctly. I am truly flabbergasted. Our Empress Kayla never fails to leave me in awe," he said.

New Baron P'Lau said, "The Vee Lok Lords chose well."

The well-dressed aristocrats surrounded Baron P'Lau in the Main Court for nearly half an hour, offering their young daughters or granddaughters. "You must convey our sincere desire to serve our Empress during her time of healing and recuperation, Baron P'Lau. It is allowed under the Imperial Law," they correctly added.

With more than a measure of propriety, P'Lau met with Empress Kayla about the matter of concern. He looked at the IV tubes in her arms, infusing plasma-rich blood, fluids, and antibiotics, and the bottle of liquid protein in her hand. He carefully began, "My Empress Kayla, out of concern for your health and recovery, several members of your Court requested you consider enacting Imperial Law Article 27 for Royal Consort Dan'L, my Sovereign." He handed her the com tablet.

Within seconds of reading Article 27, P'Lau saw Kayla's face turn red, her green eyes narrow, and she said, "Leave me!" He bolted out of her study. Article 27 of the Imperial Law allowed the Empress any number of concubines for her pleasure and allowed her leeway to grant her Royal Consort any number of concubines she deemed necessary for his happiness. It stated she could have as many Consorts as she desired, after titling her first married partner as "First Consort," and sole Father of the heirs to her throne. Furthermore, any children of the Consorts' concubines were to be raised by the Empress without prejudice in her Court. The Article detailed the exact rules governing her current and future Consorts, their concubines, and children.

Empress Kayla was more than peeved by her courtiers offering their daughters to her much-loved and faithful Royal Consort Dan'L. Her first reaction was to peel the skin off their backs and carve them to pieces with her plasma sword, to put it mildly. How dare they interfere with her marriage. After a double dose of tranquilizers from the ever-present med droid, she calmed a bit, and tried to consider the matter from a male point of view, as best she could.

For twenty-nine days, she was imprisoned and starved. Only days afterwards, she miscarried violently, further injuring her internal organs. After three weeks of intense, cutting-edge regenerative medical treatments, her body began to heal. But Dan'L was not allowed in her bed by the med droid. All her ladies-in-waiting knew this, which meant everyone in the Court knew about the situation. Another month of abstaining stared her handsome, virile Consort in the face. Or longer, depending on how her reproductive organs healed. Dan'L was not injured. Why should he be punished while she recovered?

Every day since her appointment by the Vee Lok Lords as Empress, her Royal Consort and best friend Dan'L guarded and protected her. Now, through no fault of her own or Dan'L's, she had injuries requiring months of repair and recovery. He was a powerful Borgund Ranger Master Commander, and very desirable. Dan'L had needs, too. Was she being too selfish? Could she share him? What would their marriage evolve into if she accepted concubines for his sexual needs?

Several attempts to put this matter aside and concentrate on other pressing concerns were futile. She had to deal with it now and accept the consequences. Dan'L knew something important was bothering her, watching her agitated face, and her body monitors. Before she began, the too-attentive med droid gave her another dose of tranquilizers. Kayla took a deep breath and said, "My Royal Consort, the circumstances of the last two months have forced me to be much more self-centered than ever before, Dan'L."

He looked at her and commented, "It's to be expected after all you've been through, Kayla. I thank our Creator every night you survived, and are here with me and Lukus," he said, and took her hand to hold.

She touched his face and said, "There were many changes I insisted you make to be my Consort, Dan'L. You have been loyal and faithful, above any semblance of impropriety. You are above reproach; my Borgund Ranger, my 'Faithful Son,' Master Commander Dan'L. My loving Consort," she said softly. He kissed her gently, and she stroked his face.

He watched her take a deep breath before saying, "But several in my Court feel my Consort should be…taken care of, by other willing females," she said. "It is permitted under Imperial Law. And, with my having to refuse you any sexual favors for perhaps two more months, you may need…"

Dan'L took Kayla's face in his hands and kissed her. He said, "I am your Consort, and you are my Beloved Kayla. I will wait for you to recover. Besides," he said with a cocky grin, "When a man has had the best, no other woman will do." He took his injured Kayla in his arms and kissed her passionately, reminding her heart and body what she meant to him. After their loving embrace and kisses, Dan'L said, "I will deal with the courtiers and their 'offers.' Perhaps Baron P'Lau will help this Borgund Ranger in the tact, diplomacy, and etiquette departments, so I don't offend anyone intentionally, or otherwise," he said, and they both laughed. She was relieved the matter was settled between them privately.

The former Emperor P'Lau utilized the utmost grace and finesse with the courtiers and aristocrats over the next few days. After standing silently nearby, watching P'Lau refuse several beautiful offered daughters for the Royal Consort, Dan'L asked in a whisper, "How did you do this for over twenty-five years, my former Emperor? Even diplomacy has its limits."

P'Lau confessed, "I didn't have the heart to refuse any girl offered to me by her father when I was Emperor, which is why I had more than two hundred concubines. But I was able to convince most of the courtiers to withdraw their offered daughters for you," he said.

"How so, Baron?" A curious Dan'L asked.

P'Lau got a crooked smile on his face as he answered, "I merely implied our Warrior Empress may be inclined to remove her Royal Consort's testicles with her plasma sword if he was unfaithful," P'Lau whispered. Dan'L and P'Lau laughed together and walked down the corridor to the lounge for drinks.

VIII

Rumors of unannounced Royal Hierarchical appointments circulated throughout both Royal Palaces on Home World and K'Halon Prime. The wagging tongues were having a field day. Courtiers and aristocrats speculated on Empress Kayla's new appointments and concerned themselves with who would become the newest beneficiary of the Empire. On K'Halon Prime, especially, many Royal titles and land grants were stripped from conspirators of the failed coup d'état on her coronation day. The Lords, Ladies, and Barons still in place expected some of the massive land parcels to come their way and be added to their holdings, as just reward for their loyalty to the Empire, and Empress Kayla.

To assist with keeping the Royal courtiers informed of upcoming changes under consideration while she was recuperating, Empress Kayla ordered more Main Court duties for her Kaylan Rangers, and the Novices, both Borgund and Kaylan. The courtiers loved the young Novices, with their eager-to-learn attitudes, and their enthusiasm to meet the members of the Court. The young Novices were each assigned Commanders or First Commanders to "shadow," and accompany on whatever assignment they were given. The Empress chose to keep many more Rangers in her Court during her recovery for protection.

Many social functions were held during Main Court hours, since the Empress was only able to hold Court three days a week. The banquets and frequent Court dinners were postponed during this time. High teas, luncheons, and other events were scheduled to keep the courtiers communicating with each other and the Empress' Advisors. Most of the courtiers took one or more of the Novices under their wings, explaining their family's position, land holdings, and stewardship efforts.

Lady Bette remarked, "The new Novices are learning more in the new Court social environment than I learned my first year. After this present danger is resolved and well passed, it would be prudent to evaluate making changes in our Ranger Main Court standards of assignments. My

Granddaughter, Commander Tish, has met, spoken with, and dined with every aristocrat in the Home World Main Court! Some have even invited her to spend weekends at their resorts, or hotels."

Kayla looked at her Borgund Ranger personal guard, and responded, "Commander Tish is tall, blonde, and, as our guard Master Commander Sham'S says, a 'knock-out.' Let's make certain she stays close to the Ranger Barracks. The last thing we need is for her to become enamored with a Lord or Baron, or one of their heirs," the Empress said. "Commander Tish is, after all, one of your direct heirs, Lady Bette," Kayla reminded her.

"No 'cross-pollinating,' then, my Empress?" C.S. G'Rosk asked with a smile on his face.

"No," she answered firmly. "This exercise is for us to get to know the aristocrats and courtiers better and keep Court active. Not match-making for my Rangers! Let us all keep our focus. There are undoubtedly more within our midst who are plotting our overthrow. We must not become so friendly with the aristocracy we become blind to their hidden aspirations. Please switch around the Novices' responsibilities, so the young ones do not become adversely influenced by the aristocrats and their silver tongues. Make sure they continue to report and secretly record every private interaction," she added. "Our senior Rangers would notice something a Novice might miss during such meetings." They agreed to keep close watch on the Novices' interactions, to identify the subtle machinations of the aristocrats.

Saturday evening dinner was a family affair, with tables set close to the balconies of the ground floor parlor. The talk eventually included the rumors of the Royal Hierarchy. Sitting on his Mother's lap, Prince Lukus listened to the adults talk, and became worried. He asked, "If our Warrior Class is the strongest and we are the rulers, then why do we need more Barons, Lords and Ladies, and other aristocrats, Mother? Baron Tri'T captured you and threatened to kill you if I did not step down. He was a bad man, Mother. He tried to kill you, Momma!"

His Mother carefully answered, "Lukus, not all aristocrats are bad. There are several members of the aristocracy who are dedicated supporters of the Empire, like Viscount T'Sur, Baron P'Lau, Lady Bette and Lord Vu'Duc, and several more you have yet to meet. We must not lump them all into one batch of bad people, my Son. You will study the Imperial Class System when you attend the Royal Academy next year, and then you will learn about the Royal Hierarchy. They are the stewards and guardians of the Empire," she said.

Seeing no change in her Son's distraught face, she continued, "You must realize the Imperial Class System was not haphazardly developed, Lukus. It was designed to help us serve all the people and support your Empress. There are several tiers within the System, and it's usually depicted as a sort of pyramid. Each member of their tier has responsibility to serve the Empire, the Creator, and every other member of each tier. It's how we all help each other."

"Can someone on one tier move up to another tier, or down, Mother?" The boy asked.

"A person is born into one tier or another. They move up or down according to their will, their training and education, and the opportunities they take advantage of," the Empress said.

"Most people stay within their own class tier, however, Lukus. It is very difficult to move up more than one tier, and most people are satisfied to accomplish a certain level of success. You will learn all about the tiers soon, Grandson," Javette said. "Your Mother, our Empress Kayla, is the top of the Imperial Class System, and you are directly below, as her blood heir, my Prince Lukus," she said proudly. "Your family is the top of the Warrior Class Tier."

The heavy conversation came to an end when Olm and Tara's young toddler ran out onto the snowy lawn. Prince Lukus soon followed, and his Father tossed a kickball on the lawn and played with both boys. Kayla watched them for a while, and said, "These are the precious times I treasure. Surrounded by my family, enjoying the simple things in life. They are far too few," she said. She rose, took Lukus' coat, and walked onto the lawn. She bundled her son and watched them playing together. Olm and Tara joined the game, lightly kicking the ball to both young boys, and running with them.

Javette observed, "It has only been two months since her return from captivity. Kayla is still so weak. This will tire her out for the remainder of the day. We must surround her with loving hearts and hands, G'Rosk."

"And the swift swords of justice, Javette," G'Rosk added, thinking of their upcoming trip to K'Halon Prime.

The Empress' personal guard, Master Commander Shanna, added quietly, "My knives are sharp as razors, Commanders Superior G'Rosk and Javette." They nodded to her resolutely.

The next morning, Empress Kayla was again shuttled to the Imperial Naval Base Hospital for another two hours of treatment in the ReGen-Pod. She was very tired when she returned. "I feel the machine is siphoning all my energy, Admiral Mae."

Her Royal Physician replied, "We are continuing to target your new cells in your kidneys, uterus, liver and pancreas, and we have broadened the machine to now target your bone marrow. This will stimulate production of more red blood cells. Your strength should improve noticeably in a short while, my Empress."

"So, can I run soon? Jog? Use the stair-step machine?" Kayla asked, and watched her physician shake her head "No" to each short question.

"Do you enjoy swimming, Empress Kayla? A few laps a day would help your arms, legs, back, and your core, without straining your internal organs," she suggested.

"Wear a swimsuit in front of my guards, looking like a bag of bones? I think not!" She sighed, "I still cannot complete my T'Ly routine without pain. This is so frustrating."

"T'Ly? All those kicks and jumps? Is it not your wish to recover fully and bear another child? Then you must slow down and take it easy. Your internal organs are being rebuilt cell by cell. They cannot withstand the strain of jumping and running. Please—I implore your Majesty to be patient another two months," the Admiral pleaded.

Kayla dropped into the big chair in defeat, and the much-hated med droid started another IV in her weary veins. "My arms look like those of a junky," she commented, and shook her head. "In another week, we transport to K'Halon Prime for a one-month visit. Are you up for your first trip in space, my Royal Physician?" She asked, finally smiling.

Admiral Mae's face changed noticeably, and she answered, "I cannot deny being apprehensive about flying in space. But if it is your wish, I willingly accompany you, Empress Kayla. Is there a hospital on board?"

Kayla laughed good-heartedly, and answered, "Yes, very modern, Admiral Mae. Fully stocked with stomach tranqs and sedatives. If you would prefer, we can fly alongside the Imperial Command Battle Cruiser in my ES-519, and make the trip more adventurous for you, Royal Physician," she teased.

"No!" The Admiral instantly replied, then laughed with Kayla and properly responded, "No, thank you, Empress Kayla."

At their meeting the next morning, Baron P'Lau asked, "Will you be extending your stay on K'Halon Prime beyond the Novice Ranger Confirmation Ceremony, Empress Kayla?"

"Yes, at least for one month, Baron P'Lau. We will be attending the Grand Opening of the Temple of the Creator on T'Anju, as well. I trust you will accompany us to K'Halon Prime. It will give you time to survey your lands, forest, and vineyards. This is for you, my Baron," she said, handing him a wrapped box.

P'Lau opened the box excitedly and found a set of keys on a keychain featuring a large, white polar bear key fob. "What doors do these open, Empress Kayla?"

"Your new mansion, wine cellar, barn and shuttle hangar, Great Baron of Northern K'Halon Prime," she answered with a gentle smile. "Your lands are the ancient tribal lands of Borgund, the Great White Bear, first Emperor. You are the new steward of your ancestral lands, and guardian of the Empire, my trusted friend."

Baron P'Lau knelt before his Empress and bowed his head, and then swore allegiance to her once again. He walked back to his suite and shared the news with his wife, and they both cried tears of joy.

IX

Four Space Cadre officers walked under the big Imperial shuttle, conducting their visual inspection of the fifty-passenger, heavily armored craft. Satisfied everything was in perfect order, they boarded the shuttle, stowed their gear, and settled into their pilot, copilot, helm, and navigator seats. Two Imperial Guards walked aboard and thoroughly scanned every part of the ship, paying special attention to the oxygen tanks. "No knock-out gas canisters anywhere, First Commander," the Imperial Guard reported. "All clear for boarding."

The VIP passengers began boarding for their month-long trip to K'Halon Prime. Little Prince Lukus ran up the ramp and immediately sat next to his Grandmother, C.S. Javette. The seats were all doubles in the main compartment, facing each other. M.C. Dan'L sat across from his Son, and C.S. G'Rosk sat next to Dan'L. High Ranger Lady Bette, Baron and Baroness P'Lau, and Viscount T'Sur sat in the cluster of seats next to them.

The aft seating compartment was for the accompanying Borgund and Kaylan Rangers, extra Imperial Guards, ladies-in-waiting, and the select few courtiers "hitching a free ride" to K'Halon Prime for the Main Court and Grand Opening activities there.

Entering last were Master Commanders Kend'R, Steph'N, Sham'S, and Shanna, the Ranger personal guards for the Empress. They flanked the doorway while the Empress entered, followed by her Royal Physician Admiral Mae, and six more Imperial Guards. Her security entourage waited until she was settled into her seat, and then took their seats beside and behind her in the cushy forward compartment. She asked, "Need to access the first aid kit before we launch, Admiral Mae?"

The Royal Physician reached into her medical bag, and answered, "I brought my own supply, Empress Kayla." She stabbed her thigh with the hypo pen, and said, "Stomach tranqs. Need one, my Empress?"

The Empress shook her head "No." The big shuttle lifted off from the Capital City Base and rose several hundred meters, then slowly launched towards the Imperial Command Battle Cruiser. The shuttle bounced around while in the atmosphere, and Adm. Mae held on with white knuckles. Once clear of Home World's atmosphere, the ride smoothed out. In a few minutes, Prince Lukus ran to his Mother. She put a pillow over her breastplate and put him on her lap. The boy was fast asleep in seconds, and she reclined.

Several hours later, the Imperial shuttle landed on the main hangar of the Imperial Command Battle Cruiser, and everyone waited for the Empress to make her grand entrance. More than fifteen hundred Space Cadre officers and crewmen were in presentation formation, awaiting her arrival. Her ladies-in-waiting fussed over her and changed her black cloak for a Royal Red cloak, with gold filigree. When the make-up artist reached up for more make-up, Kayla said, "Enough! The crewmen's eyes are turning yellow already!" Her guards laughed and took their places.

The Imperial Guards loudly announced, "Presenting the Great Benevolent Empress Kayla, Ruler over all Known Worlds, and Conqueror of the Unknown Domain. All Hail Empress Kayla!" She walked down the shuttle hatch to Adm. Mur and his senior officers, receiving their salutes and welcome. Adm. Mur was a good friend of the Empress and was happy to see her again. The Warrior Empress led her Rangers and Imperial Guards across the main hangar bay, returning the salutes of the fifteen hundred officers and crewmen. She stopped in front of the fighter pilot squadron, and asked their commander, "Major Flek, mind if we accompany your patrols, and take a little side trip to the G'Lenan Facility?" She had a cocky smile on her face.

"We welcome your ES-519 anytime, Empress Kayla!" The fighter pilots struck their breasts with their fists and saluted her proudly. She returned their salutes and quickly made her way to the Royal Suite, on Deck 9.

Empress Kayla was more tolerant of the VIP Welcoming Protocols this trip than she usually was, and patiently sat and smiled through the pomp with Consort Dan'L and Prince Lukus flanking her. She was rescued by her Royal Physician, who insisted she take her rest. The officers escorted the cocktail party group to the officer's lounge.

"Thank you, Admiral Mae. I am tired, and my patience was nearing its end," the Empress said, and retired to her three-bedroom Master Suite with Prince Lukus in tow.

For three days, the big Cruiser flew towards K'Halon Prime, then held its position while the Empress and the Space Cadre fighter patrol detoured to the G'Lenan Ship Building Facility. The patrol held while she flew through the massive facility in her small ES-519, checking out her newest ship: a long, black vessel of war.

"I cannot call your new attack ship beautiful, Empress Kayla. But it certainly looks fast and deadly," C.S. G'Rosk commented from the copilot seat. "A totally innovative design, that's for sure, and menacing."

She replied, "Like our Ranger uniforms, the KRS-series was designed to instill fear and awe. It's almost as fast as a standard Space Cadre fighter, carries the same firepower and payload as an attack destroyer, and has the stealth mechanism. Plus, it costs little more than half the expense of a destroyer and requires only a full crew of forty-one. Hopefully, the KRS-series will keep our cargo shipping routes clear of pirates and marauders," she said.

"I'd hate to have it appear right in front of me. Excellent project, Empress Kayla," G'Rosk said. The squadron returned to the Cruiser and completed their trip to K'Halon Prime in another day and a half.

The VIP party boarded the Imperial shuttle for their trip to the Centralia Base on K'Halon Prime. The shuttle launched slowly off the main hangar deck for its four-hour flight. Everything was smooth for the first three hours. When Empress Kayla came out of the restroom, the flight attendants were frantically going through the bins, slamming doors, and making noise. "What's the matter?" She asked.

"The Captain and copilot are sick, Empress Kayla. We can't find the first-aid kit. It should be here," the attendant said.

"Admiral Mae, please bring your bag and come to the galley," the Empress ordered into her comm link quietly. Her Royal Physician immediately accompanied the flight attendants and Empress into the cockpit.

The navigator and helmsman lay on the floor holding their stomachs and moaning. The copilot was on the floor, his face in a pile of his own vomit. The Captain was sweating profusely, but still in his seat. "Mayday, mayday. This is the Imp..." the Captain said, then threw up all over the console and passed out.

"Lock the cabin door this instant!" Empress Kayla ordered, and pulled the Captain out of his seat. "Empress Kayla to Imperial Command Battle Cruiser. We have an emergency. The pilot, copilot, and navigator are down, cause unknown. Requesting immediate assistance. Mayday, mayday." She threw off her robe and took the pilot's seat.

The computer console flashed "Red Alert," and instantly locked down every seat on the shuttle, and each passenger harness. Kayla buckled in and asked the flight attendant for a towel.

"She's down, too, Empress Kayla!" Admiral Mae cried.

"Scan the air. Is it poisoned?" She ordered and called mayday again.

After scanning, the Admiral answered, "No Ma'am, the air is clear. But these crew members have been poisoned and are dying. Cause and source unknown."

The other restroom door opened and M.C. Sham'S came out. The frantic remaining flight attendant told him in a whisper what was happening, and he beat on the cockpit door. Admiral Mae let him in.

"Welcome to the puke party, Master Commander Sham'S. Buckle in, and let's get this tub to the Centralia base," the Empress said. "Admiral Mae, please buckle in there," she said, pointing to the navigator's seat back against the port side.

"Imperial Cruiser to shuttle. Do you have control, Empress Kayla? Your craft's onboard flight computer can land you safely if all controls are working," the officer said.

She replied, "So far, so good, flight officer. Space Cadre fighters have flanked us now," she reported. When the shuttle entered K'Halon Prime's atmosphere, she said, "Shields on full for re-entry." When the shields came on, the onboard flight computer lights all went out simultaneously.

Sham'S got up and went to the power control panel to reset the computer. But it was dead and unresponsive. He checked the components, and found a small module inserted inside the power couplings for the shields. "It's sabotage, Empress Kayla. When our shields came up, this killed all power to the flight computer," he said, and showed the module to her.

She reported the information to the Cruiser flight officer, and he replied, "Transferring the comm to Centralia Space Base. Emergency, Code Red. Priority One. The Empress in on board."

Kayla looked at Sham'S, and said, "We're landing this shuttle safely, with or without the flight computer. Initiate systems check now." The two ES pilots systematically went through the systems checks manually, with Kayla in the pilot seat, pulling out panels and drawers to manually check every system. They reported each step to Centralia Flight Control, closely monitoring the urgent situation. The shuttle began to shake from atmospheric turbulence.

Flight Commander O'Wens said, "It'll take three to land your shuttle safely, Empress Kayla. How many pilots are with you?"

"Myself, Master Commander Sham'S, and Admiral Mae," she answered. Mae looked at her Empress, and Kayla pointed to the empty helm seat. "Take the helm, Admiral Mae. We need the steady hands of a surgeon. In this seat, right now."

The Admiral cautiously stepped over the dead bodies on the floor and sat in the helm control seat. Endless gauges and screens faced her. Kayla buckled her in and said, "See this monitor? Put your hands on the wheel. All you have to do is hold this line between the two red indicators. This keeps the ship steady." Kayla showed Mae what to do, and she nervously put her hands on the wheel. The maneuvers seemed simple enough.

Kayla retook the pilot seat. The many adjustments usually made by the onboard flight computer now had to be performed manually by the Empress and Sham'S. Their hands deftly flew over the panels, controlling the shuttle's re-entry safely for the next seven minutes, in constant communication with Flight Commander O'Wens and a shuttle pilot assistant. All seemed well, until it was time to ignite the thrusters to slow the shuttle down.

Sham'S said, "Thrusters unresponsive. I have to manually ignite them. Where are they?" He looked at Kayla, both wondering how and if they could accomplish the feat. They were ES warbird pilots, not shuttle pilots. She called in their situation to the Flight Commander.

O'Wens replied, "Thruster ignition manual controls are on the lower level near the hull. Each bank has a power bar. Throw the bar and they should ignite. Mid-ship first, the rear, and then forward thrusters last. Good luck," he added ominously, and shook his head. To his Emergency Officer, he said, "Notify Space High Command: The Empress is on board. Imperial shuttle re-entering the atmosphere without thrusters. Red Alert. All Emergency Units stand by."

"Take an oxygen mask, Sham'S," Kayla ordered. Admiral Mae held onto the helm wheel and kept the ship as steady as she could, trying not to watch Empress Kayla. Kayla stood at the console, both hands flying over the controls on two levels of computer screens, sweat pouring down her brow. She was running on pure adrenalin and will power.

Sham'S jumped down the floor hatch and located the mid-ship thruster bank. The bar was hard to pull up, but he did it. "Mid-thruster power bar up, Empress Kayla," he called.

She hit the power and the central thrusters came on, making the ship begin to see-saw. "Steady at the helm, Admiral Mae," she commanded, and moved over to help her. They steered the ship laterally to keep the re-entry heat as low as possible, and to maintain control of the ship.

"Rear thrusters power bar up, Empress," Sham'S reported. She hit the power and the ship turned nose down. Kayla watched Mae expertly correct the pitch and level it out. Sham'S ran to the forward thruster bank. The power bar was red hot from the heat of re-entering the atmosphere too fast. Sham'S cried out from the bar burning his hands. He put on his oxygen mask, folded his cloak over the bar, and grabbed the power bar, but it would not move.

"We need forward thrusters soon, Sham'S," the Empress called to him.

"The power bar's stuck. The entire forward area is hot. I'm trying, Ma'am," he yelled, pulling with all his might. He ran to the side tool bar for a torque wrench, levered the wrench under the power bar and pulled until his shoulder dislocated. He screamed out in pain; then, he stood on the wrench, jumped on it several times, and the bar moved. Sham'S pulled again with his one good arm, and the bar finally moved straight up.

"Sham'S, I'd really like to celebrate my Son's fourth birthday," Kayla called to him.

Sham'S leaned his back against the power bar and pushed against the wall with his legs. The bar finally moved into place, and the force of the push sent him crashing into the wall brace and cut his head. "Oww! Power's up, Kayla!"

He felt the forward thrusters ignite, and climbed the ladder as quickly as he could, holding his bleeding head. The three managed to slow the shuttle down for re-entry.

"Don't know how you did it, Empress Kayla. Now follow these coordinates, and we'll guide you down," the relieved voice of O'Wens said over the comm link.

In the cabins, the passengers sat quietly, knowing only their seats and harnesses were locked in landing position. Dan'L looked out the window and commented, "We've been locked in for more than half an hour, kind of a long time." G'Rosk silently looked at Javette.

"When do we get another drink?" Viscount T'Sur asked, but no one responded.

In the cockpit, Empress Kayla reported, "No coordinates received, O'Wens. We're still in the clouds. How deep is the cloud cover?"

"Five thousand meters, Empress. Without coordinates, I can't bring you down," he said quietly. The shuttle was off-course, due to their lateral maneuvers during re-entry.

She answered, "Then bring down our fighter escorts and we'll stay with them. I can land at Centralia when we have visual," she said determinedly.

The Space Cadre fighters flew as close as they dared to the Imperial shuttle, guiding the ship through the thick winter clouds. When they popped out of the cloud cover, the huge Centralia Base came into view, with every base light on brightly.

"Fighters break away. Imperial shuttle on final approach to base," she ordered confidently. Beginning their circling approach, she touched the controls for the landing gear. No response; just a loud, grinding noise. "Bloody hell!" She yelled and smacked the console.

"O'Wens, we have no landing gear. Prepare for full-belly landing. All emergency units stand by. I have forty-seven passengers. Give us some foam, O'Wens," she ordered.

The emergency shuttles at the base roared out, spraying flame-resistant foam all over the landing sites. The Empress turned on the interior shuttle intercom and calmly said, "All passengers brace for emergency landing."

"That's Kayla!" Javette exclaimed, and looked at her Partner, G'Rosk, and her Son, Dan'L. Prince Lukus was sound asleep. Oxygen masks came down to each passenger. The Imperial Guards and Rangers donned their masks, but some of the passengers in the back became frightened. The Guards and Rangers showed them how to put on their masks and helped them sit back and relax.

"What's happening now?" Baron P'Lau nervously asked Lady Bette.

She leaned her head back and replied, "It's just another way to land the shuttle, Baron P'Lau." Bette closed her eyes and silently prayed.

The usual landing consisted of two circular approaches over the landing site while the shuttle slowed down. Kayla and Sham'S circled five times, slowing the shuttle to the slowest possible speed before landing belly down. The shuttle floated on the foam halfway across the landing field, continually slowing. When the Imperial shuttle finally came to a rest, dozens of emergency vehicles roared alongside it.

Sham'S announced, "Please calmly exit the shuttle by the rear hatch. And thank you for flying Kaylan Air Trans." Kayla burst out laughing with him.

"We did it! We're alive!" Admiral Mae cried out. She jumped up, and the three laughed and hugged each other. "We did it!"

Admiral Mae held Sham'S' dislocated shoulder and said, "I'll set it for you on three, two…" and she unexpectantly snapped his shoulder back into place. He cried out in pain.

"What happened to 'one?' That's cheating, Doc," Sham'S said, moving his shoulder.

Admiral Mae smiled and replied, "An old Navy trick. Less tension in your joint."

Hard pounding on the cockpit door came next. The three laughing pilots held each other's arms, and Sham'S unlocked the door. Dan'L and G'Rosk looked at them, and the dead bodies on the floor. Wall panels were opened all throughout the cockpit. "What happened in here?" A worried Dan'L asked.

"Just some flight training for our Royal Physician, Admiral Mae," Kayla replied with a laugh. The three pilots walked into the fancy forward compartment arm-in-arm, laughing. Each pilot was soaked in sweat, and Sham'S had a head wound that was still bleeding.

C.S. Javette handed sleeping Lukus to Dan'L, and said, "I want to hear all about it tonight!" Her face showed her concern. M.C. Shanna looked at them with a very worried look on her face. The passengers began to exit the shuttle.

"I really need a drink," Viscount T'Sur complained, and everyone erupted in laughter.

"So do I," Sham'S said, and Admiral Mae agreed. "Party in the Palace tonight! Whoo-hoo!" Sham'S cried, and they laughed together, exhausted and grateful to be alive.

X

K'Halon Prime

Main Court was jammed packed. Word of the miraculous emergency landing of the Imperial shuttle piloted by Empress Kayla circulated throughout every Space Base and was broadcast on all four planets. Instead of a standard Court session, the agenda today featured awards and commendations for several persons involved with the VIP emergency.

Empress Kayla entered to thunderous applause and chants of "Empress Kayla!" repeated over and over. She smiled graciously, bowed, and then raised her hand to quiet the audience. Commendations and awards were given to Flight Officer O'Wens and his emergency crews, along with promotions. Next, the pilots flanking her shuttle received their commendations.

"Our many thanks, praise, and admiration go to our Royal Physician, Admiral Mae. Prior to this situation, her only piloting experience had been at the controls of robotic surgery equipment," the Empress said, and the audience laughed. "Imperial Navy Admiral Mae answered our call without hesitation, not knowing the great task we would command her to assume. The steady hands of a trained surgeon kept our shuttle at even keel during the highly dangerous re-entry into the atmosphere of K'Halon Prime, and our emergency landing at the Centralia Space Base. This feat cannot be over-exaggerated. We bestow upon our Royal Physician Admiral Mae the designation of 'Hero of the Empire,' and Helmsman's Wings!"

A blushing Admiral Mae humbly accepted the applause and cheers of the crowd. Admiral Mur pinned Helmsman's Wings on Admiral Mae and saluted her. Being designated "Hero of the Empire" was a very high honor. It meant your word was true and you were trusted above others. The Admiral was now in the top circle of trusted advisors for Empress Kayla. M.C. Shanna applauded and cheered for her lover, Admiral Mae, with tears in her eyes.

When the audience quieted, Empress Kayla said, "The last recipient of our gratitude is one whose name is known only to his Commanders Superior, his friends, and his Empress. Our Faithful Son has served with humility and in silence for many years. He has successfully completed tasks so secret and vital to the Empire, no one may speak of them. But today, we honor our fellow pilot for putting his life at significant risk to save us all. Without your strong will, determination to succeed at any cost, and willingness to endure burned hands, bleeding concussions, and a dislocated shoulder, the thrusters of our shuttle would not have ignited, and we all would have perished. We promote our Faithful Son Sham'S to Master Commander First Echelon!" More applause filled the Main Court as Sham'S received a written commendation and a sizeable bonus, and new insignia for his collar was pinned on by High Ranger Lady Bette.

"We offer our sincere thanks and appreciation to all of our award recipients today. We now welcome to our Main Court Priest K'Ramm of the new Temple of the Creator at T'Anju, and Priestess T'Char of the Temple of the Creator on Xau."

The Priest and Priestess entered the Main Court and bowed before Empress Kayla, who said, "We invite all here to attend the Grand Opening of the Temple at T'Anju in three weeks. And now, we will ask for blessings from our Holy Man and Woman." They blessed the Main Court audience and Empress Kayla. Several minutes of silence passed respectfully during the blessings, and while the Priestess burned incense on the altar.

When the Holy Man and Woman returned to their places, Empress Kayla motioned for Prince Lukus to stand beside her. The boy climbed the golden stairs, raised his arms, and cried aloud, "We celebrate our safe arrival on K'Halon Prime. Let the feast begin!" The audience laughed and applauded, and the food servants brought in tables, chairs, and massive platters of meats, fish, vegetables, and foods galore. Wine, hard cider, mead, and juices completed the feast. Musicians and entertainers performed for the audience. The exhausted Empress left early, surrounded by her personal Kaylan Rangers and Imperial Guards.

Inside her Royal Chambers, the ladies-in-waiting watched their Empress remove her breastplate and backplate and set them on the charging stand. They helped her undress and step into the shower. Kayla reluctantly let them dress her in the favorite Royal Blue lounge dress and robe. When the med droid was brought into her chambers, the attendants left.

Another IV was started with a blood drip in her left arm, and a saline and antibiotic drip in the right arm. Kayla pulled her IV stand to her desk, documenting the events of the last two days in detail in her personal journal. Once again, another attempt on her life was thwarted. But this time, the would-be assassins tried for her Son and her loving Consort too, and her relatives Olm and Tara, Javette and G'Rosk. *Would the day ever come when she could relax and enjoy the position she held?* Not in the foreseeable future. Every day was another test, whether with traitors and saboteurs, vengeful relatives of former aristocrats whose lands and titles she revoked, or subversives concealed within her Court.

An Imperial Guard knocked on her door and asked if she would be willing to receive Priest K'Ramm, and she agreed. She invited him to sit in a chair in front of the fireplace. He saw her two IV's and helped her sit first, instead. The Empress looked very pale and tired. Priest K'Ramm said, "I understand another miracle happened yesterday, my Empress."

She answered, "Yes, K'Ramm. Our Creator gave me strength and opportunity to be useful again. Yesterday's action took its toll on me, as you can see. I have not yet healed internally from my abduction and miscarriage," she admitted.

"Has any other Sovereign been subjected to the trials and tribulations you have suffered, endured, and survived, Empress Kayla? Even at the Temple, news of the attempted sabotage of your shuttle and your abduction for nearly a month while being starved have circulated. I requested passage to Home World to help you, but was denied passage by your Chief Advisor," he shared. "I am highly concerned about your well-being, Empress Kayla, and the safety of your young Son, Prince Lukus."

Kayla searched his face, and saw his genuine, loving concern for her. All female Rangers were trained in body language interpretation. The face of her priest and former lover was an open book to the Empress, and she was very touched.

"The trial of starvation was passed by deep meditation, prayers to our Creator, and our Ranger survival training, K'Ramm. And our will to survive," she added. "This most recent test found me in the right place at the precise moment of action, another opportunity I credit to our Great Creator. How else can it be explained: both Master Commander Sham'S and I went to separate restrooms and emerged just as the pilots succumbed to being poisoned. Another minute, and I would have been in my seat, locked inside the emergency harness and unable to assist. It was the will of our Creator. I knew He wanted us to succeed," she said, her eyes red with emotion.

K'Ramm reached out to her and she took his hand. They sat in separate chairs in front of the fire, holding hands. Softly he began the chant, "There is no pain. Only peace," and she joined in the chant with him. Kayla relaxed and laid her head back against the chair, chanting softly with K'Ramm.

Her door soon opened and Prince Lukus entered with his Father Dan'L and Grandmother Javette. She held her Son and introduced him to K'Ramm. The little Prince said, "I am very pleased to meet you, sir. This is my Grandmother Javette, and my Father, the Royal Consort Dan'L. We flew here yesterday, and my Mother saved all of us."

"Our Creator saved us," Kayla corrected. K'Ramm offered his seat to Javette.

Javette said, "The Creator certainly made our survival possible. But your skills and training cannot be discounted, Empress Kayla. I know no one who could have accomplished what you did. And you took zero credit for the amazing feat!"

Lukus sat on his Mother's lap. Kayla said, "Priest K'Ramm oversees the new Temple of the Creator at T'Anju, Lukus. We will attend the Grand Opening there in three weeks, my Son. He is my Priest, and my good friend," she said with a smile.

Aware of the priest who meant so much to his Kayla, Dan'L said, "Thank you for visiting my Empress tonight, Priest K'Ramm. I look forward to the Temple Grand Opening." Kayla felt the tension rise in her Consort. But K'Ramm did not take the hint and leave.

Rather, Priest K'Ramm invited the Royal Family for a private tour of the Temple the day before the Grand Opening. Empress Kayla graciously accepted, and asked, "Perhaps Priest K'Ramm would bless us all tonight?" She smiled at K'Ramm, and he understood. He blessed each one of them and anointed their heads with holy oil. He lingered over Lukus and said prayers in the ancient language over him. K'Ramm dipped his thumb in the holy oil once more and made the spiral on Lukus' forehead. The spiral was the symbol of the expanding universe, used frequently in worship of the Creator. Then K'Ramm bowed to everyone and left her chambers. Lukus quietly laid his head against his Mother and fell asleep.

"What a kind priest," Javette said. "Most priests I have met are cool and impersonal, to say the least. But he was so kind, and genuinely concerned," she added. Seeing her Grandson fall asleep, Javette bid them good-night and left.

Dan'L took his sleeping Son into the nursery and put him to bed. Kayla pushed her IV pole into the second bedroom, where her Consort slept. She held him tightly and kissed Dan'L good night. She whispered, "Only a few more days, my love." He saw her tired eyes and led her back into the Master bedroom.

"Go to bed, Kayla, and know our Creator counts every breath you take. I am yours, now and forever," he said, and helped her into bed. The med droid came over to make certain Dan'L didn't try to get into bed with her. Dan'L swatted the droid and left her room. The droid straightened out her IV lines and adjusted her controller. After she fell asleep, the droid switched out a new bag of fresh blood for her. Kayla slept soundly, dreaming of peaceful days in the sun with her family, watched over by Priest K'Ramm.

The investigation concerning the sabotage of the Imperial shuttle revealed two traitors onboard the Imperial Command Battle Cruiser, both shuttle technicians. The Imperial shuttle Captain, his crew, and forward flight attendant shared a pot of green tea and "home-made" cookies after launch. Both their tea and cookies were poisoned.

Tracing the tea and cookies was more difficult than identifying the traitors who installed the black module, which shut down the onboard flight computer when the shuttle shields were engaged for re-entry. No prints were on the module. But it was installed by someone who knew the shuttle's components well, the Space Cadre Lead Shuttle Tech. The thruster controls were sabotaged by the Assistant Shuttle Tech, both techs working in tandem to make certain the Imperial shuttle would burn up in re-entry. The two guilty men were apprehended by security officers on the Command Cruiser, and immediately interrogated under truth gas. They confessed to their sabotage onboard the shuttle, but knew nothing about the poisoned tea and cookies, or the inoperative landing gear.

A fueling tech was overheard bragging about buying an anti-gravity chopper, and it being delivered to his home on K'Halon Prime yesterday. His yearly pay was half the cost of the chopper, a very expensive toy for the young tech. The tech was reported to the Flight Crew Chief and was subsequently interrogated. The fueling tech confessed to jamming the landing gear controls after the pilot completed his visual inspection.

The third day after the shuttle incident, the flight attendant who survived came forward and confessed, "He said the cookies would make them sick. He never said they would kill the entire crew! I'm so sorry. I didn't know this would happen. He never said anything about trying to crash the Imperial shuttle. I swear to you, I never knew he planned to kill everyone. If Empress Kayla had not taken over, we'd all be dead!" The attendant broke down sobbing.

The Space Cadre security officer asked, "Who is he? What is his name?"

The flight attendant shook her head and answered, "He is called the 'Technician,' that's all I know. He gave us our 10,000-credit gold bars, and instructions to each of us. I'm so sorry." The security officer took the physical description from her and sent out a solar system-wide arrest warrant for "The Technician," a tall man in his late thirties, very well dressed, with blond hair, clean shaven, and wearing many gold rings. The flight attendant surrendered her 10,000-credit bar to the officer voluntarily.

Early the next morning, Empress Kayla invited M.C. Sham'S for a breakfast meeting. A servant brought in a large cart with several food choices and filled their plates. He served them at the table inside her private study, in front of the window. Two Imperial Guards stood their posts behind the Empress while they ate and talked, and watched the sun rise. She showed Sham'S the report from the investigation and interrogations.

Sham'S commented, "This was a very well-designed scheme. If one or more of the cockpit pilots refused the poisoned tea and cookies, the black module still would've shorted out the onboard flight computer. In case a surviving pilot or two managed to fly into K'Halon Prime atmosphere, the jammed thrusters would have required manual power shifting, like I did. But there would have been no way one man could have done both jobs. It took three of us, Empress Kayla. And the jammed landing gear was the final fail-safe. This sabotage was designed by a pilot," Sham'S said firmly.

She agreed with him, and said, "The Space Cadre traitors had four full days to sabotage our shuttle. But the guilty techs said the 'Technician' gave them the black module they installed in the power control panel before our Imperial shuttle arrived, when the Command Cruiser was resupplied for our trip. The 'Technician' had to have been on board one of the cargo ships bringing supplies and food the day before we landed on the Command Cruiser. The black module was constructed specifically for our Imperial shuttle. Whoever this 'Technician' is, he is still at large," the Empress added. They talked at length about the situation, and the pre-planned flight schedule for the Imperial shuttle, so well-known by many people.

Consort Dan'L walked into his Empress' bedroom, and she was not there. He heard her talking in her study, peeked in, and saw her sitting with a man. *It better not be that priest again,* he jealously thought, and ran to put his robe on. The Empress was whispering in the man's ear, and Dan'L became agitated. He approached the table by the window.

"Dan'L!" Sham'S said, stood, and happily greeted his good friend. Both men and Kayla spent nearly three years in Phase 1, 2, and 3 Training together.

Turning to greet her Consort, Kayla smiled and invited him to join them, and asked the server to fill a plate for him. Dan'L blushed a little. He joined them and began to eat breakfast.

"I was just going over the investigation with Sham'S, and he brought up several good points. If you can fit it into your schedule, I'd like the two of you to work on immediate recommendations to improve the safety and security of our Imperial shuttle. One change I insist on making is for the passenger seat harnesses to have some sort of emergency release, perhaps in the galley, where the first aid kit and fire extinguisher are stored. We had five pilots on board in addition to Sham'S and me, and none of you could get up from your seat. It's preposterous!" She exclaimed.

The two Borgund Rangers agreed to spearhead the shuttle modifications during their month-long stay on K'Halon Prime. In a few minutes, little footsteps let them know Prince Lukus was awake and searching for everyone. "Momma? Where are you, Momma?" He asked sleepily, shuffling into her study.

Kayla picked Lukus up and sat him on her lap. The attentive servant brought over more food and fresh juice for the boy, and breakfast resumed without the heavy conversation. "Let's invite Master Commander Sham'S to your birthday party," his Mother suggested. "He was in training with your Father and me and is a good friend."

Lukus proudly said, "I'll be four whole years old, sir. Please come and celebrate with all of us. It's in two days. I can hardly wait!" The little boy exclaimed, and they laughed with him. "Mother has to work the next two days. Then, we party!"

Sham'S accepted his invitation, then asked, "What about your Father, Prince Lukus? He goes to work, too."

Without hesitation, Lukus answered, "My Father works hard, and then comes home and plays with me. Mother works all day and sometimes all evening, too. The Empire is very big, with billions of people needing her. The Empress' work is never done," he said and put another bit of bacon in his mouth. "But on Sunday, she's all mine!" He turned and hugged his Mother, and smiled big for her.

Soon, several knocks on the door produced the first two ladies for the Empress. "It's time to begin my day, gentlemen. Master Commander Sham'S, thank you for joining me so early. Now, if you'll excuse us, please. Come on, Son," Kayla said, and the little Prince jumped off her lap and led his Mother into her bedroom.

Watching them leave the study, Sham'S said, "Your Son is quite the little man already, Dan'L. I'm sure you're proud of him. You should be."

"Very much so, Sham'S. His tutors have done a wonderful job with him. Only one more year before he goes off to the Royal Academy," Dan'L answered. "It will be hard to let him go. Kayla dotes on him, makes time for him every day, and they read together at bedtime every night. He's had more of her time, with her having to recover. She can't train him in T'Ly for a few more weeks, so I've taken over Lukus' martial arts training in the interim," he shared.

Sham'S carefully commented, "She's as beautiful as ever, Dan'L, and still sharp as a tack. When I came up the ladder into the cockpit, she was working the cockpit controls manually on both consoles, overhead, and generally being everywhere at once. I never could have done it. I keep seeing her hands fly over the controls, moving up, down, across, and even jumping over to Admiral Mae to help her. Our Empress is the most gifted, amazing woman I've ever known. Totally amazing," he repeated, shaking his head. "We owe her our lives, Dan'L."

Dan'L agreed with his friend completely. But he did not tell Sham'S how much the maximum effort cost Kayla. Admiral Mae said she'd need an extra week of therapy and massage, light exercise, liquid protein infusions, and extra rest to work out the stress on her body and regrown organ tissue. Her orders translated to another week sleeping alone, without his woman in his arms.

XI

Loud music and noisy, laughing patrons filled the large club on the wharf. It was Friday night and the dance floor was packed with happy people moving to the music. Laughter, clapping, and shouting filled the club, with the gay men partying and drinking. It was a great night to cut loose.

A tall blonde man walked past the line of men waiting to get inside the club, discreetly placed a 100-credit coin into the burly bouncer's palm and walked inside. He made his way through the packed club, keeping close to the bar area. Past the private rooms in the back occupied by men paying the male prostitutes for quick sex, was a heavy, steel door. The blonde man knocked twice, waited, and then knocked three times. A peep hole opened, and then the blonde man was admitted beyond the steel door.

"Why the hell are we here tonight? Why not just advertise with billboards all over the harbor that we are meeting here? Whose idea was this, anyway?" The blonde man asked angrily. Everyone was dressed in black suits, except one man.

The big man dressed in an ornate, heavily trimmed cape stood and answered, "I called this meeting, B'Nard. Sit down and have a drink. Remember who you're talking to, Technician," he said gruffly.

B'Nard bowed his head and sat, poured a stiff drink, and belted it down, swallowing his offended pride along with the vodka. "I meant no offense, sir," he choked out.

"We'll go ahead and start, although another Technician will be arriving in twenty minutes. Our recent attempt to destroy the Imperial shuttle was a failure. My informants tell me the Empress herself managed to land the shuttle safely," he said with disgust. "Are we incapable of even the simplest tasks? Those who performed the sabotage are in custody. Fortunately, all they gave up was a perfect description of our Technician B'Nard. Now the Empress Bitch will be able to complete her agenda on K'Halon Prime. More erosion of the Royal Hierarchy will occur soon. I need not tell you what will become of our Technicians and Alternates if we are discovered," he cautioned.

"But sir; if the Empire knew of our continued work on the 'Old Engine,' and the identity of our Technicians, they would have already been taken. We own the Centralia police and control the local security monitoring vid cams. No Imperial goons have even set foot near our warehouse, or the three underground storerooms. We are undiscovered, Lord. Should we not continue our work, as planned?" One of the other Technicians asked.

B'Nard added, "No one in the Imperial spy system is watching us. I have been on all four planets in the last six months and have never been successfully tailed. You walk within the Main Court with impunity, Lord, and carry on with your clever work. The Empress Bitch and her Rangers are completely clueless. And she will continue to be clueless, until her Empire crashes down upon her!" The men raised their glasses and toasted their Master Technician, Lord T'Yang.

The Master Technician ordered, "Then, let's keep her busy with continued minor altercations, so scattered and varied no pattern is clear. Our work on the 'Old Engine' is nearly complete. The Empress Bitch will be focusing on a minor event and be blindsided completely. The Plan of the Thirteen will prevail!" He announced, and his men cheered. They passed around bottles of vodka and drank for several minutes.

Another coded knock on the steel door produced their last member of the meeting. He bowed to the Master Technician, and revealed, "The shooter is ready, and will be in place at noon. Tomorrow, the heir to the throne will be no more." The men toasted, drank, and cheered their Master Technician several more times. Another two bottles of vodka were taken out of the case, and a cockroach ran along the floor. The flies in the room buzzed about intermittently.

Little Prince Lukus played with the many children at his party inside the private, Royal Court of the K'Halon Prime Palace. The birthday party was fun and Prince Lukus received many presents. Lunch and the opening of presents was enjoyed inside her private Royal Court. But the promised sleigh ride for the children was the Big Event, and needed to be outside, on the snowy ground near the Ranger Family Residences. Empress Kayla whispered into her comm link, "Are all sentries in place?"

Imperial Guard M.C. An'Ton replied, "Yes, your Majesty. They are on top of each building, stationed at every entrance and exit. No visitors have been admitted into the Palace at all today, Empress Kayla."

The Empress was not relaxed, and had a difficult time mingling with the children's parents during the party, her off-duty Rangers. Lukus' Grandmother C.S. Javette put on a happy face and played games with the children. All the Empress' Rangers knew the recently discovered intelligence: Prince Lukus was to be assassinated today. The intel was overheard using the "spy bugs," and was discussed by the same men who tried to kill them all in the Imperial shuttle. The Ranger parents of the children were advised of the new intelligence, but they decided to continue with the birthday party anyway, not bowing to fear.

The Empress kept the party inside her Royal Court as long as she could. Every possible precaution was taken to protect the children and their parents. Everyone wanted the little Prince to have a memorable day and meet some of the children of the K'Halon Prime Rangers. In one more year, Lukus and many of the children would be taken to the Royal Academy after their fifth birthday. They would have a less challenging time adjusting if they knew one another beforehand. Kayla put a soft armor vest on all the children before they went outside. Their Ranger parents were ordered to attend the party in uniform, their uniforms and cloaks providing resistance to laser fire.

The bright red sleigh pulled by horses entered the grounds, and the small children climbed aboard for the sleigh ride. Imperial Guards stood on the back of the sleigh and along the side runners, while the horses pulled them all around the Palace grounds. Borgund Rangers and more Imperial Guards ran alongside the sleigh full of happy children, all of them sons and daughters of the Rangers.

At the first shot of the laser rifle, Imperial Guards activated their defensive energy shields over the children, and the Borgund Rangers shielded the children with their bodies. Roof-top snipers instantly returned the assassin's fire, keeping him from firing anymore at the children. Sham'S jumped into the driver's seat and took control of the sleigh, driving it inside the gates of the stables. Dozens of Guardsmen ran to the source of the laser fire inside the guest apartments. The would-be assassin only got off a few shots at the children.

"I want the assassin alive!" Empress Kayla ordered, running to the sleigh as fast as a jungle cat. All the children were safe. The sleigh driver was killed, along with two Imperial Guards and one Borgund Ranger. The crying, frightened children were reunited with their parents, and Dan'L led everyone through the Palace corridor into the Royal Court.

In seconds, C.S. G'Rosk reported, "We have the shooter, Empress Kayla. One man in custody. He was inside the linen storeroom." G'Rosk grabbed the would-be assassin by the throat and threatened, "You'll wish my knife blade would have ended your sorry life before this day ends, you murderous bastard!" The Imperial Guards cuffed the smirking man, roughly took him to the underground prison, and hurled him inside the cell. They checked his pockets, found two cyanide capsules, and confiscated them.

Kayla consoled her crying Son and his friends, while the parents held their children close. "Are you going to kill the bad man, Momma? He shot at us and killed our Imperial Guards! He tried to kill all my friends, Momma!"

She calmly answered, "We are going to find out who paid him to do this terrible thing, Lukus. Do not worry, my Son. Stay here with your Father and Grandmother, and they will protect you and your friends. All my Rangers here will protect you and their children. Now, be brave, Lukus. It's over. Try to relax and sit at the table with your friends. Everyone all right?" She asked the children.

The little kids all nodded their heads, and they were served some hot cider and sandwiches to calm them. Their parents sat with them, grateful their precautions saved the little ones. "Let's everyone talk about the event, and how you feel now," Javette suggested, knowing the children had to work through their fear. Kayla whispered a prayer of gratitude and left her Court.

Dan'L ran up to her and began, "I want to…"

"No, my Royal Consort," she answered, knowing he would do more harm than good with the assassin. "Please, Dan'L; stay with our Son and his friends, and continue to protect them. Everyone stays here until we are one hundred percent certain this man was working alone." She kissed his cheek and left, followed by Master Commanders Shanna and L'Van, her personal Kaylan Ranger guards.

The prisoner was transferred to the interrogation room and sprayed with truth gas. Even though the prisoner was slapped around during questioning and punched twice, he said nothing. Then, a furious Empress Kayla entered the room. Her green eyes were full of fiery specks. "We have identified you as M'Tuk, a former Imperial Army soldier, dishonorably discharged three months ago, after serving four years in Ban'Ti Imperial prison for raping and beating a local Ban'Ti woman. You will tell us everything we want to know, M'Tuk," she said confidently, holding back from pummeling the loathsome prisoner into hamburger with her bare hands.

"Let me have him, my Empress. I will make him talk," C.S. G'Rosk asked. The prisoner laughed at him, infuriating G'Rosk even more.

But Kayla held up her hand to stop G'Rosk, and said, "Your record speaks for itself, M'Tuk. And now, you failed in your attempt to take the lives of Prince Lukus and his friends. All the children were under seven years of age. Imperial law prescribes harsh punishment for those who commit such heinous acts against defenseless, innocent children. Before this day is ended, you will beg for the mercy of your Empress, I promise you!" Kayla said between clenched teeth, shaking her fist in his smiling face. She led her Rangers out of the room, to the observation room behind the two-way mirror. "Begin recording. Administer truth serum to the prisoner.

Master Commander L'Van, will you honor me today?"

L'Van bowed her head and answered, "It is my greatest privilege, Empress Kayla." She removed her cloak and arm bands, put on her gloves, and walked into the room. She slowly paced in front of M'Tuk and waited a few minutes until the prisoner's eyes dilated.

M'Tuk leaned his head back and laughed at L'Van, and said, "So; the Empress Bitch sends another bitch to beat me? My lucky day! You should've let the big thug do it, instead," he said, referring to G'Rosk. L'Van stared at him, watching his eyes become glassy from the truth serum, and then she stood directly in front of him.

L'Van said in a quiet voice, "Prince Lukus slept in my arms the day he was born. His Mother, the Empress I am sworn by blood oath to obey, wants you to be cut along your belly, and slowly disemboweled. The Prince's Grandmother wants to personally skin you alive and pour rock salt over your body. The Father of Prince Lukus wants to cut your throat; but his solution is too quick and final. I have been sent in here to interrogate you, you miserable scum of a man, so that there is some life left in your body for the High Court Tribunal to sentence," L'Van said. He was no longer laughing.

Walking slowly around the prisoner, L'Van commented, "You are one of the ugliest men I have ever seen. And all this disgusting hair. How do you stand looking at your own reflection every morning?" She grabbed his long, matted hair and cut it off with a long-bladed knife from her backplate, and threw the hair on the floor. "All this hair on your neck, and a long beard, too. I have to cut it off before I puke!" She brandished her very sharp knife, and cut off his beard at the chin, then along the side of his face.

L'Van wiped her blade on his shoulder and put it back in her backplate. She took out a long, thin blade, and dry-shaved him, saying, "I'll bet you haven't had a girlfriend in years. The woman you raped on Ban'Ti probably threw up looking at you. Is that why you beat her afterwards?" M'Tuk sat very still, afraid to speak or move a muscle while her blade quickly shaved him. But his eyes showed fear to L'Van.

Once his face was shaved, L'Van ripped open his shirt, and made a face, saying, "More hair! You thoroughly repulse me, M'Tuk! No wonder women hate you. Your body is covered in thick, black, disgusting hair, like a stinking beast of the forest. Is their revulsion of you the reason you hate women?" L'Van asked, dry shaving his chest.

A few tears ran down his face and he said, "It is not my fault. The Creator cursed me! When they see my body, they all try to run away. Not one of them loves me, unless I make them. And then they hate me more. I hate them. I hate them all for rejecting me. And I hate you!" He yelled, "I hate every woman! They don't love me. Why should I love them?" L'Van uncovered his weakness. The hairy man who could find no woman willing to love and comfort him became the murderer, rapist, and misogynist he was today.

After shaving his hairy chest and shoulders, L'Van had the physician give him another shot of truth serum. Then, she drew her curved-blade knife, straddled him, and said, "Now you look better, M'Tuk. We can talk now, and I won't throw up all over you. You will answer all my questions now, won't you? I don't want to use this knife on you," she said, tapping the point of her curved knife against his balls. His eyes grew as big as saucers.

"My Empress Kayla loves all her people, M'Tuk, and most adore her, her kindness, and generosity. Why do you want to hurt her and her Son?" L'Van asked, lightly drawing her knife tip across his chest, and down his gut.

"She would turn from me if she saw me, too. They kicked me out of her Army," he said. L'Van used her knife tip and nicked his ear, and he jerked.

"Who put you up to assassinate a four-year-old boy? Who let you inside the Palace, and into the linen room? Tell me now, M'Tuk," she said, and nicked him again.

"Ow!" he yelled. "They hate her. He hates the people for loving her. They will bow to him, soon!" M'Tuk answered proudly. Slowly, L'Van drew her knife tip to his throat. "I won't tell! You can't make me. They never made me talk in prison. You can't, either!" He cried.

A slow smile came over her face, and L'Van replied, "Oh yes, you will talk. You will tell me everything I want to know. It takes a long time for surface cuts to heal, especially when they are irritated and widened, slowly." She cut a shallow gash along his belly horizontally, just below his sternum, and he winced. Taking a martial arts star-shaped blade from her breastplate, she walked it on its points inside the shallow cut, while she rocked on his lap to arouse him. He looked confused and fearful—her desired advantage.

"Who put you up to this? What was your bribe?" She asked and watched his crotch bulge. "Who paid you, M'Tuk?" Another dig in his cut with the star, followed by a thrust.

L'Van was a master of coercion. She gave him pain when M'Tuk did not answer, and "lap-dance" thrusts when he gave her information. It didn't take too long for him to figure this out. In less than ten minutes, he was recorded giving lists of Technicians' names, the location of their meeting places, and the hidden room where his two young "rewards" were imprisoned, awaiting his successful mission accomplishment. M'Tuk was nearly delirious and rolled his head in pain and excitement. She asked her final question, "Who does the Technician answer to?" She dug the tip of her star inside his cut deeper, until he shrieked.

One deeper dig, this time with a little twist, and M'Tuk screamed, "T'Yang! He is the new Master! Lord T'Yang is the one!" M'Tuk yelled out and rolled his eyes. L'Van jumped off him, wiped off her knife and star, and turned to the mirror. An Imperial Guard entered and took a shaking M'Tuk back to his cell, the prisoner crying out, "Finish me! Finish me!"

Empress Kayla ordered, "Commander Superior G'Rosk, send four of your best Borgund Rangers to find and apprehend Lord T'Yang, and anyone with him. Send two more to free the two young girls captured for this criminal, and make sure they describe their captors. Put the girls in protective custody at once." He bowed and ran to the Ranger High Command office.

The Empress tapped on her comm link for Field Marshall General Blatan and ordered the Imperial Army commandos to take and occupy the home of Lord T'Yang. "Do it peacefully, if possible, General Blatan. High Ranger Lady Bette will send you coordinates of two locations for more commando raids in a few minutes." Appropriate warrants were immediately issued, and several "Technicians" were apprehended within the hour. The mansion and grounds of Lord T'Yang were occupied by the Imperial Army, but the Master Technician was not found.

Inside his prison cell underneath the Palace, M'Tuk sat, wondering how the Technicians would kill him before the Empress' people made him reveal any more information. He had to die; he knew too much. Soon, he heard footsteps outside the solid iron door of his cell. When the door opened, more than a dozen Borgund Rangers in their black uniforms and long cloaks slowly entered his cell. Man after man said, "My son was in the sleigh with Prince Lukus;" or "My daughter was in the sleigh." M'Tuk began to tremble.

Then the group of Rangers parted, and a woman Ranger walked between them. "I have waited all day to meet you, M'Tuk the failed assassin. The children of these men were under my protection. My Grandson is Prince Lukus. My younger Kaylan Ranger sister took some information from you earlier today. But she is not as practiced as I am, retrieving information from vermin like you. You will tell me everything you know about the Master Technician, his Technicians, and the Alternates; and the Plan of the Thirteen. Before this night is through, you will beg these Rangers to use their blades on your throat, if you fail to disclose everything. Now, let us begin." They sprayed his face with truth gas three times.

C.S. Javette threw off her long, black cloak, and pulled out a knife with a very thin, long blade, and brandished it in his face. "Remove his shirt," she ordered, and a Ranger came behind M'Tuk and ripped off the man's shirt. "Tell me about the Plan of the Thirteen, M'Tuk," she said, and sliced across his chest with her razor-sharp blade. He cried out in pain and looked hatefully at her. Then, she inserted the tip of her knife under the cut edge and began to separate his skin from the underneath muscle, watching him scream. "Tell me now, or I promise you: I will skin you alive, you spawn of Hell!"

More information was obtained from M'Tuk under Javette's knife edge during the next hours. She did not skin him, but the look in her eyes terrified the prisoner. M'Tuk knew she was fully prepared to peel off every centimeter of his skin. He was sprayed every fifteen minutes with truth gas and confessed aplenty. The session was recorded by every Ranger present.

M'Tuk was recruited several years ago while he was still active in the Imperial Army and stationed on M'Wati. One of the few troops with a reputation of dishonest dealings, the Technician B'Nard watched M'Tuk closely. He took bribes from drug smugglers and helped them escape Imperial capture. He got to know many of the underground criminals and assisted with their shipments and sales of illegal drugs, and stolen Army weapons. B'Nard bought his loyalty, and M'Tuk worked for him in secret for several years.

Nothing was ever proven against M'Tuk, but his Army commander transferred him to Ban'Ti to get him outside the network he had established on M'Wati, hoping the soldier would go straight. Instead, M'Tuk resented his reassignment to the jungle planet, and became hostile with the timid farmers of Ban'Ti. He brutally raped and beat a female field worker there one day. Her family caught him, and he was court martialed, and sentenced to four years in Imperial prison. B'Nard finally had M'Tuk where he could control him.

The convicts inside the prison working for B'Nard introduced M'Tuk to former Lord Aug'R, an original Plan of the Thirteen signer, and he was taken into their confidence. By the time he was released from Ban'Ti prison, M'Tuk knew the Alternate Contingencies of the Plan, and was transported to K'Halon Prime to work for the Master Technician and his group.

The Rangers threw cold water on M'Tuk's bleeding chest and put antibiotic surgical tape over the long cut. "Is that everything, M'Tuk?" Javette asked. He nodded. "You know it had better be, or I will return. If I come back, I will not be in such a kind mood. Understand?" He nodded his head "Yes" several times.

The Rangers left his cell. M'Tuk slumped against the wall of his cell. He slid down to the floor and began to softly laugh. The Ranger bitch was easier on him than B'Nard would be, if he got hold of him. He still had his balls. She pulled out nearly everything he knew. Nearly – but not all. She didn't ask him about the Old Engine, or the next phase of the Plan.

The last rays of the sun shone inside her study where Prince Lukus played. As she read the incoming reports and the latest information obtained by Javette, Empress Kayla felt her internal "radar" becoming more active. Something bigger was in the works and set up to happen during this trip to her home planet. The Plan of the Thirteen had not been conceived and designed thirty-plus years ago and stashed away, awaiting the right time to be enacted. The Plan had been active since its original designers signed their names in blood on the parchment.

How far-reaching and vast were the deep networks of murderers, traitors, saboteurs, and spies of the Plan? In more than thirty years, thousands could have been influenced and employed. Great wealth would be necessary to keep the Plan working for such a long time. Who were the donors now? The original grantors to the Plan were known and incarcerated. But where did they hide their wealth to support their nefarious efforts?

"The Fount," Kayla said aloud, and realized what the term meant. She saw an urgent message light on her com console light up. It was Priest K'Ramm.

"Empress Kayla, I apologize for my interruption. But I have discovered something you should know. As I was looking again at the document you asked me to translate, I noticed a mark on the reverse side. It is not legible in black light, which may be why it was overlooked," he said.

She impatiently asked, "What mark? What does it say, K'Ramm?"

He answered in a whisper, "It is the old numeral for the number 'three,' and it's upside down. I think it means it's the third part of thirteen for their contingency plans, My Empress! We have to find the other documents, and I think I know where they are!"

XII

K'Halon Prime was a massive planet, one side covered in dense forests, with its three billion people concentrated in its cities and along its equatorial coastlines, where the weather was warmer. The size of the continents on the "good side" were larger than the total land masses on Home World. Those independent, tough souls who lived within the forests were close to small towns, logging and milling communities, or lived off the grid. Some towns were hundreds of kilometers from bigger government facilities, hospitals, and police protection, including several large estates of the aristocracy.

The dry, desert side of the planet was where all mining took place now, away from the mass population centers, and civilization in general. The huge mining machines and borers carved out deep canyons for the miners, then moved on to more promising sites when the metals, minerals, or precious gems were all mined out. This process left several deep mines abandoned. Although the abandoned mines were sealed, a few had been secretly and illegally reopened.

Six hundred kilometers inland from the cold, southern coast of the dry side, one of the gold mines had been illegally accessed by the Thirteen's Technicians decades ago. Initially used to store weapons and uniforms for the old Rebellion, the old mine grew to become much more. During the past thirty years, the mine and its lengthy tunnels were used not only as a weapons cache, but as the central storeroom for treasure to fund the Plan: the "Fount."

Skimming the accounts of their own factories, stores, hotels, and vineyards, the original Thirteen hid their illegal credits, coins, and gold bars in the Fount. A new vein of pure gold was discovered when they dug deeper to expand their storeroom, further adding to their wealth. A full-time crew of twenty-two trusted conspirators lived in the mine, keeping any potential trespassers away, and smelting the ore in a small furnace. Men at the Fount worked night and day, refining gold for their Masters, and the

Plan.

After the failed attempt on Prince Lukus, Lord T'Yang took refuge with another "Alternate" in Southern K'Halon Prime. The price on his head was 200,000 credits in gold. There were few places T'Yang could go now. All his titled lands and wealth were confiscated by the Empire. But he had the old steel key to the vault inside the Fount. He just had to get there without being caught.

"We have six accomplices called 'Technicians,' thirty-three associates apprehended with them; the confessed assassin, and the Palace housekeeper who let him inside the Palace linen storeroom," C.S. Javette reported. "But former Lord T'Yang has not been found."

C.S. T'Anh asked, "What of our 'flies on the wall' and 'cockroaches?' They were put in place at many suspected locations, at significant risk to our Kaylan Rangers. One of my Commanders was attacked releasing the spy bugs in the wharf district last month," she disclosed.

Kayla answered, "A secret task force is currently monitoring the 'bugs,' Commander Superior T'Anh. Their work produced the intelligence warning of the attempt on Prince Lukus' life. But nothing has surfaced regarding T'Yang. We suspect he is being harbored by another Technician or Alternate," the Empress shared.

Lady Bette said, "This is your Majesty's third week on K'Halon Prime. Your pre-announced schedule includes the Grand Opening at the Temple of the Creator; the Grand Opening of the T'Anju District Resort; the Grand Opening of the Mount Regency Ski Resort and Casino; and the Confirmation of your newly graduated Novice Rangers. A very full schedule, my Empress Kayla. The public will be present at the three Grand Openings, complete with full media broadcasts," she closed, looking at her com tablet with a frown on her face.

"Has the information been made public about the attempt on Prince Lukus, my Empress? We successfully invited the investigative journalists to help when the nuclear warhead was discovered by your future Consort Dan'L, aboard the Imperial Command Battle Cruiser several years ago. Perhaps the media can help us again," Chief Advisor Baron P'Lau suggested.

His comment set off a round of discussion among the Ranger High Command and the Advisors of the Empress. Kayla listened attentively to each comment, saving her evaluations for later. "Our media group's program, 'News from the Empire,' will be broadcast tomorrow evening. Please prepare a brief statement to be read in case we decide to alert the public," the Empress said. "We have also activated other units to pursue this and other channels. But rest assured; once critical intelligence is obtained, you will be informed immediately. You are our most trusted advisors, my friends," the Empress said with a bow of her head. The meeting was called to a close, with everyone now formulating more questions to be answered.

Chief Advisor Baron P'Lau pleaded with his Empress, "But he's so looking forward to meeting your Majesty. He must be eighty by now—maybe ninety. He wants to meet his fourth Sovereign. Please, Empress Kayla?"

"Very well, Baron P'Lau. Bring in the Minister of the Fringe Lands," she ordered with a sigh.

The doddering old aristocrat trotted in and bowed deeply to her. "My Empress Kayla. I am honored to meet you," he said. His suit of clothes was out of style, but the richly decorated fine wool and silk were the highest quality. He was, in every sense, a gentleman.

She graciously asked Minister Al'Red to join her for tea, and he excitedly sat next to Baron P'Lau. "I remember the day you both took the throne. You were only fourteen, my former Emperor P'Lau; yet you held your head high. And you, my Empress Kayla: you are the most beautiful Empress in history! This old man is your most honored servant."

For over an hour, they talked about the Reclamation Program. It was now a resounding success, and there was an extensive list of hopefuls waiting to be chosen to work reclaiming the desert of K'Halon Prime, turning it into farmland or forest. "Your T'Anju District is the 'hot spot,' according to my great-grandson. All the young people love it! They want more apartments to live there," he disclosed.

They discussed the new Temple, and the new Mount Regency Ski Resort and Casino. The minister commented, "I hope the proprietors keep strict control of the clientele, and don't allow the ruffians inside."

Kayla asked, "What ruffians, Minister Al'Red?"

"Oh, you know. Those ruffians living in the old mines. They are so arrogant and prone to fighting. The settlors complain constantly about them, and their smoke," he answered, sipping his tea.

"Smoke? What smoke? Where is it coming from, Minister?" She asked, trying to hide the urgency in her voice. "Could you pinpoint its location?"

She projected a 3D holographic map of the Fringe Lands on their table. The old Minister pointed and said, "Here, from the old gold mines. The smoke pours out all day and night. Every day. It does smell awful, I have to admit," he said.

"Like smoke from a smelting furnace?" Empress Kayla asked, and P'Lau looked at her knowingly. "Does the old mine have a name, or a nickname, perhaps?"

Minister Al'Red answered, "Oh, yes. The ruffians refer to it as 'the Fount.' Can you imagine a fountain in the desert? How absurd," he commented.

It was all Kayla could do to tactfully wrap up their meeting. Baron P'Lau helped her, sensing her urgency. She felt an overwhelming sense of impending disaster. Non-combatants, including Admiral Mae, and the Empress' ladies-in-waiting, were sent back to Home World on the earliest transport. Her Brother, Admiral Olm, accompanied them, to assist with the Royal Palace defense. Dozens of spy cockroaches and flies were air-dropped by drones at the Fount entrance. Their transmissions provided the groundwork for the Empress' plan of attack on the old gold mine.

When she was alone, Kayla conferenced in Sham'S and her friend L'Mun: "Whatever the two of you are doing has to be postponed. We have a change of plans, my dear friends." Even on their small comm link, they could see the twinkle in their Empress' green eyes. "We have discovered the location of the Fount."

Fifty Kilometers from the Fount

Midnight passed, and the sullen men in the dingy, wooden building called a bar drank in silence while listening to recorded music. "Give me another," the stranger said to the bartender. He slapped his 20-credit coin on the bar, overpaying for the swill once again.

"It's your last one, buddy. This makes seven tonight," the cautious bartender said to the stranger. "Police patrols are everywhere. They'll haul you in for drinking this much and riding, you know." He poured another double vodka for the stranger, who downed it in a big gulp, and left the bar. "Good luck," the bartender said. Every sleazy patron at the bar saw the stranger slap coin after coin on the bar, each one a new 20-credit coin. The stranger would probably be robbed before he got half a kilometer away.

The stranger staggered to his fancy chopper and straddled it. The large anti-gravity machine roared to life, and he sped off. Three men left the bar behind the stranger and followed him. The stranger had sat at his corner table all night, drinking doubles, and fingering the big coins in his pocket. The three men were going to get the rest of his loot for themselves.

Sham'S emptied the cup in his pocket where he poured the cheap vodka all night as he flew along. He looked in the mirror; three beat-up choppers were rapidly catching up to him, his original intention. Mostly miners frequented the dingy bar where he spent the evening pretending to get drunk. But the three riders after him were thugs and outlaws—just the type of men he needed working for him.

The three choppers caught up to Sham'S and signaled for him to pull over. One of the men brandished a knife. Sham'S pulled over and dismounted. The men surrounded him and demanded he empty his pockets.

"Here. Take it all. Lots more where this came from," Sham'S slurred, and pitched his credits on the ground.

The big thug with the knife grabbed Sham'S and demanded to be taken to the rest of his loot, while his buddies picked up the coins. In one swift move, Sham'S disarmed the thug, and held his knife at his throat. The other two dropped the coins in amazement.

"Now, you boys can either keep up with your petty thievery, and I'll kick your asses from here to the mines. Or, you can work for me, and make some real money. You decide. Right now," Sham'S said. The thugs agreed to work for him. "Good. Follow me," he said, and they took off through the dark desert. In an hour, they pulled up to a new building, unmarked and dimly lit. Sham'S smacked the recognition pad and led the men inside. He pointed to a round table and chairs, and yelled, "Woman, there's company here," and sat at the table with the men.

Dressed in stretch slacks, a tight tank top, and sandals, First Cmdr. L'Mun walked out with a tray of glasses and a new bottle of vodka. She sat down and asked, "Hungry?"

The thugs leered at the gorgeous blonde, and Sham'S put his arm around L'Mun. "She's off-limits. Her ass is mine," he said sternly. L'Mun ran her fingers through his curly red hair and smiled. She left the table and went into the kitchen.

They passed around the vodka while Sham'S explained their new jobs to them: "Every third day, you boys come here by ten in the morning. We wait for the signal, then ride out to the Fount. Make sure your fuel cells are full. After they leave, we walk in the secret entrance, and take the bags of gold coins. We ride into town, spend the credits, and keep our mouths shut. In two weeks, we escort the big shuttle to the harbor. No one else can know about this gig, understand? My last two hires got drunk at a bar and started flapping their mouths, and they put 'em down. Do our jobs and keep quiet. That's it," he said.

"Sounds too easy," the big man said warily. "Just spend the credits, and twice a month escort a shuttle to the harbor? Do you think we're idiots?"

Yes, Sham'S thought to himself. "Look. It's money laundering, you stupid moron. We spread it around for them. Don't you know anything? This is how they make the big bucks. They tell us which places to spend half the credits, and we keep the rest. And all the credits get circulated legitimately. Do I have to explain everything to you, or are you going to do as I say, and make some real dough?" Sham'S said, pounding his fist on the table like a boss.

The men agreed to do what he said, understanding nothing of money laundering. L'Mun brought out a tray of sandwiches and hard ciders. They stuffed their faces and drank their fill. Then Sham'S went into another room and came out with a bag. He poured the gold credits onto the table and said, "We start tomorrow, then every three days. All in?" They greedily took their loot and flew their anti-gravity choppers fast into the dark night.

"Do you think they'll be back, Sham'S?" L'Mun asked. "They're such stupid brutes."

He laughed and answered, "They'll be back for the easy money, and you, L'Mun. Next time, wear shorts," he quipped. She smacked him a good one, and they both laughed. He set the alarm and the defensive shields, in case the thugs returned too soon.

Sham'S watched L'Mun cleaning the table and felt the old longing again. Her hair was unbraided and down. She was so beautiful. He had a crush on her since Phase 1 Training, so many years ago; but L'Mun always treated him as just a friend. She was surprisingly single, as far as he knew. Sham'S wondered if L'Mun was seeing anyone now. He was a tall man with short red, curly hair, and very strong. But when it came to beautiful L'Mun, Sham'S was too shy for his own good. He swore to tell her how he felt about her when this mission was over.

L'Mun sent their report on the secret comm link number to Empress Kayla, their good friend and Sovereign. She and Sham'S sat up and planned the next phase of their mission with great attention to detail. The reign of Empress Kayla and the fate of the Empire relied upon their successful mission accomplishment. They could not fail tomorrow. Succeed at any cost.

XIII

The show emcee said, “And now, we bring to our audience across the system a special message from our Empress Kayla!” The scene shifted to the Royal Suite in the Palace at K’Halon Prime. She was seated with Royal Consort Dan’L on her right, and Prince Lukus on her left. She began:

“Greetings to all people across our Great Empire tonight. We are speaking to you from K’Halon Prime. As most of you are aware, during the celebration of the fourth birthday of Prince Lukus, a cruel, evil man attempted to assassinate your Royal Heir, along with many of his young friends. All were happy, defenseless children, riding together in a sleigh. The children were saved by our bravest Imperial Guards and Borgund Rangers, three of whom gave their lives protecting the children.”

“We are shocked and appalled at this most heinous crime and ask the help of our fellow citizens in apprehending the man involved. A sketch of the criminal mastermind as described by the captured would-be assassin will be made available to all media at the end of our broadcast.”

“If any private citizen sees this criminal, please help us. Please report his whereabouts to us at the number displayed on your screens shortly. This man is very dangerous, so do not attempt to capture him by yourselves. The everlasting gratitude of your Prince Lukus, your Royal Consort Dan’L, and your Empress are yours, as always. May the Great Creator bless all of our people,” she closed, and the Royal Family bowed their heads.

A “Wanted” sketch of an unnamed man was then shown with a toll-free comm link number below it. Then, the sentence: “A reward of 200,000 gold credits is offered for the apprehension, arrest, and conviction of this man.”

Watching the weekly “News from the Empire” broadcast, B’Nard dropped his drink and yelled, “Holy bloody hell!” He immediately called the comm link number he was ordered to never call. “Did you watch the ‘News from the Empire’? His face is all over the news, with a 200,000-gold credit reward offered. We’ll never move him now, sir,” B’Nard cried. His fellow conspirator paused the call for a couple of minutes, then came back to the call.

"This is most distressing. We will contact you shortly. Never call me again!" The Alternate sat back in his chair and wrung his hands in thought. He slowly punched in a rarely-used comm link number and said, "We need to meet. Tonight. All of us. We need his key."

After a slight pause, the voice on the other end of the call said, "At the wharf club. One hour. Cover his head and bring him. Do not be seen moving him, else we're all discovered! Do not fail!" The fat hand full of gold rings slammed off the comm link and threw it across his room in anger.

The gay dance club was closed for this Tuesday night. A sign was posted: "Closed for private party." Several disgruntled gay men complained and beat on the steel front doors, despite their being locked, and the sign posted. Two very large bouncers came outside, refused to let the men come inside, and a shouting match ensued. It was not a welcome sign for the wealthy, discreet aristocrats waiting in their shuttle. When the crowd dispersed, the aristocrats silently left their shuttle and went inside the dark club.

Three more shuttles landed, and their occupants entered the gay club. Then, eight noisy choppers landed, and their riders dressed in black suits entered. The front doors were closed and locked again. Everyone awaited the final shuttle.

In ten minutes, a matte black shuttle landed. Two private guards brought a hooded man in black inside the club, followed by two more aristocrats, looking up and down the street nervously.

"I hate this place. It's too open. Why can we never enter through the back?" One man said, and two others agreed with him.

"Our police guarantee our safety and the street cameras are all off. Stop whining. This venue has been safe for over a decade. The back alley may have some degenerates hanging about. No one suspects we meet in a queer dance club," the aristocrat in the blue jacket said.

Lord T'Yang's hood was roughly pulled off his head. "You couldn't even kill a four-year-old in the open. You botched the Imperial shuttle assignment, too. We are convinced you are incompetent, or in league with imbeciles!" The large aristocrat yelled, "And we chose you!"

For the next twenty minutes, the Master Technician Lord T'Yang pleaded for his life, to no avail. The big aristocrat yelled, "B'Nard! Do it!"

With a spiteful smile, B'Nard held the Master Technician's chin, and stabbed his heart. The man fell to the floor, and B'Nard cut his throat ear to ear. Then he handed the old steel key to the big aristocrat, and drug T'Yang's lifeless body to the back. He enjoyed it thoroughly.

"Now, we must choose another Master Technician. I nominate D'Stin," the aristocrat in the blue jacket announced. Those in power voted their newest Master Technician to rise above the other men in black suits, the "Technicians."

B'Nard was jealous of D'Stin, now having been passed over for a third time. He cleverly asked, "My Lord, is there a change in the order of Alternates? With so much happening, it is prudent to ask, sir."

With a dismissive wave of his fat, many-ringed hand, the aristocrat answered, "No. Everything remains the same."

"Let us continue the Plan, Contingency Seven. Is everything ready for next week? There can be no more failures. It is our hour of glory," the aristocrat wearing a short cape asked. "Is the 'Old Engine' ready at last?"

D'Stin answered, "Yes, my Lord, the 'Old Engine' is ready. We will ride the 'Old Engine' to fame, glory and power into the annuals of history!" The men in black suits raised their glasses to toast, but the big aristocrat stared menacingly at them.

The aristocrat in the blue jacket sternly corrected, "Alternate Seven will ride the 'Old Engine' to fame, glory and power, and rule the Empire!" The four aristocrats toasted each other. The Technicians stood silent, once again reminded they were only pawns for the remaining Alternates. As before, they obeyed their orders, and realized the only power they had was whatever the Alternates gave them.

The aristocrat in the cape said, "We will not meet here again, hopefully. You will receive your assignments tomorrow. We must not fail again!"

D'Stin answered, "Yes, Lord K'Vin." His saying the Alternate's name was his last mistake. His face became full of fear when Lord K'Vin moved his head towards B'Nard. D'Stin had nowhere to run. B'Nard cut his throat and drug his body out of the room.

"B'Nard, you are now our Master Technician. Clean up this mess. We will call you in the morning," he said, and walked out with the other Alternates to their shuttles.

"Dispose of the bodies," B'Nard said to the other Technicians. He sat and watched the two bodies be stripped of their watches, wallets, comm links, keys, and credits. The bounty was placed on the table in front of him and divided. The men put the dead into body bags and loaded them into a cart marked "Laundry." The "Laundry" cart was pushed outside the back door and emptied into the large trash receptacle. B'Nard unlocked the doors of the dance club, took down the "Private Party" sign, and opened for business.

The semi-annual Meeting of the Ministers was going on its second hour. Although her schedule for the meeting was blocked out for four hours, the Empress had no intention of listening to their droning much longer. She tapped her com tablet and ordered lunch for everyone. As the servers were bringing in the loaded food carts, several additional Imperial Guards silently entered, and joined the other Guardsmen along the wall.

Mid-way through lunch, the conversation turned to the discovery of former Lord T'Yang's body in a large trash receptacle on the wharf at Centralia. "Has your Majesty been informed of this discovery? And I understand another, unidentified man succumbed to the same fate, and was disposed of in a similar manner," the Minister of Energy commented.

The elder Minister of Environment said firmly, "This is not proper conversation during our luncheon with Empress Kayla. She is still recovering, gentlemen!"

"It is all right, Ministers. We must admit our surprise at the news," she said, hoping to draw out more information. "We understand it was in an unsavory area of the wharf."

"There are several night spots and bars there, but rarely anything more than an occasional public intoxication arrest is made," the Minister of Police said, dismissing her concerns.

"Well, perhaps you enjoy that type of diversion, but most respectable people do not frequent dance clubs offering prostitution!" The Minister of Energy exclaimed.

"Prostitution? Of which type?" Empress Kayla asked in astonishment. "We are shocked to hear this!" Now she was drawing them out.

The shy Minister of Environment answered, "All types, my Empress. Girls, boys, and those specializing in fetishes and other things not proper to speak of in mixed company, too. The clubs play their music very loud, so nothing is heard outside."

Kayla looked at the Minister of Police, A'Bek, and demanded, "Why is this illegal and immoral activity permitted? Imperial law clearly prohibits such things to be carried on in public. How long has this been going on?" Her green eyes intensely stared at him.

Minister A'Bek puffed out his chest and answered, "It is all rumor and conjecture. No conviction has even been made."

The Empress abruptly stood and ordered, "You are hereby relieved of your position and authority, A'Bek. Master Commander An'Ton, please escort this man to a private room, and see that Master Commander Kend'R interviews him at once!"

The affronted former Minister rose and was summarily taken from the meeting room. "We will thoroughly investigate this matter, and clean up our wharf, gentlemen. Thank you all for bringing our attention to this situation. Venues for music and dancing, and responsible entertainment are welcome. Illegal activities are not!" She said and retook her seat. Kayla could tell the former Minister of Police profited greatly from the prostitution. He probably allowed illegal drugs and underage activities, as well. She would get to the bottom of his scheme.

"Please excuse this interruption, gentlemen. Let us continue with our meeting. We do have a question recently raised by one of our auditors, concerning certain funds funneled to a project no one seems to be familiar with, titled, 'The Old Engine.' Have any of you heard of this?" She asked innocently.

The Minister of Mining, Minerals, and Exploration choked on his food, and coughed loudly into his napkin. Another conspirator was uncovered. Kayla looked around the table at the men. Most looked at one another and shook their heads "No." But the still-coughing Minister and the man beside him stood to leave, claiming the need for medical attention.

"Master Commander L'Van, please escort these gentlemen to another private room, and have a physician attend to them right away. Make certain they don't leave until we have made sure they are fit to travel," the Empress ordered. L'Van understood exactly what Kayla was hinting for her to do.

Empress Kayla looked around the table and said, "It seems we no longer have a quorum, gentlemen. We will reconvene at a later day and time. Thank you all for your astute observations." She stood and left the room.

Imperial Guards escorted the Empress to the holding cell where the former Minister of Police paced. From the observation room she watched him, consumed with hatred and anger, and too self-assured to be fearful. "Where is Master Commander Kend'R?" She questioned An'Ton.

"He is in the Palace now, my Empress, and on his way here. He wanted to change out of uniform for the interrogation," An'Ton replied. "I have taken the liberty to call for a physician and truth serum, your Majesty."

Arriving shortly, Kend'R was let inside the holding cell with A'Bek, the former Minister of Police, and he politely invited A'Bek to be seated. "I will not be seated! I have been Minister of Police for over twenty-five years without any blemish on my record. I demand to see my lawyer this instant!" A'Bek bellowed.

Kend'R calmly said, "Innocent men do not demand lawyers, or have lawyers at their beck and call. Innocent men are more than willing to talk about their situation, proclaiming their innocence the entire time. Therefore, I must assume there are certain guilty activities you wish to conceal from an Imperial Inquest."

A'Bek's fury grew and his face reddened as he yelled, "This is outrageous! I'll have you imprisoned for this mistreatment. Get this man out of my sight!" He walked up to the two-way mirror and screamed, "Do you know who I am? I'll have all your heads on pikes for this insult! Release me now! I demand…" and then Kend'R sprayed his face with truth gas. Two Imperial Guards rushed in and restrained A'Bek, who was fighting and kicking them with much hostility. They cuffed him to the steel chair.

Physicians administered truth serum with tranquilizers to A'Bek. The Empress insisted no corporal punishment be administered to the prisoner, and not one body blow was put on former Minister A'Bek. But Kend'R, the very able telepath, picked apart his mind. Layer by layer of lies, deceit, treachery; corruption and extortion over twenty-five years were revealed. After a stronger dose of the truth serum was injected, the most pressing questions were asked.

Kend'R stared at A'Bek and watched his eyes grow watery and glassy. He asked quietly, "Who are you, Minister A'Bek? We know you are more than merely a Minister of the Empire."

The man's face twitched and contorted, as if he was in pain; then he made a sardonic grin. Once again, Kend'R asked, "Who are you, sir? We wish to honor you today, but we must know who you are. You are a master of patience and duplicity. It must have been difficult, hiding behind the mask of a common Minister of Police all these years. They never paid you enough tribute for your excellent, most admirable deception."

Kend'R could read the man's mind, but he had to get him to confess his true name aloud for the recording. A'Bek held his head high and said, "No, they did not pay me enough. Men forget to honor those above them, seeing only this tawdry uniform. But soon, they will be made to bow down before me," he said proudly, his eyes now cloudy from the drugs.

Kend'R knelt and asked, "To whom do I pledge my allegiance, sir? I must know your name to praise you and cheer your name in the Main Court."

"Everyone will cheer A'Luz, the eldest son of Baron Z'Lun, the rightful heir to the throne! In two days, this Empire is mine! All who participated in my Father's great embarrassment will die a painful death, and their heads will be put on pikes at the main gates!"

The astonished Empress, her Ranger senior leaders, and Imperial Guards were speechless. They listened as Kend'R continued with A'Luz, extracting more information from the proud man than had been gleaned in five years. Everything was set to take place in two days or less. She had to work fast: the "Old Engine" was ready to use against her Empire.

Kayla left the observation room and walked down the corridor to the other interrogation room, where the "choking" Ministers were being held. She asked aloud, "Did any of you know about Z'Lun having any other sons, or daughters, for that matter?"

C.S. Javette answered, "We knew nothing of the former Baron having any other children. But he had many mistresses. Who knows how many other offspring could be hiding."

After turning down the hall, the Empress stopped and called Field Marshall General Blatan, and ordered," The Minister of Police of K'Halon Prime has been arrested for high treason. Prepare your commandos and troops for martial law in Centralia, and especially at the harbor there. Prepare to deploy on a second's notice but engage only on my direct command. Understood, General?"

General Blatan saluted and said, "We will prepare at once, and engage only upon your word, my Empress!"

The Warrior Empress Kayla entered the holding cell where the two "choking" ministers sat, whispering to each other and looking at her nefariously. She said, "Guard, take this Minister to a separate room. C.S. Javette, please leave at least part of his skin on him," she ordered, and watched them leave with M.C. L'Van, and a smiling Javette.

The physician shot the Minister of Mining, Minerals, and Exploration with truth serum while Kayla paced in his cell, her determination to get to the truth growing every second. She was experienced with "soft" coercion but had never had to get physically violent or abusive with a prisoner. But she and her Empire were running out of time.

"I am not only your Empress, Minister. I am a Kaylan Ranger Master Commander, and a 20th-degree Master in T'Ly martial arts. And now, you will tell me all about this 'Old Engine.' Right now," she said firmly. The Guard cuffed him to the steel chair.

The former Minister stubbornly shook his head and cried, "No! You can't make me!"

She slapped his face hard and replied, "I am fresh out of official torturers and telepaths. Now we can do this the easy way, and you will be allowed your day in the High Court Tribunal. Or, if you refuse, I will take out my frustrations from being starved twenty-nine days, nearly being blown up, and watching my four-year-old son be attacked, on YOU! Which shall it be?" She pulled out her curved knife and held it in front of his face, and he shook his head.

The Warrior Empress thrust her knife into his shoulder and twisted the blade just a little, and the man cried out in pain. "You know, I really dislike doing this to you. I find it distasteful. But if you don't talk now, I will cut you once for each day I was starved, and you will bleed until your veins are dry. Choose now!" No response. "Day Two!" She yelled and thrust her blade into his calf.

After three stabs for three days of starvation, the information began to surface. The fourth stab in his outer thigh was all the Minister needed to blab his head off, after he stopped screaming in pain. He told her everything he knew about the Old Engine and the timetable for its deployment. There was precious little time.

By night fall, the full military might of the Empire was on yellow alert, ready to come to the aid of the Empress Kayla. All Rangers and fighter pilots were ordered to their warbirds. Imperial Guards at both Palaces emptied every suite, moved all the guests and non-essential personnel out of the Palaces, and locked down the massive structures. The children in the Royal Academy on Home World Palace were shuttled to the fancy resort more than two hundred kilometers away on Paradise Island, with additional staff acquired to assist and care for them. All Palace gates and entrances were barricaded. The remaining Palace Guards were on red alert, fully armed with defensive weaponry. Imperial shuttles were ready inside each Palace courtyard for evacuation of the Guards, Rangers, and essential staff.

Empress Kayla flew her Royal Family to the new Temple of the Creator Complex in her ES-519. Priest K'Ramm sheltered Prince Lukus, and Tara and her son. She called, "Master Commander Sham'S, are you and First Commander L'Mun in position?" She saw they were wearing desert camouflage clothing and boots, their breastplates and backplates, and long coats with many pockets stuffed full of portable, incendiary weapons.

He answered, "Yes, my Empress, we are. And several thugs and outlaws are on their way to join us. Soon, we will party!" L'Mun and Kayla laughed with him. His smiling face on the view screen was reassuring to her. She acknowledged them and clicked off.

One more call to make, and she punched in the numbers. "Baron P'Lau, are you and the Council of Elder Rangers ready?"

The former Emperor proudly raised his head and declared, "I have never been more ready in my life, my Great Empress Kayla!"

"Then, may our Creator give us wisdom, strength, clarity, and endurance, and bless us all tonight!" The Warrior Empress said and bowed her head to her former Sovereign.

XIV

The "Old Engine" was the Emergency Planetary Defense System (EPDS) from two hundred twenty years ago, modernized with current technology and weaponry. It was expanded to include mobile missile launching platforms in space, and hidden missile launching systems on each planet. It utilized satellites in orbit to signal the Imperial Military on all four planets and all Space Bases to attack invading forces in space, or on the four planets.

The EPDS was abandoned over a century ago when a new generation of interplanetary communications was developed. But the old EPDS was not dismantled, as most Military Advisors believed. It was merely disengaged in favor of newer technology and faster warships, and subsequently forgotten. Billions of credits were spent over the years to upgrade and reactivate the EPDS for the evil Plan of the Thirteen.

The programming for the EPDS was discovered during a "data dump" project forty-two years ago by young Space Cadre Technology Officer T'Vic, the oldest brother of the future Baron Z'Lun. Realizing what he had accidentally discovered, Officer T'Vic secretly copied and recreated the EPDS. Over the next two years, Officer T'Vic wrote programming instructions to reactivate the system, enabling the success for the future "Plan of the Thirteen." But, after his programming work was completed, T'Vic was killed in a mysterious hunting accident the next year. His untimely death paved the way for the new Baron Z'Lun, who worked with other disgruntled aristocrats on K'Halon Prime to formulate the Plan of the Thirteen. They now had their ultimate weapon to take over the Empire.

Neither former Emperor P'Lau nor any of his Military Advisors were aware the EPDS still existed. Over the next thirty years, the EPDS was systematically restored and upgraded to cutting-edge technology. Captured original Plan of the Thirteen signers, their Technicians, and Alternates told their interrogators the old Rebellion was intentionally started to avert Imperial attention from their work on the EPDS. Technology, equipment, and weapons stolen by Rebels from Space Cadre and Imperial Army armories were diverted to the refurbished EPDS over the years. The late Rebel Leader Duma Wat believed he would take over as Emperor when the Plan of the Thirteen was activated upon the return of the Vee Lok Lords. But Duma Wat, the half-brother of former Emperor P'Lau, was merely another pawn in the Plan.

Without their slim warning, the Imperial Military and Rangers would have been activated by the "Old Engine," believing an alien force had invaded the R'Genra System. They were to have targeted the very defensive systems and ships built to protect the Empire. The goal of the "Old Engine" was the total obliteration of the Imperial Military, Rangers, and planetary defenses; the obliteration of the entire Warrior Class. If the redesigned EPDS was successfully used, hundreds of thousands of loyal men and women serving on Space Cadre ships and space bases, and on the four planets for the Imperial Military, would be killed in minutes.

At the emergency meeting of Military Advisors and Ranger High Command leaders, C.S. G'Rosk said, "Every Space Cadre line officer above Major knows the established emergency protocols and defensive plans. They were designed to defend the four inhabited planets from attacking forces originating from outside our R'Genra System. If the EPDS is activated, our missiles and laser cannons will target each other. By the time the second wave of defense on the individual planets begin, our Space Cadre will be decimated!" He said emphatically.

General L'Mar agreed, "Before the smoke clears, surviving Air Corps, Army, and Navy warcraft will empty their arsenals on each other. It will happen in seconds. Millions of loyal servicemen and women killed by their brothers in arms."

Empress Kayla said, "I thank our Creator we have warning about the restored and upgraded EPDS. Now, let us plan the new response of our military forces in space, and on the four planets."

General Blatan asked, "What of the Ranger defenses? We should discuss their plans, too, so they will be in sync with the Military, Empress Kayla," he said forcefully.

She answered, "The Ranger defensive plans will be formulated afterwards, General Blatan. They number less than ninety warbirds. The might of our Imperial Army, Space Cadre, Air Corps, and Navy must be our primary focus today." The other Military Advisors nodded in agreement. The Commanders Superior and Lady Bette remained silent, realizing the Empress wanted her Rangers defense kept secret from the Military Advisors. They knew their Empress Kayla well.

When the strategy session ended, General Blatan stated, "I trust your Military Advisors will be informed of the Ranger defensive plans, Empress

Kayla." He stared at her, in an attempt to coerce her. His tactic was obvious to Javette and Lady Bette.

The Empress returned his stare and replied, "Each Military Advisor will be fully briefed on the plans for their forces' defensive actions, General Blatan, their primary and personal responsibility. The coordination of military and Ranger defenses is not the burden of our Military Advisors." The General saluted her and left abruptly.

As she walked to her command control console, Empress Kayla made a mental note of Blatan's attempt to coerce her. Despite his track record of always carrying out her orders, there was still something about Blatan; something she could not specifically put her finger on. She did not trust the man. Her instincts were keen from years of interactions with both military and aristocratic members of the Court. She already designed defensive plans for her Rangers; but Blatan would not be told. The Warrior Empress alone would command and coordinate her forces, not her Military Advisors. The most recent intel reported the "Old Engine" would be used within the next twelve hours.

It was time to begin her defense. The Ranger warbirds launched to their assigned coordinates within the next hour and hovered in position above Home World and K'Halon Prime. Empress Kayla flew with High Ranger Lady Bette in her ES-519, with its command control console actively monitoring every Space Cadre ship and Space Base. She was surrounded by dozens of Ranger warbirds, ready to defend their Sovereign, and the people of the Empire. Scanner drones were launched from each Space Base to increase detection of hidden mobile missile launcher sites.

"All Rangers; Admiral Mur of the Imperial Command Battle Cruiser, and Admiral L'Rok of the HMS-988: this is Empress Kayla. You have been briefed on our situation previously tonight. Lock in your positions now, and the positions of the Space Cadre vessels in the solar system maps we just transmitted. Any forthcoming orders to fire on computer-generated targets are to be double-checked. We must not blow each other into the Afterlife!"

Empress Kayla said in a strong voice, "If your Sovereign is destroyed, you will refer to the encoded accompanying instructions for defense and confirmation of orders. In case we are being illegally monitored, we will not say our code word. But those of you who stood with us during our victory over the coup d'état on our coronation night will instantly recognize the code word. Remember: the cost of failure is death, and the complete demise of our Empire as we know it. We must succeed at ANY cost!" Her orders were acknowledged by cheers of "Hail Empress Kayla!" several times.

Prevention and defense were her primary focuses. Imperial forces had to maintain readiness against enemy weapons hidden throughout the Central Core of the R'Genra System, on asteroids, on Space Bases, or any of the four planets. The Space Cadre was assigned defense of the four planets and the Space Bases, and the Ranger squadrons protected the immediate space above Home World and K'Halon Prime. Air Corps, Imperial Army, and Imperial Navy stood ready to protect the four planets and their cities.

Attacks could come from anywhere. The Empress had the original charts of missile and laser cannon placements from the Emergency Planetary Defense System. Whether or not those placements would still be used for the "Old Engine" tactical attacks was a question whose answer none of her loyal Ranger High Command or Military Advisors knew.

Kayla contacted her trusted personal guards Master Commanders L'Van and Shanna, secreted within the Twelve Point Buck Lodge basement, deep in the Northern Mountains of K'Halon Prime. They were in defensive position, with scanners set for wide range, and full power defensive shields implemented by portable generators surrounded their location. The wealth of K'Halon Prime Royal Treasury was with them, also guarded by four of the Elder Rangers.

As was done the night of her coronation, Empress Kayla entrusted the great Treasury of Home World to three of the Elder Rangers and several Borgund Rangers who were not pilots to guard. The crates of gold coins, jewels, bars of gold, platinum, and thousands of 10,000-credit gold bars sat within parked Imperial shuttles inside the underground storeroom, where the Empress spent twenty-nine days of incarceration and starvation.

Her wrist comm link beeped a three-note musical tone, and she relaxed somewhat. It was the signal from K'Ramm; her Son Lukus and her relatives with him were all right. Sitting next to her, High Ranger Lady Bette said, "The conspirators planned this for over thirty years, spent billions of credits, and enlisted thousands to their cause. You have had only thirty-some hours to plan, develop, and ready your defenses. But my money's on you, my Warrior Empress Kayla, and our Rangers. May the Creator bless us all," she closed.

With a gracious nod of her head, the Empress acknowledged Lady Bette's words of encouragement. The ES-519 held position and hovered, ready to respond in the blink of an eye to the threat of the Old Engine.

The Fount

Watching the twenty "Outlaw" anti-gravity choppers approach their building, Sham'S called out, "First Commander L'Mun, ready to launch." They pulled out ahead of the outlaws on their choppers towards the old gold mine, the "Fount." In forty-three minutes, they arrived. "I told you to keep this a secret," Sham'S said to his three brutes. They laughed and kept walking to the mine entrance. *Everything is going according to my Empress' plan,*

Sham'S thought.

The outlaws ran to the entrance of the gold mine, tore down the barricade, and ripped the wooden doors off their hinges. Light automatically came on as the outlaws ran farther into the mines. Sham'S and a disguised L'Mun followed behind them, recording their incursion. The men inside were surprised by the outlaws, armed with knives, big lug wrenches, and heavy chains. The miners hit the alarm and ran deeper inside the mines with the outlaws chasing them.

"L'Mun to ES-519, we are inside, following the party. Will keep you apprised," she reported softly, and cut off the message. It would not be good for L'Mun to be discovered now. She was wearing a big hat with her long hair tucked inside, disguised as a man, but her voice was very feminine. The outlaws were all wound up and would not hesitate to stop for some sexual diversion during their raid. L'Mun and Sham'S followed the outlaws deeper inside.

In minutes, they made their way into the command center. "The attack should have begun two minutes ago! Are the ships attacking? The Air Corps should be bombing the Space Cadre bases by now. Where's the missile launchers? They should have fired on the Palaces!" Lord K'Vin bellowed. "Everybody report to me now!" He stood in front of the screens in the hidden central control room in the Fount, looking frantically at the screens.

The twenty burly, disreputable outlaws burst into the central control room, and proceeded to beat the Technicians at the computer controls. "Who are these men? Take care of them now!" Lord K'Vin ordered and hid behind the equipment. But their vicious attack continued. The outlaws beat the startled, unprepared Technicians savagely. A few of the Technicians managed to access laser rifles and began firing. Everyone took cover.

Sham'S reported, "We are in the central control room. Ready to fire upon your signal, Empress Kayla."

"Take Lord K'Vin alive, if possible, Sham'S. Then destroy their computers and get out of there immediately," she commanded.

"Can you stun him, L'Mun? I can't get a clear shot. He's hiding behind the communications console," Sham'S said. He blasted the main computer console and it exploded in flames.

L'Mun abandoned her disguise. She bravely ripped off her hat and let her long blonde hair fall out, pulled off the fake moustache, and walked to Lord K'Vin while the outlaws fought the Technicians. "Your escape shuttle is this way, Lord K'Vin. Please follow me now, sir," she whispered, and the would-be Emperor followed her past a surprised Sham'S to the exit light. She motioned for the Lord to go ahead of her and shot a stun dart into his neck. She and Sham'S carried his limp body to their choppers. "He's mine, Sham'S," she said proudly, and they laid Lord K'Vin across her chopper.

The two Rangers rode off and made their call.

"Empress Kayla, we have Alternate Seven," L'Mun said. "Will rendezvous at prescribed coordinates, my Empress." The smoke poured out of the main entrance to the mine. She fired two missiles into the entrance, completely collapsing the only exit. The outlaws found their gold but could not get out. "I think I like being back in field work, Sham'S. I've been buried in books and computers for years. This feels good!" L'Mun shouted to her fellow Ranger. He shook his head and laughed with her as they sped off to the harbor, and the Imperial Navy attack boat docked and waiting for them.

Imperial Army troop transports landed at the Fount within the hour and captured the Outlaws and remaining Technicians. The old mine was secured by Army troops, and the clean-up began. Imperial Guards and Borgund Rangers arrived to supervise recovery, packing, and shipping of thousands of gold coins and bars to the Twelve Point Buck Lodge.

XV

Kayla looked at the time, and then glanced at Lady Bette. It had to happen any moment now. "Relax, and breathe slowly, your Majesty," Bette advised with a smile. "This day will be marked in history as the end of the Plan of the Thirteen."

No sooner were the words out of Lady Bette's mouth, the emergency broadcast sounded: "This is a system-wide broadcast from Space High Command. We have alien hostile targets approaching. Your tactical computer targets have been identified. Fire at will now." The emergency broadcast repeated. Red alerts flashed on her computer control systems.

"This is Empress Kayla to all ships in the R'Genra System. Belay the previous Space High Command order. Repeat: belay the previous order. Do not fire your weapons. I repeat: Do not fire your weapons. Hold for further instructions," she said firmly. Her tactical screens showed no weapons fired, but a few destroyers deployed their fighters. The goal of the Empress' defense was to prevent the Imperial Military from destroying itself.

Then came the robo-call: "Enemy targets locked in. All ships fire at will." The sound of missiles exploding filled the comm links. The Empress ordered, "This is Empress Kayla. Cease fire. Power down missiles now. The previous broadcast is a false signal. Hold your fire. Repeat: Hold your fire!" The Space High Command channel was filled with requests for further orders. Her tactical screen indicators began flashing, showing several ships were powering up their missiles. Kayla commanded, "All ships power down missiles at once. No Space Cadre ship is authorized to launch any missiles. Hold your fire!"

She could sense the confusion of the men in command of her Space Cadre fleet of warships and fighters. She calmly broadcast, "This is Empress Kayla to all Space Cadre warships; all Imperial Navy ships; all Air Corps fighters; and our Imperial Army troops. Hostile forces have gained control of our Space High Command channels. All Imperial forces, switch to low-frequency channel 58.2. Repeat, all Imperial forces, switch to channel 58.2 for further instructions. Empress Kayla out."

The pre-recorded set of orders for the Air Corps to secure all planetary air spaces; the Navy to secure the primary harbors; the Imperial Army to ready forces on the ground; and the Space Cadre to release all tactical weapons control to the ES-519 broadcast repeatedly. The mighty Imperial Military held their positions and did not fire any weapons. Empress Kayla jammed the Space High Command channel to prevent any further EPDS orders from being broadcast.

From the computer control console in the Royal Suite at the K'Halon Prime Palace, Baron P'Lau expertly channeled all incoming urgent and emergency messages to the prerecorded message: "This is your Empress Kayla. We are in a State of Emergency. Stay in your homes and offices, my beloved people. Tune your vid screens and comm channels to emergency frequency channel 52.4 for further instructions," she said. "The situation is well in hand. Do not fear, my beloved people of our Empire." Baron P'Lau monitored the broadcasts and the defensive shields over both Palaces; both were 100%. He would not fail his Empress, or the people he ruled for twenty-six years as Emperor.

Thirty nerve-wracking, exasperating minutes passed without any further Old Engine automated announcements broadcast to the Imperial Military. With a deep breath, Empress Kayla commanded, "All Space Cadre warships stand down to yellow alert. All 'Sapphire Club' members, broadcast the 'All clear' signal now, and thank you, all of you," she said. Bette smiled at her "Sapphire Club" phrase, referencing the sapphire pins with hidden body shields the Empress gave her loyal Space Cadre officers and Rangers the night of her coronation, when the first coup d'état was thwarted. She knew the battle was not over; but they survived the first danger.

"Field Marshall General Blatan: engage martial law within Centralia and pre-arranged areas. Do not harm the general populace. Your targets are the local police, including the officers and detectives. They are to be stunned and remanded into custody. Repeat: do not harm our beloved people!" He acknowledged her orders.

Above K'Halon Prime

High Ranger Lady Bette cautioned, "This was too quick, my Empress."

Kayla responded, "It is not over, Lady Bette. I'm certain there is more to come."

Within minutes, the Red Alert sounded. The EPDS system activated again; from whom, or where, was unknown. Space High Command broadcasts began again, the same "Fire at will" orders. The Empress jammed the channel once again. But this second onslaught was very different. The Old Engine fired missiles at several Space Cadre ships.

"ES-519, we are targeted by incoming missiles. Request permission to launch defensive strike," Admiral Mur called from the Imperial Command Battle Cruiser.

"The point of origin—where is it, Mur?" The Empress responded.

The Admiral answered, "Three points: from within the White Belt; from A'Wan; and from old abandoned SB5, my Empress. Permission to launch our missiles," he asked again, with greater urgency in his voice.

She ordered, "Take them out now, Admiral L'Rok and Admiral Mur. Can we reach A'Wan from your positions?"

"Negative, Empress. They have launched missiles targeting M'Wati, now, and they're out of our range!" Mur reported.

She ordered her Borgund Rangers protecting M'Wati, "Master Commander Steph'N, initiate your plasma disrupter arc weapons and take out those missiles NOW!" Kayla watched her Ranger ES-warbirds target the large swarm of incoming missiles and destroy them with plasma disrupter arcs.

In four minutes, he replied, "All twenty missiles destroyed, my Empress. Missile launching facility located. It is deep inside A'Wan, my Empress. The small moon will be damaged and may lose orbit if we launch retaliatory missile strike from space. Requesting permission to land on A'Wan and neutralize facility," he asked. "I can do it, Empress Kayla. The other ES warbirds can stay above M'Wati and protect the planet."

She paused to consider the ramifications of his potential actions, and said to G'Rosk, "Without its moon A'Wan, M'Wati would become an uncontrolled, swirling mass of water. The survivors of the M'Wati Disaster are just beginning to have some semblance of normal lives. We've got to land and dismantle the facility on A'Wan from inside."

C.S. G'Rosk agreed, then added, "But Steph'N isn't trained on missile launch systems. No Ranger is."

Steph'N was flying with three other Borgund Ranger ES-warbirds. Empress Kayla ordered, "Permission granted to land near facility on A'Wan. But you will hold and await Imperial Army reinforcements, Master Commander Steph'N. The number of remaining missiles inside the facility is unknown. The bastards may have another wave of missiles programmed to launch at any time. We must minimize the destruction on A'Wan, and the people living there. Hold for reinforcements. Acknowledge orders, Master Commander Steph'N," she said. Several seconds passed.

"Master Commander Steph'N acknowledging your orders, my Empress. Permission to fire on any more launched missiles, Empress Kayla." He sounded ticked off to her. He was ready to take apart the launch facility single-handed, and give his life doing so, if needed.

"Yes, of course, Steph'N. I fully expect to see you in Main Court on Home World next month, my dear friend. Do your job when the Army arrives to help you, then come home," she said reassuringly to her friend.

The Imperial Army Outpost on A'Wan was ordered to send weapons technicians and security personnel to the hidden missile launching facility. It was buried deep inside a damp cave on the jungle moon, cleverly camouflaged by the jungle growth. M.C. Steph'N and three Army weapons technicians dismantled the launch system in less than half an hour. Forty-eight missiles were in firing position, targeting M'Wati targets, awaiting launch commands. A major catastrophe was averted.

The Empress announced, "Stand down to yellow alert. All ships, yellow alert. Reload, re-arm, and stand ready." She ran complete tactical analyses on all ships and their positioning, and status checks of damage to them. The four Commanders Superior at Home World and K'Halon Prime Ranger High Command offices updated reports of damage losses. "Something's amiss, G'Rosk. These men didn't rebuild this Old Engine for thirty years just to fire on the positions we've neutralized. If I had planned their attacks, I would have included both Palaces and strategic Army, Navy, and Air Corps bases on Home World and K'Halon Prime, too. There must be more to come," she said quietly. "Initiate complete evacuation of both Palaces now."

Following her instincts, Kayla ordered the Imperial Command Battle Cruiser above Home World and the HMS-988 above K'Halon Prime to launch scan probes to the moons above those planets. Within six minutes of the probes reaching the dark side of Home World's moon, a barrage of one hundred fifty missiles were launched from a concealed launch site beneath the moon's dark surface.

Admiral Mur called, "Probe scans detect one hundred fifty big heavies launched in three waves: at Capital City, the Imperial Army Base, and the Space Base on Home World. Requesting permission to destroy incoming," he asked forcefully. "Less than three minutes to targets."

The Empress replied, "Use plasma disrupter arcs. Light them up, Admiral Mur. Any missiles remaining are to be destroyed by your fighters ASAP." She watched her screens closely. Just as the first barrage of big missiles rounded the visible moon surface, the Cruiser's plasma disruptor arcs pounded the missiles in several well-timed attacks. Only four missiles escaped destruction and were quickly blasted by Space Cadre fighters.

The HMS-988 CO, Adm. L'Rok, was notified of the Home World moon attack. Since K'Halon Prime had three moons in orbit around the huge planet, there was a significant risk of another attack to be launched against the host planet. Even a battleship as large as the HMS could not target simultaneous missile barrages headed for K'Halon Prime from the dark sides of three moons successfully. Additional scan probes were launched, and two squadrons of fighters launched towards each of the three moons. But no attack was detected.

The Empress made a mental note of the opportunity to attack K'Halon Prime ignored by the Plan of the Thirteen "Old Engine" designers. Their focus was on the Imperial Military defense targets in Space, and the two planets of M'Wati and Home World. More attacks against the seat of Imperial power on Home World were expected to take place. Empress Kayla ordered all available scanners to sweep the airspace above Capital City and military bases within five hundred kilometers of the Royal Palace. One squadron of Ranger warbirds was ordered to return to Home World, to protect Capital City and the Royal Palace.

After several minutes had passed, L'Mun called, "Empress Kayla, Lord K'Vin just confessed there is another," she reported nervously, "but he won't say another what. He just keeps laughing and saying, 'There is another.'"

Kayla said, "Put him on this conversation, First Commander L'Mun." The arrogant face of Lord K'Vin soon filled her vid screen. "Lord K'Vin, this is your Empress Kayla. Your 'Old Engine' is being dismantled, piece by piece. It is our urgent and sincere desire to avoid any further bloodshed. Please help us save innocent lives, Lord K'Vin. Please tell us what the 'other' is, and help us save the people, Lord K'Vin," she entreated. "You really don't want to cause pain and suffering to innocent families and children."

His countenance began to change, as the aristocrat and father of six wrestled with his conscience. Kayla watched him, and then said, "Please, Lord K'Vin. You have so many children and grandchildren who will bear the burden of your decision today. Please, sir, I beg you to tell us now," she said with genuine sincerity. He exhaled deeply.

"The last facility is concealed in the Capital City Imperial Naval Base, directly under the Naval High Command Administration Building. Its primary target is the Royal Palace. Secondary target is the submarine base. Only a few minutes remain, Empress Kayla. May my grandchildren forgive me," he said bowing his head.

"Red Alert: Total evacuation of the Home World Royal Palace immediately. This is Empress Kayla. Evacuate the entire Capitol City Harbor and Naval Base NOW!" She ordered loudly into her comm link.

"The bastards! Focus our energies and ships all over the solar system and take out the Palace and our harbor! An excellent tactical plan, unfortunately, my Empress," G'Rosk said.

Empress Kayla switched her vid screens to Home World, where a major effort was underway to evacuate all personnel from the Imperial Naval Base and the Royal Palace. Hovering shuttles picked up as many Naval officers and crewmen as they could from the Naval High Command Admin

Building, the yards, docks, and from the rooftop of the Naval Hospital. The subs docked at the base and their support vessels were launching away as fast as they could, but moving them and the big Navy destroyer dockside would take more time than available. Crewmen and officers ran through the gates to evacuate the Base.

"Lord Vu'Duc here. We have evacuated all personnel from the Palace; the Ranger, Palace Guard, and Imperial Guard barracks, Family Residences, and Flight School, my Empress," he told her confidently.

"And where are you calling from, Lord Vu'Duc?" Kayla asked anxiously.

He replied, "On the Palace rooftop. I am awaiting the last shuttle with three Guardsmen, Empress Kayla. We got everyone else out first. The shuttle is land…" His transmission was cut off when loud, explosive sounds blasted through her speakers. The command tactical screens showed two waves of missiles imploding on the Palace Complex, seconds apart.

"Vu'Duc? Lord Vu'Duc come in," she cried, and tried once more. But there was only silence. He was gone. Kayla turned and looked at Lady Bette, Life Partner of Lord Vu'Duc for over thirty-five years. Bette held her head back to keep her red eyes from tearing. "This is Empress Kayla. All Rangers on or above Home World, report now," she ordered.

Their reports came in sporadically. From the thick of the smoke and destruction, F. C. Bek'R reported, "I'm in my ESK, and our squadron is just now approaching Capital City, Empress Kayla. The Royal Palace took a direct hit and is currently ablaze. My tactical screen shows fifty direct hits. The Imperial Naval Base at the harbor across from the Palace was also hit, Empress Kayla, and it looks bad. The Admin Building, seven other training and work centers, and two submarines in for retrofitting were damaged. The attack took place while our squadron was in the atmosphere, and we were unable to prevent the attack, my Lady," he said bitterly.

Bek'R continued his report, "The Imperial Naval Hospital was destroyed from the sixth or seventh floor, on up. If your Royal Physician Admiral Mae was at work at the Naval Hospital, I doubt she made it. Everything is on fire at the base, my Empress. Air Corps fighters now over the Palace airspace. Unable to estimate number of survivors at this time." Dozens of similar reports came over her comm link, but no information on survivors or wounded. She ordered F.C. Bek'R to resume his defense flight plans and report every fifteen minutes to her directly.

"Empress Kayla to Admiral Olm," she called. There was no response after two attempts. After a pause, she called for Ranger High Command, and all four Commanders Superior reported in: G'Rosk, Javette, T'Anh, and B'Von. Kayla ordered, "I want a complete accounting of all personnel assigned to the Home World Royal Palace ASAP. Full disclosure of the whereabouts for each man, woman, and child, by 4p.m. Take all survivors to pre-designated Imperial properties for shelter at once. Notify all local Capital City hospitals to expect incoming emergencies. The Imperial Naval hospital is out of service. Send all available shuttles to the Imperial Naval Base for rescue of survivors. All evacuations are completed at the Palace."

She added, "All personal leaves cancelled for the foreseeable future. Quarantine the Palace Complex and the Imperial Naval Base, until the full forensic reports are available. May the Creator bless everyone tonight," she closed to them. She readied her ES-519 for launch, and called, "All Ranger pilots, return to assigned bases and ships. Stand down. All vessels, orange alert. Empress Kayla, out," she said wearily. She flew to Centralia Space Base for debriefings.

With a heavy heart, Empress Kayla reported the news of the devastating Imperial Naval Hospital and Royal Palace attacks to her best friend, M.C. Shanna, and her sister-in-law Tara. Hope existed for Royal Physician Admiral Mae and her Brother Admiral Olm to be found alive and well. But their chances for survival were unfavorable.

XVI

K'Halon Prime, the next day

The private tour of the new Temple of the Creator at T'Anju was somber and prayerful for the Royal Family. Brother D'Avid led his monks in their chant, "There is no pain. Only peace," while a special ceremony was held for those lost in yesterday's brutal attacks. Priest K'Ramm said prayers for the fallen in the ancient language, while Priestess Moni joined him, burning incense and saying the responses to his prayers. It was very moving.

The Grand Opening of the Mount Regency Ski Resort and Casino and the other related events were postponed for one week, out of respect for the deceased. But the Temple opened immediately after the Imperial shuttle lifted off. Worshippers and pilgrims were welcomed inside a week before the scheduled Grand Opening. Thousands came for prayers and healing.

The Royal Palace on Home World had been constructed over eight hundred years ago, and the full complex was expanded over the centuries. It was a very large complex, with twenty buildings surrounding the destroyed Royal Palace. The Main Court, capable of holding six hundred, was demolished, as were the Royal Suite, and all guest suites. Parts of the Imperial Guard barracks were still standing, as well as scattered sections of several buildings. The portable defensive shields failed. The only building left untouched was the Royal Academy.

After a full day passed, the Imperial Naval Base still had fires refusing to die out. One hundred eighty loyal officers and crewmen were killed, and several hundred were wounded. With the hospital destroyed, the wounded were shuttled to civilian hospitals all over Capital City.

Empress Kayla walked through the K'Halon Prime Ranger Family Residence area with Prince Lukus and Consort Dan'L, while the snow fell lightly. "Your Father and I grew up here, Lukus," she quietly told him. Other Rangers, their Partners, and their children left their apartments and walked behind the Royal Family, everyone joining the walk to the chapel.

After the poignant memorial ceremony, the group began their trek back to the North Wing of the Royal Palace. A small group of boys were playing kickball near the training courts. An errant kick sent the ball rolling towards the Empress. Kayla put her foot on the ball to stop it from rolling away. The young boys ran up to the group and bowed when they saw their Empress. She asked one of the boys, "Is this your ball?" He shyly nodded. "Then come take it, if you can," she challenged, smiling at him.

She worked the ball between her feet, defensively kicking it back and forth. The boy overcame his shyness and tried to take possession of his ball, kicking it as she defended. The two players moved along the field, and the other boys came around. The Rangers' children joined in watching the two. The Empress got her boot toe under the ball, kicked it up, and head-butted the ball over the boys' heads. They excitedly ran after the ball and resumed their game.

"I didn't know you could play kickball," Dan'L said to his Empress with a big smile.

She took Lukus' hand and ran with her Son through the snow, laughing all the way back to the Palace. The somber afternoon became less painful for everyone. She invited the Ranger families to her private Royal Court for lunch. The impromptu meal was fun, filled with tasty food and frequent laughter. *We have to move forward. Ever forward*, Kayla reminded herself.

All the next day, reports of deaths, wounded, and extent of the property damages came into Space and Ranger High Command Offices. "I hate to think what could have happened if the Home World Palace had not been ordered closed, with several shuttles parked on the interior grounds. Many more would have died," Javette remarked to G'Rosk. "Kayla was right on the mark with her preemptive planning. But no one suspected the depth and breadth of the 'Old Engine's' capabilities. We nearly lost everything, and everyone, G'Rosk," she said, the emotion in her voice showing. "Our entire military, and all our Rangers. The entire Warrior Class, G'Rosk!"

"Yes, we nearly did. But we did not lose them. We must move forward, ever forward, my loving Partner, and work through this terrible disaster. We must rebuild, stronger than before," G'Rosk said, and put his arm around her. Javette nodded and kissed his hand.

Empress Kayla entered their conference room shortly with Lady Bette, Baron P'Lau, Viscount T'Sur, and her Imperial and Ranger guards. They sat, and the Guards took their places outside. In a minute, C.S. T'Anh ran into the conference room, out of breath. "My Empress, I have just received word from Master Commander Z'Bak on Home World: several have been rescued from the underground passageway just outside the Palace. The survivors include your Brother, Admiral Olm, and our Royal Physician

Admiral Mae! General Blatan is also alive, but he is injured, like the Admirals," she said, and handed her com tablet to Kayla.

Kayla looked behind her, at the relieved face of M.C. Shanna, and smiled. "Please notify my sister-in-law Tara immediately, Master Commander Shanna. She will be pleased to know she is not a widow!" Shanna left immediately. "Thank you, Commander Superior T'Anh, for the wonderful news."

Baron P'Lau asked, "Will your Majesty be extending your stay on K'Halon Prime? Or will you return to Home World to oversee the reconstruction of the Palace?"

"We will remain here for one week beyond our planned visit, Baron. It will give our Imperial Guards time to establish full security at the Farm, and for the new residence building for our Rangers to be completed," she said.

"A Farm? Where, exactly, is this Farm?" C.S. Javette asked, with a puzzled look on her face.

The Empress laughed and answered, "Elder Ranger K'Laud called it 'the Farm.' The property is actually the estate of the former Baron S'Tan. It is close to Capital City and has adequate room for many of us to stay." Seeing Javette's face relax, she added, "Not to worry, Commander Superior Javette. The time is not yet here for you to beat your plasma sword into a plowshare!" Everyone laughed with her.

"Now, let us continue with our agenda. The Novices will be confirmed tomorrow night, as planned. All our activities after their confirmation will center on the Plan of the Thirteen traitors, their attacks, and an on-going round-up of their fellow conspirators," she ordered.

Viscount T'Sur asked, "Will there be any Royal Beneficiary appointments, my Empress? With all that has transpired in the last few days, the opportunity is optimal for new Beneficiaries, and Royal Hierarchical … adjustments," he advised. "Especially on K'Halon Prime."

A few chuckles were heard. Kayla answered, "As you recommend, Viscount T'Sur. Perhaps we shall appoint a few beneficiaries after the wretched mess of the last week. Please consult with Baron P'Lau and your remaining Council of Baron members, and we will discuss your recommendations tomorrow. But the only beneficiaries we shall consider will be for the vacancies prior to the attacks," she commented. "The properties of the Alternates and the Technicians must be searched with extreme thoroughness."

"Our last item for this meeting concerns the Home World Royal Palace reconstruction," the Empress said. "We have engaged a team of experts to acquire more land to expand the Palace Complex further inland. Submit to Lady Bette any suggestions you have for additional use of the property. The new Palace will have full defensive shields, and their generators require more space. The portable shields failed to protect the Royal Palace during the missile strike. This Palace at K'Halon Prime will also be shielded, as soon as the additional land becomes available," she revealed.

"But your Majesty; these land acquisitions, remodeling, and reconstruction of Home World Palace will be very expensive. Will taxes be raised to pay for the reconstruction and improvements?" A worried Viscount T'Sur asked, his brow furrowed.

She shook her head and answered, "No, Viscount T'Sur. For your information; the gold coins illegally produced at the Fount gold mine have been confiscated by the mine's owner. An additional four thousand kilograms of gold bullion has been discovered there, too. Plus, the owner of the mine will be reopening the property for mining, with first-year profits directed to the Home World Royal Palace Reconstruction Project," the Empress said. She gathered her notes and com tablet and left with her guards.

"So, who owns the gold mine?" B'Von asked aloud.

Javette proudly answered, "My Daughter-in-law, our Warrior Empress Kayla."

The Imperial Guard ran down the corridor and loudly knocked on the door of Empress Kayla's study. Kayla took the courier pouch from the young Guard and thanked him. The pouch had a large, imprinted red wax seal. It was from the hermit monks on Ban'Ti.

Inside the pouch were twelve scrolls of the "Plan of the Thirteen," copies 1 and 2, and 4 through 13. The scribe's handwriting was similar on all copies. Each copy bore signatures in blood from the original Thirteen titled aristocrats who conspired to take the throne when the Vee Lok Lords returned. Kayla examined the documents closely, then called an urgent meeting with High Ranger Lady Bette, the four Commanders Superior, Viscount T'Sur, and Baron P'Lau. She called F.C. L'Mun and said, "I need my barrister to observe this meeting. Please bring eight new com tablets with their communications chips removed, Master Commander L'Mun."

L'Mun bowed her head in acknowledgement of the Empress promoting her and gathered the com tablets. She had the Weapons Master remove the comm chips for her. Then, she hurried to Empress Kayla's private Royal Court. She knelt at the gold line and bowed to her Empress.

"You're out of uniform, Master Commander L'Mun," Lady Bette said loudly, then smiled and pinned the new insignia on L'Mun's collar. The four Commanders Superior, Viscount T'Sur, and Baron P'Lau applauded and cheered for L'Mun. Then, the work began.

The Empress said, "Our priest and friend K'Ramm translated the first copy of the 'Plan of the Thirteen' for us. Then, the back of the document was discovered to contain so-called 'Alternate Contingencies.' After further study, Priest K'Ramm noticed the ancient numeral for the number three on the back of our original. Since he initially believed our original document was handwritten by a Temple scribe or an instructor, Priest K'Ramm followed this line of thought for his own investigation," she said.

"K'Ramm's research uncovered a Seminarian scribe who joined the Holy Caste Order forty years ago, who abandoned his wealth and family to serve the Creator. The scribe was Dok'T, an older brother of the former Baron Z'Lun. The circumstances of Dok'T's involvement are unknown, other than his writing the thirteen documents you now see before you," she said, as Consort Dan'L carefully laid each copy in numbered order on the long table. "The same scribe wrote the 'Alternate Contingencies' in ink visible only under black light on the reverse side."

"Dok'T left the seminary and moved to the caves of Ban'Ti, to live with the silent hermit monks. He took vows of silence, poverty, and celibacy as prerequisites before the monks would accept him. In his fourth month, Dok'T committed ritual suicide, leaving behind a handwritten note in his own blood that said, 'May the Creator and His people forgive this worthless wretch.'"

"According to our priest at T'Anju, the story of Dok'T is well-known, but his relationship to the Baron Z'Lun was not. We are grateful to Priest K'Ramm for translating these documents. The documents you see before you were stored in the hermit monks' caves on Ban'Ti. Master Commander L'Mun, please read the transcriptions of all thirteen documents for us now," the Empress said. She sat erect on her throne, as the 'Alternate Contingencies' were read, until copy thirteen.

M.C. L'Mun read the "Alternates and Technicians' list on the reverse side of the thirteenth copy. At the bottom of the page was written: "When the 'Old Engine' is restored and the Star People return, the Fount will be opened. From the dark wings, the Grand Master Technician will direct the play, according to the Plan of the Thirteen. The Throne of Power will belong to one of the Thirteen. We pledge our honor, our wealth, and our lives."

The list of Alternates and Technicians was checked against those captured or killed men. Four were still at large. Referencing her com tablet, C.S. Javette said, "A Lord with 'fat fingers' was mentioned on the transcripts from the spy bugs we planted inside the wharf club."

"But four aristocrats were in the last meeting: Lord K'Vin, the one with fat fingers, the one in the blue jacket, and another, who was not identified," G'Rosk said. "He never spoke."

Empress Kayla ordered, "Bring in the former Lord K'Vin, and our latest suspect." Her Imperial Guards brought in K'Vin, and B'Nard. The two men were in cuffs, shackles, and chained. The Great Warrior Empress levitated up with her golden throne, and said, "Many thanks for your warning of the last missile launching system, Lord K'Vin. Thousands of innocent lives were saved. Your cooperation will be highlighted in your defense before the High Court Tribunal." She bowed her head to him.

B'Nard's nonchalant face turned into momentary disbelief, then sheer hatred. "I knew it! You caved, you elite bastard! You patronizing wuss!" B'Nard was shot with tranquilizers and truth serum.

From the back of the Court entered Master Commander Kend'R, walking swiftly to the restrained men. He stepped directly in front of B'Nard. He said, "Every recording we have of you, every vid, and every voice recording; some aristocrat or another is giving you orders, belittling you in front of the Technicians you trained, and treating you with disrespect, B'Nard. This is your chance to take your revenge on those self-serving, pompous asses," Kend'R said quietly, removing his black cloak and arm bands.

Kend'R waved dismissively at K'Vin, and two Guards took him to the other side of the room. B'Nard's eyes were swirling from the truth serum now. "Our Empress is adored by her people but hated by most of the aristocrats. Why is that, B'Nard?" Kend'R casually asked, watching the Guards put him into a chair.

B'Nard replied, "The Empress is a bitch. Like all bitches, she is good only for breeding. She should have let one of the Thirteen or their sons be her Consort. They offered, but she picked some other Ranger. Idiot bitch," he mumbled. The Empress held her hand out to her Commanders Superior, all of whom were ready to defend her and kill B'Nard for his offensive remarks. They replaced their razor-sharp knives in their backplates and stepped back.

Kend'R laughed with B'Nard and said, "That's the trouble with women nowadays. They are free to choose and follow their girlish hearts."

"They know nothing of choosing. They let power slip through their hands like sand. A man learns about power early on, else he never has any of his own. A man knows power," B'Nard stated.

"You know all about power, B'Nard. Why do you let them treat you like their servant? You are stronger and more cunning. And much less morally corrupt. You have many who follow you," Kend'R said. "How can you stand it, man?"

He saw the emotions suppressed for so long inside of B'Nard begin to heat up, and then he said, "The Lord in the blue jacket; was he the one who turned your brother? Or was it Fat Fingers? Which one of those wealthy pigs turned him into a fag? They could've had any man in the club. Which one did him, B'Nard? Tell me who he is, and I'll get him for you," Kend'R whispered. B'Nard was almost at his breaking level, but not quite. He was very disciplined. Another shot of truth serum was injected.

Kend'R continued, "You know, when we picked up your little brother Sim'N, he cried like a girl, and yelled about his 'Benefactor,' who would get him out of jail. Which one is his Benefactor, B'Nard? Or, should I call him

Sim'N's 'Sugar Daddy,' instead?"

Kend'R moved just in time to avoid B'Nard's attempted head butt. Time to go deeper. "Shall I have Sim'N interrogated? I know one of the Palace Guards who likes gay boys. Not my style. But I bet he'd make Sim'N talk; after a few hours, that is," Kend'R threatened.

B'Nard broke, crying, "Leave him alone! Don't you touch Sim'N! It wasn't his fault. The bastard drugged him and took off with him while I was on Ban'Ti, doing their dirty work. By the time I got back, he'd turned Sim'N queer!"

"Who turned your brother queer? Who did this to the innocent boy? I'll get him for you, B'Nard. Just tell me who he is," Kend'R said urgently.

"That fat-assed Baron Lep'T. Him and his fat fingers. He makes me sick. He's got a whole basement full of boys. Why'd he pick Sim'N, and turn him queer?"

Kend'R leaned down and whispered, "I'll get him for you, B'Nard. I promise. Will he be with the other two aristocrats? Is the man in the blue jacket a fag, too?"

"Probably. They're all sticking together now, since the Empire took Lord K'Vin. They're all scared, like little girls! They know it's over, so they're all hiding out. The Empress Bitch will never find them!" B'Nard said and laughed.

"Why won't she find them, B'Nard? She's got a lot of smart Army commandos, you know. Will one of them find the other aristocrats?"

"Definitely not the Army. Maybe the Navy could find them," he said, shaking his head. "They're all on his cruise ship. No other passengers. Just them, and some girls for sex."

"And they're sailing around, drinking, partying it up with pretty girls, and having fun; and you're here. They let the Rangers find you, B'Nard. They gave you up and set sail to party. Who are they? Tell me, and I'll bring them in, and you can have the last laugh. Who are they?" Kend'R asked. He saw their faces in B'Nard's mind but had to make him say their names aloud.

From the wings, Lord K'Vin yelled, "Don't you dare, B'Nard! Don't you dare!"

Kend'R whispered, "He's the one who gave you up, B'Nard."

B'Nard looked closely at Kend'R, and whispered, "Might as well tell. They gave me up. He turned Sim'N. I'll get them for this! It's over, anyway."

"Get 'em good, B'Nard. Who are they?"

B'Nard began laughing, and then yelled out, "Lord Marl, and S'Lovik, the Silent One. He's the biggest con man I've ever met. He has everyone fooled, even his own!" B'Nard made hand signs like those of a priest giving his blessings and laughed hysterically. The Imperial Guards led him and a red-faced Lord K'Vin away.

"I knew it! How else did those twelve monks all get sent to the Temple on Xau to help the Rebels? I bet they're still alive, hiding out somewhere. And he promised to 'Clean their own house!'" T'Anh exclaimed, slapping her papers on the table.

"No wonder the donations at the Temples were embezzled for so long," G'Rosk added.

P'Lau said, "Lord Marl is the last aristocrat I would have suspected. He has done charity work since I first met him. He is the director for more than seventy orphanages." His voice trailed off, and his countenance changed noticeably when the realization of his words struck him.

"How convenient," Lady Bette said. "A child sex trader and a High Priest! If you ever wanted grounds to dissolve the Holy Caste Order, these are more than enough, my Empress."

Empress Kayla lowered her throne and said to Kend'R, "You saw who they were, and some of their evil deeds, my Faithful Son. His open confession is now the official record. I know this has been very distressing for you. You have our gratitude. Please take several days off to rest, Master Commander Kend'R," she said. "May the Creator bless my dear friend Kend'R."

Warrants were issued for the arrest of Baron Lep'T, Lord Marl, and S'Lovik. Several Borgund Rangers were assigned to accompany the Imperial Navy in their apprehension. The Empress looked at C.S. Javette, and ordered, "Commanders Superior Javette and T'Anh: you will immediately have our Kaylan Rangers personally contact all seventy orphanages formerly under the directorship of Lord Marl, regarding any missing or mistreated children. Work with our Minister of Human Services on this investigation and be extremely thorough. The defenseless, innocent children need our help and protection," she said firmly.

The Empress then stood and said, "Baron P'Lau and Viscount T'Sur, please join me in two hours for a complete overhaul of the Royal Hierarchy!" She marched out of her Court with her Consort and Imperial Guards.

After reading the transcriptions of the new copies of the Plan in her study once again, Kayla realized how great a manipulative power monger Baron Tri'T had been. One of the original thirteen signers of the Plan suffered a debilitating stroke while visiting Tri'T on M'Wati, prior to the Nuclear Devastation. Without consulting the other signers of the Plan, the dying Baron enlisted Baron Tri'T as his replacement, called only the mysterious "Figure Thirteen." He met the birth qualifications: Tri'T was born prematurely on K'Halon Prime while his pregnant mother was visiting friends.

No wonder Baron Tri'T was so driven to survive after the M'Wati Nuclear Disaster. He had the deceased man's notebooks with all the Plan's information and secrets, and the keys to his safe deposit boxes, full of wealth. And, more importantly, Tri'T had the chance to be selected as Emperor.

The rescued survivor of the M'Wati Nuclear Disaster was given a hero's Royal Homecoming on Home World by Empress Kayla. As an Imperial Hero, Baron Tri'T sought out Baron S'Tan, the Master Technician of the Plan of the Thirteen, and divulged his identity as Figure Thirteen, the previously unknown replacement. He shared his new wealth with S'Tan, and they arranged the kidnapping and imprisonment of Empress Kayla.

Recalling Tri'T's words to her that his fellow conspirators wanted to kill her rather than hold her in captivity, Kayla understood why he insisted she be kept alive. Tri'T wanted to banish her and Prince Lukus to the desert wastes of the Fringe Lands on K'Halon Prime, forcing them to work the harsh desert soil, living in dire poverty. Such public punishment of a former Empress would have sent a strong message to anyone challenging Tri'T's rule as Emperor. His plan to become the new Emperor came within seconds of becoming a reality—if not for the efforts of Master Commander Kend'R, her telepath and good friend.

Deciding to prevent her loving family and Royal Consort Dan'L from being exiled in abject poverty, Empress Kayla had the Royal Treasurer separate her gifts of wealth from the Vee Lok Lords from the Empire's wealth within the Treasury. Kept in secure crates bearing her Imperial Seal, her crates were locked in the secure, underground cell where she was kept for twenty-nine days. The Empress later divided her personal treasure into three caches and stored them in secret underground "Kaylan Treasuries" on the Central Core planets: Home World, K'Halon Prime, and M'Wati. Only she, her Mother-in-Law C.S. Javette, and Baron P'Lau knew the location of the Kaylan Treasuries. Whether or not she survived any further attacks from the Plan of the Thirteen traitors or other enemies, her family would have the wealth to survive on the Central Core planets.

Empress Kayla softly knocked on the office door later and peeked inside. "How is our Prince Lukus today, Master Tutor Tan'K?"

He bowed and replied, "Prince Lukus is very advanced in his reading. We are discussing long division, Empress Kayla."

"I hate long division!" The little Prince exclaimed.

She suppressed a smile and said, "You must excel at mathematics to qualify for Flight School, my Son. Why not give it another try?"

Lukus sighed and said, "Okay, Mother. I will." He resolutely turned to his com tablet and resumed his problem. "Stupid long division," he mumbled. She laughed to herself. He was a headstrong boy, but open to suggestion. She went next door to her Suite.

When P'Lau was Emperor, there were twenty-two Lords or Ladies with lands and titles, and twelve Barons. As of this morning, only five Lords and one Lady remained; four Barons, including P'Lau, and Viscount T'Sur. Millions of square kilometers of land on the three Central Core planets were seized by the Empress since she came to the throne. T'Sur was correct: either she divided her lands and shared power or became a dictator.

Kayla looked at her reflection in the mirror. Being known to history as the "Warrior Empress" was an accurate description. Only a strong warrior could have survived her first five years: a coup d'état the night of her coronation; an attempted assassination in Main Court; several power plays from heirs of former aristocrats whose titles and lands she revoked; and the recent events of the last several months.

But being called a "Dictator," or possibly a "Despot," did not reflect her beliefs or her intentions. She wanted to rule an Empire of Peace, and usher in a Golden Age of Knowledge and Awakening for all her people. Several carefully chosen Imperial Beneficiaries were needed. Now, more than ever. The people needed to know their Empire would serve and protect them.

She had to make the call pressing on her heart, first. Kayla conferenced Priest K'Ramm and Elder Priestess T'Char with her. "In the name of our Creator, thank you for speaking with me, my friends. News has been obtained in our Royal Court not yet made public. We feel the need to share this with our Holy Servants of the Creator." After taking a deep breath, the Empress revealed, "A long-time associate of the Plan of the Thirteen conspirators has named a member of the Holy Caste Order as a powerful Plan Technician."

The look of surprise on K'Ramm's face was expected, as was the stoic countenance of T'Char. "Please, Empress Kayla. I know it is difficult for a believer to accept, but we must know," T'Char said gently.

"The confessed associate named S'Lovik and called him the 'greatest con man' he'd ever met. S'Lovik was known as the Silent One," she revealed.

T'Char enquired, "Has our former High Priest been apprehended? He must face his brothers and sisters and confess his sins before being sent to the Afterlife, my Empress. It is our Holy Caste law," she stated.

"S'Lovik and two others are being pursued on the high seas, as we speak. When he is apprehended, you have my word he will be given to the Holy Caste Order for his penance. But we must have him back," Kayla said. "So many need closure."

They agreed to speak again when S'Lovik was in Imperial custody, and Priestess T'Char clicked off. Priest K'Ramm asked, "Did you receive the parchments, Empress Kayla?"

"Yes, K'Ramm, just this morning. They were most helpful. We thank you for your assistance again," Kayla said. She sat back and asked, "More than thirty years of planning; billions of credits; thousands ensnared in their Plan; and over one billion innocent people killed. Were these men always so evil? Or did they become evil in their quest for power?"

"Only the Creator knows their dark paths, my Empress. I thank Him every day for your being on the throne of power. No other Emperor or Empress in our long history has been faced with the trials placed upon you, Empress Kayla. Without your strong will and determination, we would be facing anarchy, or complete destruction," he surmised.

She said, "We are supported by strong and loving hands of many loyal friends, my dear Priest." They stared into the vid screens and both smiled, briefly remembering their time together, so many years ago.

"Well—it is time to realign our Royal Hierarchy, Priest K'Ramm," she said, pulling from his gaze with a blush. They bowed to each other and clicked off.

XVII

K'Halon Prime

The Viscount said with a smile, "Two new Barons, four new Lords, and one Lady. We have made great strides today!" Their long, tedious meeting was successful.

The Empress agreed with him, and then added, "There are two small parcels of lands adjacent to the Baronies we wish to bequeath to Friends of the Empire. The first ten square kilometers is in the lower quadrant of the former Baron Tri'T lands on M'Wati. We will make this area a gift to the Holy Caste Order for their new Temple of the Creator. Their former Temple was in N'Well, and is gone," she disclosed. Both the Viscount and Baron P'Lau agreed.

"And the second grant is adjacent to your lands, Baron P'Lau: the area in the Northern Mountains known as the 'Twelve Point Buck Lodge.' We wish to bequeath the hunting lodge, surrounding cabins and buildings, and another ten square kilometers to our Council of Elder Rangers," she said. "A small token of our gratitude for their guarding the Royal Treasure of K'Halon Prime and Home World." She saw him considering her decision. "Is there a problem, Baron P'Lau?"

He answered, "Yes, there is. The Council of Elder Rangers has been a silent, unassuming pool of advisors for both your Majesty and myself, when I served, and for Emperors through the centuries. None of them accept a single credit when they perform as advisors, trusted Rangers, or Treasury Guards. Whatever task their Sovereign asks is completed without any expectation or acceptance of reward. I am concerned the Council will refuse this grant, your Majesty. I volunteer an additional two hundred square kilometers for them, with the hope our proud and noble Council of Elder Rangers will accept," he offered.

She was happy he not only agreed, but enhanced her land offer to them, and said, "Then, let us make them a gift not only will they accept, but proudly share with others!" They discussed the matter further and decided to build a much larger, modern lodge adjacent to the original property, so more retired Elder Rangers would be able to enjoy the remote outdoor retreat.

Membership in the exclusive Council of Elder Rangers was by invitation only. To qualify for membership, a Ranger must have attained Master Commander rank or higher and served a minimum of thirty years in good standing.

"Where is our tailor?" The Empress asked for the third time, in an uncharacteristically loud voice. "The Confirmation Ceremony begins in fifteen minutes!" She stood in front of the full-length mirror, dressed in her formal Kaylan Ranger uniform red dress and knee-high, red high-heeled boots, with her new, dark red, nano-titanium breastplate and backplate. The new armor was heavily accented with solid gold trim, emphasizing her female form.

Several colors of nano-titanium armor were made for Empress Kayla, including ivory, dark blue, green, and black, as well as Kaylan Ranger dark red. The gold-trimmed armor immediately identified Kayla as the Empress. No other Ranger body armor was decorated in pure gold like that of the Empress Kayla. Rank insignia for her uniform was unnecessary.

The tailor ran into her dressing room with her new Royal Red cloak. "The seamstresses just finished the sable trim, my Empress. Do you like it?" He asked excitedly.

"We ordered no furry creature to be killed to trim our clothing. Heirloom pieces are one thing; our new clothing is another," she said tersely.

"It is faux sable, as you ordered, your Majesty," he replied.

She smiled at last, swirled the new cloak around her shoulders, nodded to her tailor, and walked swiftly to the Main Court. Courtiers, military officers, and VIPs were lined up on the sides of the Main Court, watching the Borgund and Kaylan Novices march in. The Novices were all sons and daughters of proud Warrior Class parents, most of them Rangers themselves. This was a solemn, very important day for the new Novices.

Empress Kayla was escorted in by twenty Imperial Guards and took her throne. C.S. Javette announced: "The Great Empress Kayla, Ruler over all Known Worlds and Conqueror over the Unknown Domain. Your Novice Kaylan and Borgund Rangers appear before you, to confirm their lives and service to you." Every Novice knelt on their right knee and bowed their head.

The four Commanders Superior and High Ranger Lady Bette stood at either side of the Novice Rangers. A loud bell chimed, and the Novices put their right hand over their heart and said in unison: "I swear my service, my loyalty, my will, and my life to the Great Empress Kayla, and to our Creator." Each Novice removed their left-hand glove, took a knife from their backplate, cut their left palm, and held their bleeding left palm high for all to see: their blood oath. Then they put their gloves on again.

"Draw swords!" C.S. B'Von commanded. The Novices drew their plasma sword, and the fiery white-hot swords gleamed and crackled pure energy, as they held them high above their heads with both hands. "Salute!" He cried. They sharply pulled their swords down to their left breastplate with both hands, in the Royal Salute.

"Sheathe swords!" C.S. G'Rosk ordered, and they returned their swords to their backplates. The Novices stood, and the large audience in the Main Court applauded and cheered for them. Their lives and service officially belonged to Empress Kayla.

When the crowd quieted, Empress Kayla said, "My newest Faithful Sons and Beloved Daughters, you have made your Empress very proud today. You represent the highest tier of your Warrior Class, following in the footsteps of the great Borgund and Kaylan Rangers who served the Empire for over 2,500 years. Be proud of your calling and Confirmation today. Know this: We all serve the Empire, and the Creator of us all."

The High Priestess stepped up and blessed the Novices, in the ancient language. The Empress personally handed each Borgund Novice a solid gold belt buckle on a black leather belt, resting in the finest black silk, set inside a black box. The heavy buckle bore the Imperial seal, with an onyx stone prominently set in the center.

Empress Kayla then ordered the Novice Kaylan Rangers to remove their left-hand gloves. She placed their long, gold and jewel-laden Confirmation Ring on their third finger. Empress Kayla returned to her throne, levitated up two meters above them, and declared, "Our young Kaylan Novices are now our Beloved Daughters, and our Borgund Novices are our Faithful Sons. Congratulations to our brave protectors!" Everyone in the Main Court applauded and cheered again, and the ceremony was complete.

When the applause for the fourteen new Borgund and three Kaylan Novices died down, the Empress raised her hand to quiet her Court, and said, "As most of our honored guests and Rangers know, we made a few modifications in the Royal Hierarchy, as well as in the Ranger system," she said with a slight smile. A few laughs were heard from the guests.

"Our Rangers have protected and served this Empire for more than 2,500 years, many making their ultimate sacrifice for their Sovereign, and our people. Ours is a proud tradition, and deservedly so. Yet our Borgund and Kaylan Rangers serve with modesty, not flaunting their achievements on the ancient uniforms. The uniform of the Rangers is instantly recognizable anywhere in the Empire," she stated, then paused for a few seconds.

Empress Kayla continued, "But we are ushering in a new era. We are incorporating several modern technologies into our Ranger uniforms, to provide the ultimate protection for them, and utilize new advances in weaponry." She moved her right hand, and four Rangers walked out. "Borgund Rangers, this is your new formal uniform." Master Commander Sham'S proudly turned to the audience. With a touch of his new armband, a full shield activated around his body. Then, he deactivated the shield, and ran down the Court incredibly fast.

"As you can see, we are now incorporating power cells in the boots, defensive shields to protect those who protect us, and new arm band controls. Now, our Kaylan new formal uniform," she said, pointing to Master Commander Shanna. They had the same body shields, power cells in their knee-high high-heeled boots, and the modesty panels in front of their red dress was more ornate. "Both uniforms feature greater helmet features, as well."

Then the daily all-black uniforms were shown with the same upgrades. She said, "Weapons Master, if you please," and he brought four human-figure targets, placing them along the wall. "Guards, stand aside," she quietly ordered. "Did we mention the new arm bands?" The four Rangers raised their arms and shot laser fire from the new arm bands, and the crowd erupted in applause. "Our Imperial Guards were provided similar new armbands with shields and lasers."

"Their new Ranger breastplates feature new weapons, but they will not be demonstrated here, to protect our guests," she said to a laughing audience. "And our final improvement: the new, expanding plasma sword." The four drew their fiery, white hot swords, twisted the ornate handles, and they expanded another one point five meters into a spear. They demonstrated several martial arts spear movements, then held the plasma spears aloft, and bowed to their Empress, acknowledging her as the Master of this weapon.

"The recent attacks on our Imperial Naval Base in Capital City have created a leadership vacuum at the highly-strategic facility. We have assigned several senior Rangers to assist, until more Naval personnel become available to fill the vacuum. Also, to insure protection and increase Imperial presence, a Ranger High Command will be established on M'Wati," she announced.

"And for our last announcement: we present our newest ESK-class warbird," she said proudly. The huge vid screens came down and showed the new warbird. It was shaped in a futuristic, crescent-shaped design no one had ever seen. The test flight demonstrated the warbird's increased maneuverability and firepower. The audience applauded and cheered loudly. Kayla watched the excited faces of her new Novices, many of whom would someday pilot the new warbirds. "Do you approve of our latest changes, my Faithful Sons and Beloved Daughters?" Applause and loud cheers burst from the Rangers.

"Thank you all. Now, Viscount T'Sur and Baron P'Lau have asked for a few minutes of your time," she said, and the men came forward.

The elderly Viscount said, "Many changes have already taken place in our K'Halon Prime Main Court and the Imperial Class System. Some will be easier for the Old Guard to accept than others," he said with a smile, and the audience laughed softly, nodding their heads.

"But the greatest change of all has taken place at the very top of the Imperial Class System: our Great Benevolent Empress Kayla, chosen by the Galactic Vee Lok Lords," Baron P'Lau said.

T'Sur continued, "To honor and acknowledge our Sovereign, who has proven herself to be both Great and Benevolent, and the Warrior sent to us by our Creator to lead our Empire through these troubled times; the Great Council of Barons and your Viscount present a new crown to our Warrior Empress."

P'Lau held up a red box and opened it with much flourish. Both men lifted the new crown and raised it high for all to see. The vid cameras in the court focused on the crown and projected it on the huge side screens.

Viscount T'Sur proclaimed, "Forged from the veins of pure gold from the new mine on Ban'Ti; and platinum from the deep mines of M'Wati."

P'Lau continued, "Diamonds from the heart of Home World; and a great, Royal Emerald from K'Halon Prime. We crown you our Warrior Empress Kayla!" They placed the new crown on her. The crown gleamed and glistened across her forehead, with the big Emerald in the center, surrounded by large, perfect diamonds.

The entire audience and all Rangers clapped and cheered loudly for the Warrior Empress. Kayla barely managed to hold back her tears of surprise and gratitude. This new crown became her favorite, made especially for her. She held out her left hand, and little Prince Lukus stepped up beside her, wearing his Royal Blue robe. He raised his arms and cried, "Let the feast begin!"

The servants paraded a whole roasted deer for everyone, followed by dish after dish of delicacies. The feast was accompanied with fine wine, musicians playing, and entertainers dancing. The day was a memorable occasion for the newly confirmed Novices and their proud families. Traditional folk dancing was a big part of the celebration.

Kayla left the festivities early, as usual, and retired to her chambers. Her ladies ran her hot bath in the large tub and sprinkled rose petals in the water. They put her long hair up, and talked excitedly about her new crown, placing it carefully on a new pedestal. Kayla stepped into the bath and let the hot, bubbling water relax and soothe her body and mind.

In a few minutes, running footsteps forewarned everyone to get prepared. "Momma! Momma!" Little Lukus cried, tearing off his robe and clothes. He jumped into her large tub, causing a big splash and laughing with all his might. Her attendants were used to the boy's antics and tossed their readied towels on the floor around the water-jet tub. Lukus sprinkled rose petals on his head, and over his Mother's submerged body.

She cautioned, "Next year, you'll go to the Royal Academy, Lukus. You'll be too big for me to allow you to play in my bath." She ran her fingers through his curly hair. "You'll be a big boy then, and it won't be appropriate."

"But that's next year, Momma. We can play together now!" The boy said and swam around the large tub. Her attendants and his Mother laughed, watching him toss more petals in the air.

Consort Dan'L peeked in and said, "Here you are, Lukus. Is there room for me?" The young attendants giggled at him and blushed. Kayla shook her head "No."

"We left a little something in your room for you, my Consort," she said with a smile. He left, and the attendants helped Prince Lukus out of the deep tub, wrapping him in a clean towel. Then they led him off to bed.

Kayla finished and dried off, then put on her favorite red and gold robe. She dismissed her ladies and walked into her bedroom. The sparkling wine was chilled perfectly. Dan'L came in wearing his new silk robe. He started to kiss her good night, as he had done for two months. Then he noticed the hated med droid was gone, and chilled wine rested in an ice bucket.

Slowly walking to her Consort, Kayla said, "I'm not quite at the Ranger P.T. level, but I hope I pass your inspection, Master Commander." She had not let him see her body since the night she was rescued, when she was so emaciated from starvation. Kayla opened her robe a little for him, watching his eyes dance with excitement.

Dan'L looked at his wife's shapely, healed body, and whispered, "My beautiful Kayla!" He picked her up and kissed her, and took her promptly to bed. The reunited lovers shared much lovemaking and enjoyed their fine sparkling wine. Sometime in the night, they fell asleep, their bodies and legs tangled in sweet bliss.

The Royal Family and accompanying Imperial Guards and Rangers boarded the triple safety-checked shuttle and flew to the Imperial Command Battle Cruiser. Their trip to Home World was packed with meetings and vid conferences for the Empress. Her Consort had the pleasure of escorting his Son all around the huge ship. Both Dan'L and Kayla served aboard the Cruiser when they were young Rangers.

Prince Lukus stood on a chair in the Flight Ops Control room, watching the Space Cadre fighters launch for their patrols. He heard, "ES-519 ready to launch," and excitedly said, "It's Mother!" When she launched the distinctive ES-519 off the deck, Lukus jumped and clapped, and high-fived the Flight Ops Captain.

At dinner, Admiral Mur presented Prince Lukus with a Space Cadre Officer's duty cap, with the Cruiser's logo on the front, and "Honorary Flight Ops Captain" on the back. The young boy proudly wore his cap every day, and the crewmen saluted their Prince. He returned their salutes perfectly.

Home World

In three days, everyone landed in the shuttle at "the Farm," a big, twenty-bedroom mansion on the estate formerly occupied by the traitor Baron S'Tan, the "Grand Master Technician" of the Plan of the Thirteen. The Royal family settled into the Master bedrooms, with recovering Admiral Olm and his family next to them. Lady Bette was assigned the big bedroom suite down the hall. There was ample room for the two Commanders Superior G'Rosk and Javette, and several Master Commander Imperial Guards and Rangers to be housed in the mansion. Dozens of single Guards and Rangers doubled-up in the small hotel a few kilometers down the road.

Auxiliary housing for Rangers with young children, previously housed in the Family Residences within the Palace Complex, was generously provided by Viscount T'Sur. He donated an all-suite hotel for the families until their housing in the rebuilt Palace could be completed.

XVIII

Weeks of human and robotic forensic teams searching the Imperial Naval Base and the Royal Palace for survivors came to an end. Admiral Olm felt incredibly lucky to have been rescued with the Royal Physician Admiral Mae, General Blatan, and several Palace servants. They all ran through the underground escape tunnel leading to emergency shuttles near the forest and became trapped inside when the tunnel collapsed. Even though she could not move her body, Admiral Mae gave instructions to help others injured. She and Olm both suffered fractured vertebrae in their lower backs, with internal injuries. Olm would walk with a cane for many years to come.

The missiles used in the final phase of the attack were the largest non-nuclear tipped missiles in the Imperial Army arsenal. They proved highly destructive and took out their targets with pin-point precision. Within six weeks, much of the rubble had been cleared from the Naval Base, but it would take much longer to clear the Palace Complex. The Palace was over eight hundred years old, constructed with massive solid stone blocks for several of the buildings, some of which still stood in place.

Reconstruction of the Naval Base Hospital was first priority on the base. The twenty-story facility had several floors standing, but not safe. The Empress ordered the hospital torn down and rebuilt from its foundation. Several Admirals complained about their Administration Building taking second priority, but orders were to rebuild the Hospital for the care of long-term wounded first. The ReGen-Pod on the second floor was not damaged, thankfully. Many hours of treatment for the wounded were performed, including several for the "Mistress of the Machine," Admiral Mae.

For the Home World Palace, the immediate priority was rebuilding the Main Court and North Wing, and the Royal Suite on its third floor. Since the Royal Academy was not bombed out, it suffered primarily cosmetic damage. But the Empress kept her Academy students on Paradise Island until most of the rebuilding of the Palace was completed. Her students were protected at all times.

M.C. Shanna jogged upstairs to the Royal Apartment in the mansion at the Farm, wondering why she was summoned on her day off. Empress Kayla insisted she rest, after weeks of guarding her without time off; now this summons. The Imperial Guards admitted her into the private study.

The Empress entered with her Ranger guards and said, "Please forgive us for calling you on your day off, Master Commander Shanna. But our guest requires a tour of our 'Farm' this morning, and specifically requested you," she said with a little smile. She stepped aside, and Admiral Mae walked to the front cautiously, using her cane to steady herself.

Kayla felt the surge of energy between the two women. She said, "We have tired you unintentionally, Admiral Mae. Perhaps Master Commander Shanna and one of our Imperial Guards can escort you to your guest suite. If you're able, please join our dinner tonight at seven," she said. The Royal Physician was helped to her guest suite by a Guard and Shanna. The Guard returned in a few minutes.

Mae carefully sat on the sofa and patted the cushion next to her. Shanna took off her cloak, armor, and arm bands, then rushed to sit next to her. "It's been forever," she said softly. "When did you get out of rehab? What can I do to help you, Mae?" Her lower back brace showed beneath her uniform. Shanna helped her take off her jacket.

Mae answered, "They released me this morning. I can't believe we're here, together, Shanna. I thought I'd never see you again." She tried to get comfortable, and said, "The day of the attack, I spent the morning at the Naval Hospital, as usual. Then, on a whim, I ferried across the harbor, and hopped on the moving sidewalk to the Palace to meet with Admiral Olm. He updated me on his sister's progress, then everything began exploding! Imperial Guards led us to the roof with Lord Vu'Duc for a rescue shuttle, but they were killed in front of us when the second round of missiles hit," she said with emotion.

"Then, Admiral Olm took my hand, and we ran down emergency stairs in the dark. Several others were running in the tunnel with us. When the last barrage of missiles hit, Admiral Olm took me in his arms and dove to the dirt floor. The tunnel behind us collapsed. General Blatan crawled back to make sure we were OK," Mae said, her voice shaking.

Shanna held her hand while Mae finished her story. "Olm was calm and in control during the bombing and kept all of us from panicking. We were in the dark, and everyone was injured, including me. I couldn't even crawl, Shanna. The injured people tried not to cry in pain, as did I, but we couldn't help it. The poor servant girls were hysterical. It was a long, frightening two days." She tried to keep her composure, and said, "If I'd stayed at the Hospital, I would have been killed, Shanna."

Mae dabbed her eyes and whispered, "All I could think about was

Empress Kayla, and her being held in that dim cell for twenty-nine days. I told them all that if our Empress could survive, so would we. I spoke harshly to the frightened servant girls, Shanna, and I feel ashamed about it. But our ordeal was a trifle compared to what our Empress suffered," she said.

Shanna commented, "The servants had no emergency training, Mae. You commanded them when they needed to hear the voice of a leader in control. I'll wager they credit you with saving their lives, Admiral. You did well," the battle-hardened Kaylan Ranger said to her. She covered Mae with a blanket, and exhausted Mae slept until dinner.

In the grand dining room of the mansion, a special awards ceremony was held. Empress Kayla vid-conferenced every Ranger in the solar system. She sat in a large chair, surrounded by her personal Ranger guards and six Imperial Guards. She thanked everyone for joining the meeting, and then said, "We have been informed the Royal Palace Main Court at Home World will not be ready for another four months, due to structural complications. The needs of the Empire require several actions to be implemented much sooner."

She pointed to the descending vid screen and said, "We previously announced the creation of a Ranger High Command on M'Wati. To fulfill the command requirements for this new division, we promote and appoint Commander Superior Steph'N," she proudly said, and he bowed his head to his friend.

"To assist our Imperial Navy during the reconstruction of its Hospital and Submarine Base, we are sending Master Commander L'Van, Commander Tish, and several Novices to assist their efforts." She leaned forward and stated, "Also promoted is our new Fleet Admiral L'Rok, of the Space Cadre."

"The safety and security of every citizen in our Empire is first and foremost on our mind. Therefore, we have appointed the man best suited and imminently capable as our Temporary Imperial Security Advisor: Commander Superior G'Rosk," she announced. C.S Javette proudly joined in the loud applause for him.

"Many more commendations, awards, and bonuses will be merited when our Main Court reopens. But there is one more announcement to be made today," the Empress said. "After serving tirelessly for a minimum of thirty years for our Empire, our Great Council of Elder Rangers serves upon the request of their Empress, without hesitation. Not one Elder has ever accepted any remuneration, award, or bonus for their important contribution to the survival of the Empire," she revealed.

"But, after the maximum efforts of the Council of Elder Ranger members, including sacrificing two of their lives during the attack on the

Royal Palace of Home World, your Empress must insist the Council accept at least one gift. We hereby appoint the Council of Elder Rangers as Royal Beneficiary, and bequeath the area known as the 'Twelve Point Buck Lodge,' and the surrounding two hundred square kilometers from Baron P'Lau, to your esteemed Council this day," she said.

A red-faced K'Laud and R'Shon bowed their heads, finally accepting a Royal Gift for their Council members' selfless contributions. The applause was nearly deafening. The short ceremony ended with dinner and wine, both of which High Ranger Lady Bette declined. Empress Kayla walked outside in the cool evening air with her. "What is troubling my former Commander Superior tonight, Lady Bette?" Kayla asked.

The eldest Kaylan Ranger stopped and looked at her young Sovereign, and asked, "Is this the night I am 'put out to pasture,' Empress Kayla?"

Empress Kayla tactfully answered, "I know several of the appointments were made without consulting you."

"All of them, my Empress," she answered. "I thought making such recommendations was my duty," Bette added.

Kayla said, "Yes, and I hope my appointments meet with your approval. I have always valued your insight and experience, and still do. But I did not consult you intentionally, Lady Bette. You were given several weeks grieving time, and I did not wish to burden you during this time with your family," Kayla answered, with a bow of her head.

Lady Bette returned Kayla's bow of respect. They continued walking for a while, then Bette asked, "Then, may I assume my duties as High Ranger, my Empress? The work will do me good. Lord Vu'Duc is in the Afterlife. I must move forward," she said determinedly.

"Whenever you are ready, I welcome your wise council and guidance. The Empire and your Empress need our Lady Bette, as long as you wish to serve," Kayla answered.

"Then, let's return to the banquet, if any food and wine are left," she said with a smile of relief. "Now, about Master Commander L'Van being sent to the Imperial Naval Base," she began, and Kayla burst out laughing. The two women returned to the dining room arm in arm.

C.S. Javette entered her suite and hung up her cloak. *Another fifteen-hour day, and many more to come,* she sighed. She put her armor on its charging stand, stripped, and headed for a hot shower. Then she put on a short gown and laid down to sleep.

G'Rosk came in several hours later, ditched his cloak and uniform and showered. Then he crawled into bed next to Javette. In the early morning, he awoke, and saw Javette peeking out through the curtain. He stood behind her and looked, seeing Empress Kayla and Dan'L running with her Imperial Guards. "Just like in Phase 2 Training," he said.

"They've been best friends since the Royal Academy," Javette said. "Dan'L favored Kayla since he was a boy."

G'Rosk put his arms around Javette's waist, and said, "Sometimes best friends become lovers." He lightly kissed her neck.

"And Life Partners," she whispered, leaning back against him. G'Rosk caressed her body, and she turned in his arms. Javette held his face and kissed him again and again, until he drove her to their bed. On this perfect morning, the lovers skipped their early morning runs and workouts. They had far more enjoyable things to do.

XIX

Sham'S tried to brush off the dust from his black cloak, but there was too much. He was covered in dust, dirt, and gunk. Supervising civilian workers was difficult; but their job bosses were impossible. *How did anything get built?* An ice-cold hard cider sounded perfect.

His comm link beeped, ordering him to appear before Empress Kayla ASAP. He requested one hour's delay to clean up, but she replied, "My office, NOW!" He ran to his shuttle and flew immediately to the Farm.

Kayla took one look at Sham'S in his dirty cloak and uniform and could not hide her smile. "Let our working man wash up," she invited. She ordered a bucket of hard ciders on ice, and a double hot roast beef sandwich for him, his favorite. Sham'S washed his hands and face in her bathroom, and an attendant took his cloak for cleaning.

"Master Commander Sham'S: you have toiled tirelessly today, and many days since our Ranger training together. Without hesitation, you served when and wherever your Sovereign sent you, and completed your missions successfully. You stood many times within your Borgund ranks while others received awards and commendations, and made no complaint," she summed. "You have been our faithful friend since Phase 1 Training. Today, we ask our Master Commander to take on a heavy yoke. Do you volunteer to serve us?"

Without asking what she needed or wanted him to do, Sham'S knelt before his friend, and said, "I swore my service, my will, and my life to you the day of your appointment by the Vee Lok Lords, my Great Empress Kayla. I am yours to command," he said, with a bow of his head.

Kayla touched his dust-covered head and said, "Then we command you to assume control of Ranger Training immediately. The Phase 1 trainees will graduate in two weeks on Xau, and you must be there to separate the wheat from the chaff. Help them choose the right career path. Mentor our Ranger trainees through Phase 2 and 3 Training, and present them for confirmation, Commander Superior Sham'S!"

The big smile on his face absolutely melted Kayla's heart. Sham'S stood and struck his left upper breast hard with his right fist, saluting his Empress. "When shall I leave for Xau, my Empress?" He asked.

"Soon. But let's finish this bucket of hard ciders, my friend. Then you can take a good shower," she added. They toasted and downed the ice-cold hard cider together. Every man has his day, and today was Sham'S' day.

After he cleaned up, newly promoted C.S. Sham'S pinned the impressive gold insignia on his collar. He felt a surge of pride and satisfaction. Bolstered by his success, Sham'S went to M.C. L'Mun's apartment. Sham'S revealed his love for her, and asked L'Mun to be his Life Partner.

L'Mun agreed, asking, "What took you so long? I nearly tired of waiting, Sham'S!" In the night, they sealed their pact making love. They sent their Life Partnership Agreement Application to Empress Kayla the next morning. She approved it immediately, along with L'Mun's request to transfer to K'Halon Prime Royal Palace. It was only an eight-hour shuttle flight from K'Halon Prime to its third moon, Xau. She'd be much closer to Sham'S, there.

K'Halon Prime

Low-flying Imperial Navy search drones and aircraft scanned sections of the ocean of huge K'Halon Prime. Plotting all possible courses away from the harbor of T'Anju a private yacht could cruise at its top speed, every available Navy watercraft was utilized to locate and apprehend Baron Lep'T, Lord Marl, and High Priest S'Lovik. Submarines launched underwater probes in the vast waters.

Air Corps fighters assisted in the search by scanning the ocean from 5,000 meters. Each vessel appearing on their scanners was contacted, identified, and its position and course plotted. Satellites above K'Halon Prime were directed to use their high-intensity scanners and GPS mapping computers to assist in the search for the Baron's yacht.

While the search for Baron Lep'T's yacht continued, Imperial Army commandos took control of the Baron's mansion and grounds. He did indeed have a "basement full of boys," as B'Nard said. Eight boys from ten years old to fifteen were kept in his "dormitory," as it was called. They were fed and clothed well, and had vid games, broadcast screens, and other entertaining games. The refrigerator was stocked with snacks and drinks, including hard cider, wine, and Brandywine. A locked cabinet held various containers of tranquilizers and pleasure drugs. The room in the back was for "bad boys," complete with fetish sex toys, leather harnesses, whips, and a rack where the bad boy was chained for his punishment.

The wife and children of Baron Lep'T lived separately in a penthouse in

Centralia, far away from the Baron. Baroness Lep'T knew her husband secretly favored boys and moved away from him many years ago. She knew nothing of the Plan of the Thirteen, or its many contingency plans. Lep'T's immediate family made every effort to avoid his company. When the Borgund Rangers asked her about his "dormitory," and the eight kept boys, she was shocked. She voluntarily submitted to interrogation under truth serum, and her innocence was verified. The Baroness was disgusted after hearing of her estranged husband's involvement in the Plan of the Thirteen.

Lord Marl's wife and grown children, however, fired on the approaching Imperial Army commandos. The mansion was fortified heavily with small laser cannons and grenade launchers. At the end of their underground escape tunnel was a secluded launch site in the thick forest, where his shuttle was kept. Army commandos hid near the shuttle and captured Lady Marl and her adult children, and their security men. Lady Marl swallowed a cyanide capsule rather than being taken alive.

Former High Priest S'Lovik maintained an apartment in Centralia, in addition to his rooms in the Home World Temple of the Creator. The Rangers and Army officers investigating his apartment used a robo-scanner. The one-bedroom apartment had a false wall, behind which was a black-painted room full of occult items: the requisite black candles; various dried bone charms; a long, black cape and mask; and several books, one of which was an ancient book of spells, written on dried human skin. The High Priest of the Holy Caste Order was also the High Priest of Dark Magic.

Reports were sent to Ranger High Command and Empress Kayla. The High Priestess, Elder Priestess T'Char, and Priest K'Ramm were copied on the investigative report on S'Lovik, and vid recordings were attached. They gave no response. The top tier of the Holy Caste Order was clearly in shock and were fasting and praying. Their Holy Hierarchy fully expected Empress Kayla to dissolve their Holy Caste Order and force them back into the Imperial Class System.

After weeks of searching the seas, the yacht of Baron Lep'T was located. Imperial Navy scuba commandos were dropped into the icy water while three Navy assault boats surrounded the yacht. When they boarded, the commandos found a scene of recent slaughter. Hot food was on the galley stoves. A lone cigar lay in an ashtray, still lit.

One of the crew called a "May Day" signal, but only once; his dead body lie on top of the comm console. Every member of the crew was shot with a laser blast. Three teenage girls were lying dead on the sun deck in their bikinis, their bodies still warm. S'Lovik was in his suite, his mouth foaming from a cyanide capsule. Lord Marl lie dead in front of the fireplace in the lounge. He had tried to burn his journals and notebooks, but the commandos took them off the low gas flames and recovered them.

Baron Lep'T sat in the captain's chair on the bridge, panting to breathe, his fat fingers on the trigger of his laser rifle. All officers on the bridge were dead. When the Navy Commander discovered Lep'T, he raised the rifle to fire, but it was out of ammo. Lep'T smiled and said, "She won't get me," and reached into his pocket for a cyanide capsule. But the Commander stopped him from putting the suicide capsule in his mouth.

A shouting Lep'T was cuffed, arrested, and taken by the Navy commandos on their attack boat. He fought to leave his yacht, screaming, "Kill me! Kill me! Don't let her get me!" But he was stunned and carried to a brig cell.

When Empress Kayla was notified of the seizure of the Baron and his yacht, she ordered, "Return the yacht to Centralia harbor for full investigation. Tow it, if necessary. Sedate the prisoner. Fly Baron Lep'T directly to the Imperial Army Base near Capital City on Home World at top speed."

Home World, Imperial Army Prison

No visitors were permitted for the former Baron Lep'T. Empress Kayla entered his cell, surrounded by eight Borgund Rangers. "We 'got you' after all, former Baron Lep'T," she said with an intense look on her face. "We hope you enjoy cold porridge, because it's the only meal served on this prison level. But it's more than we had for nearly one month," she reminded him.

"My attorney will have me out of here by this afternoon," he shouted. "I have more power than you know, Empress Bitch," he bragged.

"Your attorney resigned as of yesterday. Your Royal Beneficiary status has been revoked. All your lands, property, businesses, factories, and every credit of your wealth have been confiscated by the Empire. We gave an annual allowance to the former Baroness and her children, and let them keep their penthouse in Centralia, since they were innocent of your deeds. If another attorney volunteers to represent you, he or she will be permitted one visit. It is Imperial law," she stated.

She walked slowly in front of him and tried to set aside her disgust. "The Plan is finished. We will allow you time to confess to our High Court barristers, should you choose to do so. Then, you will be interrogated with truth serum, to dredge the deepest and darkest secrets you hide. All will be revealed, in time. And we have so much time with you. It will take over one year to plan your prosecutorial case, the Tribunal has informed us."

He rose with difficulty from the floor. Then he looked at her with pure evil in his eyes, and said, "You won't get anything from me, Empress Bitch! I have powers you cannot begin to fathom! My people will have me out of here in an hour!" He continued his tirade, until she heard enough, and turned away. "We should have killed you when we had the chance."

"Fast the traitor for three days on water only. No visitors. No one, is that understood? Full 24-hour vid surveillance every day. Take his belt and shoelaces, and have the guards put a proper prison uniform on him. He is on suicide watch. Sedate him, if necessary. And keep him in the dark for one week. It's good for soul-searching!" The Empress said and walked out of his cell. The prisoner screamed at her as she left, and during her walk up the stairs.

No attorney came forward to represent Lep'T. To keep the law, a public defender was appointed for him, but the former Baron refused his service. The prisoner did not confess. Interrogations began after his forced fast, and it took three full days to get any information from Lep'T at all. He admitted to being an integral part of the Plan of the Thirteen; but Baron Z'Lun felt Lep'T was too young to be a signer at only fourteen years of age.

The Empress did not want Kend'R to be brought in for Lep'T's interrogation. She knew Kend'R had read the minds of those he interrogated and saw many more of their evil deeds than they openly confessed. Kayla did not want her friend to suffer by connecting with the sadistic, evil mind of the sodomist and pedophile. She wanted to spare Kend'R the heinous experience.

XX

C.S. Sham'S and M.C. L'Mun hurried aboard the Imperial shuttle, followed by crewmen pushing anti-grav carts with their battle armor cases and luggage onboard. Already seated were Admiral Mae and M.C. Shanna. "Thanks for letting us hitch a ride, Admiral Mae," Sham'S said.

She smiled and answered, "I don't want you and L'Mun to be late for your Partnership Ceremony." The anxious Partners-to-be smiled with her and chatted as the shuttle launched towards the Capital City Space Base.

In a few minutes, a loud explosion was heard. L'Mun looked out the window and exclaimed, "It's the power station! There are dozens of apartment buildings around. We'd better see if they need our assistance." They landed close by the fire. The three Rangers grabbed their helmets and ran, while Admiral Mae offered medical assistance to the Fire Captain. He gladly accepted their help. Admiral Mae triaged the injured while the Emergency shuttles landed their personnel.

The Rangers and shuttle pilots helped evacuate the apartment buildings closest to the power station. Then the main gas line ruptured from the explosion, threatening an entire twelve-block sector of apartment buildings, restaurants, and small shops. The local police cordoned off the evacuees to allow rescue and repair workers room to work.

"I think everyone's out. Thanks for your help," the Fire Captain said to Sham'S. The Imperial shuttle passengers began walking back. Then, an exploding gas line suddenly ripped through the sidewalk, followed by one of the apartment buildings exploding in flames. "Everyone back! The main gas line could blow!" The Fire Captain yelled. Even the journalists were pushed back. M.C. L'Mun helped contain the people in a safe area.

Next door to the burning apartment building, a young girl screamed through an open window. Sham'S put his helmet on and ran into the building to rescue the young girl. His Ranger uniform and cloak were fire-retardant, as well as resistant to laser fire. Tall Sham'S ran up the interior stairwell, broke down the door, and took the terrified girl in his arms. He wrapped her in her coat and ran outside with her. The people cheered and applauded for them.

Another gas explosion near a second building occurred, followed by the partial collapse of the lower floors. The faint cries of a baby were heard. Shanna ran top speed into the burning building. Mae saw the flames erupt in the collapsed lower floors. The entire building was engulfed in the fire, and her heart pounded in her chest.

Wrapping her cloak around her, Shanna climbed the stairs towards the sound of the baby's cries. She kicked down the door and saw the mother dead on the floor, her arms protecting her infant. Shanna wrapped the baby in his bedding, and then inside her cloak.

Shanna was halfway down the stairs when the ceiling collapsed in a storm of fire. She jumped off just in time to avoid being crushed, but they were trapped by burning boards and flooring. Drawing her plasma sword, Shanna cut through the burning timbers and framework, holding the baby tightly. When she cut an opening big enough, she ran through the flames to the street, a second ahead of another explosion. The flames and smoke billowed behind her as she ran with the little baby, using her plasma sword to deflect the falling planks of fire.

The media cameras caught the rescue scene: Shanna holding the baby in her arm, slashing the burning, falling boards and ceiling with her plasma sword, and emerging from the collapsing building; now a veritable inferno. The Firemen and medics ran up to her and took the baby, and she sheathed her plasma sword. They hosed Shanna down, and the smoke rose off her body. When she took off her helmet, she asked, "Is the baby all right? Is he still alive? His mother died protecting her son."

The infant was carefully unbundled from his blankets and began crying again. Everyone breathed a sigh of relief. The journalists crowded around a smudged-face Shanna, congratulating her and asking dozens of questions. The trained Emissary of the Empress Kayla handled the media frenzy well. She gave all credit for saving lives to the Firemen and rescue personnel. "This terrible incident could have been much worse without the immediate response of your Capital City Fire and Rescue. They evacuated hundreds of residents you see behind you. The Firemen and women and medical personnel are your heroes and deserve the gratitude of the people today." She led the media group to the Fire Captain, who took over the interview.

The three Rangers, Admiral Mae, and their shuttle pilots boarded the shuttle, as the rescued evacuees cheered and applauded. Sham'S and L'Mun were dropped off at the Space Base, and the shuttle continued to Admiral Mae's home on the harbor.

After Shanna came out of the shower, she relaxed on the sofa with Mae, watching the Evening News. The lead story was the explosion of the power station and subsequent gas line eruptions. Featured in the segment were short scenes of Sham'S rescuing the little girl, the spectacular scene of the baby's rescue by Shanna, and her interview.

Her comm link began ringing with recognized tones. "Oh crap!" She mumbled and jumped off the sofa.

She sat her comm link on the table, kneeled, and answered the call from Empress Kayla, "We gave you the weekend off to relax, Master Commander Shanna. Is this how our favorite Kaylan Ranger chooses to spend her free time, assisting the Capital City Fire and Med crews, and rescuing an infant from a raging inferno?"

Shanna tried to suppress her smile but failed. "Not usually, my Empress Kayla."

Both the Empress and Shanna laughed. Then Kayla said, "We are very proud of our Kaylan Ranger, and our Royal Physician Admiral Mae. Enjoy your weekend," she said with a big smile, and clicked off.

"Why did you say, 'Oh crap,' Shanna?" A curious Mae asked. "You're her favorite."

"We're not supposed to talk with the media or be on-camera—for any reason," she answered. "I'm certain my Commander Superior will have a few words to say about it. Why didn't they interview Sham'S?" She asked and sat down again.

"Sham'S rescued the girl and risked his life in the process. You and Sham'S both were heroes today. But your rescue of the baby was incredibly dramatic, Shanna. My heart nearly stopped when the burning building collapsed with you inside. Seeing you emerge from the inferno, fighting back the falling debris with your plasma sword; it was truly incredible! The media recorded your thrilling rescue and caught the entire astounding scene," Mae explained, and put her arm around her reluctant heroine.

Another call beeped on her comm link, from Sham'S, "Hello, hero Shanna. Thought I'd give you a head's-up. High Ranger Lady Bette just chewed my fanny royally for being on-camera. She's gonna have a field day with you, my friend," he said, as L'Mun laughed in the background. "Good luck!"

The expected beep from Lady Bette came next. Before she answered, Shanna asked, "Can I have one of your vodka shots, Mae?" Mae made drinks for them, while the newest media-darling got read the "riot act" from Lady Bette. After the too-long call, Mae and Shanna enjoyed their drinks and cuddled. Then one more call beeped. "My Commander Superior, now," she groaned.

C.S. Javette said, "You know why I'm calling, Shanna. If Lady Bette asks, tell her how severe I was with you. You have made all Rangers very proud today. Dinner's on me next week. Javette out." Shanna and Mae toasted, and resumed enjoying their weekend together.

Brother D'Avid called Empress Kayla unexpectedly in a few days. "My Great Empress Kayla: Information regarding our former High Priest S'Lovik has caused much disturbance in our Holy Caste Order, as you might expect. His deception affected many brothers and sisters. I wish to inform you fourteen of our monks at the Temple of the Creator on Xau have confessed their involvement to their brothers and sisters of the Holy Caste Order. Their full roster of deeds performed includes storing weapons and hiding traitors of the old Rebellion, five years ago; helping S'Lovik embezzle donations from the Faithful; and assisting the traitors of the Plan of the Thirteen against the Empire."

"The five senior monks have committed ritual suicide to atone for their transgressions," he said, bowing his head. "But Elder Priestess T'Char has recommended we turn over the disposition of the youngest monks and one nun to your good judgement," he said.

Considering his new information carefully, she asked, "Have any of the young monks or the nun admitted being influenced by the former High Priest S'Lovik? Young people sometimes have a strong desire to please authority, and can be more easily coerced," she said. This matter required tactful treatment. No offense could be made to the Holy Caste. Kayla knew they were working feverishly to prove their worth to their devout Empress, and to retain their independence.

Brother D'Avid answered, "Each of them took instructions from S'Lovik, or Brother D'Ridi, the confessed ringleader, who worked for S'Lovik directly. The young nun was S'Lovik's lover whenever he visited the Temple on Xau."

Kayla said, "Those young monks and nun were clay in the hands of S'Lovik. Let me ask one more question of you: Do you and the esteemed Elder Priestess T'Char feel there is a good possibility these monks and nun can truly repent, perform their penance, and live as dedicated Holy Men and Woman of our Creator?"

After a few moments of thought, Brother D'Avid answered, "They have each confessed and asked forgiveness from their brothers and sisters. The monks anticipate being sent to the caves of the hermit monks on Ban'Ti for penance."

"And the nun?" Kayla asked.

He sighed deeply and replied, "Priestess T'Char said Sister B'Kah is disillusioned and has lost her faith in the Creator. She was very distressed when she heard of S'Lovik's practice of the Dark Magic."

"Then, let us be fair with each one. The young monks and the nun are to be given opportunity to confess their involvement in the old Rebellion and the Plan of the Thirteen, in the Main Court of Home World. We want them to view the devastation of the Royal Palace Complex with their own eyes and see what their Master intended to happen to millions of innocent people throughout the Empire. We will personally deliver sentencing afterwards," she said. "Elder Priestess T'Char may accompany them, along with yourself, if you desire, Brother." He agreed, and they clicked off.

The transport landed on the Capital City Base one week later, after making a tour of the destroyed Imperial Naval Base. Each monk and the nun looked out the window at the ongoing repair and reconstruction efforts. "More than one hundred eighty people were killed here, and hundreds more injured. The rubble has already been cleared away," Brother D'Avid told them. They transferred to an Imperial shuttle.

"Wait until you see the Palace," their guard said.

Flying slowly over the Palace Complex, the young monks saw nineteen demolished buildings, and men and machinery actively working to carefully remove the rubble. The nun reached for the air sickness bag and vomited violently when she recognized Coroner's shuttles on the grounds. When their Imperial shuttle landed, the monks and nun were made to walk among the rubble for more than an hour to witness destruction for themselves, close up. The monks were escorted to prison cells in the Imperial Army Base.

The young nun was taken to the small chapel on the Base. Sister B'Kah was led to an alcove near the front and told to sit. She was terribly afraid of what they might do to her. The trembling nun watched four Rangers dressed in black garments walk inside the chapel and stand by the door. A tall woman in a long cloak entered, dropped some credits into the offertory urn, and walked to the altar. Elder Priestess T'Char met the tall woman at the altar and they bowed to each other. Then both women walked toward the alcove.

Priestess T'Char said, "Kneel before our Great Empress Kayla." The frightened nun kneeled and bowed her head.

Kayla said, "Please rise, and be seated." The young nun sat on the bench, and the Empress sat next to her. T'Char quietly walked away. "Please tell me how a devout nun was turned into a criminal saboteur, and a traitor against the fourteen billion people of our Empire," the Empress said.

Sister B'Kah began to softly cry, and Kayla handed her a new handkerchief. After a few minutes, she told her story of being sent to the Temple on Xau, away from her family on Home World. The visiting High Priest soon chose the lonely, young nun for an assistant. He seduced her with promises of love everlasting.

"S'Lovik said we would build a new Temple on M'Wati, and minister to the people there. He said we would be together always once the Empire was broken up and each planet became independent. But he never said anything about violence, and fighting, and deaths. He lied to me! I know it now, Empress Kayla. I read the report and saw the vids of his secret apartment. He used me! I was so stupid. How many people died because of my ignorance and blind love for the heretic?" She burst into tears.

Kayla waited a few seconds, then replied, "Fortunately, no one died as a result of the work you performed for the traitor S'Lovik. We discovered the hidden weapons cache just in time and removed the weapons of destruction from the Holy Temple. But what neither you, nor I, nor our former Emperor P'Lau knew was, the men S'Lovik worked with used the old Rebellion to distract our Imperial forces, to hide their true purpose. The destruction here in Capital City you saw today is what they intended to happen in every city, on each planet. They planned the destruction of the Empire, many people, and our self," she disclosed.

The young nun looked at her Empress for the first time, as Kayla studied her face. Trained in understanding body language, Kayla watched the nun try to grasp the full scope of what she heard. "How could the Creator let such men work for evil this way, Empress Kayla? He could have stopped them! So many killed. So many," she said.

Kayla answered, "We are all given free will. Those men turned away from our Creator. But He blessed us with many who worked long, tireless nights, and fought many battles to turn the tide, and become victorious. Our goal is to usher in a New Peace and Reconciliation: A Golden Dawn of Harmony, Peace, and Justice for everyone," she said.

Looking at her Sovereign, Sister B'Kah said, "S'Lovik said you were evil. But I see no evil in you, Empress Kayla. What shall I do? What happens to me now? How can I possibly atone for my sins? What penance could I possibly perform to appease the Creator?"

"Discuss these questions with Priestess T'Char. She is very wise. We only ask you to appear in our Main Court and disclose your involvement. The people need closure. We all serve the Empire, and the Creator of us all," Kayla said, and walked out of the chapel.

XXI

Thunder rumbled, and rain beat against the balcony door. Her wet cloak dripped onto the new flooring. Shanna tried to hide her nervousness, pacing while she waited in the Royal Suite foyer. Someday the Palace reconstruction would be finished, and she could walk from her office to the Royal Suite inside hallways. But for now, she had to dash from one building to another in the pouring rain.

"May I take your cloak?" The lady attendant asked, noticing Shanna's puddle of raindrops on the floor. She removed her wet cloak for the attendant.

Soon she was invited into the private study for her friend and Empress. She thanked Empress Kayla for her time, and began her rehearsed request: "My Empress, I would first like to thank you for your tolerance of this Kaylan Ranger's sexual orientation. Never have I felt any prejudicial treatment from you, either as my Empress, or as my Commander, when I was a new Ranger."

Kayla commented, "Our Creator loves variety in His people. You worked very hard as a new Ranger, Shanna. Every day your work is an example of total commitment and focus, for which I am truly grateful."

"Thank you, Empress Kayla. What I am here to ask you is whether a Life Partnership between Admiral Mae and myself would be approved. If Admiral Mae agrees," she added.

The Empress smiled at the corner of her mouth. She asked, "You seek your Empress' approval before asking your Admiral? Should it not be the other way around, Shanna?"

They laughed softly together, and Shanna answered, "I need to know whether a non-traditional Life Partnership request will be approved before I broach the subject with her. I know of no other such partnership for one of your Rangers, your Majesty," she answered anxiously. "I am sworn by blood oath to my Empress for my service, my will, and my life. Without your approval—and your blessing—it would be futile to ask Admiral Mae,

Great Empress Kayla."

Shanna watched her Empress' face as she considered her request. "The Holy Caste Order forbids marriage between same-sex couples. But, as a Ranger, you cannot marry. You are mine," Kayla said with a smile, and a wiggle of the ring finger on her left hand. Every Kaylan Ranger wore their Confirmation Ring, a long, pure gold ring bearing the Imperial seal, filled with precious gems—including the Empress. Shanna raised her left hand and smiled.

"And because you belong to your Empress, my beautiful, brave Shanna, I will set a precedent, and approve a Life Partnership Agreement Request from you and Admiral Mae. Assuming, of course, you are bold enough to ask her, and she is wise enough to agree!" Kayla answered. They laughed together, and a relieved Shanna knelt and thanked her Sovereign. On her way out, the attendant returned her cloak, dry and freshly pressed. She swirled her cloak over her shoulders and ran outside in the rain to her office, happily letting the raindrops pelt her smiling face. *Kayla said yes. Would Mae?*

The glass of white wine was room temperature by now and tasted funny. Shanna sat in the bar waiting anxiously for Mae to arrive at the exclusive restaurant. She was rarely late; maybe she changed her mind about meeting for dinner. Shanna pushed away the wine glass and wondered if Admiral Mae would agree to Life Partnership with her. Was *she* ready for this step?

Empress Kayla tolerated their relationship; but how would Admiral Mae be treated by her stuffy Imperial Navy Admirals and staff at the Naval Hospital, if they became Partners? Shanna's friends knew she was gay, and it was okay. But several other Rangers snubbed her. Admiral Mae commanded over two hundred Naval Hospital personnel. Would she jeopardize her position?

"What's bothering you, Shanna?" Mae asked, sitting at her table. She was so deep in thought she didn't see Mae enter the restaurant.

"Just some work stuff. Let's get our booth, okay?" They were seated at a private booth overlooking the ocean. They ordered drinks and then enjoyed a fabulous dinner together.

After a pause, Shanna said, "As a Ranger, I live wherever my Empress chooses, either on Home World, or one of the other planets; or a Space Base. I've been lucky to have lived at the Palace here for the last few years. But that could change, according to the needs of the Empire. Even the Rangers with kids and partners sometimes get split up for a while."

Mae said, "I know, Shanna. Until I was appointed Royal Physician, it was never a sure thing I'd get to stay assigned to Home World. Is something up?" She asked, now looking intently at Shanna.

Shanna put her left hand on the table, touched her Confirmation Ring, and said, "This ring was placed on my finger on my Confirmation Day, when I swore my life, my service, and my will to Emperor P'Lau. When Empress Kayla ascended, I swore my blood oath to her for my life, my service, and my will. Every Ranger belongs to our Empress, including me."

Mae sat back and said, "This conversation is getting heavy, Shanna. Just tell me plainly what is up, please." She emotionally braced for unwelcome news: Shanna's reassignment off-Home World; or them breaking up. *Did she find someone else?*

Leaning forward, Shanna said, "I need you to understand my position, and life commitment, Mae. It's important. You need to know these things before we go on. Before you decide," she said.

"Decide what, exactly?" Mae asked defensively.

She reached into her jacket pocket and took out a blue box wrapped with a gold ribbon. "Before you decide to be my Life Partner, Mae." Shanna slowly pushed the box in front of a stunned Mae.

Mae opened the box. Inside were two plain gold bands. "No gemstones are permitted, or any fancy bands. They have to be plain, Mae," Shanna explained. "If you need time," she began, looking at her.

"Can we do this? Is it permitted for a same-sex couple? Marriage between us is not permitted, I know," Mae asked, trying to remain calm.

"Marriage is not available to any Ranger. I belong to Empress Kayla. But we are permitted to have a Life Partner, Mae," Shanna answered with a smile. "I already asked permission from my Empress."

She asked with a surprised look, "You asked her permission, first?"

Shanna laughed and admitted, "She was kind of surprised, too. But it's never happened before; a same-sex Partnership in the Rangers. The few gay Rangers usually keep separate apartments and are very discreet. Empress Kayla must approve our request, if you say 'Yes.' So, I made sure she would approve, if you agree," she explained, with a sexy smile.

"You know I'm divorced, Shanna," Mae admitted. "My parents never liked my former husband, so divorcing was no problem. But they haven't …embraced my becoming gay."

"They'll like me, Mae; don't worry. I'm a trained Emissary," she said confidently. "My Father knew I was gay long before I did."

"I never dreamed you'd do this, Shanna. I'll need time to consider this; a lot of time. About two seconds!" She answered, "Yes, my beautiful Shanna. Let's become Life Partners. I'll thank our Empress Kayla for sharing you!" They held hands, laughed, and talked about the future.

Their Life Partnership Agreement Request was sent to Empress Kayla the next morning. She approved it and attached the note: "We have created the legal precedent for your Life Partnership. In doing so, we fully expect to be invited to your Ceremony!"

Southern Home World Mountains—one month later

The mountain resort was fully booked, and Viscount T'Sur walked around the outdoor reception area to make certain everything was perfect. He donated his resort's banquet facilities to his Empress' favorite Kaylan Ranger for her ceremony. He peeked in the prep salon to look at the beautiful ladies, and they summarily ushered the gentleman away—with another glass of sparkling wine, and many smiles.

The musicians were playing soft, mellow music, while guests and family members of Admiral Mae were shown to their seats. The first two Imperial shuttles landed, and off-loaded dozens of Imperial Guards and twelve Borgund Rangers in white coats and ties. "Do I look okay?" A nervous Bek'R asked, and his friends assured him he looked sharp. The bright sunshine provided a glorious day.

Air Corps fighters escorted the last Imperial shuttle containing the Royal Family, Lady Bette, G'Rosk, and Javette. They disembarked without the usual fanfare and were shown to their place of honor. Baron and Baroness P'Lau, and Admiral Olm and Tara followed, with more Rangers. "We should've had the ceremony in the Royal Court," Elder Ranger K'Laud mumbled, and got an elbow in his ribs from his partner, Elder Ranger C'Lu. They were seated while the Imperial Guards took their posts behind the Royal Family. Only the working Imperial Guards and Rangers were in uniform today.

The Rangers in their white jackets fidgeted while they waited, straightening their ties. The music changed to the processional, and the Ranger groomsmen took their places along the sides of the aisle. The bridesmaids were escorted by the Rangers in the white jackets. Admiral Mae's Mother, Captain Grace, entered, and then retired Colonel Jas'N proudly walked his daughter Mae to the front, followed by retired Master Commander Mak, escorting his daughter Shanna.

Shanna wore the very expensive sky-blue dress ensemble she wore the night of Empress Kayla's Coronation, while impersonating her at several parties, and during the failed coup d'état. She looked stunning in the blue dress and high-collared coat; the dress decorated with threads of pure spun gold. Mae wore an ivory dress ensemble, also trimmed in gold. Her face glowed with pride, and she looked radiant.

Being a civil ceremony, the exchange of Partnership vows was short. Rings were placed on each woman's right hand, in accordance with Ranger Partnership regulations. When the justice said, "I now pronounce you 'Life Partners.' You may kiss," Shanna and Mae kissed tenderly in front of their family and the audience. The Rangers and guests cheered and applauded their perfect kiss and the reception began. Sparkling wine was served to everyone, along with a wonderful dinner.

Sitting close to the Empress, Mak said, "Begging the Empress' pardon, but you look so familiar, your Majesty." After several minutes' conversation with her and G'Rosk, they discovered Mak had shadowed her Father, Master Commander Tom'S, for two years, as a new Ranger. "You're little Kayla? Please forgive me, your Majesty. Your late Father Tom'S was the best fighter pilot of all of us. We fought several campaigns together. Your Mother was beautiful, and the fiercest fighter of any Shi'Lon Ranger I'd ever seen," Mak revealed. "You have her long black hair, my Empress."

Empress Kayla smiled graciously, and introduced Mak to her brother, Admiral Olm. Mak was honored to meet the Son of Tom'S. Mak then bowed to his former Emperor, now Baron P'Lau. Kayla enjoyed the afternoon relaxing with the guests and new Partners. She listened while Grace and Jas'N argued about which one of them Shanna liked better, and softly laughed.

When Bek'R danced with Shanna, he whispered in her ear, "I'm so proud of you. Doing this took guts. But you still hold my heart, my beautiful Shanna." They looked at each other, briefly remembering their past times together, and smiled.

All the guests had fun, including Viscount T'Sur, who was honored more than once for his generous wedding gift. He shyly waited until Mae and Shanna came to ask him to dance, and proudly took a turn with each beautiful woman. The new Partners escaped early and shuttled to a southern beach resort for their short, three-day honeymoon.

XXII

Home World Royal Palace

Three hundred anxious military VIPs, new aristocrats, and Royal courtiers stood in the morning sun, awaiting the Grand Reopening of Main Court. The Empress waved away her ladies, put on her dark blue breastplate and backplate, and her new, matching arm bands. Her ladies placed her favorite Warrior Empress Emerald crown on her thick, black hair, and put on her Royal Blue robe.

"You're magnificent, Empress Kayla!" Consort Dan'L proudly said with a big smile and held his arm out for her. "There must be fifty media broadcasters downstairs, and even more outside. Hundreds of cameras. But no pressure, my Empress." They laughed and walked down the long, winding staircase together, the cameras buzzing; then her personal Borgund and Kaylan Ranger guards took over.

At the stroke of ten o'clock, the new, gleaming doors of the Main Court opened, and the audience hurried to their places, noticing the decorating changes their Empress made. The old Main Court was over eight hundred years old, dark, and had a musty smell from the ancient building stones. The floor was also stone and dark marble columns supported the high ceiling.

The new Main Court was the same size and shape, and also had exposed wooden beams and a few stone walls. But modern lighting was recessed everywhere, highlighting the oiled, natural wood-paneled walls and seating areas. Instead of hard wooden benches, cushioned seating provided greater comfort for the courtiers. The titled aristocrats sat in open opera-box areas, complete with small vid screens inside the boxes. The draperies were deep red, complementing the red marble columns and floor.

"This is so beautiful! And the decorator colors are so subtle, yet harmonious touches to enhance the audience experience," a media announcer said into the camera. "Today will be a very formal entrance of all the Court VIP's!"

One sour-faced courtier complained, "How much will our taxes be raised to pay for this opulence? Just look at those red marble columns and floor. A ten percent increase, at least." He settled into his comfy seat and scowled.

With four deep chimes, the Official Advisors entered, the last of whom was Chief Advisor Baron P'Lau. Next, the Great Council of Barons entered, each man dressed in his finest clothing. The Lords and Ladies entered and took their places behind the Advisors. Viscount T'Sur entered and stood with his Barons.

Two columns of Imperial Guards marched in, wearing their deep purple robes and carrying powerful pulser spears. They flanked the Court floor along the columns. Fifty-seven Kaylan Rangers in their formal, red uniform dresses and cloaks marched in, their red, high-heeled boots making a distinctive sound. Then one hundred sixty-two Borgund Rangers marched in, their heavy boot steps resounding through the Court. Main Court was nearly full.

Imperial Guards surrounded the throne area, then Empress Kayla entered, followed by her personal Rangers and Imperial Guardsmen. Thunderous applause and cheering continued for several minutes. When she sat on her new levitating throne, all her Guardsmen and Rangers knelt on their right knees.

High Ranger Lady Bette announced, "Our Great Benevolent Empress Kayla, Ruler over all Known Worlds and Conqueror of the Unknown Domain. All hail Empress Kayla!" The Rangers perfectly performed their Royal Salute, then sheathed their plasma swords and stood. They led the cheer, "Hail Empress Kayla! Hail Empress Kayla!" The audience applauded loudly again.

The Empress bowed her head and raised her scepter to quiet the crowd, and said, "Thank you all for attending our Grand Reopening of the Main Court. Our Home World Royal Palace is arising from its ashes!" More applause and cheers. "The basic design from the original blueprints is the same, but we made a few modifications," she said with a little smile. "Do you like them?" Approving applause and cheers filled the Court.

Very large vid screens shimmered into view, without any visible mechanical support. Three-D models of the buildings for restoration were shown, and she very briefly described them. Then she said, "Our new design required the acquisition of more land. Our Royal Palace will now receive the protection of defensive shields, already fully functional." The model was covered by an iridescent energy shield. The audience approved.

"Before we continue to the awards presentation, there is one side note we wish to make. We have heard and read the comments from around our Empire, estimating the costs associated with rebuilding our Royal Palace, and the full Complex, eventually. We have even heard absurd rumors of exorbitant tax increases to be levied on our people, and it bothered us a great deal," she said.

She raised her new throne a meter off its landing and proclaimed: "Not one credit of taxpayer funds has been used to rebuild this Main Court, nor will any taxes be raised to pay for the Palace rebuilding and improvements! The traitors involved with the attacks on our Space Cadre vessels and bases, M'Wati, K'Halon Prime, and Home World have had their Imperial Beneficiary status revoked. These evil traitors caused the deaths and destruction, and their former wealth will pay for our rebuilding!"

The entire Court erupted in applause, and the cheer "Hail Empress Kayla!" resounded again. Many awards, commendations, and bonuses were merited over the next two hours. Each recipient humbly bowed, thanked their Empress, and returned to their place. After a short half hour break, everyone reassembled. The Rangers now stood on either side, leaving the Court floor open for more business.

High Ranger Lady Bette announced, "We are blessed to present our Holy Caste Order priests and priestesses." Thirty priests and priestesses entered the Court lining the center. A very elderly priest announced, "Our Holy Caste Order now presents our new High Priestess T'Char, and our new High Priest K'Ramm! They will bless this Main Court and all within its walls, and everyone in our Great Empire," he said. The big fire altar was brought in, and incense burned.

Dressed in their finest white and gold robes and tall hats, the highest members of the Holy Caste Order walked up three steps on either side of the throne. In unison, they prayed over the Main Court, blessed them, and everyone watching throughout the R'Genra System. Then, they blessed Empress Kayla and Prince Lukus, and the Royal Consort Dan'L. It was very moving. The priests stepped off to the side, behind the Empress.

"The Leader of all monks, Brother D'Avid," Lady Bette announced, and he came forward.

The Brother spoke, "With the permission of our Benevolent Empress Kayla, the Holy Caste Order wishes to present those among our Caste who have transgressed against the Empire, its people, their Empress, and our Creator. They have come to seek the just sentence of our Empress for their deeds," he said. The young monks and nun walked into the Court, each one bound by their hands, but wearing their religious clothing.

Each monk confessed his involvement with Brother D'Ridi, who directly plotted against their Leader Brother D'Avid, and the Empire. They confessed their work for former High Priest S'Lovik in storing weapons and traitors and helping embezzle donations from the Faithful. The young nun confessed her involvement, and her relationship with the former High Priest. Then, they knelt and bowed their heads, awaiting judgement and sentencing.

Empress Kayla began, "We are honored by the highest tier of the Holy Caste Order bringing forward their monks and nun. The Holy Caste Order chose to bring these young men and woman to our Main Court, although there is no Holy Caste law requiring them to do so. Rather than have our heavily burdened High Court prepare cases against them, these young people came before us to confess their guilt," she said.

"Each guilty one kneeling before us does so of his or her own volition, voluntarily. Their guilt, deeds, and involvement have been entered into the Official Record. The young monks and nun before you have shown remorse for their deeds, and contrition. It is not our wish to interfere with Holy Caste Order and their laws. But the people of our Empire require closure," she said.

She rose in her levitating throne and flew in front of the monks, and asked, "What punishment is deserved for your crimes against the people of our Empire, and what restitution will each of you pay?"

One young monk rose and said, "I pledge my service to our Empire, to assist the laborers repairing and rebuilding the Royal Palace and the Navy Base. I promise to work hard for as long as it takes, my Benevolent Empress Kayla." The other young men each stood and repeated his promise.

Then the nun stood and said, "I pledge my service to the people of the Empire and our Creator, to assist the wounded to heal, and the displaced to find good homes. I promise to work hard for as long as it takes to rebuild and recover, my Great Empress Kayla."

The Empress rose higher in her throne and asked the Main Court audience, "Shall we allow the penitent Servants of our Creator the chance to rebuild our Royal Palace and our Imperial Naval Base for us? What say you, my people?" Cheers and applause grew from a scant few to a loud volume of acceptance.

"Then we accept your offers. Let the record reflect their promises. May the Creator bless his Holy Servants," the Empress said, and lowered her throne to its place. The monks and nun were led out of the Court to apartments near the Temple.

When the crowd quieted, Empress Kayla moved her left hand, and Prince Lukus stepped up beside her. He raised his arms and said, "May our Creator bless every person in our R'Genra System. Let the feast begin!" Cheers, laughter, and applause rang through the Court, and the servants rushed in with long tables, more chairs, and dozens of dishes of sumptuous foods. Large decanters of wine served all the courtiers and aristocrats, and the people became very merry. Kayla left the feast early, while the party continued for the better part of the evening.

When Dan'L returned to their suite, he laid his sleeping Son on his bed, and the nanny watched the boy. "The Empress changed and went outside, Consort Dan'L," her attendant said. Dan'L looked out the window and saw Kayla in workout clothing going through T'Ly routines with High Priest K'Ramm on the private lawn. His jealousy began to rise; then he saw his Mother Javette join in, followed by G'Rosk, Shanna, and several other Rangers. He shook his head, changed clothes, and ran downstairs to join everyone.

The young monks kept their promise, working from dawn to dusk every day, clearing the rubble, bringing in materials, and performing any task assigned to them, until both the Royal Palace and Imperial Naval Base were nearly completed.

The nun assisted in the local hospitals with the survivors, tending to their needs. She worked in whichever facility needed her the most. When the Naval Hospital was rebuilt, she volunteered there, until every survivor was healed and released.

Neither the monks nor the nun accepted any form of payment, other than room and board. Empress Kayla donated one 10,000-credit bar for every month they worked to the Temple of the Creator on Xau.

XXIII

Lord T'Sel waited anxiously in the parlor of the new Royal Suite. Only months ago, young Empress Kayla was nearly starved to death. His advancing age and unfamiliarity with the new Vee Lok technology made him bow out, and turn the Empress' recovery over to the younger, more advanced Imperial Navy Physician, Admiral Mae. She was the new Royal Physician.

F.C. Bek'R opened the Suite door and escorted Lord T'Sel to the Empress' private office. He looked at the Suite's new décor, momentarily distracted by the novel changes in color, textures, style and lighting. The Empress found her missing guest.

"Do you like our changes, Lord T'Sel?" Kayla asked.

He blushed, realizing he became too absorbed in the décor, and apologized, "My eyes have seen the same Royal suite for more than forty years, Empress Kayla. You kept the rooms and layout the same, but your décor changes everything! It is so modern and brightly lit. It looks like a new high-rise hotel penthouse, with tasteful trim and fabrics. Amazing," he commented.

They enjoyed talking over lunch. Kayla watched him become more energized and his face look happier. "How do you like your estate, Lord T'Sel? Have you visited all your properties yet?" She asked.

His face fell and he looked tired again. He said, "My wife loves the mansion. My grown sons and daughter, their spouses, and my grandchildren enjoy the mansion and its grounds, the horses, and all the wondrous woods surrounding us."

Kayla asked, "Has your Empress unintentionally burdened our former Royal Physician? Our wish was to reward you for a lifetime of service to three Sovereigns, Lord T'Sel."

"For which I felt necessary, my Empress. My only purpose now is signing checks," he said. "The income flows in; the payments go out." He sighed again.

She pursed her lips and said, "Well, we have a new challenge for our former Royal Physician, if you are interested." He lifted his face and eagerly awaited her saying, "We are in serious need of someone who can probe the minds of the most heinous criminals in the history of our Empire. These two men have expertly lived two lives for over thirty years: one as loyal, titled aristocrats; the other as hidden traitors, and funders not only of the old Rebellion, but also the Plan of the Thirteen. One of these men is an original signer of the Plan, a very cunning deceiver. Both planned the total obliteration of the Imperial Military forces, our Imperial Guards, our Rangers, and our self!"

He asked, "I assume truth serum and the usual interrogation techniques have been employed. Any corporal punishment? Torture? Hypnosis?"

She stood and walked to the window and replied, "Truth serum and gas; the usual interrogation methods by my Rangers and Army specialists; and some light corporal punishment. I am no fan of torture, although the Ranger method of coercion with blades has been used," she revealed. "But these men are so evil and corrupt; we cannot break them. One, in particular, actually became sexually aroused whenever more physical methods were used. He's disgusting," she said with a grimace.

"A sado-masochist, Empress Kayla. They are most difficult to break. If he were tortured, he'd probably enjoy it, to a certain degree," Lord T'Sel said. "Is he straight or homosexual?"

"He prefers pre-teen and teen-age boys and kept eight of them in his basement. He even had a room for 'bad boys' to beat and sexually abuse," she divulged. "But he also had three mistresses, with whom he was sexually active. His wife moved away from him many years ago. Small wonder."

The former Royal Physician held his chin for a moment, and then said, "He will need a specialist, or two. One who understands his perversions and needs for conquest. It is power and dominance, at its most basic level, you understand. What about the other man?"

She sat again and answered, "He is no pervert. But he is very private; highly reserved in his family and personal life, and business dealings. He concealed his involvement well for over thirty years, even from his own wife and family. Only his personal shuttle pilot knew anything of his involvement. A very intelligent man, too. But he still has a moral compass remaining. He revealed the secret missile launching system at the Naval Base that destroyed the Royal Palace. Our only warning," she shared.

"My sources told me you evacuated the Palace days before the attack, Empress Kayla," he said. "Do not discount your pre-emptive efforts. You saved thousands of lives, my Lady," and bowed his head.

"Yes, but not all. We lost High Ranger Lord Vu'Duc, two Elder Rangers, and several Imperial Guards. And the Palace Complex. The Imperial Naval Base personnel were hardest hit, with several hundred injured, and over one hundred eighty killed," she said. "Will you assist us gathering the information these men are still concealing from us?"

He bowed his head and said, "Whatever assistance I can offer is yours, Empress Kayla. It will be my greatest privilege to break these evil men and open their minds. When shall I begin?" He excitedly asked.

"The sooner, the better. Right now, if you are able. We have to make absolutely certain there are no other undiscovered conspirators plotting death and destruction of our people," she answered emphatically.

He stood and said, "Let me make a few calls for a specialist for the sado-masochist. Then, I'll begin with your 'Private Prisoner.' Hypnosis, accompanied by a psychotropic cocktail injection should pierce his internal wall," he said with confidence. The anteroom for the private Royal Court was selected. It had comfortable furnishings, with a concealed vid screen for observation. Lord T'Sel made his special calls, then ordered drugs for the hypnosis session. He was not told the name of his prisoner.

Four Imperial Guards led in a gray-haired man, who looked pompous, even in his beige prison uniform, shackles, and cuffs. The two men instantly recognized one another. "Lord K'Vin, please sit on the sofa. Our Empress wishes us to take a trip together today," T'Sel said.

K'Vin snorted and said, "They already drugged me with truth serum many times. They failed, former Royal Physician."

T'Sel responded, "But I will not fail, Lord K'Vin. We will tear down your wall of resistance, brick by brick, memory by memory. Then, we will strip your logical construct to its most rudimentary. If you are cooperative, you will emerge with your mind and personality mostly the same," Lord T'Sel said. "But resistance will be painful and may damage you irreparably, my old friend."

The Guards restrained K'Vin and laid him on the sofa. A male nurse gave him an intravenous injection slowly. "What are you giving me, T'Sel?" He asked suspiciously.

"A cocktail of psychotropic drugs and tranquilizers, Lord K'Vin. If you relax and let it work, the experience may be quite enjoyable. Fight it, and the trip will have other outcomes. There you go. Now, just watch my crystal as it swings back and forth. Back and forth," he repeated softly.

K'Vin went into deep hypnosis. The Physician kept the session primarily regressive and his tone of conversation light. All the way back to the Royal Academy K'Vin tripped, to his boyhood friends there. "Who is your best friend, K'Vin?"

His smile was wide and full, and he answered, "Z'Lun is my best friend, of course. His room is across the hall. We study together and play kickball, you know. He is so popular with the fellows and girls. Z'Lun knows everyone and everything about them."

For three days, Lord T'Sel drugged K'Vin with psychotropics and tranqs, and hypnotized him. His patient enjoyed the experience; but the doctor only got so far. "The man is truly a trained master of mind control. I have never dealt with anyone so resistant, Empress Kayla," he admitted. "We are going to have to increase the dosage and submit him to extreme sensory stimulation, I'm afraid. I'll need access to a holographic room, to induce fear. The man is so controlled; he must become genuinely terrified to break. It is the next step in the process. It will not be pleasant for him."

The Imperial Army Commando Training Facility became the new location for Lord K'Vin's session. "Is this where I get beaten to a pulp by her Imperial Army?" A smirking K'Vin asked, while the Army med techs hooked up his IV, and fully restrained him on a hospital bed. No one answered his question.

The drug and tranq cocktail strength was doubled in his IV, and the room lights were dimmed. A brain scanner was placed on his head, while various holographic images flashed in front of his eyes, projected all over the ceiling and walls of his room. Happy little children playing; beautiful girls in colorful dresses; boys playing in a university kickball tournament; these were the first, pleasant images. Then slowly, more darker images flashed intermittently among the nice ones. The change from light to dark was almost imperceptible for ten minutes. Classical music accompanied the pleasant images, and then faded away.

Slowly, horror was introduced: clip after clip of frightening faces, burned and disfigured by war; deserted, abandoned buildings with blood splattered all inside the floor and walls; vids of actual smoke-filled battles, with Army troops and Rebels fighting one another, dying in agony; horrific vids of the survivors of the M'Wati Nuclear Disaster. The music became louder, with heavier bass and percussion, until K'Vin screamed to turn off the sound.

"Why are you showing this to me? Turn it off! I do not want to see this movie anymore!" He screamed. Drugs were injected in his IV once again.

An anonymous male voice said, "You are not watching a movie. These are actual video recordings from the old Rebellion, which you funded from the very first battle, Lord K'Vin. You sat in your beautiful mansion with your wife and family, eating gourmet food, drinking vintage wines every night, while loyal Imperial troops and Rangers gave their lives to protect the people of our Empire from your Rebels. The attacks are real; the blood is real; and the destruction is real, you pompous fraud! You almost feel it now, don't you?"

Lord K'Vin yelled, "That's what they're paid to do. Fight! Turn it off!" More vids were shown of dismembered bodies; more spilled blood; men begging for food and water, with swollen, cracked lips; and a school being bombed. "Stop it! Stop it!" He yelled.

The male voice said, "You paid for all this mayhem and murder. You and your Plan of the Thirteen traitors paid for the Rebellion, to distract the Imperial forces and our Emperor P'Lau while you recreated the most destructive device in our history. You caused these needless deaths; yet sat safely behind your table, stuffing your aristocratic face full of exquisite food and wine, while our Army troops and Rangers tried to save the people of the Empire from the murderous Rebels. You paid for this. Now watch it!" The vids of battles flashed faster and faster, until the final one: the huge mushroom cloud destroying the M'Wati capital city of N'Well.

"He was never supposed to use the nuclear option. He was only supposed to threaten that spineless Emperor P'Lau with it and force him to step down. We told him specifically not to use it. Duma Wat never did what we told him to do! The Royal Bastard was never going to be the new Emperor. I don't want to see anymore. Stop it! Stop it!" K'Vin yelled.

Then the vid was shown of Baron Z'Lun, holding Empress Kayla roughly by her arm, trying to get her to abdicate. He threatened to blow up Home World and K'Halon Prime, yelling, "Say goodbye to your Empire, little Empress," and pressed a detonator switch again and again.

The anonymous voice said, "Your best friend tried to nuke K'Halon Prime, your home, and Home World. You paid for the destruction of both planets and the deaths of another ten billion people!"

One lone tear rolled down K'Vin's face. Then he said, "It wasn't Z'Lun. He loved the people of K'Halon Prime as much as I do! It was that animal U'Ret. Not Z'Lun!" They replayed the vid of Baron Z'Lun pressing the detonator again and again, and looped it repeatedly, until K'Vin screamed at the top of his voice and tears ran down his face. Then the vids stopped.

"Not true. You said it was U'Ret. Not true. How could you do this, Z'Lun? You lied to me! To me!" He bawled uncontrollably, thrashing his head side to side, fighting the restraints.

The male voice said, "Your unwavering faith in your childhood friend Z'Lun kept you fully committed to the Plan of the Thirteen. Your blind devotion to its grand purpose to restore K'Halon Prime to the seat of power for your would-be Emperor Z'Lun cost the lives of more than one billion innocent men, women, and children of the Empire. You, Lord K'Vin, are as guilty of genocide as U'Ret, Duma Wat, and your friend, Z'Lun!"

Former Lord K'Vin, titled aristocrat, Imperial Beneficiary of more than ninety thousand square kilometers of prime farmland, vineyards, and lands of his beloved K'Halon Prime, was shattered. "We worked for victory for so long. We donated our fortunes to the Plan and the Old Engine. With the Imperial Military and Rangers destroyed, the Warrior Class would be no more. We would have blamed the weak Empress Kayla for their obliteration. We failed. We failed," K'Vin repeated, and started crying again.

"When they finally break this way, it is almost sad. That is, until we remember what he is responsible for enabling. Lord K'Vin never fired one shot; yet he indirectly caused one billion deaths, and the crippling of an entire planet, M'Wati," Lord T'Sel commented to Empress Kayla, observing with him.

"Our parents were killed fighting Rebels. Dan'L's father was, too. We fought in many battles in space, on various planets and asteroids, and space bases, fighting the Rebels of Duma Wat. All were funded by this man and his best friend, Z'Lun. Their coup d'état was defeated the night of our coronation. We were nearly blown up with our family. Our Son was attacked on his fourth birthday. His 'Old Engine' nearly destroyed our entire Imperial Military, the Home World Royal Palace, and the Naval Base," she said emphatically. "The annihilation of our Warrior Class was his ultimate goal."

After a few seconds to compose herself, the Empress ordered her Rangers, "You will continue to gather information from the former Lord K'Vin, using whatever means necessary. The people of our Empire must be safe from those he employed for over thirty years to do his dirty work. Find out if there are any other weapons primed and ready to be used against our people. Traditional, nuclear, chemical, biological; or otherwise. Find them. Make him confess everything!" She stormed out of the observation room.

The former Baron Lep'T lie on the floor of his cell, looking for all intents and purposes like a beached whale. Imperial Guards pulled him up, cuffed him, and led Lep'T down another flight of stairs. "Ah—finally! I get to see the old dungeon! What's on the menu? Whips and chains? The post of pain?" He asked, sounding more excited than sarcastic.

The Guards pushed him inside the old dungeon, but the ancient iron torture devices were gone. They closed and locked the door behind him. A very muscular, bare-chested bald man in leather pants, and a woman with long red hair stood on either side of a tall, black, free-standing cabinet. They wore black cloaks of satin. Lep'T's eyes lit up and he laughed. "So, you've come to play with me? A brute and a dominatrix. How pedestrian. All you will get out of me is semen." He strutted towards them with an arrogant smirk on his face.

The man walked up to Lep'T and chained him to the post. The dominatrix said, "Foolish pig. We are here to perform our finest work. We are not here for your pleasure. We will begin the punishment of an evil, self-serving killer of men, women, and children; and defiler of children of the Creator." She threw off her cape exposing her leather bustier, short leather pants, and thigh-high leather boots.

The bald man whispered in Lep'T's ear, "You know nothing of pain. You will give us your pain. Your blood will spill and flow like a river. Your tears will gush forth unending, and no one will answer your cries. Your weak semen will hide inside, too afraid to rush forth. All you have done to those weaker than you in the past is child's play. We are here to give you a glimpse of the punishment waiting for you in the Afterlife!" They slowly opened the black cabinet.

Lep'T's sarcastic grin went away. He had never seen such tools. No sex toys here. He tried to cry out, but the dominatrix put a muzzle on his mouth, and a collar of spikes around his neck. She looked him in his eyes, and said, "May your past sins engulf you. May our Creator grant you twice what you wished for our Empress Kayla, and her beloved people!"

The observation room emptied. No one could watch Lep'T receive his own medicine; the pain he inflicted on young boys and women for decades. The bald man and dominatrix were hard-core S & M professionals, promised full pardons for their past crimes if they succeeded extracting a complete confession from the former Baron Lep'T. They took him into the world of deep, darkest sadism. He screamed and cried for hours, several days unending.

XXIV

Handwritten confessions from both Lord K'Vin and Baron Lep'T were addressed to, "Our Beloved and Benevolent Empress Kayla." Neither man was too injured—mentally or physically—to miss their day in Main Court before the High Court Tribunal Justices. Both men waived their right to trial, and their sentencing took place. Their guilty pleas resulted in each man being sentenced to death by lethal injection.

Hoping to avoid another mob riot, the Empress had both guilty men removed quickly from her Court by the Imperial Guards. Then she announced, "Hundreds of canisters of sarin gas, cholera, anthrax, and various other chemicals and biological weapons were located from the confessions of the two guilty criminals. At significant risk to our Imperial Army Hazard Materials Teams, the deadly canisters were removed. They have been incinerated and destroyed, and the ashes placed in sealed containers, launched by one-way probes into the Unknown Domain."

"To further remove any potential planet-killing destructive force from our R'Genra solar system, we have ordered the complete disassembly of all nuclear warheads. There will be no nuclear, biological, or chemical weapons threatening our beloved people of the Empire!" She said with passion in her voice.

The Main Court audience of six hundred courtiers, aristocrats, military VIPs, and Rangers applauded loudly. Then, cheers of "Hail Empress Kayla!" were heard throughout the Court. She stood and bowed her head to her people, raised her arms, and left the Court. Only her Imperial Guards saw the tears falling down her face.

"Did we get all of it? Have all the concealed arsenals of the old Rebellion and the Plan of the Thirteen been seized and destroyed? We wish no more threats of any kind for our people. We must move forward toward peace!" Empress Kayla said.

"Yes, Empress Kayla. The men confessed all they knew," Lord T'Sel said confidently.

"All we could get out of them, anyway. Your efforts were remarkable, Lord T'Sel," Lady Bette said. "I hope we asked all the right questions."

C.S. Javette commented, "The bald man and woman who worked on former Baron Lep'T were cool, professional, and frightening. I know coercion. But my efforts pale, in comparison," she admitted. "And I have absolutely no desire to learn any of their methods! I could not stand to watch them." They agreed with her.

The Empress commanded, "Focus now on the Technicians who worked on their 'Old Engine.' Forensic reports delivered to us this morning revealed all missile launch units are Space Cadre design from the last three to five years. We want to know how hundreds of medium and large missiles were procured. Were they stolen? Where are the reports of theft? Who made them; who transported them to the hidden launch sites; and who installed them? Find out, and let us discover where else additional missile sites and weapons caches are located. This is a top-priority assignment for our Borgund Rangers and the Space Cadre," a stern Empress Kayla ordered her Ranger High Command and Military Advisors. The Commanders Superior were dismissed, but the Military Advisors were told to remain.

Reading the recent missile and "Old Engine" forensic executive summaries once more, the Empress breathed deeply to contain her anger. "We read this morning's report from Space High Command. The 'Plan of the Thirteen' conspirators worked their treason and sabotage during our reign. They are still at large. Some may be actively serving aboard our vessels in space, or at Space Cadre High Command," she said, searching the faces of her highest Military Advisors. "We must make certain the Old Engine threat is no more!" They blankly stared at her.

"You will find these traitors, bring them to Home World, and turn them over to our Temporary Security Advisor C.S. G'Rosk for interrogation. We want the traitors who rebuilt those missile launchers, stole the missiles, programmed the computers, and loaded the missiles found," she ordered. "Whoever issued the commands for the Old Engine attacks is your priority target. He is to be found and brought before me."

The Military Advisors looked at their reports quietly. The Empress stood, slammed both hands on the table, and yelled, "Why are you here reading? Get these traitors and criminals NOW!" Her uncharacteristic anger lit a fire under the men, and they ran back to their offices.

The Royal Consort entered her private Royal Court, passing the Military Advisors. No one stopped to speak with him. He casually asked, "What's got into your Advisors, my Empress? They looked like they're running from a fire," Dan'L commented.

"The fire's under their behinds. Here, Dan'L. Read this forensic report, and let's discuss it with Olm tonight at dinner. They rebuilt the bloody missile launchers during my reign. Right under our nose! Bloody hell!" She exclaimed, and ordered the guilty conspirators imprisoned on Ban'Ti re-interrogated. "We must ask the right questions to obtain the right answers," she said, and he nodded.

Home World Palace Prison

The short man was taken to B'Nard's cell underground, but not permitted to enter. He saw the many cameras on the prison walls and realized privacy would be impossible. "So, you've come at last," B'Nard said, rising from his cement bed. He walked up to the energy bars to speak with his visitor. "What happens now? They'll execute me when they're tired of asking me questions. Fat Fingers and K'Vin are scheduled to die in a few days," he said sarcastically.

The visitor whispered, "We have one more chance. The Imperial idiots sent the shooter to Ban'Ti. He knows the codes for the Aux Comm. We have enough Technicians there to overrun the prison and take control. The Ram wants you to ask to be sent to Ban'Ti. You can control them."

B'Nard whispered through clenched teeth, "Look, Mon'T, he has no one to order around anymore, no one but you left to do his dirty work, and no gold to pay anyone now. Got it? The Fount is gone. No more gold. No more credits. Don't work for free, Mon'T," B'Nard advised. "We gave them everything, and we lost. It's over. Give it up."

Mon'T smiled and whispered, "The Ram is going to fix everything. He said for you to go to Ban'Ti prison, organize everyone, and wait for the signal. Overtake the prison, release all our men, and escape. The Ram will have a ship ready for everyone," Mon'T whispered. "He said he's ready."

"Then what? We all fly to Home World and piss on the new Palace? We are out of weapons and launchers, Mon'T. We need weapons to fight," he countered.

"He has the big Rebel arsenal at Aux Comm, remember? Plus, more. The Empress Bitch did not find Auxiliary Command. If they can escape and make it to Aux Comm, we have her on her knees! He is our last Alternate. We are sworn to help him, B'Nard. We can make Aux Comm in three days!" Mon'T cried.

"Be quiet, you fool! At least I can only die once. I'm sentenced to death. Ban'Ti will have to rise up without me. Get out before the Ram gets you arrested too, Mon'T. She'll find everything, eventually. She is not the weak little girl they thought. Run far away, Mon'T," B'Nard whispered, "And never look back!"

Mon'T asked, "If the Ram gets you out, will you honor your oath to the last Alternate? They know nothing of the Ram, or the location of the Aux

Comm, B'Nard."

B'Nard said cynically, "If the Ram gets me out and onto his ship, I'm back in business. But he'd better have his ducks in a row, or the Empress Bitch will get all of us." Mon'T smiled and bid B'Nard a good day.

Paradise Island

Supernatural beasts emerged from the dark mist on either side of a huge stack of wood for a bonfire. Carrying ancient weapons of torture and death, the beasts began to chant in an unknown language. The beasts parted when their leader, a figure with the head of a ram and body of a man, slowly walked towards the bonfire. Evil half-man, half-goat beings carried a bloodied woman bound by poisonous, thorned vines to the wood pile. The tortured woman was tied to a long stake, and the stake hoisted upright into the middle of the wood stack. The half-goat beasts threw pots of burning oil onto the wood pile and lit the bonfire. Flames grew from a few flickering fires into a roaring blaze.

A crying boy was brought forth, held aloft by the half-goats, and presented to the Ram. He held the boy so the woman on the stake could watch and sliced his throat. He cut off the boy's head and threw it into the flames at the feet of the burning woman. Her wails of sorrow filled the night, while cheers and more chants came from the beasts at the fire's edge. They kneeled before the Ram-man, raised their arms and bowed to him, while the burning woman screamed in agony. Her flesh began to melt away from her arms and face, and she screeched from horrendous pain.

Dark smoke from the bonfire rose towards the night sky. When the final shriek of death was uttered by the tortured, burning woman, the dark smoke became pure white iridescence. It curled into patterns of infinity signs and spirals, turning inside and out, like billowing, iridescent white clouds. The evil sacrifice was accepted by the Creator of All Things, as He embraced the souls of the tortured woman and her son, and welcomed them into the Afterlife.

Kend'R awoke from the nightmare with a loud cry. He sat upright in his bed, gasping for breath. His body was covered in sweat, his heart raced, and his hands shook like a man with palsy. Rising quickly, he dunked his entire head into a basin of water to fully awaken. Kend'R pulled his mind and psyche out of the nightmare. *Was it a premonition from the Creator?*

Surrounded by three-dimensional holographic star charts and his ephemeris, Kend'R checked and double-checked his calculations, and finally put his forehead into his hands. There was no error. The stars do not lie. Conceal, perhaps; lie, no. He had to talk with her tonight. He took a deep breath and keyed in her private comm link number. Kend'R said, "My beloved Empress, I know you are very busy. But it is imperative I meet with you tonight."

"Master Commander Kend'R; can it not wait until tomorrow? I am buried with tasks and reports," she objected.

"Buried," he said. "How prophetic, my Lady. Please, I beg you, Empress Kayla. I cannot say what I must over the comm link. We must meet. Now. Please, Empress," Kend'R pleaded. "I must see you this very night, as soon as possible!"

Her friend had never been so insistent to see her. His track record was infallible; she had to go. "Are you at the Palace, Kend'R?"

"No, it's not safe or secure there. We must meet secretly. How fast can you be ready for a quick trip outside the Palace, Empress Kayla? I will pick you up myself," he whispered. There was a brief pause.

"Fifteen minutes. Myself, and two Rangers," she said. "Landing site five, at the main site."

"Perfect. Thank you, Empress Kayla." He closed down and password-protected his programs and 3D charts. He grabbed his long cloak, com tablets, and notes, and hurried to his shuttle. They all thought it was over. But another chapter had begun, one whose author was unknown, and whose plot was crystal clear. His Empress and her young Son, Prince Lukus, were targeted for a horrific death by a nefarious enemy.

Empress Kayla ran onboard Kend'R's shuttle with M.C. Shanna and C.S. Javette. They flew back to his "sanctuary," on Paradise Island. All three women wore their black Ranger uniforms, as did Kend'R. He said, "I am permitted to use this bungalow on the Island for meditation. Sometimes I need to get away."

The women knew Kend'R had used his telepathic powers to read the minds of diabolical criminals and traitors and needed solitude to recover. They landed quietly on the dirt site and jogged into the small bungalow. They scanned the property: all clear. Kend'R led the women inside, opened the 3D holograph and his programs, and invited them to sit.

He took a deep breath and said, "I know none of you believe in any of this," and they chuckled. "But it is as clear to me as your faces, my Empress, and Kaylan sisters. You are once again purposefully being diverted from the true path, my Empress. One who has been hidden for many, many years has come into the light to strike you down. He is very powerful, cunning, and ruthless. He is being aided by another," Kend'R said. He began to sweat, and his face became red—a fact Kayla noticed.

She said, "Easy, now, my friend. Now—who is aiding him?"

"Your chart says one you trust without any reserve will bring you to your enemy. He will entrap you, my Empress. They are waiting to ensnare you. This shows the betrayal of one you trust who will bring you before him. His power is surrounding you, even tonight, Empress Kayla. Before the morning light, you will be in his grasp!" Kend'R said to her, pointing at the alignments which prophesized his warning. Then, he very briefly relayed his nightmare to her in whispers, watching her emerald green eyes narrow.

M.C. Shanna said, "Then we will help you escape, my Empress. Somewhere you've never been before. We can hide you away!"

"Not without my Son," Kayla said, "And my Consort."

"He is waiting for you to return," Kend'R said, holding his temples in anguish. "I cannot see his face! But I hear his laughter in my mind. He is very close to you now, and close to your Son."

"We leave now," the Empress said. She turned to Kend'R and asked, "How will I know my betrayer?"

Kend'R closed his holograph and answered, "He will help you escape. Then he will turn on you, like a savage beast. And then it will be too late. I implore you to escape now, my Empress, and do not return to the Palace. Any of you. Please—fly away now!" He closed everything down, and they all ran out of the bungalow and into the shuttle.

C.S. Javette said, "My Empress, my beloved Sovereign and Daughter-in-law; Kend'R is right about my not believing in astrology and predictions. But what if he is right? If they apprehend you again, they will not keep you in a cell for a month. These men are clutching at their last straw. Like a wounded animal in the forest, they know they have little chance to win. They will be ruthless, and their actions will be brutal and final. If you die, your Son has no chance to live. Kend'R is right. We must not let you go back tonight, my Empress," she concluded firmly.

"Please, my faithful friend. Think of your Empire, my Lady. Without our Warrior Empress, all is lost. Please, Empress Kayla," Kend'R begged. He went to her seat and knelt before her, with tears in his eyes. He begged, "Please! It is not the time to fight. It is time for you and your Son to flee!"

She keyed in the top security comm link for her Consort. "Dan'L, listen closely. Lock all the Royal Suite doors immediately. Take our Son down the passageway now. Talk to no one. Do it now, my love! Run as fast as you can. Trust no one you know. Trust no one new. Run, Dan'L. Run!" She cried and clicked off.

Javette took over piloting the shuttle. Kayla sat next to Shanna, looked out the window at the lights of the Royal Palace, and prayed.

Home World Royal Palace

The food server wheeled his cart from the lift to the Royal Suite door and was stopped by two Imperial Guards. "I have a cake, fruit, and whipped cream dessert for Prince Lukus," he said, and raised his hand to knock on the door.

"No one is permitted to disturb the Empress when her doors are locked. Be gone with you!" The Guard said quietly, but firmly.

The servant bowed his head and said, "The Prince will be very unhappy about this." He pushed his cart a couple of meters back to the lift, turned, and blasted both Imperial Guards with his laser pistol. He ran to the Royal Suite door, fired on the locks until the door opened, and rushed inside. The Suite was empty. Prince Lukus' bed felt warm. "They're gone, and on their way to you. Don't screw this up!" He threatened into his wrist comm link. Six Imperial Guards rushed in and captured the servant and notified Ranger High Command.

F.C. Bek'R arrived at the Royal Suite first. He ordered the "servant" taken to a cell underground and started a complete search. He peeked into the middle bedroom closet and saw a light under the hidden door panel. "Bek'R to C.S. G'Rosk: Someone's gone down the passageway. Request we have a team stand by the emergency shuttles, sir!"

Running as fast as he could with Lukus in his arms, Dan'L sped through the old escape passageway, still full of debris. It ended at a secret shuttle landing site among the trees. *What is going on?* He started to turn the final corner around the debris pile and stopped. He put his hand to Lukus' mouth and listened, hearing men's voices whisper.

"They should be coming soon. He said to stun them, remember. The boy must be kept alive," a man said.

Dan'L reached into his backplate and pulled out his plasma pulser pistol. He kept to the wall and crept along, silent as the darkness. Dan'L held the pistol in front of him and took the final two steps to the stairway leading to the secret landing site. When a man lowered his laser rifle to fire, Dan'L fired, creating a large blast which took out all three men. He grabbed two of their laser rifles and carefully climbed the stairway.

Using the barrel end of a laser rifle, Dan'L raised the door open a bit. "Did you get the kid?" A voice asked. Dan'L carefully sat Lukus down, threw open the door, and blasted his way outside. When he saw five dead men, he came back for his Son, picked him up, and ran into the parked shuttle.

They lifted off and flew away. "You all right, Lukus?" Dan'L asked. He heard muffled sobs and turned to see a man holding his hand over Lukus' mouth, with a laser pistol pointing at his head.

"He's fine, Consort. But you're dead!" The man said. Dan'L dove to the floor, pulling the wheel back to a near-vertical lift-off. The man stumbled and fell, firing his laser wildly as the shuttle climbed.

Drawing his long cloak around Lukus, Dan'L protected the boy, and fired a poison dart from his breastplate. But the assailant wore body armor and the dart bounced off him. Dan'L unclipped his cloak and drew his plasma sword. He instantly cut off the arm holding the laser pistol and stepped on the screaming assailant's chest.

"Who sent you?" Dan'L demanded.

The shuttle's red alert began beeping. Dan'L kicked the assailant unconscious, sheathed his sword, and took control of the shuttle, barely missing a landing space transport. He rose to 5,000 meters and set autopilot, then cuffed his assailant, and shot another stun dart into his exposed neck.

"Are you all right Lukus? It's over, Son," Dan'L said, trying to console his crying boy. He held Lukus on his lap in the pilot seat and called Kayla.

"Consort to Empress. We made it out, but there were men waiting for us, and one in the shuttle. Our ES warbirds are most likely waiting traps, Empress. Any suggestions?" he asked.

She replied, "Rendezvous on Island 1034," and clicked off.

"1034? Where is…" he started to ask, but she was gone. There was something familiar about "1034," if he could just remember. He *had* to remember. 1034…1034…

XXV

Aboard Kend'R's small shuttle, Kayla told them the news about Dan'L and Lukus escaping the Palace. She told Kend'R, "I see how difficult this is, my friend. Perhaps, if you could relax, the face of the Ram-man might enter your mind. I'm certain he is the new Alternate for the Plan of the Thirteen traitors." She sat on the floor with him and they began to chant, "There is no pain. Only peace." The familiar chant of the monks soothed Kend'R as they flew through the night. Finally, he exhaled fully, and relaxed. He laid on the floor of the shuttle most of their flight.

It was time to call an old friend. "General Hal'Bek, this is Empress Kayla," she began.

In a few seconds, a gruff, sleepy man in a T-shirt answered. "Is this some joke?"

She smiled and answered, "No joke, my General and old friend. Your 'Princess in a black cape' is in dire need of your help tonight."

The General laughed with her, bowed his head, and said, "My Princess and my Empress have but to command your humble Army General. How may I be of service, Empress Kayla?" She was assigned to the Army outpost on Xau for two years, and became good, trusted friends with Hal'Bek, the CO there at the time.

He arranged for the shuttle to land on his Imperial Army Base located 1034 kilometers from Capital City, on a medium-sized island. The Empress and her three Rangers were escorted to top-security, underground emergency quarters. She and C.S. Javette briefed the General on their escape.

"Let me get this straight. Our Empress and three senior Rangers came here because of his horoscope?" The General asked incredulously.

"No, General Hal'Bek. We are here because of Empress Kayla's horoscope, not mine. And another shuttle will be appearing in your scanner range, in four and one-half minutes," M.C. Kend'R said with confidence. "They have a prisoner on board for your brig, too."

"My Empress, when this is over, I want to hear the whole story over Brandywine and cigars," he said, shaking his head. They both laughed. The Army security team soon brought Consort Dan'L and his Son to the emergency bunker. When little Lukus saw his Mother, he ran to her and jumped in her arms, holding onto her tightly. She introduced her Consort and Prince to the General, and he ordered sandwiches and tea for them.

"It took me a while to figure out Island 1034, my Empress," Dan'L admitted. "But we made it." After everyone had a bed and a snack for the night, the Empress called her Temporary Security Advisor, C.S. G'Rosk.

"Empress Kayla here, C.S. G'Rosk. Your Partner and I are here with trusted friends. What is happening at the Palace?" She asked quietly.

He reported the capture of the servant, and the dead men who tried to seize Lukus and kill Dan'L at the passageway exit. "The servant has not yet talked, Empress Kayla. The Head of Staff does not recognize him; but, somehow, he looks familiar," he said.

"Send over his picture, but do not let him see us," she ordered. She stared at the "servant," and said, "Pull off his fake beard and moustache, G'Rosk." Kayla's eyes squinted hatefully when she saw the man's face.

The face of Prince Lukus' private tutor, Professor Tan'K, was exposed. G'Rosk and the Rangers recognized him, and another round of interrogations began, with a few body blows, this time. He had worked with her Son for nearly two years, to prepare Lukus for the Royal Academy. Thank the Creator there was always an Imperial Guard present. She silently wondered if she would ever fully trust any of those working in close proximity to her and her family again. Not likely.

From across the room, Kend'R laid down on a cot, holding his pounding head, and said, "He's not going to talk, my Empress. He has a cyanide cap in his right lower molar, and just now cracked it open."

"G'Rosk!" Kayla warned, but it was too late. Tan'K collapsed on the floor with white foam coming from his mouth.

Gen. Hal'Bek stared at the reclining Borgund Ranger Master Commander and asked, "How did he know?"

M.C. Shanna answered, "Only the Creator knows how, General Hal'Bek. I used to disbelieve him, but no longer. He has never been wrong. The Master Commander is a certified telepath and is blessed with many gifts."

Kayla said, "We all should get some rest. We are presently unable to be proactive, so we must be refreshed, ready to react at a second's notice. Orange alert, all hands. We will rest for a little while, then bring you up to speed, my friend. Thank you for your assistance."

"I will take the first watch, Empress Kayla," Shanna said. She borrowed a laser rifle and two belts of ammo from the Army security team and stood her post in front of the Empress' door. No half-man, half-goat beasts were getting past her.

Kayla laid down after taking off her armor and put her arms around her Son. She said a prayer of gratitude and fell asleep.

Consort Dan'L asked the General, "Ever heard of the 'Plan of the Thirteen,' General Hal'Bek?" The two men quietly talked about the ultimate threat to the Empire that, up until Kend'R's prescient warning tonight, everyone assumed was finished.

Home World Royal Palace

Ranger High Command had been active all night, gathering and disseminating intel from across the solar system, and within their own Palace walls. Just before 3a.m., G'Rosk received orders, supposedly from Empress Kayla. He asked, "Lady Bette, do these read like one of our Empress' texts? They don't to me."

Scanning them, she surmised, "Too wordy for my Empress. Contact C.S. T'Anh and get her input, too, G'Rosk."

The former Commander Superior for Kayla's first five years of service as a Ranger read the texts, then shook her head "No." She said, "Even as a Novice, Empress Kayla was direct, short, and concise. These are too high-handed, Lady Bette, and C.S. G'Rosk. Does this mean they have her?" She asked worriedly.

At Island 1034, an emergency signal awoke C.S. Javette, and the Ranger leaders shared their concern. She dressed and went to Kayla's room, where Dan'L stood watch. "I must speak with her now, Consort," she said, and he opened the door.

Kayla looked at Javette and asked, "What now?" She was informed of the attempted deception, and they ran to the command center down the hall.

"This is Empress Kayla. You will disregard all orders, intel, or communications supposedly sent from your Sovereign the last few hours. We are declaring a state of emergency, yellow alert, for all Imperial Military, Ranger, and Imperial Guard units throughout our R'Genra System. Our comm system has been compromised. All forthcoming orders must be triple verified at Level Twenty. Take no action without Level Twenty verification. Empress Kayla, out." She roughly smacked the comm link button and called, "Master Commander Kend'R!"

In the Palace, a righteously pissed-off High Ranger Lady Bette ran down to the prison level, demanding to see B'Nard. The surprised prison guard turned on the lights in his cell, and then muttered, "The Creator help me!" B'Nard was gone.

Bette called for the Sergeant-at-arms, pushed the incompetent prison guard into the empty cell, and slammed the door shut. "You are all confined to this level until further notice. Give me all your security vid recordings from the last forty-eight hours. NOW!" They scrambled for the recordings and gave her copies.

"Why weren't these vids shown to us? Why was this visitor permitted to talk with B'Nard? He was not to receive any visitors at all. Enhance their whispered conversation, transcribe it, and give it to me at once!" Lady Bette ordered the security techs in her office.

In a few minutes, Mon'T's conversation with B'Nard was transcribed for Lady Bette, and she read them with C.S. G'Rosk. "It's starting all over again, G'Rosk. And we are woefully unprepared. They have us at a severe disadvantage this time. Who is the new Alternate? And what—where—is the 'Aux Comm?' Call a state of emergency meeting at once. Have everyone present, live or by vid screen. I'll call Ban'Ti Imperial Prison myself," she ordered.

The Ban'Ti Warden assured Bette no one could escape his maximum-security facility. He was overly confident, bordering on arrogance with the second highest-in-command of the Empire. "I am ordering you to conduct a live bed check on all Imperial prisoners now, Warden. This is top priority. I will hold while you conduct your prisoner checks," she said.

After eight minutes, a sweating, red-faced Warden whispered, "They're gone! All four hundred Imperial prisoners are gone, Lady Bette. The entire wing is empty. I don't know how, but they're gone!"

A very angry Lady Bette slapped the comm link off and called Empress Kayla. The news did not shock her; in fact, Kayla merely nodded her head. Then she said, "The new Alternate is not young. Neither is he 'new.' He has been working alongside us for our entire reign, a trusted ally, sowing seeds of mistrust and misinformation among us. His identity is currently unknown. But realize this: he has the complete trust of each of us, Lady Bette. We implore you to trust no one. Trust no one you know, and trust no one you do not know. We will see you shortly, with the blessings of our Creator."

Empress Kayla calmly called her friend Admiral Mur, Commanding Officer of the Imperial Command Battle Cruiser, "Greetings, my friend. We are in need of passage. Is our finest ship and crew of the Space Cadre ready?"

He proudly answered, "Your loyal officers and crew are always ready, Empress Kayla. When shall we depart, and what is our destination, my Sovereign?"

She answered, "Departure within three days. Destination is classified. Empress Kayla out."

"Commander Superior Steph'N, how are you this fine day?" The Empress casually asked, calling on the main comm channel. His good friend and Empress never opened this way.

Steph'N looked at her, trying to read her face for more information, then answered, "I am well. How may I serve my Empress Kayla today?"

She chit-chatted with him for a few minutes, as if everything was fine, and there were no threats. Then she asked, "Have they completed the installation of our new facility? We wish to know where our auxiliary command console will be installed. M'Wati has no more available land for Imperial use. The purchase of more land there is not in our fiscal plan. Can you suggest other alternatives? We must have back-up for all our new data, Commander Superior Steph'N. Contact me in two weeks with your suggestions. Empress Kayla out."

C.S. Steph'N replayed her message, then noticed her tapping the stylus on her com tablet. He started from the beginning again and cut her vocal track. Kayla strategically interspersed the old marine electronic code in her message; the old dit-dot-dit. Remembering the old code from his undercover work many years ago, he deciphered:

"They completed installation of new auxiliary command. No Imperial use. Not our plan. Other Alternates. Must have back-up. Contact me with suggestions."

He swallowed hard. The 'Plan of the Thirteen' was still active. He checked the tapping stylus again; there was no error. The Empire was at risk again. His friend Kayla and her young Son were in grave danger.

Checking the restricted Imperial News feed, C.S. Steph'N read about the big prison break-out at the Ban'Ti Imperial Prison. At first, he disregarded the information, because the high-risk Imperial prisoners were supposedly re-captured by "Imperial forces," the news said. Then he thought about it. Which "Imperial forces" re-captured those traitors, murderers, and rapists? Space Cadre? Imperial Army?

Steph'N said aloud, "They weren't re-captured. They were rescued!" And they were going to the Auxiliary Command center, wherever it was. He yelled, "Master Commander Va'Pal! First Commander Stek'R!" The new building on M'Wati could wait. In less than one hour, three ES-class warbirds were heading for the White Belt, in search of the Auxiliary Command, and the escaped Technicians of the Plan of the Thirteen.

The update meeting with General Hal'Bek was completed. Trying to sound casual, Kayla asked, "How do you get along with Field Marshall General Blatan? He's the only senior military officer I've ever met from Ban'Ti. Not many people there volunteer for military service, I understand," she added.

"Off the record?" He asked, and she nodded. "He's a strange duck.

Never has any officer meetings of any kind. The Navy, Air Corps, and Space Cadre all have Year-End Holiday Award Meetings. We haven't had one since Blatan became Field Marshall. He travels to all the bases more than any senior officer I've known. But no intermingling of his direct reports. No one remembers him from the Royal Academy or Army Officers School, either. And that's strange."

He sat forward and continued, "I have not been invited to one single event at either Palace since he has been in charge. We all think he wants us to feel isolated, with him as our only important contact person. It's not the Army way, Empress Kayla. We are brother officers. You remember. Even our little outpost on Xau had officer get-togethers. But not General Blatan," he said, and shook his head. "Not the Army way at all," he repeated.

"No, it's not, General Hal'Bek. I'll be sure to rectify the situation. The great Imperial Army is vital to the Empire. Each officer and soldier should feel important. You definitely are to me, and have been since we met, so many years ago. Thank you for your frankness," she said, and left their meeting.

Kayla ran into M.C. Shanna returning from chow hall. She was shaking her head and laughing, then saw her Empress. "Those new Commanders were hysterically funny, Empress Kayla. I needed a good laugh. They had vids of themselves as old ladies, and the CO, too. They even aged me to eighty! Makes we want to stop sleeping and use my best years now, while I look half-way decent. Admiral Mae would leave me behind, for sure!" She laughed and showed the new app to her Empress. "It can even take an old person and make them young again."

Kayla said, "Come with me, now, Shanna."

XXVI

Island 1034

Trying to sound lighthearted, Kayla called Baron P'Lau, "Baron, when we were appointed Empress, you gave us a com tablet with the Royal Hierarchy list, the courtiers, and so on. Do you still have a copy? I seem to have misplaced mine. We would appreciate the download as soon as possible."

"Of course! Would you like the current one, and the old one from my Mother, Empress Tan? They are quite comprehensive, Empress Kayla," he said with pride. Her former Emperor kept excellent records.

"Please download everything to our private number now. And many thanks to you, Baron P'Lau," she said with a smile. In a few minutes, more photos and data on the Royal Hierarchy downloaded than she ever dreamed possible. Working with the aging app with Shanna, they patiently age-progressed the face of each living aristocrat, courtier, military major and above, and their partners and spouses in the list. Then it suddenly dawned on her: *What if someone who was thought to be dead returned?* They could assume a new identity; but without extensive facial reconstructive surgery, they would still retain the basic facial features.

Kayla called Javette to join them. "Show Baron Z'Lun and his siblings, Shanna. Now, do the aging on his oldest brother, killed in the hunting accident." No luck there. "How about the middle brother, the one who went to the seminary on M'Wati?"

Shanna located the only photo of Dok'T, a Royal Academy class photo. She isolated his face and used the aging app on the picture. The women stared at the face on the screen. "Make his hair totally white, and give him a bushy moustache," Kayla instructed. They looked at each other in recognition of the face. "The new Alternate, hiding within our own Court." She told the women to keep silent about their discovery and walked to the command center to be alone.

In half an hour, the Empress called Baron P'Lau again, "Please set up a formal dinner for tomorrow night, at the new Imperial Naval Admin Building executive dining room. We would like the Viscount, Home World Barons and Lords, as well as Field Marshall General Blatan and our other Military Advisors present, in addition to yourself, Baron P'Lau. We wish to have a private, congratulatory pre-Fifth anniversary dinner, and plan our Royal Anniversary for our people, Baron," she said. He became excited and promised a wonderful evening. "We will bring four guests with us, Baron P'Lau. See you then."

Warrior Empress Kayla met with General Hal'Bek one more time prior to her departure. "You're taking a significant risk meeting with those men, Empress. They'll most likely try to kill you again, probably after dinner. I know your Rangers are excellent fighters, but no one can beat missiles, grenades, or plasma pulsers, my Sovereign," the experienced Army man said.

She agreed, then said. "We grow by facing adversity and defeating those who wish to harm us. I will not hide and let my enemies grow stronger, and gather more to their cause, thinking the Empress is a frightened, weak little girl! They will face me, Hal'Bek. It is much easier to kill thousands with missiles and bombs than to kill someone while looking into their eyes," she reminded him.

"I wait for your signal, my Empress Kayla. Your Son, my little Prince Lukus, will be safe here. I give you my word," the General said. He struck his left chest to salute her, and she returned his salute. Then she swirled on her cloak and left. M.C. Shanna remained to guard Prince Lukus.

During the trip to the Palace, the Rangers discussed the situation in depth. "He's got the whole Imperial Army under his control. He spent the last five years grooming the officers to obey him without question. This is very dangerous, Empress Kayla. Does he know we're suspecting him, Kend'R?" Javette asked.

"No, he is too self-assured at this point. We may have the advantage if he is revealed in a public setting. But you are correct; he has the entire Army under his thumb," Kend'R agreed.

"If it is him, he knows all Imperial defenses, as well as defense protocols. But General Hal'Bek is not only a career officer; he is a graduate of the Army Officers School. He knows many other officers currently in command positions. If Hal'Bek is right about their not trusting the deceiver's methods, he will convince them to obey our commands. We will only have one chance to seize the traitor. We must not fail," the Empress said firmly.

C.S. Javette landed the small shuttle next to the construction site at the Royal Palace. She, M.C. Kend'R, and Empress Kayla walked down the hatch. Kend'R stopped, called to the Empress, and pointed at three workers nearby. They walked over to the workers, stepping on and over large building stones.

"You can't keep it. It belongs to her. We have to tell the Empress!" The first man insisted to his two co-workers.

Kayla leaped off the foundation block behind him and asked, "Tell the Empress what?"

The three men immediately knelt before her, and the first one said, "We removed this broken foundation stone block and found this, Great Empress Kayla!" He pointed into the hole where the broken foundation stone had been. An old trunk containing hundreds of emeralds, diamonds, rubies, and gold and platinum jewelry with precious stones was exposed.

The second man raised his trembling hand and gave her a large sapphire, saying, "I took it for my wife, my Empress. She had twins and is overwhelmed. I thought it would... I'm sorry, Empress Kayla," he choked out. "Please forgive me!"

Kayla called for Chief Advisor Baron P'Lau, and they all waited while he and dozens of Imperial Guards arrived at the scene. P'Lau was astonished. The area where the treasure was uncovered was part of the Flight School now; but it previously was the old harem for Emperors past. The Empress looked at the three workers and said, "Your honesty will be rewarded this very day. Baron P'Lau, please issue each man one 10,000-credit bar in gold and have them escorted to their homes within the hour."

The three workers thanked her on their knees. The man who initially pocketed the gem bowed his head and said, "Thank you for your mercy, Great Empress."

"Use it well. Everyone needs the mercy of their Empress, and mercy from our Creator at some point in their life," she wisely said.

The old trunk of gems was reinforced, and carefully raised. Beneath it was a cache of gold bars six meters deep and three meters wide. The new-found treasure was removed, inventoried by the Royal Treasurer, and placed into crates. "This is a wonderful sign, my Empress. A first of many good things to come," Baron P'Lau remarked.

"If we survive to put it to good use, my friend," she said quietly, and left her trusted former Emperor to oversee the movement of the new fortune for the Empire. She ordered it stored in the underground vault at the Farm, for now.

As she walked to the Royal Suite with Kend'R and Javette, she asked, "Have you charted our horoscope for today, Master Commander Kend'R? I hope Baron P'Lau is correct."

Kend'R only saluted her and nodded. He jogged to the Ranger Barracks with his com tablets and notes. His lack of words told her more than any star chart could.

The gourmet dinner at the new Admin Building on the Imperial Naval

Base was the first formal event to be held at the facility. No expense was spared. All the Barons, Lords, Viscount T'Sur, and the official Military Advisors mingled and sipped cocktails, awaiting the arrival of the Empress and her four guests. Navy security was very tight. Each VIP was required to go through scanners twice before being shown to the dining room. The gentlemen were mingling enjoyably with each other.

The big, fully armed Imperial shuttle carefully landed in the middle of the Naval Base, barely able to open its hatch amid the reconstruction equipment and materials. Twenty Imperial Guards escorted the Great Empress Kayla and four guests into the building, past the entry scanners, and up into the dining room. The Empress was dressed in a Royal Blue and gold gown, wearing her signature gold-trimmed dark blue breastplate and backplate armor. Under her long blue robe's wide sleeves, she wore the new Ranger arm bands. The Empress was beautifully coiffed and made up, but ready to fight.

The Imperial Guardsmen entered the large, formal dining room, and silently lined the walls. The maître' d announced: "Presenting the Royal Astrologer, Master Commander Kend'R; Temporary Security Advisor Commander Superior G'Rosk; High Priest K'Ramm; Elder Ranger, former Commander Superior C'Lu; and our Great Benevolent Empress Kayla."

The Royal Guests entered and flanked the Empress at the dining table, and the other guests took their places. Everyone was smiling and cordial, happy to be included for this pre-Fifth Anniversary Dinner Celebration. The Imperial Guards used their small scanners quietly on each man, and their Commander gave his Empress a nod of approval.

Several minutes of welcoming protocols took place, then the Empress sat, followed by her guests. The men complimented her fabulous up-do hair style, and the heirloom jeweled crown she rarely wore. No one mentioned her arm bands; if anyone saw them, they said nothing. Kayla was the Warrior Empress, after all. She graciously accepted their compliments with a warm smile.

Course after delectable course of gourmet foods was served, each with its own wine flights, which the Empress and her guests declined. The conversation was light and centered on planning the Fifth Anniversary Celebration for the people. Each planet would have its own celebrations.

"The Celebration has already begun at the Royal Palace on Home World, with the new treasure uncovered today," General Blatan said. "A phenomenal discovery, my Empress."

"Yes, isn't it?" She answered and looked at Baron P'Lau.

"What was the total value of the wealth, if I may ask, Empress Kayla?" Viscount T'Sur asked politely.

She calmly replied, "When the Royal Treasurer has completed his inventorying, the antique jewelry, precious stones, and gold will be tallied in today's credit values. The amount will not be published, nor the location of the treasure. It is no longer at the Palace," she disclosed. "Our Royal Historian is examining the gold bars for more information, cross-referencing the historical records in an attempt to date the collection. Each bar has a seal stamped on it, as I'm sure you've heard." She watched each man mentally attempt to calculate the value of eighteen cubic meters of gold bars and a trunk full of precious stones.

After dessert was served, Viscount T'Sur smiled and said, "Let me say how wonderful it is to once again spend time with our esteemed Elder Ranger, former Commander Superior C'Lu. The years have been much kinder to you than myself. You are as beautiful as ever, C'Lu," he said, and bowed his head to her. She smiled and thanked him.

Elder Ranger C'Lu looked at General Blatan, and commented, "Pardon me, Field Marshall General Blatan; but you look very familiar to me. Are you or your family from K'Halon Prime?"

The General did not look at C'Lu, intentionally. He answered, "No, I am from Ban'Ti, Ranger C'Lu," and sipped his wine.

The Viscount noticed the rude behavior of General Blatan, and commented, "Our Elder Ranger C'Lu served in the Main Court under Empress Tan, her Father, and her Son, our Emperor P'Lau. She is famous for her photographic memory, General Blatan. Perhaps one or more of your family members attended Main Court during her active service?"

The General's face turned red. He replied, "I am an only-son, and we are from Ban'Ti."

For the first time all evening, High Priest K'Ramm spoke, "I spent one semester of seminary on Ban'Ti, General Blatan, studying within the library archives in the caves of the hermit monks. To be quite honest, your face resembles one of the men in the portraits in their library, without your moustache, of course," he said.

Blatan did not like the spotlight on him. Trying to change the subject, he asked, "Have you planned the security measures for the Fifth Anniversary Celebration, G'Rosk?"

G'Rosk began a superfluous synopsis of the special security measures planned for the Royal Palace. All the while, Kend'R lightly tapped on the tabletop with his finger, as if he was edgy, or impatient. Kayla picked up his code and turned a little in her chair towards him. Kend'R tapped, "It is him. He is the last." She nodded ever so slightly in recognition.

Elder Ranger C'Lu once again looked at Blatan, watching him converse with G'Rosk. Then, she stood and said, "Dok'T! The second son! The one who joined the Holy Caste Order and went to seminary. It is you!"

With a face as red as C'Lu's formal Kaylan Ranger uniform, General Blatan jumped up from his seat and glared at C'Lu, and then Empress Kayla. She folded her arms, touching her arm bands.

He said with an evil smile, "You set up this game, Empress, and now you will suffer the consequences. I know your defenses on each planet. The Imperial Army Commanding Officers answer to me alone. Enjoy your last meal, Empress Bitch!" He reached under the table to fire his concealed one-shot laser tube at her.

Empress Kayla instantly touched her arm band and her personal shield covered her and K'Ramm. Kend'R protected C'Lu with his shield, and Blatan's laser blast killed no one. Imperial Guards restrained Blatan. She calmly sat while he was stunned and removed from their dinner.

"Who is Dok'T?" Admiral L'Rok asked, completely amazed.

C'Lu answered, "He was an older brother of former Baron Z'Lun, the middle son, who allegedly turned his back on title, land, and wealth to become a priest. It would seem he only performed a decades-long charade," she commented.

"Gentlemen, we ask you to pardon our small theatrics. My guests were completely ignorant of our reason for inviting them here tonight. But we had to make certain of the deceiver's true identity, and my esteemed guests uncovered the charlatan. Now: each Military Advisor will receive top-secret orders over your secure comm channel. Our best and last defense against the Plan of the Thirteen begins immediately!" The Empress rose, and her party left with her, leaving behind her shocked dinner guests.

The Imperial shuttle lifted off, en route to the Farm. Kayla called General Hal'Bek and said, "Congratulations, Field Marshall General Hal'Bek. You are now my Imperial Army Chief of Command. Contact your Brigade Generals on all four planets by vid conference in thirty seconds. We have no time to lose!" She sent a pre-recorded announcement of Blatan being relieved of command, and Hal'Bek promoted to Field Marshall.

Looking at her four guests in the Imperial shuttle, Warrior Empress Kayla thanked them for attending her dinner. With a smile at the corner of her mouth, she announced, "High Priest K'Ramm, please pray for us and our families. Rangers: lock and load!" The Imperial shuttle dropped off Elder Ranger C'Lu and High Priest K'Ramm, then sped back to the Palace.

The prison transport en route to Ban'Ti was ordered to return to Home World, only half a day's flight away from the jungle planet. The shooter M'Tuk noticed the change of course. There were eight other convicted Technicians on board with him. The last visitor on Home World told them all the Plan was back on. Mon'T promised they'd escape and be rescued from Ban'Ti. He looked out the narrow window, but no ships were approaching. No matter. They'd come for him one way or another. He knew where the Aux Comm was, and the entry codes for access.

XXVII

The chart of the R'Genra solar system showed the orbital positioning of each planet. The Central Core planets were M'Wati, Home World, and K'Halon Prime. Separating the three Central Core planets from the relentless R'Genra sun was the White Belt, a large asteroid belt of broken planetary matter, space junk, thousands of assorted sizes of orbiting asteroids, and ice crystals. It was a dangerous place to travel.

Sitting just inside the White Belt was little Ban'Ti, the jungle planet. Travel from Ban'Ti to the Central Core planets in an ES-class warbird took three to five days, depending on the planets' orbital positions, and the ability of a skilled pilot to detour through the White Belt. The much larger space transports at this time of year took three weeks to travel from Home World to Ban'Ti.

It took C.S. Steph'N and M.C. Va'Pal two days at hyperspace twenty to approach Home World sector in their ES warbirds from M'Wati, currently at its farthest orbital point from Home World. Steph'N calculated all possible courses from Ban'Ti towards Home World an unidentified space vessel could take in hyperspace. No one at Ranger High Command knew what the "Aux Comm" really was. It made sense to him for Aux Comm to be another command computer center to activate what remained of the EPDS, the "Old Engine." But the only ones who knew were on the ship full of escaped Imperial traitors and criminals, en route to Aux Comm.

Young F.C. Stek'R flew ahead of Commander Superior Steph'N and Va'Pal, flying with spy drones instead of missiles, and not using his stealth system. He launched the spy drones at points directed by C.S. G'Rosk every few hours. The spy drones could reconnoiter and identify any electronic signal in a wide area. If Aux Comm was functioning now and running, they could pinpoint it in seconds.

But if Aux Comm was dormant or not powered up yet, the spy drones would most likely not find it. Space Cadre Fleet Admiral L'Rok said the best place to hide a big missile command and launch system would be deep inside an asteroid. There were many previously mined asteroids in the White Belt, partially hollowed out. If the hidden system was activated when the White Belt asteroid was close to Home World's orbit, there would be little warning of an impending strike.

Remembering his two years of undercover work with the Rebels, Steph'N recalled the many strikes on Imperial ships, merchant and transport vessels, and even Space Bases the Rebels made. Most attacks were lightning fast, ruthless, and utilized tactical plans designed by former Space Cadre officers turned traitor. Many attacks were successful, even with the Rebel's old, inferior ships.

C.S. Steph'N called C.S. G'Rosk at Ranger High Command and asked, "What if Aux Comm is not what we think it is? The criminals know this is their last chance. Have we planned for incoming missiles tipped electro-magnetically? A planet-wide EMP strike would render Home World defenseless. We'd be reduced to primitives and anarchy," he said. "All they'd have to do is get the missiles within communications satellite range and ignite the laser beams. It's what I'd do, if I only had a handful of men, ships, and missiles left," Steph'N said. "We should also assume they have more than one ship. There may be several ships stored at the Aux Comm from the old Rebellion, and probably an arsenal of missiles, too, sir."

G'Rosk answered, "Our planetary defense shields should protect against such an attack."

But Steph'N countered, "Sir, I understand. But I worked with engineers, technicians, and programmers for two years who had little more than out-of-date equipment and ships. The former Space Cadre-trained men were very clever and adept at reconfiguring old technology into new weapons. If I was at tactical command for them, I'd make every missile count. They will use our own defenses against us, C.S. G'Rosk. By the time we've analyzed their attack, it's over; and we're finished. I'd mix up the missile war heads with EMP's, plasma disrupter arcs, and chemicals. Three minutes, and Home World is neutralized. Not destroyed; incapable of defense," he closed. "Battle over."

Listening to their conversation, the Empress interjected, "Then, while you're flying towards your assigned area, design two different tactical attacks. Notify us just prior to transmission, so we can receive them securely, Commander Superior Steph'N. We will send you any updates we receive. One thing we know: if we cannot stop the Aux Comm plan in space, there may not be ample time or the ability to use planetary defense fighters and systems. We have no information of its capabilities and effectiveness. The destruction of the Space High Command Communications Satellite Network must be prevented. We must prepare as much as we can, in every conceivable scenario. Good hunting, 'Major S'Loc,'" she said with a smile, saying a name only Steph'N would know.

S'Loc was the Chief Engineer Steph'N impersonated for more than two years, deeply imbedded with Duma Wat and the Rebellion.

A confused G'Rosk asked, "Major S'Loc?"

"A private joke, my former mentor. Now, update High Ranger Lady Bette with C.S. Steph'N's attack ideas. We must prepare to defend against what we do not know, and what we fear, as well as our own military tactics," she ordered.

Three musical tones on her comm link chimed. It was another signal from Dan'L: he, Lukus, and M.C. Shanna were all right. After she promoted Hal'Bek to Field Marshall General, her family was secretly moved to the Farm, to their quarters in the wine cellar. Her emotional "umbilical cord" for her Son pulled tightly; his Father was protecting Lukus, but she was not there with her Son. She smiled, remembering little Lukus' words: "The Empress' work is never done."

No time to relax in a bath of rose water tonight. She dismissed her attending ladies, changed out of her Royal clothing, and left her hair up in its great style. Kayla saw the red love mark on her neck from Dan'L and smiled. They made fabulous love last night, both knowing it could very well be their last moments together. She wanted another child. Neither she nor Dan'L wanted Lukus to be their only child. But Kayla was not certain she physically could have any more children. If they came out of this ultimate threat as victors, she was spending several days on Paradise Island with her Consort. A big "If."

After dressing in her Ranger black trousers and blouse, Kayla knelt to pray. She gave thanks and praise to the Creator of all Things and begged for a night of victory. She prayed for peace for all people, and their safety. "Please help me. Show me the path to peace for all our people. Please guide me in making the correct decisions and taking the actions to swift victory. Please use your Daughter to bring victory and peace to all people of our R'Genra System."

Kayla meditated for several minutes, and the words in the Holy Books came into her mind: "Prepare for defeat even as you prepare for victory. Failure to prepare for defeat leads to pain, remorse, and death. Victory and defeat are one in the same. Those who fail to prepare meet defeat." She took a deep breath, exhaled slowly, and prepared for defeat mentally.

The Empress considered what defeat would mean for her Empire. Every Ranger knew the consequence of failure: Submit, and swear loyalty to a new Emperor, or embrace death. Escape plans for Prince Lukus and his two personal Master Commander Kaylan Rangers Shanna and L'Van were in place, but Kayla knew she would not be alive to see them be successful. If they did manage to help Lukus escape a new "Plan of the Thirteen" Emperor, none of them could return to their former life, their partners and families, or ever talk about the past. Both Shanna and L'Van swore to protect Lukus, knowing the price to be paid.

Contingency plans for post-EMP scenarios were in place, ready to be engaged when and if necessary. Thousands of generators and many more solar panels hidden deep within the three Central Core planets would restore power for brief periods, until repairs and replacement parts for power plants could be made. The Empress scanned the "Contingency Report" from her Imperial Army coded dispatch to be implemented in case of an EMP, satisfied the preparations were adequate. If the Royal Palace were back to full function, there would be a larger centralized area for temporary housing and shelter; but it was not ready. She had to work with the facilities she had ready and available.

She refused to think about defeat anymore and concentrated on total victory for her fourteen billion people of the Empire. Imperial Military forces were all on orange alert and standing by for further orders. There were no more gaps to be filled, at least until they knew what they were fighting. Kayla swirled on her black cloak and walked to the underground prison.

Lord T'Sel had Dok'T restrained on a gurney, and under deep, drug-enhanced hypnosis. He looked at her and shook his head "No," meaning no further information had been revealed.

There was no other choice. Too much was at stake. The Empress summoned her telepath, Kend'R. To her surprise, he was sitting in the guards' office, and walked up to her with a smile on his face. "I am ready, my Empress," he said confidently, and walked inside the cell.

"Give the prisoner another dose of truth serum," she instructed, and called for the elderly Lord T'Sel to come outside and relax. Kend'R removed his cloak and walked around the cell for a few minutes. Then, the master telepath began his work. Kayla and T'Sel went into the observation room.

Kend'R unfastened Dok'T's head and feet restraints. "They have treated you with great disrespect, General Dok'T. For all their actions, I humbly apologize. Their ignoble methods have only served to annoy my General. They will be punished appropriately, General Dok'T," Kend'R said, and bowed to him. "Let me help you, sir."

Dok'T said, "They will feel my wrath, and soon will be reduced to lost children crying in the dark wilderness. My brother Z'Lun did not receive just punishment, in this life anyway. They should have killed him privately for his failure, not forced him to grovel and beg for death on M'Wati! Baron S'Tan botched everything!" He rolled his head back and forth.

"S'Tan caused much pain. He worshipped the dark magic, as did several Alternates," Kend'R said. "They had secret rooms with evil books, masks and capes of black."

"Dark magic! It is all black candles and excuses for sexual perversion!

The old gods have little power. But they are good for controlling the weak-minded. Had they focused on the Plan, we would have the throne of power now. So many served in silence while they ruined the lives of young girls and boys, wallowing in sin. Unforgiveable sin!" He cried out. Dok'T's eyes were welled in tears. Kend'R saw the path to break Dok'T become crystal clear.

"You served tirelessly, restoring the 'Old Engine,' and managing Technicians, while the chosen few sinned and turned their backs on our Creator," Kend'R said.

"They strayed so far away. No wonder they failed and she caught them. Hopeless fools! Perverts and miscreants, working for sexual deviants!"

"Will you punish our Empress now, General? She took back the lands and wealth of your ancestors," Kend'R asked.

Dok'T raised his head and said, "She is one of the Warrior Class. They have ruled unfairly for centuries. I care not if she takes back all the land. When I am crowned in two days, I will give the Royal lands to all the people. They will be free at last!" He kicked and tried to get up again, to no avail. Empress Kayla noted his "two days" comment.

"But if the Empress gives away all her lands to the people, they will try to rule themselves. History is clear: men will fight and kill each other without clear and strong leadership," Kend'R waxed prophetically.

"The people need their Creator," Dok'T corrected, and began humming.

Kend'R felt a strong urgency inside him and signaled for the physician to inject his prisoner with truth serum again. Afterwards, he said, "Lord Aug'R will use the Auxiliary Command to punish Home World. Will you permit this to happen? Our Creator does not like bloodshed of the innocents," Kend'R whispered.

"They will do what they like. I will set them free," Dok'T said, and began chanting.

"My General, if Lord Aug'R and B'Nard use the Aux Comm, you will be destroyed, too. You and millions of innocent children will be destroyed. You cannot set them free. They only worship power, money, and sex. Help me stop them, so you can set them free of their evil desires!" Kend'R pleaded and fell on his knees beside the gurney. He was deep inside Dok'T's mind now but needed more information. Kend'R listened to Dok'T's deep, melodic chants, and changed his approach.

"I must set them free," the prisoner said, now rolling his head.

"And save the innocent children from their destruction, their perversion, and their dark magic. Please help me, Holy Monk!" Kend'R pleaded.

The prisoner's eyes opened wide, and cried out, "The children! So many innocents! I must save them!"

"Help me, Holy Monk Dok'T! How can I stop them from killing the innocent children? Please, tell me, sir. Please tell me. Please tell me," he chanted.

"Save the innocents! 32, 14, 9, and seven come eleven. Send the sinners to hell, and the children to heaven." Kend'R recognized the numbers as launch codes.

He was nearly frantic. Kend'R grabbed Dok'T by the face and asked, "Holy Monk, Servant of our Creator; how can I stop the Aux Comm and save the innocent children?"

Dok'T cried out, "You cannot reach the Aux Comm in time to stop it. It has already begun. But you can stop some of its fury!"

Kend'R pleaded, "How can I stop its fury? We must save the innocent children, Holy Monk. Help me stop it!"

"Stop them from killing the innocent children! Their lives must be spared!"

"How, Holy Monk? How can I save the innocent children? Please, Servant of our Creator, please tell me. I beg your indulgence and your mercy. Please help this worthless wretch save the innocent children, Holy Monk!" Kend'R begged, on his knees, in supplication.

"Only the great arcs can stop the weapons of evil. The great arcs will render them useless," he answered.

"Where are these weapons of evil, Holy Monk? I will help you stop them. I will help you save the innocent children. Where do I find them, Holy Servant of our Creator?"

The tears began pouring down Dok'T's face, and he cried out, "Pointing at your face, my son. They are mounted on the platform base above us now, pointing at all the sinners. 32, 14, 9, and seven come eleven. Send the sinners to hell, and the children to heaven!" He began to sob incoherently, and screamed, "Fury soon released!"

Kend'R ran outside, drenched in sweat, and said, "Empress, have Admiral Mur destroy our orbiting platform base above us now, Empress Kayla. The launch codes have been remotely programmed from the Aux Comm and cannot be unlocked. They will be activated any second. Destroy the platform or be destroyed!" Kend'R cried out and collapsed.

"Admiral Mur, this is Empress Kayla. Fire plasma disrupter arcs on our orbiting platform base now. Take it out. Right now, and that's an order, Admiral Mur!" She yelled, running up the stairs three at a time. "Then get my ship out of there!"

"Imperial Command Battle Cruiser firing plasma disrupter arcs now, Empress Kayla," he reported. Inside the Ranger High Command offices directly above the prison, they watched the orbiting platform base get hit by plasma disrupter arcs from the big Cruiser. At first, the flat landing platform took the direct hit and broke apart. Then, an extraordinary series of explosions went off, culminating in a massive, final explosion of incredible intensity.

The Rangers cheered; all but the Empress. "Find out how many were aboard the platform, Lady Bette. I need to know how many loyal souls I just sent into the Afterlife tonight," Kayla said, and walked out of their offices. *More innocent blood on my hands,* she thought.

Back on the prison level, Empress Kayla came to Kend'R, slowly recovering from his ordeal. "The orbiting platform is destroyed. The souls sent to the Afterlife are my responsibility, my loyal friend Kend'R," she said softly. "Not yours – mine."

He laid his head back and said, "I saw the ship carrying Lord Aug'R. Hundreds are with him, Empress Kayla. They have a command destroyer with full weapons systems, and other leftover ships from the Rebellion," he said. "B'Nard and the other Technicians are in attack-striker ships; very fast, and well-armed. Not certain how many ships, but several. The rendezvous is set for 3 a.m. at Aux Comm, when it's within range of Home World. And somehow, Lord Aug'R has nuke-tipped missiles and many drone fighters. That's all the tactical intel I have, my Empress," he said, and held his head in pain. "Aux Comm is now fully functioning."

Kayla kissed his cheek and whispered, "Go to your bungalow, my friend. Know that you have saved us all tonight. May our Creator bless my Kend'R," she said, tears running down her face.

Kend'R saluted and bid her good night. She walked back into the Ranger High Command office. "How many, Lady Bette?" She asked and sat on a chair.

Bette answered, "One Commander, two Officers, and seven crewmen, my Empress. All sacrificed to save millions of innocent lives," she said, trying to soften the blow.

"Full honors to each one, and a bonus to each surviving spouse and child. Make it so, Lady Bette," she said quietly. Kayla looked at their tactical screens, and said, "Aux Comm is fully functioning. It begins now."

The Warrior Empress stood and commanded, "Yellow alert, above Home World, M'Wati, and K'Halon Prime. All ships, make ready battle stations. Get the other Ranger High Command leaders and our Space Cadre Fleet Admiral L'Rok on the comm link for me. We have at least one destroyer, several attack-strikers, drone fighters, and probably many more remnants of the Rebellion under Lord Aug'R's command; and all fully armed. All Ranger pilots to their warbirds. This ends tonight!" She said, pounded the table, and walked out.

XXVIII

Dan'L tightened his new breastplate and backplate. His original armor was more comfortable, broken in from several years' wear, and many battles. This new armor was Royal Blue trimmed in gold, and contained the new, updated weapons. It was proper armor for the Consort of the Empress, and one of her senior Borgund Rangers: her "Faithful Sons."

"You look scary, but fancy, Father," four-year-old Prince Lukus observed. "Do I look scary, too?" He asked, and stood in a fighting pose in his new, soft body armor.

"My Prince Lukus looks protected, and brilliant!" Dan'L said with a smile, and they high-fived. "Now you must be very good for Master Commanders Shanna and L'Van tonight, Lukus. They are taking you through the underground tunnel, into the storeroom. The Elder Rangers are there, waiting for you, too. You must be brave, Lukus. You are my Son, and the Son of the Great Warrior Empress Kayla!"

Prince Lukus puffed out his little chest and promised to be brave and good. He kissed his Father's cheek, and his Kaylan Ranger personal guards led him down the hall to the lift. Master Commander Dan'L swirled on his black cloak, put on his new arm bands and helmet, and left the Farm. He was shuttled to the Space Cadre Base in Capital City, with a full load of Ranger warbird pilots.

Shanna whispered to L'Van, "If they are not victorious tonight…"

"Then you and I will never see our partners or my daughter again, Shanna," L'Van finished her sentence. "May our Creator bless us all, and our Prince Lukus!"

The Borgund and Kaylan Ranger pilots waited in four lines while their warbirds were towed out of the Imperial Ranger hangars for them, already fueled and fully outfitted with all weaponry. "Wait up, Master Commander Dan'L," a familiar voice yelled. He turned and smiled to see C.S. Sham'S run up to him.

"What's this about, Dan'L? I was ordered to break all hyperspace records two days ago and come here, and now we're scrambling fighters and warbirds," Sham'S whispered. "What's up?"

"Nothing much. Just the last battle against the Plan of the Thirteen armada. It's over tonight, one way or another, Sham'S—according to our Empress," Dan'L said. They looked at one another, realizing they had to win the battle tonight. "Succeed at any cost."

A Flight Crew Chief yelled, "ES warbirds up next!"

While Dan'L and Sham'S were speaking, two women Rangers ran past them. "Take your warbirds, Borgund Rangers!" C.S. Javette ordered, running alongside Empress Kayla.

"Yes, Mother," Dan'L said softly, watching Sham'S laugh. "As you order, Commander Superior Javette!" He replied loudly. The men ran to their ES warbirds, now being pushed towards them. Two by two, sixty Ranger traditional fighters and twenty-two ES-class warbirds launched into the night.

Space Cadre fighters were rolled out of their hangars on the opposite side of the landing field. Their pilots climbed inside but did not launch. Those fighters would only be launched from their Capital City Base to protect Home World. Hopefully, the Space Cadre battleship group and Ranger warbirds would keep the threat contained in space and defeat it there. But the planetary defenses on all four worlds were ready to launch in seconds if needed to protect their planets.

"Field Marshall General Hal'Bek to Empress Kayla. Have spoken directly to all Divisional Generals. We are in defensive positions on each planet with missiles locked and loaded, and troops ready. Standing by for further orders, Empress Kayla," he said firmly. She acknowledged his information. The General of the Air Corps announced his fighters were scrambled and ready to launch. Imperial Navy battleships and destroyers were in position to provide support and protection to each planet, and their capital cities.

"G'Rosk to Empress Kayla: we have downloaded C.S. Steph'N's tactical plans into our computers, for use upon your command. I hope he is wrong. None of us know what to expect. They may have more weapons hidden inside Imperial bases and installations, like the Home World Platform Base. We must be prepared to destroy our own bases and outposts, Empress Kayla. Two hundred years of construction and trillions of credits, my Empress," he said, with a look of grave concern on his face.

"And tens of thousands of lives. Order the immediate evacuation of all non-essential personnel off the bases and outposts, to reduce the number of potential victims," she said. Kayla studied Steph'N's tactical plans. His Plan One could work perfectly with her Plan B, if necessary.

The Empress expanded her tactical screens. Her ES-519 was now modified as a flying command control operations station. She was both

Battle Commander and pilot. All Ranger pilots were on course to intercept the recently discovered Technicians' command destroyer, directly on course for SB4, in between the White Belt and Home World. Ranger fighters and warbirds were her first line of defense. SB4's fighter squadrons would flank them, collapse the battle theater, and leave no place for the enemies of the Empire to escape.

Kayla looked at the time: 12:07a.m. Less than three hours for the Plan's Technicians to rendezvous at the Aux Comm. She ordered, "Bring Lord T'Sel back to interrogate Dok'T. Have one of our guards assist him with corporal punishment, if needed. Address Dok'T as a Holy Monk. Uncover all he knows about Aux Comm. We need more information from him, any way we can get it. Do it now! Find out where the bloody Aux Comm is located, G'Rosk."

Her comm link signaled afterwards with a message from C.S. Steph'N. One of the spy drones had picked up a faint signal from an asteroid on the Central Core side of the White Belt. He was changing course to investigate. She forwarded the message to G'Rosk and Lady Bette.

Unexpectedly, a message from C.S. Sham'S came across, "Empress Kayla, is our defensive strike force protocol? What I mean is, are we Rangers doing everything we are supposed to do according to the Space High Command Tactical Defense Instruction Manual? The battleships and destroyers on my screens remind me of our Flight Training exercises. Every Space Cadre and Ranger pilot knows the defensive plans, my Empress," he said.

She answered calmly, "Yes, Sham'S. You are correct. But even protocol plans allow for some level of alteration. Good observation, my friend," she said. She winked at him, and he signed off. She wanted her enemies to think she was using textbook maneuvers. Only the Empress knew the true Plans B and C. Kayla had a big surprise up her sleeve, ready to be activated upon her command—her KRS-201, flying in stealth alongside her Ranger warbirds.

All his spy drones were launched, so F.C. Stek'R changed course, as ordered. Soon, the monitors began beeping. Many more pings began, coming from the spy drones launched three hours ago. He notified C.S. Steph'N and buckled in his pilot seat. He activated stealth mode and joined the Ranger formation. All he had were his laser cannons—no missiles.

"Asteroid 347.65 is pinging, Ranger High Command. Changing course to investigate," M.C. Va'Pal reported. She was less than forty minutes away, flying in stealth mode.

"Heavy pinging from 347.65, Empress Kayla. Advanced scouts will investigate. Faint pings detected from second location, to be investigated, as well, my Empress," M.C. L'Mun reported. Every Ranger was working tonight, even the Empress' barrister.

Everyone was on the live vid comm, ready to coordinate the next orders. The Imperial Military High Command was notified to move to red alert. It was 2:47a.m., thirteen minutes to the Aux Comm Rendezvous.

"Unidentified craft exiting White Belt near asteroid 347.65. They were hiding behind the big rock, Empress Kayla. Scanners show one destroyer and three attack-strikers. No fighters; not yet, anyway," Va'Pal reported. "They are heavily armed."

"Cut the chatter, VaPal, and remain in stealth," C.S. Steph'N ordered. *They probably picked up her comm link now,* he worried. Va'Pal was his Life Partner. Steph'N breathed deeply and buried his emotions. "Succeed at any cost."

F.C. Stek'R broke his comm silence, too, and reported, "Empress Kayla, two squadrons of fighters just launched from 347.65. And another destroyer just came out of hyperspace. It has seven attack-strikers accompanying. Four more squadrons launching from second destroyer. It's an old, big mother, not an attack destroyer, and she's right in front of…" The unmistakable sound of a loud explosion followed by silence told them Stek'R and his warbird had been located by his communications and destroyed.

"Ranger High Command to all warbirds. We have a command destroyer, an attack destroyer, ten attack-strikers, and six squadrons of fighters launched. Hold one moment." Pings from the spy drones near the smaller asteroid in the White Belt began signaling rapidly. "Drone attack fighters have been launched from several points within the White Belt, TMTC (too many to count). Assume attack formation."

She jumped on her comm: "Empress Kayla to all warbirds: Belay the order to assume attack formation. Remain in stealth mode and hold your position," she ordered. There was more to come. She would not have her warbirds group together and become easy targets. Her Battle Plan required precision timing, and she was the one issuing the orders.

From her frontal command position, Kayla studied the Plan Technicians' attack so far: hide and pounce. They used the old drone fighters from one hundred years ago, probably upgraded with today's weaponry and technology. Expendable first line attackers, trying to kill her Rangers. Her Plan was to defend against the Technicians' destroyers with her Ranger fighters and warbirds, using SB4 fighter squadrons to flank them, and its Battleship's fighters as back-up, when the Ranger fighters needed to refuel. The Battleship HMS-1221 fighters were primarily to defend the big Space Base against the attackers.

The Technicians' attack would activate SB4's alarms soon, and forty-eight fighters would launch to defend the Base. Kayla sat bolt upright. *What if SB4 had hidden missiles ready to fire on them? Would it be necessary for their eight squadrons of fighters to launch prior to enabling the hidden missiles?* She ordered the SB4 Base Commander and Battleship HMS-1221 to signal red alert, but not to launch any fighters, or fire their weapons at any time without her direct command. The Base and Battleship Commanding Officers nervously acknowledged her orders. As a precaution, she conferenced Ranger High Command on her call. She displayed the SB4 schematics.

"Empress Kayla to SB4 CO: Follow my orders to the letter, CO. Leave every fighter in the hangar. Do not launch. Repeat: do not launch. Send a team of security officers below Main Hangar Deck A with robo-scanners at once. Report to me immediately. Leave all fighters in place! Intel reports hidden missiles and weaponry directly below hangar decks, to be launched when your fighters launch. Get going with those scanners!" She ordered, her hands working the tactical screens. As a precaution, she ordered the Battleship HMS-1221 to scan for hidden missiles near its hangar decks. The Battleship CO reported all clear after a few minutes.

"Pull up the specs on SB4 now," G'Rosk ordered. The Base was one of the first built. Its hangar decks were modeled after Navy fighter carriers, with the capability to elevate up and down. There was ample room to mount missile launchers beneath the hangar deck. Once all the fighters launched and the deck was clear, the deck platform could be raised seven meters. SB4 would become a very large missile launch site, and probably be destroyed in the process. It took only a matter of minutes for the recon to be reported.

"SB4 CO to Empress Kayla. Your intel was correct. There are four hundred medium and one hundred-twenty big heavies in launch position, concealed behind false partitions. We never would've found them without your order to search with the robo-scanners, my Lady. We are disengaging firing computer control and power sources. Estimated time to completion is three hours. For all our families, thank you, Great Empress Kayla!" The Commanding Officer said, relief showing on his face. She bowed her head to him and clicked off. Three hours without the SB4 fighters crippled her attack plans. Kayla made tactical adjustments to her Battle Plan B, adding parts of C.S. Steph'N's Plan One. The untested KRS-201 became the pivotal element of surprise. The newest destroyer in the Space Cadre fleet was now the critical focus for their defense. She sent the signal to Admiral Kur of the KRS-201 to move into position.

"Whose intel did the Empress use about SB4? I don't see anything on the classified reports," C.S. B'Von said, searching his com tablet.

"Her gut," Lady Bette answered, slowly pacing in the Tactical Room.

Kayla checked the screens for positioning of her Ranger warbirds. Her loving Consort Dan'L was in position directly behind her, with Sham'S flanking. Commander Tish, Bette's granddaughter, was holding the opposite flank position as directed. C.S. Javette had the rear command and monitoring position. She was surrounded by her dearest and most-trusted friends, all excellent, battle-tested pilots. Everyone was depending on her to win this battle.

Kayla punched her comm link and said, "One threat has been neutralized. Many more face us, while unknown threats await the right time to attack. Remember the fourteen billion innocent people asleep in their beds, unaware of the current situation threatening their lives and their future. Stand strong on their unwavering trust, and the trust of your Empress. We are Rangers. We do not surrender. We do not fail. We succeed at any cost! My Faithful Sons and Beloved Daughters, this is the battle you prepared for every day of your lives. The moment is here. The time is NOW! May our Great Creator bless our Rangers!" Her voice rose in its strength and emotion during her rally cry.

Cheers of "Hail Empress Kayla!" came over her comm link for several minutes. She breathed deeply and waited. Dok'T, the former Field Marshall General Blatan of the Imperial Army, knew all standard Imperial battle plans. Kayla knew he designed the attack plans for the Technicians' armada. The Empress designed her own battle plans, to keep her warbirds and battleship one step ahead of the attacking armada coming her way. But with SB4's fighters unable to join her original Plan B attack, the Ranger fighters and KRS-201 carried the responsibility to defeat the enemy. The Battleship HMS-1221 in orbit around SB4 had to keep its fighters ready to defend the critical Space Base.

The six-minute wait was nerve-wracking. The signal finally beeped from the KRS-201, the beginning of her Plan B sequence of actions. Kayla ordered, "All Ranger standard fighters, form dual columns, four by four, one thousand five hundred meters separation." Her Rangers split into two long columns.

"Does anyone know the battle plan here?" C.S. B'Von asked, frantically flipping through his com tablet for orders.

"Empress Kayla knows, and that's good enough for me," G'Rosk remarked quietly. "The fewer who know battle plans, the greater the secrecy—and surprise for the enemy." He watched B'Von toss his com tablet on his desk in frustration.

Two beeps from the KRS-201 came over Kayla's comm link. She ordered, "All ES warbirds pull behind the two Ranger columns and align with them, four by four." The invisible ES warbirds' positions were now known to the incoming attack armada. "Drop stealth, warbirds, and hold steady," she ordered calmly. "All shields up!"

The third signal came next. "C.S. G'Rosk and Lady Bette, ready the 'Plan B' tactical attack plan, but do not yet download," she said. One more signal to go. In another twenty seconds, all ships were in position.

The Technicians' armada was nearly within missile range. This would be a very close call. Their timing must be precise. Here came the fourth and final signal from the KRS-201. On the open broadcast channels, she announced, "This is Empress Kayla to all attacking, illegal vessels. Power down your weapons and come to a full stop for boarding. This is your only opportunity to surrender. You have three seconds to comply." *One, two, three.*

"This is the Great Lord Aug'R, and we will not surrender. Tonight, your Empire is mine!" He clicked off. Her sensors beeped, notifying her she was targeted.

"KRS-201, fire at will!" She ordered. From the center of the two columns of Ranger warbirds, a long, menacing, next-generation destroyer materialized from stealth, and began firing its massive laser cannons on the Technicians' old destroyer. Hundreds of their drone fighters accelerated to attack speed, heading right for the Rangers.

While the destroyers battled each other, the Ranger warbirds engaged. Kayla warned, "Rangers, remember the drone fighters' purpose: to separate you from your formation and target, and get you to empty your lasers. Use your shields!" She cried, "Save your missiles for your targets!" The enemy fighters were in traditional formation, while the drone fighters leading the enemy attack flew their programmed attack patterns against the Ranger warbirds.

In another twelve seconds, Kayla ordered, "KRS-201, engage second phase of your attack Plan B now." The long destroyer moved out weapons' arms from both sides of its hull and fired a series of plasma disrupter arc blasts. The Technicians' attack destroyer exploded in a blinding burst, taking many of its own fighters with it. Another wave of plasma disrupter arcs was fired, effectively vaporizing dozens of drones and attacking fighters in wide, powerful arc blasts.

"ES-317, you've got three drones on your tail. Drop down and I'll get 'em," Sham'S called to Dan'L, who wisely responded immediately. Sham'S and Dan'L made quick work of clearing a path through the drones, and then attacked the unmarked fighters. Dan'L was an excellent warbird pilot. He, Kayla, and C.S. Steph'N fought successfully in several space battles together over the years. All were deadly accurate with their weapons, fast, and focused on victory.

The warbird sorties continued for more than one hour. The Rangers were ordered to make each shot count. They were severely outnumbered. F.C. Bek'R took advantage of enemy fighters pulling away from sorties to regroup in formation, and blasted them with his plasma disruptor arcs. He took out eleven enemy fighters and several drones in one well-placed shot. M. C. Dan'L congratulated him on his tactic and notified his Empress about Bek'R's success.

Space Base 4 called her with the "All Clear" for the hidden missiles' control systems, thankfully releasing their fighters for launching over an hour earlier than expected. The Empress ordered four squadrons of SB4 fighters launched to provide cover for her Ranger warbirds, while they flew for re-arming and refueling on the main hangar deck of the Battleship. In seven minutes, the Space Cadre SB4 fighters joined the battle, and the Ranger warbirds began quick trips to the Battleship HMS-1221 to refuel and re-arm. Empress Kayla led the last two squadrons of ES warbirds for refueling, and they were refueled and re-armed in record time.

"Empress Kayla, SB4 reports the big destroyer is powering up a ballistic missile. A nuke's coming in, my Empress," L'Mun reported.

"Download tactical attack Plan B immediately," she ordered. Their ES tactical screens changed, and several missiles armed automatically. "All Space Cadre fighters return to your main hangar on SB4 right now." The fighters broke away and returned just in time.

"The big one's just launched," L'Mun reported anxiously. "Time to detonation: forty-two seconds!"

Kayla watched the incoming ballistic missile head for SB4 in an attempt to blast it apart. The ES warbirds' missiles fired on the big nuke, rocketing towards them at nearly hyperspace speed. Then, Plan B activated their shields on full, and shot each Ranger fighter and warbird, and the KRS-201, into hyperspace. Eighty-one blips disappeared from the scanners at Ranger High Command.

"Where'd they go? Did the nuke get them all?" C.S. T'Anh cried out. She had not seen either Plan B or Plan C. Her counterpart B'Von put his head in his hands from sheer frustration.

"They're in hyperspace now," G'Rosk called out. "Give them a few minutes."

The Rangers' tactical Plan B missiles exploded the nuke-tipped ballistic missile, and it blew up far away from SB4. The flash was devastating, taking out several of the Technicians' fighters and drones in its conflagration. The frontal wave of the explosion was felt on SB4, and the Battleship; but no damage was sustained.

"Twenty seconds to go… They're coming back in 3, 2, 1; now!" G'Rosk announced. Seventy-seven blips returned. The Ranger warbirds came back to their pilots' control, and the sorties resumed.

Empress Kayla breathed a sigh of relief. They avoided being caught in a nuclear firestorm. But four warbirds did not automatically drop out of hyperspace. She checked the warbirds' ID numbers, and her heart sank. The ES-317 was missing. For a moment, she felt as if she was falling. The ES-317 was Dan'L's warbird.

Her comm link beeped, "ES-519, this is Javette. You must continue forward; ever forward, my Warrior Empress Kayla!" There was no hiding the tears in Javette's eyes. But she was right. They had to fight on and win.

Win for Dan'L, her Son, and fourteen billion people sound asleep in their beds.

"KRS-201, this is Empress Kayla. Take out their last attack-strikers and that bloody destroyer! Pave our way to victory, my creation!" Admiral Kur acknowledged her orders and opened his ship's arc arms again. He fired both arms, relentlessly pounding the Technicians' last vessels, until his plasma banks were empty.

The attack-strikers and fighters protecting the Technicians' big destroyer took the brunt of the arcs, not the destroyer itself. The KRS-201 was not finished, however. It had a few more tricks up its sleeve. "Admiral Kur, ready plasma fusion bombs, and realign position for phase three of Plan B," she said. The long weapons arms folded back.

"Engage stealth mode now, KRS-201, and finish the destroyer," Kayla ordered. "When you have the shot, take it, Admiral Kur." The KRS disappeared. "All ES warbirds, full shields, and form double delta formation now. Close ranks," she ordered. The ES warbirds pulled out of their sorties and regrouped in the center, directly in front of the old destroyer, and protected the standard Ranger fighters. In seconds, the big KRS reappeared behind the Technicians' destroyer and fired plasma fusion bombs into her engines and rear laser cannons. The explosion was incredibly brilliant and blinding for several seconds. The Technicians' fighters nearest the destroyer got caught in the explosion and disintegrated.

"Well, Empress Bitch, you surprised us once again. Like all good bitches, you surround yourself with lots of good, powerful men. But I am not done with you. The Aux Comm, like the Old Engine, has many moving parts," Aug'R said, beginning to cough. "By the end of this day, we will all meet in the Afterlife!" He said with a raspy laugh. Then, the remaining forward section of his destroyer exploded.

"All Rangers, regroup in your squadrons. Set course for asteroid 374.65. Engage," she ordered firmly.

The door to Ranger High Command opened, and M.C. Kend'R walked in. "Where are we?" He asked. Lady Bette gave him a punitive look and pointed at L'Mun.

She gave him a quick update, and added, "Rangers all on course for asteroid 374.65, to finish it."

Kend'R nodded and took a seat. The words of Dok'T echoed: "32-14-9, seven come eleven; send the sinners to hell, and the children to heaven." He saw imminent destruction in his mind, and then cried out, "It's a trap! 374.65 is wired to blow with baby nukes. He'll take them all with him! Tell her. Tell her now!" He cried frantically, "The White Belt will kill them all!"

Lady Bette called Empress Kayla to break off the attack and reverse course immediately, per Kend'R's intel. On their scanners, seventy-seven blips turned and reversed course. Then the massive explosion happened in three waves, each one bigger and brighter than the next. Explosion one was bright blue; the second explosion was yellow-tinged, with several smaller explosions near the edges. The third explosion was immense, filling her entire view screen with brilliant fiery red and orange-colored destruction. The scene reminded Kayla of the Holy Book's pictures of the depths of Hell: red and orange flames, with black, billowing clouds of smoke engulfing the immediate space in front of them.

Her warbird was caught in the force of the explosion and blown backwards; it rolled, yawed, pitched, and spun wildly from the explosions. Kayla. continually adjusted its helm, trying to bring the ES-519 back under control. All scanners went blank. Her onboard computer crashed for several seconds, then rebooted automatically. Fortunately, her ship shields stayed powered-up, and deflected or destroyed the sporadic asteroid fragments coming at her ship at high speeds. No communications were possible for several minutes.

Dead silence in the Ranger High Command office. Then the scanners came online. Fifty-nine blips appeared on their scanners. In the White Belt, the humongous explosion sent hundreds of asteroids out of their regular orbits, crashing into one another and space debris, and bursting into thousands of fragments, like a spinning dance of death. It was the most devastating series of explosions they had ever seen. The disruption within the White Belt would go on for several years, preventing any travel inside the asteroid belt.

"Red alert. All Space Cadre ships and fighters near Ban'Ti, M'Wati, and the White Belt." L'Mun ordered, "Full shields, now." Weeks of firing on errant asteroids hurling towards the two planets near the White Belt—Ban'Ti and M'Wati—would have to take place. Pulverized space debris began to appear everywhere in front of the squadron. Every warbird raised their shields.

The Empress knew she lost more good Rangers in the explosion, but could not identify any of their missing fighters yet. There were five confirmed kills and nineteen warbirds and fighters Missing In Action (MIA). She said a prayer of gratitude more of her Rangers were not killed and tried to visually count the warbirds near her. It was over.

Space Cadre destroyer attack groups in position above the planets began defensive maneuvers to protect M'Wati and Ban'Ti. Their ship shields provided the first line of defense against the small-to-medium asteroid fragments. Laser cannons pulverized the larger pieces of rock away from the two planets.

Battleship HMS-1221 near SB4 deployed its fighters for search-and-rescue missions. The remaining Ranger warbirds refueled and re-armed at SB4. Their pilots ate and rested, and then began their return trip back to Home World in seven hours. The final expense paid in Ranger pilot lives and warbirds was still being tallied during their flight home. But everyone was satisfied with the obliteration of the Aux Comm. The destruction could have been much worse, if the arsenal of deadly weapons and warships from the Aux Comm had been unleashed on Home World. The seat of the Empire would have been decimated.

XXIX

Home World

In Dok'T's prison cell, Kend'R waited while Lord T'Sel gave the prisoner another shot of truth serum, then said, "I'll take it from here, my Lord."

He began, "Once more, I have come to serve you, Holy Monk Dok'T. Space Base 4 is whole, and its hidden missiles are neutralized. Asteroid 374.65 has been destroyed from within, and caused great disruption within the White Belt, Holy Monk," Kend'R said.

Dok'T said, "The Creator is with her. I assume she yet lives?"

"Yes, but at the cost of many of my Ranger brothers and sisters," he answered. "It is a sad day, Holy Monk."

"They will be welcomed in the Afterlife, and receive the Creator's mercy," Dok'T mumbled.

"Yes, it is good to receive mercy. And your mercy is what I have come to seek, Brother. They think it is over, but you and I know better, do we not?" Kend'R asked.

Dok'T smiled, "No. It is not over. One step leads to another. You are correct, my son."

Kend'R asked, "Please, tell me how to finish it, so that no more innocents die. We must save them, Holy Monk. Please tell me Brother Dok'T: What steps remain?" His patience was gone. Too much was at stake. "Tell me everything, Holy Monk. Tell me now," Kend'R said forcefully, and held Dok'T's face in his hands, staring into his eyes and probing his mind for several minutes. Flashing images of ultimate destruction and death burst forth from Dok'T.

"That is all," Dok'T said, rolled his eyes, and passed out. The force of Kend'R's mind probe took all his energy, and left Kend'R nearly limp.

"Help me upstairs, now!" Kend'R said to the young prison guard. Into the Ranger High Command, the guard led an ashen Kend'R. G'Rosk rushed up to him and helped Kend'R sit at his desk. "Call her for me, now. Please, sir, I must speak to her now," Kend'R asked weakly.

"This is Empress Kayla. Kend'R, all you all right?" She asked with a worried voice.

He nodded, and said, "The Aux Comm Program is in many levels, and two steps remain: you must not land at the Capital City or Centralia Bases. They have been activated to blow when the warbirds land. The last is the worst: no one must cross the threshold of the Royal Palaces. They are also a trap. The Aux Comm is like your shuttle accident; one failure, then another, and another. The activation sequence cannot be cancelled or aborted, my Empress."

"What about those people currently in the Palaces? Can they escape? What about the Guards?" She asked, nearly desperate.

He shook his head and answered, "Everyone in both Royal Palaces will die. It is the final step of the Aux Comm programming. No one may cross the threshold—in or out, my Empress." Kend'R started to fade, and said, "Do not land on the bases. Do not cross the threshold of the Palaces. Do not land. Do not cross," then his head fell onto the desk with a thud.

"Notify the Imperial Guard High Command at both Palaces. Emergency lock down procedures. Lock the doors from the outside. Close and barricade the Main Gates. Sound the red alert at Centralia and Capital City Space Bases!" Lady Bette ordered loudly, "Get our Palace broadcast channel up NOW!" She ran to the vid screen to deliver orders in person.

Orders were implemented at both Palaces. Palace Guards on sentry duty, and Rangers and Imperial Guards returning from early morning runs were not allowed re-entry. Anyone outside was taken to the Main Gates and not permitted re-entry. Both Palace Main Doors and outer gates were locked and secured. Every door and window were remotely locked, and could only be re-opened by Lady Bette, Baron P'Lau, or Empress Kayla. Tension mounted over the next few hours, with no explanations given. Imperial Army troops, technicians, and medical shuttles were deployed to both Royal Palaces.

In three hours, she called, "General Hal'Bek, this is Empress Kayla, requesting landing for fifty-eight Ranger warbirds, and shuttles for our Rangers!" They landed safely on Island 1034, and pilots assembled near the arrival building on the tarmac. The Empress called role, checking off each pilot silently. Nineteen of her original pilots were Missing In Action (MIA), including C.S. Javette, C.S. Steph'N, M.C. Va'Pal, F. C. Stek'R, and her Royal Consort M.C. Dan'L. Every pilot looked around their squadron for the ones MIA.

Kayla took off her helmet and said, "Space Base 4 fighters are conducting search-and-rescue attempts for our missing warbirds, and search-and-destroy for the Technicians' fighters. Both Palaces and the

Space Bases near them are on emergency lock-down. Refer to your information downloads. We will be shuttled to the Farm, courtesy of the Imperial Army," she said, and nearly smiled. "Thank you all. This was a maximum effort of men, women, and machinery. We thank the Creator for our dedicated, loyal Rangers and Space Cadre personnel. May He bless all of us tonight," she closed.

Kayla put her helmet on again and followed the Army Captain to his private shuttle. "Sham'S, Tish; you're with me," she ordered, and they boarded. Silently they sat, each looking out the window, wondering where their friends and loved ones were. Two Elder Rangers met her shuttle when it landed and led the Empress to the underground storerooms' emergency quarters. Master Commanders Shanna and L'Van were very relieved to see their victorious Empress Kayla return. Kayla thanked them, took off her armor, arm bands, and boots. She showered, put on a clean uniform, and laid down next to her Son Lukus.

Prayers were said for the MIA pilots. In the morning, little Lukus awoke in his Mother's arms. "Where's Father?" The boy saw the tears fall down her face, and asked, "And Grandmother Javette?" Then he cried with his Mother, until the soft knock on the door came.

"Please excuse the interruption, Empress Kayla, but Commander Superior G'Rosk is on the vid for you," M.C. L'Van said.

"Give me a minute," she choked out. Both Mother and Son tried to compose themselves. Lukus would not let go of Kayla, so she picked him up and went to the vid. She hit the button and asked, "Do you have any good news for us, my dear friend?"

His red eyes told her she wasn't the only one in emotional distress. He started to speak when Lukus asked, "Did you find Grandmother? Or my Father?" G'Rosk turned away, and L'Mun took over the call.

"My Empress, Space Cadre search and rescue have located several of our warbirds adrift in the White Belt. They are towing them back to SB4. Five have been damaged badly and will have to be identified when in the Base hangar. The Base released twenty-four spy drones programmed to search for our warbirds deeper in the White Belt. No further information, my Empress," L'Mun concluded. Kayla bowed her head and turned off the screen.

Master Commander Shanna contacted her Partner, Admiral Mae, unable to explain anything of the last few days. L'Van became overwhelmed with emotion when she picked up her three-year-old daughter Marta, at the Farm. The fate of her partner M.C. Kris'T was unknown.

Imperial Army security scans revealed active sensors under each Home World Royal Palace doorway, including the secret door for the emergency escape passageway. Lower floor balcony doors and top floor windows of the Royal Suite also had sensors affixed. The sensors would have detonated four plasma fusion bombs recently buried alongside the new foundation stones of the Palace, reducing the reconstructed stone Palace to ash. The civilian construction managers, supervisors, and their crews were ordered arrested and detained for interrogation.

At the K'Halon Prime Royal Palace, only the Main Court doors were affected, with much smaller, less potent bombs planted in the kitchen's storeroom. It was obviously a hurried job.

The Space Cadre Base at Capital City had twelve plasma fusion bombs imbedded under the transport landing sites. So many large, deadly bombs would have taken out the entire Base, three kilometers surrounding the Base, and left a hole over twenty meters deep.

Like the weak bomb attempt at the Palace on K'Halon Prime, the Centralia Space Cadre Base had three missiles primed to explode upon any vessel landing near the second site. All those missiles were cleared in one day. But the Home World Base and Royal Palace required careful extraction by Imperial Army Bomb Bots and their explosives technicians.

New uniforms and clothing were delivered to all the personnel forced outside of their barracks and homes by the Aux Comm Battle. Everyone showered and changed into their new black uniforms and felt better. Time to make the call: "Commander Superior G'Rosk, greetings to you my friend. How many warbirds and pilots have been recovered?" Kayla asked.

He answered matter-of-factly, "A total of eight, my Empress. Three are confirmed deceased, four have been rescued with minor injuries, and one is in serious condition at SB4. No further infor… one moment, please," he said. L'Mun whispered in his ear. He cleared his throat.

"Just tell me, G'Rosk," she said impatiently.

"Four more Ranger warbirds have been recovered. All have considerable damage to their craft. No pilots responsive. One is the ES-317, Empress Kayla." He looked into her weary eyes.

"Continue your prayers to our Creator, as will I. Keep me informed, Commander Superior G'Rosk," she said and slapped the com button. The ES-317 was the warbird for her Consort Dan'L. He was her best friend for the better part of her life; her Consort, lover, protector, and Father to her only Son, Lukus. Neither of them was even thirty-three years of age. But suddenly, she felt old and worn, like the tired, torn uniform she just threw away this morning. How much pain did G'Rosk feel for Javette?

Kayla bolted from her emergency office. Fresh air was what she needed; she couldn't breathe. She jogged through the storeroom, ahead of her startled Imperial Guards, and ran up the five flights of stairs three at a time. She ran full speed from the building's concealed opening in a haze, her long black hair flying behind her. She kept running through the bare fields of harvested grain, until she saw the skyline of Capital City.

The lone Imperial Guard able to keep up with his Empress stopped beside her, both panting. "You're a very good runner, Empress Kayla," he said. "We called for your shuttle, if you'd like to fly back, ma'am," he said between breaths.

She smiled at her young Guard and nodded. "How far did we run?" She asked. Two more Guards joined them, and she repeated, "How far?"

The First Commander looked at his comm link and answered, "Seven point three kilometers, Empress Kayla. We all needed a good stretch this morning, my Lady," he added, and they all began to laugh. They hopped into the shuttle and flew back to the Farm.

After another hot shower and new uniform, Empress Kayla tackled the work on her desk again. Lady Bette called in the report: Steph'N, Va'Pal and Stek'R's damaged warbirds were found, with all pilots deceased. Kayla was prepared for the information; but the confirmation of Commander Superior Steph'N's death made her very sad. Two more Ranger warbirds were located, and those pilots were also deceased. Lunch upset her stomach even more.

Thank the Creator her friend Sham'S made it. She, Dan'L, Sham'S, and L'Mun were inseparable in Phase 1, 2, and 3 Ranger Training. And Steph'N arranged for her escape from Duma Wat on old SB 5 with T'Anh and Dan'L, when she and Dan'L were Novices. Steph'N and Dan'L were her best friends for several years. She was running out of friends. Could she let anyone close to her again? The odds did not seem to favor those who were her best friends. Kayla felt toxic.

The preliminary report of the forensic work on the Palace showed fingerprints on the sensors belonged to one of the Palace Guards. She became angry at his betrayal, and, without thinking, hit the speed dial for Javette. When no one answered after three beeps, she hung up.

C.S. Javette was Dan'L's Mother, and Grandmother to Lukus. She and G'Rosk were Life Partners for almost eight years, now. Javette tried to shield a young Novice Kayla from C.S. T'Anh's jealous, resentful tirades, and unfair treatment during her first five years. Javette was still beautiful, once the most beautiful of all the Kaylan Rangers. Young Borgund Novices swooned if Javette merely said, "Good morning," to them. Her friend and former mentor, G'Rosk, must be devastated about Javette being MIA.

Kayla's Mother, Master Commander Rosa, died when Kayla was only seven years old. She was closer to Javette than she had ever been to any woman. Javette was dedicated and intense but had a great sense of humor. She was a kind and caring Grandmother and loved to dance. They were the best of friends. Javette was irreplaceable.

Kayla left the underground storeroom with her papers and com tablets, and ordered everything moved into her Master Suite at the Farm. The emergency facility was bomb-proof, but she couldn't breathe or think positively down there. She walked the long tunnel into the Farm's wine cellar, consumed in thought.

Two hours later another update came from L'Mun, "Space Cadre expects the towed ES-317 to arrive at SB4 within the hour. They will update us when it lands on the hangar. No word on C.S. Javette, or any other pilots, my Empress. I promise to call you at once," L'Mun said. She thanked L'Mun and clicked off.

Dinner with Lukus and M.C. Shanna was quiet, and Kayla couldn't eat. Her Son talked about his new "Farmer" clothing from Lady Bette, pointing out how plain it was compared with his usual "Princely" clothes. He finally made his Mother laugh and jumped down to hug her. *Funny how children always try to please their Mothers, even in dire circumstances*, she thought.

The Empress offered Shanna some time off, but she refused. "Your Kaylan Ranger will only accept time off when the Royal Palace is reopened, my beloved Empress. Until then, the Prince is under my personal protection." Kayla agreed, and felt better to leave Lukus in the care of her personal guard.

"The Empress' work is never done," Lukus smiled and said. He took Shanna's hand and left with her.

When asteroid 374.65 was destroyed from its hidden arsenal within by the Aux Comm programming, the explosions were so violent and powerful, the Ranger warbirds nearest the asteroid suffered an EMP. In addition to damages from the explosion itself, the surviving fighter pilots had no power in their warbirds, no communications, and no distress beacon. Every fighter had portable emergency trackers, but they were useless inside the craft. The pings just resounded within the interior of the ships loudly. Only if the pilot was physically able to open a hatch or window manually and affix the tracker onto the hull, could it become functional. If the pilot was injured or otherwise unable to get the hatch open, no rescue pings could be transmitted from an EMP-affected fighter.

Each ES warbird and traditional fighter carried one or more spacesuits with their own oxygen supply for three hours. Added to their fighter's eight-hour emergency supply, the pilots had eleven hours to be rescued. Deep meditation was taught to each pilot to breathe as slowly as possible. But time to find pilots alive and functioning was nearly gone.

Kayla was startled by another beep, "Royal Consort Master Commander Dan'L was removed from his ES-317 alive, but badly injured. His right leg was nearly crushed. He suffered significant blood loss," G'Rosk anxiously reported, "but the initial prognosis is favorable, Empress Kayla!"

She managed to thank him for the news. After a prayer of heartfelt gratitude to her Creator, Kayla became physically ill and began throwing up. She rested for a few minutes, then ordered Shanna to bring Lukus to her office. Upon hearing the good news, the boy ran around the room in circles, jumping on all the furniture, making both women laugh. There were still five more MIA pilots. The odds were getting worse every hour.

Space Cadre called in her next update: "Wreckage of enemy attack-striker found, with three men unconscious, but still alive."

Kayla said firmly, "I want them revived and brought before me - alive!" She did not feel "Benevolent" today. Suddenly, she ran to the bathroom and vomited violently. *What a time to get a stomach virus,* she thought.

An unusual call came in to SB4 on its open channel: "Space Command, this is mining colony Alt'Ar. We just picked up a distress ping. You got any ships missing in the White Belt?"

The ping was located on an asteroid thousands of kilometers from the battle location. Space Cadre fighters landed next to it and called, "ES-201 has been located. Pilot is sitting on the fuselage awaiting rescue. Will send more info when pilot is on board."

C.S. Javette was in her Ranger black battle armor, with less than ten minutes of oxygen remaining. The force of the 374.65 asteroid explosion sent her warbird careening off course, hit by errant asteroid fragments. Her ES was beat to an unrecognizable form after ricocheting off several asteroids in the final explosion. Javette always flew with three space suits, plus her Ranger battle armor—a habit which saved her life.

She made her own report, "C.S. Javette to Ranger High Command. Have been rescued by SB4 fighters and am returning to their base. The ES-201 is inoperable. Requesting immediate transport to Home World, ASAP."

"This is G'Rosk. Are you all right, Javette?"

"I know it's you, G'Rosk. And no, I'm not all right. My ES-201 was knocked around like a kick ball! It's completely unresponsive, and probably scrap by now. Please inform Empress Kayla I will have to requisition another warbird, G'Rosk." She saw him breathe deeply and sigh.

The Empress was already on her call, and asked, "Are you hurt, Javette?"

"I'm a little banged up and have a concussion. And my nails are ruined! Just bring me home, my Empress," she answered, and gave a tired smile.

Ranger High Command was in much better spirits. Lukus was told his Grandmother was alive and feisty, and the boy jumped for joy. Javette and Dan'L were put on a Space Cadre fighter the next day and flown to Home World. Still, four more warbirds were MIA.

By morning, wreckage from three traditional Ranger fighters was found, with all pilots deceased, including M.C. L'Van's Life Partner, M.C. Kris'T. Three weeks for grieving time was given to Empress Kayla's personal guard, M.C. L'Van, for the loss of her Life Partner M.C. Kris'T. She was escorted to her parent's home with little daughter Marta.

The last MIA was F.C. Bok, who was found on a tiny ice asteroid, barely alive. Space Cadre pilots revived him and brought him to SB4.

To top everything off, Empress Kayla doubled over from throwing up. This was happening too many days for stomach flu. A concerned M.C. Shanna called for the Royal Physician this time. After a quick scan by Admiral Mae, her true condition was announced to the startled Empress: She was six weeks pregnant, with twin fetuses. She smiled with Admiral Mae, and ordered the information kept secret. Once the bombs and sensors to activate them were cleared, Kayla moved back into the Royal Suite in the repaired North Wing of the Home World Royal Palace.

XXX

Upon landing at the Army Base, Consort M. C. Dan'L and C.S. Javette were shuttled to the Home World Royal Palace. Royal Physician Admiral Mae scanned the emergency work on Dan'L's leg and approved. He was in a full-leg tension cast, with metal pins and tightening screws attached. "After a few days' rest, we'll shuttle you for ReGen-Pod treatments for your leg and kidneys," she said. "It will accelerate your recovery, Consort Dan'L."

He was uncomfortable and kept trying to sit up. He asked, "Will I heal completely and be able to resume my position as Master Commander? You know our P.T. standards. Will I be able to run again? Dance with my wife?"

She slowly shook her head and answered, "Better to know now than later, Royal Consort. You should recover within three to four weeks. But complex, multiple fractures like these are Ranger Career-ending. You will be able to run, but not at all like you did before, I'm afraid. Dancing occasionally should be no problem," she said. "You're very lucky, as I'm sure you were told. Your femoral artery somehow escaped being lacerated by your bone." She gave him a mild tranquilizer, seeing how her prognosis upset him.

The Admiral gave the information to Empress Kayla. "Dan'L and I both are Rangers, Admiral Mae. It will be a difficult transition for him, but he will make it. Once a Borgund Ranger, always a Borgund Ranger!" Admiral Mae was not so sure as her Empress.

The tight head bandage was finally removed from Javette's head. The body bruises from being slammed into many asteroids would take longer to go away. She immediately went to the salon to have her hair and nails done. The small indulgences made her feel better. Her recovery accelerated when her twelve-year-old daughter K'Rissa received a special weekend pass from the Royal Academy to visit her Mother, and her brother, Consort Dan'L.

Funeral celebrations for the eleven deceased Rangers were held, paid for by the Empire. The celebrations were sad and poignant. Not all of them were recipients of high awards in the past, but each was given a special commendation for valor and bravery in the "Aux Comm Battle." In addition to the eleven funerals, fifteen more Rangers would receive medical disability discharges from service upon their recovery and release, including Royal Consort Master Commander Dan'L. Each surviving spouse or discharged Ranger received an annual pension from the Empire, as was the law.

Aboard the Prison Transport En Route to Home World – Three weeks later

The short prisoner was escorted back to his seat and buckled in for the remainder of their journey. But, unlike his two fellow prisoners, he was not chained and shackled. The leader of the three men said, "You're disgusting, Mon'T. You didn't have to do it. Even you must have some pride," B'Nard said, and spit on the floor.

Mon'T smiled and reached into his pocket. Slowly he pulled out the keys he took from the prison guard he "serviced." B'Nard's look of disgust turned into a smile. "The price of freedom depends on the jailer," Mon'T whispered. B'Nard, M'Tuk, and Mon'T chuckled.

Their prison shuttle was nearing Home World Royal Palace. The Empress ordered the only enemy survivors of the Aux Comm Battle brought before her Main Court. A frantic incoming call to Space Command was whispered, "We have been hijacked. Three prisoners have taken control of transport, on heading for the Royal Palace. Notify all emergency units. They intend to crash the shuttle on the Palace!" The wounded guard was caught and killed.

Home World Royal Palace

Three men parachuted down, abandoning the shuttle before the shield barrier came up. "All defensive shields over the Palace now," C.S. Javette ordered. Defensive laser cannons targeted the incoming shuttle as it flew towards the rebuilt Palace and destroyed it.

"Capture those escaped prisoners. I want them alive!" Empress Kayla ordered, watching the situation from her private study. The Palace Guards were fired on by B'Nard and M'Tuk, both former Army commandos. Somehow, the three escapees made it onto the Palace interior courtyard near the Royal Academy. An Imperial Guard's pulser spear killed Mon'T and wounded M'Tuk, but he continued running behind B'Nard.

Suddenly, the situation developed into a nightmare. The second year Royal Academy students were at recess, playing outside. B'Nard captured a Royal Academy child and held his laser pistol at her quavering head. All Guards and Rangers were ordered to hold their fire. Shouting at the top of his voice, B'Nard yelled, "Bring me the Empress Bitch, or the girl dies!"

Kayla was notified at once. She immediately put on her armor and arm bands and swirled on her long black cloak. "You can't do this, Empress Kayla! He wants to kill you! We can't let you go out there!" Her Imperial Guards protested.

She declared, "I have enough innocent blood on my hands. My fate belongs to our Creator. I am your Empress, and you will let me pass!" She ran down the stairs, across the courtyard towards the Royal Academy.

"She's doing WHAT?" G'Rosk yelled and looked out the window to see for himself. Every available Ranger and Imperial Guard was ordered onto the courtyard. Dan'L transferred into his anti-grav chair and left his room. The Guards stood in formation behind B'Nard, waiting for further orders.

"Use the kid as a hostage, and let's get out of here, B'Nard," M'Tuk said. "If we make it to…"

"Shut up!" B'Nard yelled. "You knew when we parachuted down here, we were both dead. I want her standing before me, begging for her life! I'll take the Empress Bitch to the Afterlife with me!"

Empress Kayla ran until she could see B'Nard's face: hard and determined, with his brow sweating. He showed no other emotion. A very self-controlled man. A cold, calculating killer, who would not hesitate to end the life of a terrified child in his grasp. He had nothing left to lose.

"Release that innocent child, B'Nard. She has done nothing to you," Kayla shouted. "I order you to release her this instant!"

He snorted and said, "You wanted me to face you, and here I am, Empress Bitch!"

"Hiding behind the skirt of an innocent girl. The Creator is watching you, B'Nard. Now, release the child, and I will let you and your partner M'Tuk go. You have my word," she said, trying to calm both men. M'Tuk sprinted away and stumbled.

"Run then. You coward! The Empress Bitch will catch you at the Main Gate," B'Nard said to M'Tuk, now crawling on the grass.

Kayla slowly walked two steps forward. "What do you hope to accomplish by this fiasco? Dozens of laser rifles are pointing at you. The courtyard is surrounded by Imperial Guards and Rangers. You will not escape today, B'Nard. Now, make one final act of compassion, and release the child. Let her go, and I swear as your Empress, you will not be killed by their laser blasts. Release her, B'Nard."

B'Nard laughed and said, "I will release her, on one condition. Take off your fancy red armor and plasma sword and fight me. You want to rule like a man, then fight me! We will both die today!" M'Tuk hobbled to the end of the courtyard. Imperial Guards closed ranks in front of him, and he wisely threw down his laser rifle and raised his hands in surrender.

Kayla asked, "As the one challenged, do I get to choose the weapons?"

The 20th degree T'Ly Master excelled with every martial arts and conventional weapon. She was ambidextrous with hand weapons, as was every Ranger. In truth, Kayla preferred the spear for martial arts contests. But this was no mere sparring contest; one of them could lose their life in this challenge. There would be no rules of engagement today.

"No weapons. Just you and me. Fist to fist. Can you handle it, Bitch?"

"I will fight you hand to hand," she said. "I accept your challenge, B'Nard. No body armor. Put down your laser pistol and release the girl." She unbuckled her dark red body armor and let it fall to the ground. "See? I am without my armor. Release the child, B'Nard. Release her and fight me, if you dare." She subtly folded her hands, her thumb near her shield controls.

B'Nard said loudly, "Your Empress gave me her word. I am releasing the girl. Don't shoot," he cried. He raised his hands off the little girl, dropped his laser pistol, and the little girl ran to the Imperial Guards.

Her long black cloak was thrown off, and Kayla asked, "Why do you want this fight, B'Nard? The Plan is finished. Aux Comm is destroyed. Why not surrender, and live?"

"Because no man has been able to kill you. I am the man who will end your reign. The records will say, 'Great Empress Kayla was killed by B'Nard!' Your destiny awaits, Empress Bitch!" He moved closer, assuming a martial arts pose.

Kayla faced off against him in a T'Ly defensive stance. "Come claim your glory and make a name for yourself, B'Nard. I'm bored waiting on you!"

B'Nard attacked her fiercely. The man was a former Imperial Army commando and knew T'Ly. He was powerful, taller, and quite strong. But Kayla was exceptionally fast. Kick after kick, punch after punch was thrown, but none landed on her. She defended against him by blocking his attacks and did not hit him, and it angered B'Nard even more. "Hit me, you Bitch! Are you afraid to hit me?" He yelled.

She taunted, "I don't like embarrassing little boys with frail egos." He came after her with fury and nearly landed a double-kick on her two-month pregnant belly. She turned just in time. From the sideline, Admiral Mae watched the fight, terrified he was going to hurt Kayla's developing babies, and possibly render the Empress badly injured.

Kayla's goal was to keep her defensive moves going until he showed signs of becoming tired, but the fiend relentlessly came after her again and again. He was running on pure adrenalin. Then, an opening came. Kayla jumped up, spun, and kicked his head. A gaping cut was left where her high heel wounded his head, and it bled noticeably.

"Your first mistake, Empress Bitch!" B'Nard said, savagely spun and threw a kick at her. She blocked him, and kicked his lower gut so hard, the sound of his cry of pain filled the courtyard. Then he pulled a knife from his boot and threatened, "I'll cut your pretty face so bad no man will want to look at you."

Kayla laughed at him, pulled up her skirt and took out a knife from her high-heeled boot. "Give it up, B'Nard. Your Empress is a Kaylan Ranger. We do not surrender!"

"You're just a Bitch, and no Empress of mine!" He yelled and charged her. He was good with a blade, but not as fast as his opponent. Kayla sliced the side of his face, and he screamed. Their fight became faster with both fighters thrusting and slashing at each other. Kayla's long silk skirt and blouse offered no resistance to lasers and knife cuts. A full-on knife thrust would severely wound her—and her unborn twins. She was even more careful and fast in her defense.

"I tire of you, B'Nard. This sparring contest bores me," she taunted again. He rushed her, and Kayla kicked the blade out of his hand. She head-butted him in his face and he stumbled. Kayla jumped again and gave him alternating midsection kicks three times in mid-air. B'Nard fell on his butt, a look of pure amazement on his face. He lunged at her once more, and Kayla jumped, spun, and kicked him senseless. When he staggered, she jump-kicked his back with both feet, and he fell on his belly.

The Warrior Empress put her high-heeled boot on his neck and declared loudly, "Who's the bitch now?" The cheering Rangers on the sidelines rushed in, picked up B'Nard, and cuffed him. M'Tuk broke free from his distracted Imperial Guard. The Empress raised her arm and shot M'Tuk with the laser in her arm band. The man who attempted to assassinate her Son was dead.

"You had those on your wrists the whole time. Why didn't you just shoot me?" B'Nard asked incredulously.

"It's something you know nothing about, B'Nard. Honor," she said, and her Guardsmen took him away. Empress Kayla put on her dark red armor, and then swirled on her black cloak.

A Novice Imperial Guard whispered to Dan'L, "Pardon me for saying, Royal Consort; but I've never seen our Empress fight. She's a beautiful woman, but when she fights, she's …"

"Hot. Yes, I know," Dan'L said, and gave a stern look at the Guard. Then he laughed and said, "Her green eyes show red specks of passion and fire. She is fierce!"

"Yes, but she should not have taken the chance, after all she's been through the last year," Admiral Mae said with concern in her voice. She never mentioned Kayla's pregnancy.

The Empress walked back to the group of Ranger leaders and her Consort, the look of satisfaction on her face. An unhappy G'Rosk said, "A dangerous move, Empress Kayla. B'Nard could have killed the girl, and you, too, with his laser pistol."

"G'Rosk, you taught me never to cower in the face of danger in Phase 2 and 3 Ranger Training. I did what was necessary to free the girl," she said emphatically. "I kept my word— even to a terrorist. And I kicked his ass!" She added and walked to the Royal Academy.

Kayla went over to the child B'Nard had terrorized, knelt, and told her, "You were incredibly brave, Jenna. I am so proud of you! Would you join me for lunch today? We'll have tea and cakes, and ice cream for dessert," she said, and held out her hand. They walked to the Palace, and the little girl and her classmates were treated to an afternoon lunch with the Empress and Prince Lukus, and Consort Dan'L. Jenna received presents galore for her bravery. Prince Lukus escorted little Jenna and her classmates back to the Royal Academy, accompanied by dozens of Imperial Guards.

When he was alone in his office, G'Rosk entered his notes into the official Ranger High Command record and closed the formal entry thusly: "The Great Warrior Empress Kayla personally vanquished the last of the 'Plan of the Thirteen' Technicians." He sat back and smiled, thinking of his former protege, *Kayla beat B'Nard wearing a long silk skirt and high heeled boots!* G'Rosk went to the underground prison level to supervise the interrogation of the recaptured prisoner.

XXXI

The anniversary of Empress Kayla's fifth year as Sovereign passed during the reconstruction of the Royal Palace. But, since their Royal Wedding took place only a few months after her coronation, Chief Advisor Baron P'Lau recommended combining the two events into one "Fifth Anniversary Celebration Cruise." Each planet would be visited by the Empress on the Celebration Cruise, and their capital cities planned extensive festivities for her visit.

Royal Consort Dan'L floated in his powered, anti-gravity chair beside Kayla, with Lukus riding on his lap. She strolled through the Main Courtyard with them, observing the continuing repairs. Dan'L had been silent the entire time. He asked, "What will I do, when I can't be a Borgund Ranger anymore, my Empress? It's all I ever wanted to be my whole life."

She took his outstretched hand and answered, "There are many projects that could use your expertise, my Consort. I will discuss the possibilities with both you and Admiral Olm, when you recover and retire out. He can no longer serve in the Space Cadre and is as disconcerted as you. Please concentrate on healing, Dan'L. We'll find something to occupy your mind and your time, never fear."

He grinned and asked, "Article 27?"

His Empress backhanded his arm and replied, "You had your chance. Too late now, my Royal Consort!" They laughed together and continued their stroll. She said, "We will travel to K'Halon Prime after our Home World Main Court reopens and hold a few days of Court there. Then M'Wati for two weeks. We need to visit their new capital city, Lova. A few days on Ban'Ti; then inspections of our Central Core Space Bases. A good itinerary for our Fifth Anniversary Celebration Cruise, don't you think?"

"As long as I'm out of this tension cast by the time we reach M'Wati, I'm all in! I want to go diving there," he said, and Lukus agreed.

"Of course. I won't be showing until we return, anyway," she said with a cagey smile.

Dan'L's face lit up. "That's the best news I've heard in weeks! Boy or girl?"

"Admiral Mae said it's too early to tell. But perhaps, one of each," she said.

"Twins? Now I really have to find a new job!" He said, his face getting serious. Kayla smiled at him, and they continued their walk.

Javette and K'Rissa joined the Royal Couple, and G'Rosk jogged over to catch up. Soon, they arrived at her private Royal Court, nearly completed. "It's beautiful, Empress Kayla! The colors are delicate and brighten your Court considerably. Such a contrast from the deep wood and red marble in Main Court," Javette commented. K'Rissa and Javette looked all around the new Royal Court at the modern design, beautiful lighting, and new colors.

"When it's finished, the white ceiling will have a rose quartz trim. Pink marble columns and floor, with gold accents, and a touch of M'Wati blue," Kayla said with a smile.

G'Rosk asked sarcastically, "And pink chairs?"

Kayla gave him a sideways glance and replied, "Only for you, my Temporary Imperial Security Advisor. Everyone else will be seated on gold-trimmed white wood with white leather cushions." The group laughed at her response. She would have a big chair with pink cushions made for him in a few days, which G'Rosk would call "the Hot Seat."

Admiral Olm carefully limped in with Tara and their youngest child to join them for lunch. Kayla felt wonderful with her entire family there together. Everyone was thankful Kayla, Javette, and Dan'L survived the Aux Comm Battle.

The next morning, Empress Kayla met with C.S. Sham'S, and ordered him to resume managing the Phase 2 and 3 Ranger Training. "We lost eleven Rangers in the Aux Comm Battle, and another fifteen will be retired out tomorrow. It is imperative you mentor the best of our Phase 1 Trainees through their Phase 2 and 3 Ranger Training course, Sham'S. Work them as hard as they worked us, and help them over the roughest trials. The Empire needs its Rangers!" He asked to attend Main Court's reopening first, and she agreed.

Home World Main Court opened with a full agenda: Ranger and Space Cadre awards in the morning; lunch banquet; and then High Court Tribunal. The awards and commendations were proceeded by vid recordings of the earlier attack on Home World Royal Palace, and then the Aux Comm Battle. After the posthumous awards were given to the surviving spouses and families, Rangers and Space Cadre received promotions with their awards and commendations. The morning's ceremony was solemn, with everyone keenly aware of their missing Ranger and Space Cadre brothers and sisters.

Admiral Olm received an award for Valor, for helping Admiral Mae and several others escape the attack on the Royal Palace. Then, he was retired with a medical discharge and full honors. The Court gave him a standing ovation.

Master Commander Dan'L joined eleven of his fellow Borgund Rangers and three Kaylan Rangers. They were awarded medals of Valor and Bravery for their defense of the Royal Palace bombing, and the Aux Comm Battle. They were given full medical retirement honors, and raised their plasma swords for one final time to salute Empress Kayla. The Court was called to attention, and everyone saluted the retiring Rangers, some of them in anti-grav wheelchairs. Applause filled the Court. Afterwards, the disabled Rangers were taken to seats of honor for the banquet. Many of the medically retired Rangers were offered strategic positions at Main Court, or in top-secret Imperial government agencies.

M.C. Kend'R received an undisclosed bonus and commendation for Valor, Bravery, and Excellent Performance under Duress. He was also awarded "Hero of the Empire" status, an enviable achievement. It meant your word was true, and you were trusted above others. Kend'R was now officially one of the top advisors to Empress Kayla.

Privately, Kayla asked Kend'R what he wanted as a reward for his all-important telepathic endeavors. She said, "Victory was possible because of your efforts, Master Commander Kend'R. You utilized your gift from our Creator to save us personally, as well as the Empire. What do you desire as a personal gift from your Empress to show her gratitude?"

He smiled at his friend and answered, "My Empress and many of our Rangers and Space Cadre defeated the Plan of the Thirteen traitors in the Aux Comm Battle, my Lady. My reward is to serve the Great Warrior Empress Kayla. I neither need nor desire anything else, my Sovereign." She bowed her head in acceptance of his decision.

The banquet was magnificent, with many roasted meats and fine foods placed on the long tables for everyone. Out of respect, the retired Rangers were given the first plates, and served fine wine, for those who could drink. After the food and wine were cleared away, a thirty-minute break took place before the High Court Tribunal session.

Former Field Marshall General Blatan, also known as Dok'T, stood silently while his guilty plea was entered for all ninety-one charges. Dok'T waived his right to trial and requested immediate sentencing. The Tribunal Judges sentenced him to death by lethal injection.

Great Empress Kayla made an official statement to her Court: "For the last five years, General Blatan served the Empire and protected our people, and executed our orders to the letter. Our greatest shock was discovering his dual identity two days before the Aux Comm Battle was initiated. For the entire span of your twenty-six years of service in the Imperial Army, you secretly worked to overthrow this Empire by restoring the 'Old Engine,' and training terrorists for the assigned day of revolt."

"As former Monk Dok'T, and Servant of the Creator, we ask you now: Do you wish to fulfill your Holy Caste Order's law; to be brought before your brothers and sisters to confess your sins, and perform penance by ritual suicide?" She asked. The Court audience was silent.

Dok'T looked at her, momentarily stunned by her offer. Then he replied, "This former monk wishes only to meet with our High Priest to confess and be allowed penance by ritual suicide. The offer from the Great Benevolent Empress Kayla is greatly appreciated." He bowed deeply to her. She nodded, and Dok'T was returned to his cell. Main Court was adjourned for the day, with many wagging tongues discussing the former General Blatan's deception.

Dok'T later met with High Priest K'Ramm and made a full confession, which was recorded. He confessed to being persuaded by his brother Baron Z'Lun to write the "Plan of the Thirteen" documents, promising to carry the Plan to its completion. When the individual thirteen documents were completed, the original signers drew their own blood and signed each document. As the years progressed, the Alternative Contingencies were developed, and Dok'T helped Z'Lun by writing them on the reverse side of the original documents. He sealed and stored them within the M'Wati seminary vault and thought no more about them. He thought the documents were merely faulty aspirations of young men.

Discovering the thirteen signers committed large sums of credits, enlisted Duma Wat to create the Rebellion to distract Imperial attention—and were deadly serious—Dok'T's conscious weighed heavily on him. Z'Lun met with him about the Plan and told him he was the last Alternate. Z'Lun gave Copy Three to the "Grand Master Technician," Baron S'Tan, for reference and safekeeping. Dok'T left the M'Wati seminary and went to the hermit monks on Ban'Ti for penance, to spend the rest of his life there. He thought he had disappeared.

But Z'Lun found Dok'T, reminded him of his promise, and brought him back to civilization. He faked Dok'T's suicide and gave him a new identity: Blatan. Two decades in the Imperial Army allowed Blatan the experience and skills needed to perform the work and train the Plan's Technicians, as he had promised Z'Lun. With much help from the Great Council of Barons, Blatan moved through the ranks and became a three-star general. Blatan spent many hours rebuilding the Old Engine, using eager, young Rebels to divert shipments of missiles from Baron S'Tan's weapons manufacturing factories to their secret launch sites.

Blatan followed the orders of the young Empress Kayla. When she and her Rangers defeated his Brother Z'Lun's coup d'état, he carried out her orders to overtake his lands, factories, and wealth. Z'Lun failed and deserved to be punished. One by one, traitorous Imperial Beneficiaries discovered to be involved with the Plan had their titles, land, and wealth stripped. Blatan felt they deserved such punishment for failing.

Only when Baron Lep'T reminded Blatan he was the last Alternate and was honor-bound to fulfill his sworn promise to the Plan, did the final chance to take the throne call him to action. Unlike his twenty-plus years of behind-the-scenes work, this forced him into the spotlight. In less than one month, the Empress uncovered his deception.

Because he failed his promised duty to the Plan, Dok'T felt he also needed to be punished; but he wanted to be given the chance for confession and penance before meeting his Creator. Following the ritual requirements, the head and face of Dok'T were shaved clean. When Dok'T signed his confession in blood, Empress Kayla was notified. Kayla came to his prison cell with several Rangers to witness his penance and stood next to K'Ramm. He told her of the ritual suicide steps in soft whispers.

Dok'T watched the beautiful Empress whispering with K'Ramm, and realized they knew each other very well. He asked the priest if he could confess one more thing privately. K'Ramm bent down to listen, and Dok'T whispered, "You were her lover. You took her innocence, my High Priest," and softly laughed. "Penance is due from us both."

The Empress did not hear Dok'T's words. She watched K'Ramm kneel, unroll a leather sheet, and hand Dok'T a ceremonial knife. While High Priest K'Ramm said the prayers in the ancient language, Dok'T held the knife with both hands, and thrust it into his abdomen deeply. He breathed short breaths while K'Ramm prayed, and pulled the imbedded knife across his belly, and then back the opposite direction without a sound. Then, Dok'T removed the ceremonial knife, took the white cloth from K'Ramm, and wiped the blade clean; a perfect act.

"May the Creator receive your soul, and grant you mercy," K'Ramm prayed.

Dok'T was bleeding profusely. He handed the cloth to K'Ramm. Then, he turned the knife around and offered it to K'Ramm, and said his final words, "Join me in your penance."

The emotional exchange between the men was noticed. Kayla watched K'Ramm's face; he was seriously considering it. She swiftly took the knife from Dok'T. High Priest K'Ramm snapped out of his haze, looked at Kayla, and the tears flowed from his eyes. Dok'T fell over on his side and died.

Kayla and F.C. Bek'R helped K'Ramm stand. She ordered her Guards to take him to a guest suite, and said, "Suicide watch for our High Priest. Notify High Priestess T'Char at once."

After a few hours, Empress Kayla went to K'Ramm's guest suite. She knocked politely, and he opened the door. She told her Guards to remain outside.

"My dearest friend K'Ramm, are you well? I confess I was frightened for a few seconds, seeing you with Dok'T. Have you ever assisted in ritual suicide before?" She asked.

He quietly answered, "No. It was my first. I meditated to prepare, but the power and emotion of the act nearly overwhelmed me. Dok'T saw my great pain and tried to lure me to join him. But, thanks to you, I came to my senses. Once again, I thank you, Empress Kayla," he said with a bow of his head.

"The thought of life without your friendship, counsel, and your smile makes me highly disconcerted, my friend. I depend on you and have the highest regard for my High Priest. Are you beyond your struggle? I will not rest until you move beyond this event, K'Ramm," she said, and reached for his hand.

He took her hand and led her to a chair. She sat, and he sat on the floor beside her. This time, Kayla began the chant, "There is no pain. Only peace," and they chanted together for a long time. Kayla walked to his door.

K'Ramm stood next to her and confessed, "I have loved you since our moment at the spring on Xau, when the blue dragonfly led me to you."

She looked into his deep, blue-gray eyes and softly said, "I know, K'Ramm. We were sworn to higher powers. I was sworn to Emperor P'Lau, and you to our Creator. We both knew it could not last forever, K'Ramm." She touched her heart and whispered, "Your love is with me always, cherished, and safe inside my heart. My love also goes with you, the love and respect of a devoted friend, who will not be without her Priest K'Ramm." She smiled tenderly at him.

K'Ramm said, "I will always love you, my precious Kayla. Go to your Royal Consort, and sleep in peace." She touched his cheek and left his room.

XXXII

The Fifth Anniversary Celebration Cruise to all four planets was an enormous success. The Royal Family was young and energetic, and hugely popular with the people. Parades and celebrations were held in the capital city on each planet. The people showered their Empress Kayla with cheers and applause wherever she appeared, and she felt truly thankful. They were her beloved people, whose lives and happiness were entrusted to her by the Vee Lok Lords when they appointed Kayla as Empress.

Consort Dan'L's tension cast was removed en route from K'Halon Prime to M'Wati. Admiral Mae gave him special healing laser treatments to strengthen his leg bones for the celebrations, and to enable his wish to go diving. Prince Lukus swam with his Mother in the warm waters above the dive spots his Father chose and played with the little tropical fishes in the tide pools. The accompanying Rangers and Imperial Guards took turns enjoying the waters and beaches with the Royal Family. The Empress spent some time shopping for new fabrics for summer dresses. Cotton and silk from M'Wati were the best quality, and she loved those fabrics.

Empress Kayla met with new M'Wati Imperial Planetary Governor Tessa in the Regency Resort, a new, five-star property built and owned by the Empress. Work on a new hilltop Royal Residence and a surrounding complex in Lova was well underway, but far from completion. When Empress Kayla was not in residence, Regency Resort suites were rented out, so the property and its lush resort grounds could be enjoyed by the people of M'Wati. As with every new business venture paid for by the Empire on M'Wati, all profits went directly to the M'Wati Restoration Project.

The trip to Ban'Ti took one full week longer than usual, because the Imperial Command Battle Cruiser was not permitted to "cut through" the White Belt. Chaos was having its way with the White Belt's asteroids, still causing major disturbances and collisions as a result of the explosion of asteroid 374.65. Years would pass before the White Belt would be deemed safe to traverse.

Inspections of four Space Bases took place, as well as a visit to the G'Lenan Facility. The second KRS-series destroyer was being constructed. The Empress' design proved lethal and very effective during the Aux Comm Battle. It was given more laser cannons and hangar space to accommodate three additional squadrons of Space Cadre fighters.

The Royal Historian, Treasurer, and Archivist submitted their report on the new treasure discovered under the foundation stone of the old harem at Home World Royal Palace. Several small samples taken for analysis revealed the jewelry pieces were created in the first century of the Empire. They were dated by metallurgical analytical tests prior to Imperial Year 100. The gold was not from the R'Genra solar system. Seals embossed on the gold bars were previously unknown and were recorded.

The precious stones were estimated to be from the same time period, but the analysis was incomplete. No samples were taken in order to not damage them. Baron P'Lau and the Royal Historian concluded the treasure was hidden during the original construction of the Home World Royal Palace and were originally the gifts to the first Emperor Borgund from the Vee Lok Lords. Emperor Borgund's treasure was kept separate from the wealth of the Empire by his dynastic Royal Heirs, all directly from his bloodline.

The antique jewelry was priceless, and the precious stones in the treasure were each perfect, without any flaws or inclusions whatsoever. The gold bars were worth sixteen billion credits, in today's intrinsic value of gold; but priceless to a numismatic gold collector. Empress Kayla stored the new treasure with her own gifts of gold and precious jewels from the Vee Lok Lords when they appointed her Empress.

The priceless treasure was placed into specially marked boxes and crates sealed electronically. They all bore the personal seal of the Empress and were accounted for separately from the Royal Treasury assets. Passed down from Emperor Borgund upon his selection by the Vee Lok Lords, Empress Kayla ruled the antique treasure was too precious to be used for mere Royal Treasury purposes. She presented one twelve-kilogram bar of gold to Baron P'Lau, the last ruling Emperor from the lineage of Emperor Borgund. P'Lau was speechless, and very proud.

During the Celebration Cruise, reconstruction of the Home World Imperial Naval Base and the Royal Palace Complex continued. Viscount T'Sur donated personal funds for a new "Royal Aquatic Center," to replace the 210-year-old pool and gymnasium destroyed in the bombing of the Palace. It featured a competition-length swimming pool with moveable bleacher seats. A full exercise floor complete with free weights, exercise machines, treadmills, and the like was on the opposite side of the showers. The building had a retractable dome over the pool, to take advantage of

Home World's temperate climate and sunshine.

Home World Royal Palace, Six Months Later

The fifth birthday party for Prince Lukus had come to an end. His friends and their parents had all gone home. Grandmother Javette patted the cushion between her and G'Rosk, and Lukus sat with them on the sofa. Admiral Olm and Auntie Tara wished Prince Lukus well on his upcoming transition. Olm said, "The journey on which you're about to embark is a time-honored tradition for all children of the Warrior Class, my Nephew. Everyone in your family is incredibly proud of our Prince Lukus today. Remember who your parents are and make them proud you are their Son!" He shook Lukus' hand, smiled, and left with Tara.

The Royal Suite parlor became quiet. Grandmother Javette put her arm around Lukus, noticing his nervousness rising. "Be brave, my Prince," G'Rosk whispered to the boy.

Dan'L stood by the window, while Kayla sat across from her Son, all of them waiting anxiously, and smiling for him. "You are ready, Prince Lukus," his Mother said confidently. "My Son is brave and smart, and all will know you as their next Emperor Lukus!" She gently rocked the double cradle containing her newborn twin Sons, only one month old. She fully recovered from the emergency surgery to give birth to her twin Babies, but their delivery was difficult and exhausting. Whether or not the Empress could ever bear another child was unknown at this time.

His Father Dan'L said, "You have been shot at, and had a laser pistol pointed at your head. Your Mother has trained you in T'Ly for the last two years without mercy," he added with a grin. "This will be a piece of cake for you, Lukus." Then the room got quiet again.

The knock on the Suite door sounded like a bass drum beating. M.C. Shanna let in the Imperial Guard M.C. Anton, who handed a red card with gold writing on the envelope to Royal Consort Dan'L. He read aloud with pride, "My Beloved Prince Lukus has been chosen by the Great Benevolent Empress Kayla to attend the Royal Academy, where he will study, train, and gain wisdom and knowledge. May the Creator bless Prince Lukus."

Everyone stood with Prince Lukus. The boy hugged his Grandmother Javette, G'Rosk, and his parents once more, and dutifully walked out of the Royal Suite with Imperial Guard M.C. Anton. For the next ten years, Lukus would attend the Royal Academy as a full-time student and live away from his parents, just as each of them did upon their fifth birthdays. By Imperial Law, every child born of Warrior Class parents belonged to Empress Kayla and was to be given to her around their fifth birthday for training and education.

One of the favorite duties of Empress Kayla was the monthly greeting of the new inductees into the Royal Academy. Their first evening, the group of five-year-old children from across the Empire were taken to the private Royal Court and seated at large banquet tables. With full pomp and protocol, a formally dressed Empress Kayla entered her Court and welcomed the anxious children. She greeted her young Royal Academy class of five-year-olds, congratulated each boy and girl, and comforted those who were afraid and cried. The Empress looked beautiful and powerful. She knew them all by name and handed wonderful gifts and toys to each child in red velvet bags.

The feast was delicious, accompanied by magicians, entertainers, and little pigmy goats and miniature horses to delight the children. It was a wonderful evening. Prince Lukus sat with the other children talking and smiling with them and had fun. He knew many of the other children already and felt comfortable with them.

After their feast, the Empress presented each child their own trunk of school and court clothing and shoes, sized to fit them perfectly. The happy children were escorted to the Royal Academy on anti-grav platform scooters and whisked to the opposite side of the Palace Complex. They were allowed one live vid call home to speak with their proud parents before bedtime. Prince Lukus' parents were happy for him, and assured Lukus they would see him on school holidays and for his birthdays. Lukus kept his composure during the entire day and listened to other children cry themselves asleep.

Although the Royal Academy was inside the Palace Complex, it was forbidden for him to walk back to his Mother and Father in the North Wing of the Palace. He had to stay in the Academy, like all the other children. The little Prince silently determined to be the brave Son of the Great Empress Kayla and Borgund Ranger Master Commander Dan'L. He would not cry. He would not show fear. One day, he would be the Emperor, and his classmates would remember him as a brave, excellent student, and a friend.

Home World Royal Palace, One Year Later

Two Birthday Parties for Empress Kayla took place in the Royal Aquatic Center. The Ranger and Imperial Guards' families enjoyed the pool until 4p.m. Palm trees and tropical plants were brought in and the bleacher seats removed. Meats, fowl, and fish were grilled on open barbecues, served with many other delectable foods. Empress Kayla shared exotic fruits from Ban'Ti with everyone, and the mixologists concocted great seltzers and smoothies to enjoy, all alcohol-free.

Sitting in an area under the open dome, Empress Kayla sunned with Javette. Shanna and Admiral Mae were in the chaise lounge chairs right behind them. The Baby Princes Tom'S and K'Ser were in their carriages next to Empress Kayla, shaded from the afternoon sun, and sound asleep.

Commander Tish was Prince Lukus' favorite friend today, and he kept her busy in the pool, jumping into the deep end, and being "rescued." When the boy was just two years old, he jumped into the old pool, and Tish rescued him and saved his life. But now Lukus was in his first year at the Royal Academy and was a good swimmer. The young Prince just wanted to jump in the water and play with his friend Tish.

Cmdr. Tish brought Lukus out of the pool and wrapped him in a towel. The Prince ran to his Father, busy visiting—and flirting playfully—with several young Kaylan Novices. Tish escorted Lukus back to his Mother. When Consort Dan'L finally joined his family, Kayla asked, "Have all my new Kaylan Novices met you now?" She saw his charming antics with the women.

Dan'L teased, "Yes. I think we need to discuss Article 27 again." Kayla shot him a look, and he began trotting away from her, laughing. Javette heard his remark.

"Commander Tish; please watch Prince Lukus and my Baby Sons for me a while longer," the Empress requested. She grabbed her robe and jogged back to the Royal Suite in the Main Palace, pursuing her Consort. Dan'L ran limping into the Palace, hopped in the lift, and went upstairs. She entered the other lift, punched the third-floor button, and ran to their suite.

Kayla slapped the recognition pad and entered, and jumped into his arms, saying, "I have you now, my Royal Consort. You're mine!" They laughed together and kissed. Dan'L laid her on his bed, and they made love. Later, she called for Tish to bring Lukus, Tom'S, and K'Ser to her. It was time for everyone to get ready for the big, elegant Birthday Party.

The formal Birthday Party was filled with happy aristocrats, Barons, Lords and Ladies, and their spouses. Viscount T'Sur and the guests were enjoying the beverage of their choice. The pool dome was open, and extra tables and chairs were set up on the lawn directly in front of the new Aquatic Center for all the guests.

The Empress and her chosen Favorite Ladies entered: Javette, Shanna, Tish, and Tara. Each lady was dressed in a sleeveless, flowing, M'Wati silk dress of white, with a long cape attached at the shoulders. Golden belts loosely tied matched their gold high-heeled sandals. They looked very sexy. The guests said "Ooh" and "Aah," as the Empress and her Favorite Ladies slowly entered. Viscount T'Sur had a smile from ear to ear, and he said, "My Great Empress, you and your ladies look like goddesses from the old storybooks! So beautiful!" They walked with such poise and grace, they seemed to float through the crowd of guests. Shanna wore a long blonde wig for the evening and was stunning. Only Admiral Mae and F.C. Bek'R recognized her.

The maître'd announced: "Presenting Prince Lukus, and First Consort Dan'L."

Dan'L gave the maître'd a disapproving look, and whispered, "Royal Consort, not First Consort," and the maître'd merely nodded. Prince Lukus and his Father were dressed in white jackets and trousers, and M'Wati blue-patterned ascots. They looked very dapper.

The guests were excited to talk with the Empress and see the new Royal Twin Princes. Many Happy Birthday wishes were expressed. When Dan'L and Prince Lukus joined the Favorite Ladies with her, the Barons and Lords congratulated him on becoming a Father of Twins. He was very proud of his Empress, as always, and held his one-year-old Baby Sons in his arms.

The Favorite Ladies were so popular, every guest wanted to see their beautiful gowns and talk with them. A very late Captain Leni ran up to his Empress, bowed low, and apologized for his late arrival. Dressed in his Space Cadre summer uniform with its white jacket and wearing many medals on his chest, the handsome officer held out his arm to his friend Kayla and escorted the Empress and her Favorite Ladies to his Father, G'Rosk.

"As usual, you're late, Leni," G'Rosk said to him disapprovingly.

"You look very handsome, *Captain* Leni. When were you going to tell us about your promotion?" A smiling Javette asked.

He smiled proudly and answered, "I was promoted this afternoon, Javette, which is why I am late."

The Empress sat in her raised chair and looked at Leni. "We need a Captain for our new KRS-class destroyer. It should be ready for its maiden run in four months. Could you suggest a qualified officer with superior tactical experience for our consideration?" She smiled broadly at her friend Leni.

"Yes, my Empress. I know just the officer for your consideration, Empress Kayla!" He saluted her and bowed his head. She introduced Captain Leni to her Favorite Ladies, saving Tish for the last. Tish had watched the Captain enter and escort his Empress to her seat, and could not take her eyes off the tall, good-looking Leni—and Kayla noticed. Captain Leni offered his arm to Tish and took her to the cocktail bar for a drink.

"I saw that maneuver, my Empress," Lady Bette said quietly. "Playing Matchmaker with my granddaughter, Empress Kayla?" She asked, with a crooked smile.

"Our newest Captain needed a Kaylan Ranger escort for his protection, Lady Bette," Kayla replied, and her Favorite Ladies laughed. Baron P'Lau brought several aristocrats forward to meet the Empress.

Dan'L whispered to Kayla, "I was introduced as 'First Consort,' not Royal Consort."

"Yes, I noticed, Consort Dan'L," she replied nonchalantly. "Didn't you wish to invoke Article 27?" Now she had him going. She watched his face, as he looked around at all the men fawning over his exquisite Empress, waiting to talk with her. Most would give anything to become a Consort to his beautiful Kayla. He'd forgotten Article 27 allowed the Empress to take concubines and other Consorts, as many as she wanted, as long as she permitted her Consorts the privilege of having concubines. Kayla looked at Javette, watching her Son Dan'L size up the competition, and both women began to laugh softly.

Kayla ordered fresh juice seltzers for them all, with a plate of sliced Ban'Ti fruits. Prince Lukus properly used his long appetizer fork to pick out his favorite fruit, and offered it to his Grandmother, Javette. He was the perfect little gentleman tonight. The Birthday Party was very festive, and a wonderfully relaxed event for everyone.

Viscount T'Sur came to Empress Kayla to say good night. Imperial Guards helped him walk across the grassy Courtyard into the Palace Guest Suites, to his top-floor apartment. The elderly gentleman stopped and looked out of the full-length window at the end of the hall for several minutes at the continuing party, everyone having an enjoyable time at the new Royal Aquatic Center he built.

The eldest Steward of the Empire felt a tremendous sense of satisfaction tonight. The Royal Hierarchy was being rebuilt gradually, and thoughtfully. Disaster had been averted once again by the Great Warrior Empress Kayla, her devoted Rangers, and the Imperial Military. T'Sur watched Empress Kayla slowly walk through the crowd with Prince Lukus, her Baby Sons, Consort Dan'L, and her Favorite Ladies towards the exit. The Viscount smiled to see the many aristocrats, courtiers, military brass, and other VIPs cordially bid her good evening. Kayla was the most beautiful woman he ever knew. She was truly extraordinary: Empress, Warrior, Mother, and Wife. The people adored Empress Kayla, and so did he. Viscount T'Sur smiled and walked to his apartment.

In the morning, his Imperial Guard entered and found the elderly Viscount T'Sur passed away in his overstuffed chair. He was holding a com tablet with suggestions he made for his Empress. The page was titled, "Rebirth of the Empire."

EPILOGUE

K'Halon Prime

The city lights of downtown Centralia glistened through the full-length windows of the penthouse. From seventy-five stories in the air, Lev'K surveyed the largest city on big K'Halon Prime. The ten-block section of the old harbor where the multi-colored glass and steel office complex sprawled used to belong to his family. One day, it would all be his.

Three off-duty Palace Guards were shown into the living room, and Lev'K quickly got to the point. "You know why you're here tonight. You're tired of being treated like slaves by the Rangers and Main Court elites, and the arrogant Empress Bitch. You're over-worked, under-paid, and ignored. But no more," he said.

Handing a roll of gold coins to each Guard, the tall, very thin Lev'K said, "Here's 10,000 credits in gold for each of you. Don't talk about it or flash it around. Our agreement is strictly between us. Do nothing to draw attention to yourselves," he cautioned. "In three weeks, you'll bring me the Royal Palace blueprints, files on all Imperial Advisors, and complete personnel files of active-duty Rangers and Imperial Guards. Agreed?" He asked, looking closely at each man. They each agreed.

"You'll receive another 10,000 credits in gold whenever we meet, and you bring me the information I want. Another 1000 credits every month will be deposited on these plastic debit cards," he added, handing them to the men. "See you in three weeks," Lev'K finished, and showed the men out.

Lev'K walked into the den and opened the closet door. He touched his comm link and activated the android inside the closet. The droid projected a holograph of its internal schematics. "You passed through Imperial scanners at the transport station, Unit ST-507. You and I will design artificial intelligence systems just for you. Then, you will create ten thousand next-generation androids, each with its own individual human face," Lev'K said to his creation.

"The individual faces will increase production time by 27.687%, master," the android said. "The Imperial Battle Droid programming is not currently compatible with any facial movements, or Imperial protocols, master."

The advanced robotics engineer Lev'K replied, "Full compatibility is the task of another designer. We will increase your memory 23% for your new battle codes. Your offspring will be autonomous, ST-507. You will create the new Imperial Rangers, Guards, and Space Cadre. You will bring the Empress Bitch to her knees. You will right the wrongs she inflicted upon your master, ST-507. Then, I will have you create the new Imperial Army, and I will lead the Empire into the future!" Lev'K paused for a sip of his vodka and laughed vindictively.

www.ingramcontent.com/pod-product-compliance
Lightning Source LLC
Chambersburg PA
CBHW070815120626
46556CB00002B/513

* 9 7 8 1 7 3 3 1 5 4 3 2 1 *